Praise for Babs Horton

'I loved this book. The story is earthy, harsh, grievous even – and yet so funny, so cunningly and powerfully told, so lit up by the sense of what it was like to be a child then, full of terror and delight, caught in the snare of adult mysteries. Above all, Babs Horton captures the physical intensity of being a child – the smells, the tastes, the ghoulishness and sudden ecstasies'
Helen Dunmore

'Convincingly fuses a nostalgic glance back to the long, hot summers of childhood with a detective story and a dollop of old-fashioned romance ... Small-town secrets provide plenty of darkness to dapple this atmospheric tale'
Daily Mail

'The ever-surprising developments of the story are written with original and lyrical prose'
Good Book Guide

'A mystery shot through with elements of the magic of folk tales ... Unusual and cumulatively moving'
Big Issue

'Mystery, fairy tales and wonderfully observed characters are all wrapped up in this magical novel'
She

'A wonderful read, billowingly lyrical, suspenseful and psychologically intriguing. Award-winning Horton weaves an alluring magic'
Western Daily Press

'The story casts a net of magic over the reader's imagination ... Horton is a voice with a fresh take on the world'
Weekend Australian

By the same author

A Jarful of Angels
Dandelion Soup
Wildcat Moon

Brought up in London and Wales, Babs Horton now lives in Devon where she is Writing Fellow at the University of Plymouth. Her debut, *A Jarful of Angels*, won the Pendleton May Award for the Best First Novel of 2003, and was short-listed for the Authors' Club Best First Novel Award.

Recipes for Cherubs

Babs Horton

POCKET
BOOKS

LONDON • NEW YORK • SYDNEY • TORONTO

First published in Great Britain by Simon & Schuster, 2008
This edition first published by Pocket Books, 2008
An imprint of Simon & Schuster UK
A CBS COMPANY

1 3 5 7 9 10 8 6 4 2

Simon & Schuster UK Ltd
Africa House
64–78 Kingsway
London WC2B 6AH

www.simonsays.co.uk

Simon & Schuster Australia
Sydney

A CIP catalogue record for this book is
available from the British Library

ISBN 978-0-74349-596-7

Typeset by Rowland Phototypesetting Ltd
Bury St Edmunds, Suffolk
Printed and bound in Great Britain by
Cox & Wyman Ltd, Reading, Berks

For Marie Viola Horton

Acknowledgements

I would like to thank my husband John, Laura and Jack for support and laughter. To Pat and Terry Cowan, Pat Gigg and families for their generosity and warmth. My gratitude to Giuseppe Puccio of Palermo Sicily, who took the time to write and cheered me up when I was down. Thanks also to the smaller people in my life who make me smile; Sophie, Cassi and Olivia.

I want to thank Angie Smith of Ridgeway School, Robin Pritchard and Heather Chapman of Plymouth College, Martin Edmonds of Tamarside Community College who foster a love of literature among their students. For memorable and hair raising times in the middle of Dartmoor I am indebted to my friends Nicky Evans, Sarah Fish, Ian Gee, Cathy Haddy, Mandy Gilkes, Paul Hingston, Tom Maguire and Pip Murphy. My thanks to Father David Mead of The Retreat for peace and sanctuary at a hectic time.

As always I owe a debt of gratitude to my agent, Clare Alexander. Kate Lyall Grant for advice and reassurance. The Simon and Schuster team, especially Melissa Weatherill, Libby Vernon, Joe Pickering and Stuart Poulson and Rafi Romaya who designed the cover. This was a year of new beginnings and goodbyes. I would like to thank the Royal Literary Fund for my fellowship at the University of

Plymouth from which I have gained new inspiration and precious time to write. Thank you to John Hilsdon and Tony Lopez for making my move there effortless. Finally, I would like to remember friends who are no longer with us; Tony Gigg and Diane Rawlings; God bless.

Geniuses are like thunderstorms.
They go against the wind, terrify people,
cleanse the air.

Kierkegaard, *The Journals*

Part One

Chapter 1

SUMMER 1960

Kizzy Grieve turned over in bed, opened her eyes and winced. One too many port and lemons at the club last night had left her with a thick head. She got out of bed, wandered over to the window and looked out into Ermington Square. In the communal gardens, the nannies were already out with their young charges. Some pushed cumbersome prams and others held the sticky hands of squirming toddlers.

Kizzy shuddered. How she would hate such a tedious job, being stuck all day with mewling babies and crabby toddlers. The trouble with small children was that they looked so cherubic and peachy-skinned but only when they were sleeping – for most of their waking hours they were a pain in the proverbial. A schoolmistress shepherded a crocodile of little girls across the road, and their chattering voices made Kizzy frown and put her hand to her aching head.

Only one more week and her daughter Catrin would be back from her convent school for the summer holiday. The prospect of eight whole weeks with her sourpuss of a daughter was more than she could bear to contemplate. What on earth would they do in London for all that time?

If Catrin were an ordinary sort of child it would probably have been quite fun; they could have gadded about together like sisters, spent hours in the shops trying on clothes and then lunched in the most fashionable places.

She lit a cigarette and inhaled deeply. Sometimes she wondered if Catrin were a changeling. Wasn't it the cuckoo or the magpie that laid its eggs in the nests of other unsuspecting birds? Maybe someone in the private maternity home had deliberately switched babies and she'd got the short straw, Catrin.

Someone out there now would have a delightful, pretty daughter full of the joys of living, when by rights they should have been lumbered with bloody Catrin with her baleful looks and nitpicking, fussy ways. Whatever did she have to be so miserable about? She had a nice home to come back to in the school holidays, a lovely bedroom and a generous allowance. She went to a half-decent school – Kizzy would have preferred to send her to Benenden or Heathfield but Catrin's godfather, Arthur Campbell, had stipulated that as he was paying the fees she had to be educated and brought up as a Roman Catholic.

Catrin wasn't that bad-looking really, not exactly the face to launch a thousand ships but if she just made the best of herself, used a little powder and lipstick, she'd be presentable. The trouble was, she wasn't interested in make-up, clothes or boys or any of the usual things that normal thirteen year olds were interested in. Kizzy had never known a girl with such an inability to have any fun at all. Why, if she herself were thirteen again she'd be having the time of her life – and she wouldn't make the same mistakes she'd made the first time round.

It would be better for both of them if Catrin didn't come home, but that bloody Sister Matilde had been most unhelpful when Kizzy rang to ask if Catrin could spend part of the summer holidays at school. She'd said in that oh-so-sanctimonious voice of hers, 'A little time spent with her mother is well overdue.' Time with her mother! That was quite clearly the last thing Catrin wanted, and she made it pretty damned obvious whenever they were together, with her sulks and flounces. If the truth were told, Catrin liked school better than home, loved being among the nuns, and it wouldn't surprise Kizzy if she ended up taking the veil or vows or whatever it was they took. It would suit Catrin down to the ground, the perfect life of fasting and long periods of huffy silence.

Sister Matilde was just being spiteful and interfering. After all, Catrin had stayed at school for an extra week at Easter when Kizzy went to Paris. She knew some of the other girls were staying at school for the summer. For a start the Palfrey twins were because she'd met their mother outside the Army and Navy stores. That stuffy-faced bore had said that her husband had a new posting to Khartoum and the girls couldn't possibly spend the summer there.

Kizzy stubbed out her cigarette angrily. It really was most unfair. She sat down at the dressing table and felt the tears of frustration rising. She pulled open a drawer, fished around for a handkerchief, found one at the back of the drawer, yanked it out impatiently, and a crumpled photograph fell into her lap.

It had been taken on the front lawn of Shrimp's Hotel at Kilvenny in Wales. There was bossy Aunt Ella staring defiantly out at her with those piercing eyes. Next to her stood dear Aunt Alice smiling sweetly at the camera. Kizzy was next to Aunt Alice; how young she looked in the photograph – and positively ravishing, too, even if she said so herself. It was a pity the photograph was black-and-white because the silk dress she was wearing had been the most glorious shade of poppy red. It had cost an absolute fortune,

5

too, but good old Aunt Alice had insisted on buying it for her for the wedding despite Aunt Ella's protestations about wasting hard-earned money on frippery. It had been a divine dress and she'd loved the scalloped hemline and the delicate embroidery round the neck. Oh, and those sling-back patent shoes she was wearing were gorgeous. She was sure she still had them somewhere but she hadn't seen the dress in years.

She sighed; if only she could turn the clock back, she would do things so differently and certainly wouldn't lumber herself with a child. There was Gladys Beynon, who used to be the cook at Shrimp's Hotel; she used to bake pastries one would cheerfully die for. The afternoon teas at Shrimp's Hotel had been wonderful; seed cake and cream horns, scones with clotted cream and raspberry jam. Oh, those were the days, when one could feast on fattening things and never put on an ounce. Kizzy's stomach rumbled at the thought of food; she must take one of her little wonder pills in a moment to suppress her appetite. She was creeping alarmingly close to nine stone and that wouldn't do at all.

She was about to stuff the photograph back into the drawer when something caught her attention. Next to Gladys Beynon there was a shadow on the wall of the house, the shadow of someone standing just out of view. There was the unmistakable outline of a boater hat set at a rakish angle and an outstretched hand holding a cigarette.

She put down the photograph with a trembling hand and sat staring into the mirror, watching the tears welling up in her eyes, her mouth crumpling. Then she shook her head, pulled back her shoulders, wiped her eyes and lit another cigarette. It was no good crying over a shadow in a photograph. She'd been just a silly, gullible girl barely five years older than Catrin was now.

She'd fallen for his charms all right, got herself pregnant and been left stranded.

She went downstairs and gathered up her post, glancing cursorily through a couple of depressing postcards. There was one from Marguerite, who was already settled into her villa on the Costa Brava, and another from Lily, who was having an absolute ball at a house party in Cannes. Damn! All she had to look forward to was a summer with Catrin.

Then as she picked up the last postcard her hand began to shake uncontrollably. The card had a picture of a cherub on the front, a smiling, rosy-cheeked cherub with flashing green eyes, his head tilted to one side, looking up towards the cerulean blue of the heavens. She turned the postcard over but there was nothing except her name and address printed in capital letters on the other side.

She stood up, sat down again with a thud, the adrenalin rushing through her and making her tremble with excitement. She must get a grip on herself and think logically. This must be someone playing a cruel joke. But it couldn't be. No one could know about the cherub and its significance to her; it had been their special thing. How her heart used to flutter whenever a postcard like this had arrived at her boarding school, and everyone had commented that there was never any writing on them. She'd smiled secretively and told them that an eccentric old uncle, who could never be bothered to write a message, sent them to her. She held the postcard to her nose and sniffed. There was a definite smell of onions . . .

In the kitchen she threw everything out of the drawer in her haste to find a candle and a box of matches, and with her heart racing she held the wavering flame beneath the postcard. Beads of perspiration grew on her forehead and her head thumped painfully. Gradually, as the heat warmed the postcard, faint writing in that once-familiar hand began to appear on the paper: *'Napoli Centrale. 15 Iuglio – mezzanotte.'*

She closed her eyes and tried to breathe normally.

She'd waited years for a message from him and none had ever come until now.

She turned the postcard over and looked at the postmark. Naples.

She put it down next to the photograph and looked at them both. It was such a coincidence that she should come across the photograph by accident and then moments later to receive the card. It was a sign, an omen.

She began to pace about the room. She was in an absolute quandary. It was imperative that she got out of London and down to Naples by 15 July, but that was in five days' time, the day before Catrin was due home from school. She couldn't possibly go gallivanting about Europe with her daughter in tow.

Then she had an idea, a ridiculous one, perhaps, but she was desperate. She'd be pushing her luck after all these years and all the bad feeling that last summer she'd been at Shrimp's, but that was an age ago and surely the Aunts couldn't bear a grudge for ever.

Shrimp's Hotel was an idyllic place for a child to stay – why, there was plenty of fresh air, exercise and good food. Needs must when the devil drives and all that; it was time to forgive and forget, whether Alice and Ella Grieve wanted to or not.

Even if they didn't want to see Kizzy again they might welcome Catrin with open arms; after all, she was a blood relative, a Grieve. Aunt Alice had always had a wonderful way with children, such patience and fortitude. Aunt Ella, on the other hand, could be a bit of a tartar, and not one you could twist around your little finger, but she was all right in her own way.

The Aunts would do Catrin a power of good; they would certainly feed her up a bit, put some flesh on her bones. God knows she needed it. It was one thing being thin but the last time Kizzy had seen Catrin she had looked almost skeletal. She supposed it was all that abstinence the nuns instilled in them. Still, a holiday at Shrimp's would put a bit of colour in those bloodless cheeks and if a miracle occurred it might even put a smile on her face.

It was a perfect idea – an enormous cheek, maybe, but what the heck; a lot of water had passed under the bridge since that last summer at Shrimp's. Aunt Alice must surely have got over it by now and was probably rather relieved that things had turned out as they had. It was definitely time to let bygones be bygones.

She hunted around for her telephone book and rifled through the pages until she found the number. Shrimp's Hotel: Kilvenny 311.

She took a deep breath and dialled, but there was no reply. She replaced the handset with irritation. Of course, it was the start of the holiday season and the Aunts would be run off their feet. Oh well, tiresome though it was, she would have to write to Aunt Alice and tell her when Catrin would be arriving. And Catrin should be delighted; after all, not many thirteen year olds would get the chance to stay in a top-notch hotel for the whole summer. Shrimp's really was quite something. It was a little on the old-fashioned side as far as the furnishings were concerned, but the food was wonderful and there were always so many interesting and sometimes very attractive guests.

It was about time Catrin got to know her only living relatives, and she might even be an asset to the Aunts. It was a perfect solution to Kizzy's problems from her point of view and she had rarely found it necessary to consider the views of anyone else.

She dressed hurriedly, smiling to herself as she did so. Life was strange: one minute one could be in the depths of despair and the next, one was positively euphoric.

How unbelievable that she was going to Italy. At last she'd be able to find out what had happened to him, why he'd left her like that. Then they would have the most marvellous reunion; she imagined herself lying on an airbed in a swimming pool, cool drink to hand and nothing to do all day. Absolute bliss.

She picked up the telephone and dialled the number of Catrin's school. She would speak to the headmistress and tell her of the new arrangements for Catrin at the end of term.

Half an hour later Kizzy Grieve shut the front door and crossed the square, walked jauntily along the Edgware Road on her way to the travel agent's to buy a rail ticket to Kilvenny and to arrange her own travel down to Italy. Then she thought she might go shopping and buy a few new summer outfits for Catrin as a little treat. One needed to look the part at Shrimp's.

Chapter 2

In Shrimp's Hotel Ella Grieve shuffled slowly along the attic corridor, calling out as she went. 'Olive! Maureen!' She opened the doors to the rooms but to no avail; there was no sign of any of them anywhere. Where were the blasted maids this morning? The door to the last room was open and she put her head round the door and immediately wished she hadn't.

Honestly, young people today were so slapdash. The bed was still unmade and the sheets were positively filthy. Dirty clothes had been strewn across the floor, an opened but empty blue glass bottle of scent was discarded on the dusty dressing table and a pair of laddered stockings hung over a chair back. A bluebottle buzzed angrily against the windowpane and dead moths littered the windowsill.

Ella picked up a crumpled dress, shook it and watched the dust fall from it. She turned it over in her hands, then flung it crossly to the floor. Absentmindedly she brushed a cobweb from her hair, walked across to the window and stood looking out to sea.

The sun was rising, a soft pink glow bleeding into the misty horizon. Golden-winged gulls followed the wake of a small boat heading towards the shore and a cormorant was fishing over near Bleaky Rock.

Down on Kilvenny beach a thin stream of smoke rose from the chimney of the Fisherman's Snug, a dilapidated thatched hut built up against the sea wall, where the fishermen used to congregate for a mug of hot, sweet tea or something stronger. Ella sighed wistfully. She and Alice had loved to sneak in there when they were girls, to mingle with the old men of Kilvenny while they cooked fresh sardines, bacon, cockles and lava bread on an ancient stove. It made her hungry just to think about it. She used to love to squeeze in among them and listen with wonder to all their stories of Kilvenny in days gone past, while Alice hid under the table and talked to her imaginary friends.

The fishermen had long since abandoned the place and no one went there now except that odd little boy she'd seen hanging about there of late. He'd been up here once, trying to peep in through the windows, but she'd yelled and banged on the glass and he'd fled. A frightened rabbit of a boy running away, hell for leather through the waving grass without looking back once.

Rooks were circling above the ruined tower of Kilvenny Castle and she could hear young Tony Agosti whistling as he washed down the pavement in front of the Café Romana.

Ella turned her attention to the garden below. She must speak to the gardener and get him to mow the lawns; a sprinkling of daisies and buttercups was one thing, but it was getting to be a bit of a jungle down there. Was that Mrs Ellis in the hammock beneath the mulberry tree? And surely that was young Charlie Heddon going down the rocky path to the beach with his sun hat askew and his shrimping net bobbing about all over the place.

For goodness sake, Ella, stop dreaming, she chided herself. Mrs Ellis would be over a hundred by now and Charlie Heddon must be in his forties at least. Hadn't she heard that he was married and living in Canada? These days her eyes seemed to play tricks on her. She blinked and looked again. The garden was empty except for a blackbird pecking at a snail over by the rockery and a rabbit rifling through the vegetable garden.

It was early still and the hotel guests were sleeping. In an hour or so the water pipes would gurgle and clank as they rose and took their morning baths. Early smokers would wander out on to the terrace for a puff, and others would walk briskly down to Kilvenny for the daily newspapers that Luigi Agosti sold in the Café Romana.

Ah, well, it wouldn't do to stand about idly staring out at the morning. What in God's name had she come up here to do? She was getting terribly forgetful. She supposed it was because there was always so much on her mind, so many tasks to do at Shrimp's Hotel in the high season.

She searched in the pocket of her overalls for the list she had made earlier, but to no avail. She was forever making lists and promptly losing them.

The menus for tonight's dinner needed writing up, and she must check that Gladys Beynon had sent Alice up to Duffy's Farm to fetch the cream and butter. There really was no time to waste. Tommy Roberts would arrive soon with a delivery of lobster and crab and no doubt on the lookout for a free breakfast.

As soon as breakfast had been served there would be even more work to do. Gladys, the cook, would be up to her eyes in the kitchen. There was luncheon to prepare and after that she would be making potted shrimps, scones and cakes ready for afternoon teas.

Ella must check that the chambermaids had cleaned the bedrooms; the newly starched sheets must be properly turned back, fresh flowers arranged in vases on the side tables. The windows had to be opened to air the rooms and fires laid in case of a sudden chill in the evenings.

That was the thing the guests loved about Shrimp's, the old-fashioned hospitality, the fact that nothing was ever too much trouble.

There were several new guests arriving tonight for the summer ball and she must let Halloran know what time their train was arriving. She rummaged in her pocket for the guest list, but where had she put it?

Ella climbed slowly down the attic stairs and paused on the landing to pick up a discarded patent leather shoe. She saw a mouse scurrying into the airing cupboard. There seemed to be a plague of them this summer. She must remind Halloran to put out some more traps; the little devils must be getting in through the cellar again. She didn't want her guests upset by mice.

Ella made her way through into Alice's room and gazed around. The fire was already laid and Alice's book lay on the chair just as she had left it. She stood for a moment looking at a painting on the wall, a very good copy of that Italian fellow's famous masterpiece, *Woman and Child*.

It used to hang in the old nursery in Kilvenny Castle when she and Alice were children, and Alice had insisted on bringing it up here to Shrimp's when they moved. Alice had loved that painting and used to blow kisses to the woman each night before she went to sleep. Ella put up her hand and touched the woman's cheek, then turned away hastily.

She climbed stiffly down the main staircase and paused midway, looking down into the hall. The grandfather clock had wound down for the second time this week. Whatever was the matter with Alice? She must have words with her because it was one of her jobs to wind the clocks. The guests liked to hear the old grandfather clock marking out their hours of leisure.

She wandered into the dining room to check that

everything was ready, and tut-tutted with irritation. The silver cruets hadn't been polished to her satisfaction and in a pot, mustard had congealed to a sticky blob. That wouldn't do at all. The standards at Shrimp's had to be impeccable: attention to detail and thoroughness were what they were known for.

In the hallway she stood in front of the gilt mirror and frowned. What was going on here? The mirror needed a damned good clean – why, she could write her name in the grime. She would not tolerate this kind of sloppiness and she would give Alice the sharp edge of her tongue when she caught up with her: she was too slipshod about her chores these days. Where in God's name was Alice this morning? She had been most odd of late, disappearing for hours on end.

Ella looked at her reflection in the tarnished mirror. One day soon she really must venture down to the village and get her hair cut; it was far too long for this hot weather. She turned away from the mirror and looked with dismay at the enormous pile of post on the doormat. She picked up a letter whose handwriting looked a little familiar, then tossed it back on to the pile. There was no time for reading the post now. She checked her wristwatch. Goodness, look at the time. She must make sure that the kitchen staff were getting on with the breakfast. Then, when all was as it should be, she would sound the gong and another busy day would begin at Shrimp's Hotel.

Chapter 3

Sister Matilde hurried through the crowds on Paddington station clutching the hand of a young girl. As they ran, the nun's grey habit swirled in the draught and her face grew red, beads of perspiration forming at the point where her wimple met her creased forehead. She was too old to be chasing up and down railway platforms but she was always given this job at the end of every term because she was the only one of the convent sisters who had the confidence to drive the battered old Austin through London. London traffic held no fears for Sister Matilde; in another life she'd driven in Paris and Naples and had nerves of steel.

She'd made two separate trips already today, had seen seven girls off on their trains and now she was running late. She had to get this last child safely off, and then if time were on her side she might get to see the art exhibition at the Royal Academy and still make it back to the convent in time for Benediction.

An announcement drew nun and girl to a sudden halt.

'We regret to announce that the four-fifteen train to Swansea is ten minutes late.'

'Damn. Here am I working myself up into a lather and the train is delayed,' said Sister Matilde.

Catrin Grieve looked up at her and smiled shyly. Sister

16

Matilde was her favourite of all the nuns at school. There were lots of rumours about Sister Matilde, that she had been a professor or maybe it was an artist before she had become a nun. The older girls said she'd had a failed romance with a duke and that's why she'd taken the veil and come to St Agnes's. She was very clever, could speak French and Italian, play the piano and the organ, and knew everything in the world about art and books. And yet she was forgetful, too. She could never remember anyone's name for more than five minutes, so she was likely to call you anything. She was also a little bit mad. On the last day of term, when she was supposed to be playing the school out to 'God Save the Pope' she'd played 'Paddy McGinty's Goat' by accident. It was hilarious. All the nuns twittered with horror and the girls hugged themselves, desperate not to laugh. Sometimes clever people were like that because their brains overheated and that made them do peculiar things.

'Do you have the piece of paper with the telephone number of the place where you're staying, Cynthia?'

'I'm Catrin, Sister, not Cynthia, and yes, it's in my purse.' she replied for the tenth time since they had left school.

Sister Matilde looked down at the girl, reached out to push a stray curl under the brim of her boater.

Cynthia, Celia, whatever her name was, had lost such a lot of weight during the last term that there was hardly anything left of her. There was something not right at all with this child. She used to be such a lively, bonny girl, full of vim and vigour, but she'd lost her sparkle of late. And as for that dope-brained mother of hers, she could do with her face slapping. It was bad enough that the girl had no father; the least the mother could do was be around for her in the holidays. And yet she'd telephoned a few days back, saying that Catrin would be going to stay with some old aunts for the whole summer holiday.

17

Old aunts indeed. The girl needed to be with her mother. Girls of this age needed to fight with their mothers, lock horns, sulk and then make up again. It was part of growing up, for God's sake. It was shameful the way some parents acted towards their children. It was one thing to choose a boarding-school education but quite another to try and offload them in the holidays when there was no need. No need at all in this case, because there didn't seem to be any shortage of money. Hadn't Sister Lucy said that they lived in a grand house in one of those elegant London squares? Too much money and not enough sense, probably. The mother hadn't even had the decency to visit Catrin and explain the new arrangements for the holidays; she'd just sent a taxicab to deliver the train tickets and a suitcase full of expensive clothes which, according to Sister Lucy, were all two sizes too big.

As far as Sister Matilde was concerned, the woman was a well-to-do floozy. One of those hair-brained women out dancing until all hours of the night and throwing cocktails down her silly neck. Or else gallivanting about the Continent with unsuitable men in tow. She'd bet she was the type to flaunt herself in those new-fangled bikini articles that were all the rage, along with mini-skirts and the other ridiculous paraphernalia that was creeping in.

'Be sure to say your prayers every night and find a Catholic church as soon as you can so that you can go to mass every Sunday. I expect those aunts of yours are good Catholics?'

'I don't know, Sister, I've never met them.'

'You've never met them?' Sister Matilde was horrified.

'No, Sister. I didn't even know they existed until a few days ago. I didn't realise I had any family apart from my mother.'

Sister Matilde frowned down at the girl's worried face.

'Well, well, I'm sure they'll be lovely people, and it'll be good for them to have a youngster around the house.'

'I'm not staying in a house, Sister, it's a hotel.'

'And what, pray, is the name of this hotel, Cecilia?'

'It's called Shrimp's Hotel, Sister, and it's near a place called Kilvenny in Wales.'

Sister Matilde stared at the girl before her without really seeing her.

She caught hold of her rosary and held it tightly. Sweet Jesus.

Sister Matilde had hoped fervently that she'd never hear that place mentioned again. She wiped a bead of perspiration from her brow.

'Tell me your name again, child.'

'Catrin. Catrin Grieve.'

Sister Matilde closed her eyes, felt her heart beating erratically, her stomach twisting into a painful coil.

For a moment she was back in Kilvenny, hearing the sea crashing against the rocks below the hotel gardens, a swing creaking in the wind. The cry of rooks rising up from the tower of the castle, and the first touch of warm lips upon her own.

Dear God in heaven, can I never be allowed to forget?

'The train now standing at platform one is the four fifteen, London Paddington to Swansea.'

Sister Matilde straightened up and put all unpleasant thoughts from her mind.

'Come on, let's find you a seat. Remember, now, make sure that you eat well during the holidays. I want to see you hale and hearty when you come back to us in September.'

'Yes, Sister.'

Sister Matilde climbed on to the train and settled the girl in an empty compartment. She lifted the suitcase on to the luggage rack and handed Catrin a brown paper bag which

19

contained some food for the journey. She smiled, thinking that the meagre rations of convent food would be the last tedious meal that Catrin Grieve would eat all summer. Whatever unpleasant connotations Shrimp's Hotel had for Sister Matilde, the food there had been exquisite. Thinking of the small earthenware ramekins of potted shrimps and the homemade brown bread made her stomach rumble. Squab pie and sticky almond pudding. Hopefully Catrin Grieve would renew her appetite and put on a few pounds over the summer – she sorely needed to.

She leant towards Catrin, touched her gently on the forehead, then slipped her hand into the pocket of her habit and absentmindedly took out one of her holy pictures and put it into Catrin's blazer pocket.

'God bless you and keep you safe.'

'Thank you, Sister.'

Then Sister Matilde got off the train just as the guard blew his whistle.

She stood watching the train pull slowly away from the station.

Catrin waved to Sister Matilde, who looked at her through the window. She had taken off her boater and for a moment her face, framed by a halo of unruly curls, was bathed in a shaft of light, softly illuminating her small features. It was a curious moment of déjà vu. Somewhere, a long time ago, a face just like this one had looked at her . . .

During the return drive to school, the nun had a terrible feeling of foreboding – and that feeling was to remain with her for a long time.

Chapter 4

In the doorway of the Café Romana, Tony Agosti lit a cigarette and inhaled deeply, pulling up the collar of his jacket, for the night had turned suddenly chilly.

Every night before he locked up the café he loved to stand outside listening to the rhythmic lapping of the waves down on the beach and the first tentative calling of owls over in Gwartney's Wood. He breathed in the familiar smell of the wild garlic and nettles that grew in profusion alongside the creek. There was a whiff of pungent herbs from the castle's kitchen garden, and the sweet night fragrance of roses.

Hell, he was going to miss this place if he was forced to sell up and move away. But things were looking dire at the moment; the takings were rock bottom again this week and he couldn't carry on like this for much longer. There was no way he could survive selling half a dozen meat pies and a few ice-cream sundaes. It would be for the best if he bit the bullet and broke the bad news to Nonna sooner rather than later.

If only it were that easy, eh? How did you tell your ancient grandmother that everything she and her late husband had worked for was about to go down the pan? How could he tell her that one day soon he'd have to uproot her and move away from Kilvenny, although God knows where they'd go?

Sweet Jesus, his grandfather would turn in his grave if he knew how tough life had become here. Luigi Agosti had walked all the way through Italy and France and got on a ship which had brought him to Wales. He'd worked in the docks in Swansea and then somehow or other he'd made his way out here to Kilvenny and put down roots. At first he'd worked all hours at the herring smokehouse further along the coast, scrimped and saved until he had enough money to open the Café Romana, where he soon built up a thriving trade. The café had been busy from morning till night. Work used to start at dawn making tea and toast for the early shift workers waiting for the bone-shaker bus that took them to the herring smokehouse. He missed the smell of fish that used to fill the air when the breeze was in the right direction, but now the crumbling remains were all that was left and the bus had long since been sent to the knacker's yard.

Later in the day, the women of the village used to venture out to Bryn Jones's shop, then on to Watkins the Butcher's, finishing up in the Café Romana for the daily dose of gossip and tea with side orders of ice creams and Welsh cakes. In the night the teenagers came, sloping down from the farms, smoking filched Woodbines, spitting and talking too loud, on the lookout for a pretty girl and to buy a soda or a chocolate nut sundae.

His reminiscing was interrupted by the distant sound of the late train chugging sluggishly towards Kilvenny station. The locals euphemistically called it the 'late train' as though there were early trains and lunchtime trains and not just this train which came once a week to Kilvenny and rarely stopped unless you asked the guard first. It was all the talk that next year the line would close for good and Kilvenny would lose its last link with civilisation and sink further into isolation and decay.

He watched the steam from the engine rise into the night sky and drift above the one remaining tower of Kilvenny Castle.

He strained his ears, heard the train creak to a halt, a carriage door slamming and then the train moving off again, building up a head of steam as it clattered on round the coast.

He wondered who could be arriving in Kilvenny at this time of night, for as far as he knew no one had travelled out recently and few visitors ever made their way here except by accident.

He stepped out of the doorway and looked towards the bend in the road where whoever had arrived on the train would surely appear soon. Ten minutes passed and no one came, which was odd because there wasn't anywhere for miles if one turned left instead of right out of the station.

Unless ... unless whoever had arrived had decided to walk down to the village through Gwartney's Wood for old time's sake.

He put his hand in his jacket pocket and felt for the dog-eared postcard he'd kept there all this time. A frisson of excitement made his heart beat erratically and he shivered with anticipation.

He screwed up his eyes waiting for someone to appear. First there would be the sound of whistling and the telltale smell of a foreign cigarette on the night air. Then suddenly they would step into the pool of light from the crooked gas lamp. But no one came.

He pushed open the café door and the bell above it tinkled gaily. He looked round sadly at the faded posters on the walls and the battered boater that he'd worn that summer long ago. There too was the little statuette of

St Joseph of Arimathea, the patron saint of foundlings, in his niche; a poignant reminder of his grandfather's childhood in Italy.

He climbed the narrow stairs with a heavy heart. Before he went to bed he'd check on Nonna, and if she were still awake then he'd break the news to her gently.

Nonna lay asleep in the big bed; her silver hair undone from her braids was spread out over the starched white pillow like a frozen river in the moonlit room. Even in sleep she clasped her rosary tightly, the pink beads pale against the dark skin of her old hands. The room smelled as it always did, of lavender and coffee dregs, of the orange-blossom scent one of Nonna's nieces sent each birthday from Italy.

Nonna stirred in her sleep, moaned softly, reaching out across the bed as though she were expecting to find her husband still lying there beside her although he'd been dead and buried these fourteen years.

Tony backed out of the room, covering his mouth with his fist to stifle a rising sob. Tonight he would let her sleep peacefully but one day soon, unless a miracle happened, he would have to break the bad news to her.

Chapter 5

It was dark when the train pulled in to Kilvenny. Catrin stepped awkwardly down from the carriage, set down her heavy brown suitcase and looked around fearfully. She was the only person who had got off the train and there wasn't another soul in sight.

The station was the smallest she had ever seen, lit by one old-fashioned gas lamp whose meagre light spread gloom and despondency across the weed-clogged platform. There was a ramshackle waiting room which looked as if it would collapse like a house of cards under the first rough breeze.

The train whistled, belched out a cloud of writhing steam and moved slowly away, abandoning her to the misty dark.

She stretched her arms above her head and yawned. Any minute now Aunt Alice and Aunt Ella would dash out from the shadows to meet her for the first time. They would fuss and kiss and hug and do all the other rubbishy stuff that aunts were supposed to do.

She stamped her feet impatiently. She just knew that she was going to hate it here; all her mother's garbled stories on the telephone about how wonderful it was would be a pack of lies. That was the thing her mother did best: tell lies. Her mother must think she was an absolute idiot. The reason she was being sent to stay with these long-lost aunts was nothing to do with it being good for her; it was about her mother getting her own way. Again. She was off gallivanting about in Italy while Catrin was sent here to spend eight weeks in the middle of nowhere.

Why hadn't her mother ever mentioned these Welsh aunts before, if they were so damned wonderful? Because they wouldn't be, that's why. They'd have false teeth which jiggled when they talked, they'd stink of mothballs and perm lotion, and worst of all they'd be stuffy, boring and as old as the hills.

In the dilapidated waiting room a clock ticked spasmodically.

She walked to the door, peeped inside and withdrew her head quickly; there was a strong smell of tom cats and stale tobacco but there was no one waiting for her.

She made her way out of the station, past the unmanned ticket office where a yellowing CLOSED sign hung haphazardly across the cracked window. She brightened. The aunts must have sent a car to pick her up – her mother had said the old gardener used to collect guests who arrived by train and he'd no doubt be waiting patiently outside the station.

The lane was deserted. A high moon wobbled above the swaying treetops and a lone gas lamp spluttered, casting a watery pool of light around her feet. Moths flickered in and out of the light, their fragile wings fluttering feebly against the dusty bowl of the lamp.

Moonlight dappled the lane and a chill breeze made her shiver and pull her school blazer tighter around her.

Surely someone would come soon? After all, they knew she was arriving on the late train.

It seemed an age since Sister Matilde had seen her off at Paddington. Thinking of Sister Matilde brought a lump to her throat. She wished that she could have stayed at school for the summer instead of being sent here to some stuffy old aunts she'd never met and didn't want to.

If no one came in the next five minutes, she'd damn well find a telephone box and ring her mother. She'd just have to jolly well come down here and pick her up, except that wasn't possible because her mother was already on her way to Italy. Catrin brushed a tear from her cheek, screwed up her fists, felt anger rising inside her, a thick, tight band in her stomach which pushed against her lungs and made it hard to breathe.

She would love to have gone on holiday to Italy even if it was with her mother. Sister Matilde had told Catrin's class loads of stories about when she'd stayed in a convent in Italy. She'd described the cool, ancient churches smelling of incense and wild flowers, and how when the church bells clanged, the startled pigeons flew up into the blue summer skies. She'd told them of the beautiful paintings and the marvellous statues she had seen and how she had drunk icy limoncello and eaten marzipan cakes in a shady café in a tree-lined piazza. She had made it feel so real, so enticing, that Catrin could almost smell the lemons and limes stacked in the baskets on the market stalls, could almost breathe in the aroma of thyme and rosemary that filled the air. In her mind's eye she could see the old women dressed all in black who sold eggs from wicker baskets while chickens pecked the cobbles in search of crumbs.

A bird squawked as it flew overhead and Catrin jumped, all thoughts of Sister Matilde and Italy disappearing.

Hell's bells, why didn't somebody come?

It was the first time in her life that she had been out in the dark in a strange place on her own, and she didn't like it. There were worrying noises everywhere; the cracking of a twig might mean someone was lurking in the bushes waiting to pounce. It was well known that tramps and tinkers prowled around the countryside at night, with sharp knives and black hearts.

At school the doors were always locked and bolted because you never knew who might try to get in. Once a naked man had climbed over the convent wall and chased Sister Lucy through the cabbage patch.

There was a rustle of leaves as a mouse or maybe a rat scurried into the undergrowth. A spider writhed on a dangling thread from the branch of a tree and bats squeaked somewhere beyond the pool of light.

A cloud passed over the moon, the gas light dimmed and it grew so dark that she almost screamed in fright.

She put her hand in her blazer pocket and for comfort took out the holy picture that Sister Matilde had given her. She stepped closer to the lamplight and looked at it in surprise. The nuns usually gave out pictures of sad-faced virgins, horse-faced saints or a sorrowful Jesus in the garden of Gethsemane. This was a tiny painting of a large, fat cat sitting beneath a tree on a withered lawn strewn with fallen apples. She looked more closely and realised that they weren't apples but pomegranates.

It wasn't a holy picture at all.

Why would Sister Matilde give her a picture of a fat cat?

It wasn't even a cute cat, but an ugly fierce-looking thing with its mouth opened as if it was snarling. It must be Sister Matilde's idea of a joke.

She slipped the picture quickly back into her pocket and felt for her rosary.

An owl called, a long and quivering hoot which made her skin erupt with pinpricks of fear. Another owl answered mournfully.

Surely someone must come for her soon.

In the distance a church clock chimed the hour and a dog howled dolefully.

She wasn't going to hang around a moment longer. She'd grit her teeth and walk down to Kilvenny village, find a blasted telephone box and ring Shrimp's Hotel.

She walked quickly down the lane, keeping to the middle, out of reach of the long, hairy arms of any bogeymen hiding in the bushes.

The air here in Wales was different from London; there was a heady whiff of stinging nettles, damp earth and coal smoke mingling with the salty tang of the sea. There was no sound of traffic, no cars tooting their horns and no orange streetlights to guide you.

The narrow lane curved round to the left and emerged into a narrow street and signs of civilisation. A hand-painted sign on the side of a house read 'Cockle Lane'. She looked around hopefully but there was no telephone box and not a person in sight. Kilvenny was like a badly lit ghost town.

The houses on either side of Cockle Lane were the smallest she had ever seen, more suitable for midgets than real people. It would almost be possible to climb down from the upstairs windows into the street without a ladder. The front doors were all firmly closed and the curtains drawn across the tiny windows. Some of the houses were empty, the windows boarded up with wood and corrugated iron.

Crackly gramophone music drifted out into the night and the smell of someone making toast made her stomach ache with longing.

Further down the road there was a war memorial with withered poppy wreaths scattered haphazardly round the base. The weak light of a flickering gas lamp illuminated the list of names.

KILLED IN ACTION 1939–1945
Arthur, David John
Grieve, William John
Grieve, Charles Arthur
Lawrence, Dafydd
Roberts, Ianto

She wondered if William and Charles Grieve were relations of the aunts. There was so little that she knew about her family until her mother had conjured up these aunts, like rabbits from a hat.

On the right-hand side of Cockle Lane there were a few shabby shops. Daniel Watkins, High-Class Butcher and Poulterer didn't look very high-class with the chipped pottery pigs leering out from behind the greasy window-pane and the green paintwork on the door blistered and peeling. Next to the butcher's was a tall, narrow building with a washed-out sign hanging above the door, 'Kilvenny Proprietary Library'. The curtains on the arched window to the left of the door were open and Catrin edged towards it.

She peeped cautiously in through the window, marvelling at the hundreds of old books that lined the walls from floor to ceiling. Then she saw the old man. He was sitting in an enormous chair, his feet curled beneath him, oblivious of everything except the book he had his nose stuck firmly into. A fat white cat slumbered in his lap and he looked so content and cosy that for a moment Catrin's chest filled with rage. How she would like to get in there, tip him out of the chair and rip the book to pieces.

He picked up a cup from a side table, without taking his eyes off his book. He reached out for a biscuit and popped it into his mouth, dropping crumbs down the front of his grey shirt. He took another and another.

Greedy guts. Her mouth watered and she swallowed hard. Gutsy pig. Biscuits were bad for you and they spoiled your appetite.

Suddenly the cat opened one large green eye and stared at her, and she moved stealthily away from the window in case the man looked up and caught her snooping.

In the window of the Café Romana she caught sight of her reflection. She looked like a character just stepped out from an old-fashioned storybook for girls, with her boater hat and old-fashioned uniform.

The café was shut but a light shone behind the counter and illuminated the room in a soft blue aura. It was an Aladdin's cave with rows and rows of sweet jars on shelves behind the counter. Humbugs and liquorice twists, sherbet and coconut macaroons. Toasted teacakes and chocolate éclairs. She licked her lips longingly. She'd given up sweets and chocolate for Lent last year and hadn't eaten any since. Sweets made you fat. What was it they said in the slimming magazines she smuggled into school? *A moment on the lips means a lifetime on the hips!*

An enormous glittering soda fountain bore the words 'Sarsaparilla, Lime and Lemon'. Posters advertising Capstan cigarettes and Fry's Five Boys chocolate hung on the walls, along with faded pictures of mouth-watering ice creams: tutti fruttis, vanilla and chocolate sundaes and gigantic knickerbocker glories.

Her stomach protested noisily, even though she didn't really like ice cream that much because it was full of fat and sugar.

The last thing she had eaten was a thin piece of toast scraped with margarine at breakfast this morning. She thought of the picnic lunch that she'd thrown away. One greasy Spam sandwich, a small russet apple and a slice of dried fruitcake.

She dragged herself reluctantly away from the café window.

Further down the road she stopped outside Meredith Evans, Photographer for Weddings and Special Occasions.

There were photographs of stiff-lipped bridegrooms and simpering brides. There were dribbling babies and horse-faced young men dressed in their best suits and a wide-eyed little girl sitting underneath a table smiling shyly out at the camera. There were eerie-looking men in top hats and frosty-faced women with parasols and wonky teeth. An owl called, a drawn-out, wavering hoot that gave her goose pimples and she had to bite her lips to stop her teeth chattering.

The sign outside the Old Boot Inn groaned ominously above her head, and the sound of a creaking accordion drifted out through the shuttered windows, along with a smell of warm beer and cigarette smoke which made her stomach turn over.

Sister Lucy had warned them about keeping away from public houses because they were places where the weak-willed went. Decent women should never, ever go into one and only a certain type of woman ever did. They were called loose women and had beehive hair sprayed stiff with lacquer. They wore chipped red nail polish, and painted circles of rouge on their cheeks. They had bosoms which wobbled dangerously, high heels and stockings with ladders in. Mary Donahue said the ladders were for men to climb up at night.

To her left the ruined walls of an ancient castle were silhouetted against the sky, a sky quite unlike the London one she was used to. There were more stars here in Wales than there were in England, millions of them spread out across the heavens like a secret code.

Much of the castle was ruined, but one wing still

remained and the latticed windows glittered in the moonlight. Spooky.

Ghosts would walk in there at night. Long-faced women wearing faded velvet dresses, smelling of lilac and sobbing for their lost loves. Ugh.

Down in the dungeons the ghosts of toothless, stinking beggars would clank their chains and beg for stale bread and water.

She hurried on until the road petered out into a concrete slipway which led down to the beach. A lopsided signpost in the shape of a finger pointed across the beach, and she could just make out the writing: 'IMP'S OTEL'.

A muffled cough startled her and she turned and saw a wooden hut built against the sea wall, a higgledy-piggledy place with a worn, thatched roof and three small windows. A brass sign above the door declared it to be The Fisherman's Snug. It looked snug, too, with smoke curling up from a tiny chimney and a candle in an enamel holder burning in the middle window. How lovely to be shut up in there on a stormy night, listening to the wild winds and the crashing of the sea. A startled face appeared suddenly at the window, a pale-faced man with eyes as bright as stars.

Their eyes met momentarily and Catrin moved quickly away into the shadows and waited with bated breath. The candle was suddenly blown out and the face disappeared, although she was sure the man was still watching her.

As she hurried across the beach her sandals sank into the soft, wet sand and water seeped up into her cotton ankle socks and made her feet itch uncomfortably. Wearily she climbed the steep steps at the far side of the beach, stumbling as she went, trying to stem the tears of exhaustion.

At the top of the steps she put down her suitcase and looked with dismay at the meadow of waving grass she would need to cross. Away beyond the meadow a large house loomed up stark as a cardboard cut-out against the sky. At last. Shrimp's Hotel.

Moonlight silvered the meadow and the long grass shivered in the breeze as she made her way tentatively forward, the grass tickling her bare legs, the heads of silken poppies brushing against her goose-pimpled skin. She was afraid and yet filled with a curious excitement which sent a peculiar shiver tootling up her backbone.

Shrimp's Hotel was all in darkness, but hopefully the aunts would still be up. The thought of a warm bed and a long sleep spurred her on despite her aching legs and the suitcase almost pulling her arm out of its socket.

She struggled on, stopping by an oak tree where a lop-sided swing dangled from a large branch.

There were swings in the park near the school but they were only allowed on them if no one was around, and even then Sister Lucy made them tuck their dresses firmly round their knees so that they wouldn't show their underwear. Men could go mad if they caught a glimpse of women's underwear.

Sister Lucy said men were sorry creatures who didn't have any self-control where young girls were concerned. Good Catholic girls must never flaunt themselves in front of eejits and dirty-minded young men.

Once, in the playground, a wasp flew up the frock of a senior girl and she screamed and lifted her skirts to get it out and Sister Lucy had accused her of being a wanton hussy and taken all her merit marks away in one go.

Catrin looked longingly at the swing and wondered what it would feel like to sail through the air in the dark.

It would be daft. Wonderful.

What if someone should see her?

She climbed tentatively on to the wooden seat, leant back

and pushed against the ground with her feet. The swing moved, slowly at first and then faster and faster. Higher and higher she went until she felt as though she was leaving the earth and merging with the stars.

She heard a mouse rustling through the grass. An owl called, unseen but close.

She was unafraid. Flying.

She giggled. If Sister Lucy could see her now she'd have a blue fit: 'Have you taken leave of your senses, Catrin Grieve? Showing your washing to the whole wide world. Get down from there this instant.'

Catrin threw back her head and laughed, felt the breeze, deliciously cool on her face, lifting her dress above her bony knees.

There was a creaking as the swing lurched, the rope crossed over and the swing twisted round in the air.

Round and round she went, faster and faster, until the world was out of control. Trees and house, moon and sea. Stars spinning above the tower of the ruined castle.

The rope snapped and she was thrown high into the air.

Her feet were above her head, stars twinkling above her brown crepe-soled sandals.

She hit the ground, rolled over and over, brambles ripping at her bare legs until finally she came to rest. She lay on her back struggling to catch her breath. Her heart was beating fast, the blood rushing to her head, and a drumming sound echoed in her ears. When the shock began to subside, her breath came in scratchy gasps.

Whatever had she been thinking of?

She could have killed herself falling like that and yet she was fine, although she'd be bound to have a few bruises to show for her madness in the morning. If anyone at Shrimp's had seen her they'd think she was some kind of simpleton.

The hairs on the nape of her neck twitched, a million

antennae warning her that someone out there in the darkness was watching her. What if there were dangerous halfwits wandering around in the dark? Lunatics broken out from asylums?

She ran now, the suitcase banging painfully against her legs, until she reached the front door of the hotel and looked up at the darkened windows.

There must be some terrible mistake. She dropped the suitcase and hastily made the sign of the cross.

Chapter 6

Meredith Evans closed the door to his dark room and shuffled through into the parlour. He heard the church clock chime the hour, switched on a side lamp, poured himself a full tumbler of whisky, drank it down, smacked his lips appreciatively and turned on the wireless. A crackling filled the room, followed by an ear-splitting whistling punctuated by the familiar voice of the weatherman, who sounded as if he were at the far end of the world and talking through a pipe. He turned the dial with impatience but the whistling got louder so he turned it off, poured another tumbler of whisky and went out into the front of the shop.

It always looked better there at night than in the daytime. The layer of dust on the counter and the cabinets was transformed to silver by the moonlight and looked more like freshly sprinkled fairy dust than the result of years of neglect.

The photographs on the walls acquired a different patina, the faces of hard-faced old maids were softened by starlight, and even Hester Grieve took on a benevolent smile, the glint of malice in those slanting eyes dimmed by shadow.

Absentmindedly he opened the door of a large cage in a corner of the room. It had been empty for years but sometimes, in the gloom of the shop he thought he could see that wily old monkey looking back at him accusingly. The monkey had been a crafty little beggar but he hadn't been clever enough to undo the clip that kept him chained inside the cage. Meredith cursed; he'd made good money round the coast taking photographs of kids with the monkey perched on their shoulders until some idiot had set him free. And he had a bloody good idea that the idiot he had in mind was Ella Grieve.

He turned and looked up at the portrait of Alice Grieve and smiled, ran his hands lovingly round the ornate frame. Damn, she was a beautiful woman if ever there was one. If he'd known he was going to lose her to another man he'd have bought a bigger cage and locked her up in it for her own safety.

He turned away from the photograph, looked out through the shop window – and his mouth fell open, his spectacles dropping down to the end of his nose. Who in the name of God would be looking in through the shop window at this time of night? He shoved his spectacles back into place and looked again. There was definitely someone there, someone wearing a straw boater. Jesus! Were there ghosts abroad tonight? He looked again and with relief saw that it was not a man but a child. That was ridiculous, though. There were never any children wandering around the village in the pitch dark – there were barely any children here at all, these days. He'd taken a drop too much whisky again, and he was starting to imagine things.

He turned away from the window, laughed a little nervously, and chided himself for his foolishness. He mopped the gathering sweat from his forehead with a dirty handkerchief and steadied himself against the counter. If he turned round slowly and kept calm, urged his brain not to play tricks on him, he would see that he was mistaken, that there was no one there.

He turned his head.

Jesus and all the Saints! It couldn't be! Yet those eyes couldn't lie.

Pull yourself together, Meredith. Dead people didn't stand staring in through the dusty windows of photographers' shops. Dead people couldn't walk.

He backed away through the shop, knocking his shins on a camera stand and cursing loudly. He reached for the whisky bottle and took a hefty slug, the amber liquid trickling down his unshaven chin. Hurriedly he turned out the light and, still clutching the whisky bottle, climbed the narrow stairs to his bedroom, where he pulled back the curtains and stared down into Cockle Lane. There was no one there. He looked towards the beach, and beyond the beach he saw the stark outlines of the tall chimneys at Shrimp's Hotel – and he shuddered.

Chapter 7

Ella Grieve woke up with a start. She sat up, rubbed her eyes and looked round the room. Who on earth would be knocking on the front door at this hour? All the guests had a night key in case they stayed out late. Maybe old Igor Evanski had been down to the Old Boot, taken a little too much liquor and mislaid his keys again.

Pull yourself together, Ella. That was ridiculous. Igor Evanski, the piano tuner, had been dead for years. She and Alice had been to his funeral in Hampstead and Alice got squiffy on gin and lemon. It was all in the past. Done and dusted.

Ella got up from her chair, found the matches, lit a candle stub and made her way out through the kitchen.

She glanced down at the pile of unopened post that lay on the doormat. She really must get to grips with it one day soon.

The frenzied banging on the door began again.

She put her head on one side and listened. Someone was sobbing.

'Who is this?' she called irritably.

The banging stopped.

'Aunt Alice, let me in, please.'

'Aunt Alice? I'll give you bloody Aunt Alice!'

'Please, please, just let me in.'

'Whoever you are, go away. Alice isn't here.'

There was an uneasy silence.

'Is Aunt Ella there, then? Please fetch Aunt Ella.'

Who could this be, calling her Aunt? No one had called her Aunt in years.

Ella stiffened. It couldn't be Kizzy Grieve; she wouldn't dare come back here after what she'd done.

The sobbing got louder, the banging weaker.

Ella bit her lip, held the candleholder more tightly to stop it shaking.

'Is that you, Kizzy Grieve? I told you years back I never wanted to clap eyes on you ever again.'

'It's not Kizzy, it's Catrin.'

'I don't know any Catrin. Now get away from here.'

'I'm Catrin, Catrin Grieve. My mother is Kizzy, she wrote to you, she's your niece.'

'I have no niece.'

'But she *is* your niece. She's called Kizzy for short – really she's Katherine Isobel.'

Ella stood looking at the door, clenching and unclenching her fist. 'What do you mean, she wrote to me?'

'She wrote and asked if I could stay here with you for the summer.'

The voice beyond the door was edged with panic.

Ella could barely move for shock. She looked down at the pile of letters at her feet. No wonder she'd thought she recognised the handwriting on one of them, but they had been lying there unopened for weeks.

The bare-faced cheek of the woman. How dare she presume to send her stupid child here for the summer?

'Are you still there?' Catrin whimpered.

'Of course I'm still here. I'm not a bloody ghost. I didn't open her letter, and if I had I wouldn't have replied. And

41

just supposing I had replied, I'd have told your blasted mother to go to hell.'

'But I've nowhere to go, and ...' Catrin's voice trailed off and she began to sob.

Ella turned her back on the door and shuffled back towards the kitchen muttering to herself. Then she paused and called, 'The bolts are too stiff to draw back on the front door. You'd best come round the side to the kitchen door.'

Catrin stumbled round to the side of the hotel and found the door. She heard the rasping of a rusty key being turned, and the kitchen door opened with a rheumaticky creak. She looked uneasily at the old woman who stood in the doorway holding a candle aloft.

Her face was streaked with grime, her bright eyes narrowed with irritation, her tangled hair hanging down almost to her waist. She was dressed in a filthy brown overall tied round the waist with a piece of greasy string. On her feet she wore ancient wellingtons, one green and one black.

This couldn't possibly be one of her aunts. Her mother had always said that she came from a very respectable family. This must be a tramp broken into the house and pretending to be one of the aunts.

Ella looked the girl up and down and her mouth dropped open in astonishment.

Dear God! There was something about this girl that reminded her of Alice when she was a child, Alice who had metamorphosed from the ugly duckling to the swan, physically if not mentally.

So this was Kizzy's daughter.

She was a skinny girl with a head of curls and a pale, tear-stained face. She had eyes as big as an owl's and a chin which wobbled like junket. She stood there, her bony knees knocking together in fright, clasping a boater hat between white knuckles.

She didn't look anything like Kizzy or her father, thank Christ.

Ella couldn't take her eyes off the girl. 'Don't just stand there gawping. You'd better come in.'

Catrin followed Ella into the kitchen and looked around, her eyes wide with trepidation.

'I can't understand what you think you're doing coming out here and waking folk up at this hour.'

'I'm sorry. I told you, I was supposed to be staying here and I don't understand why my mother sent me all the way here when she hadn't even heard from you to say it was all right.'

'Why did Kizzy Grieve ever do anything in her life? Because it suited her purposes, I daresay.'

Ella rubbed her forehead with dirty fingers and chewed her lips in consternation.

'Why ... why wouldn't you want me here?' Catrin stammered.

'Why wouldn't I want you here? I don't want anybody here.'

Catrin looked around her fearfully, searched her blazer pockets for a handkerchief to stem her tears.

'I like being on my own,' Ella went on. 'I've got used to it since Alice went and died on me.'

Catrin bit her lip and when she spoke her words were muffled. 'My mother never said anything about Aunt Alice dying.'

Ella laughed, a cracked, harsh laugh, and Catrin flinched, took a step backwards.

'Your mother! Your mother never cared about anyone except herself. Alice thought the world of your bloody mother, and look where it got her. Your mother hasn't been back here in years; she wasn't welcome after what she did. She broke Alice's heart – oh, Alice might have forgiven her, given time, but time was one thing she hadn't got.'

'What did my mother do that was so awful?'

Ella watched the girl closely, saw the fear rising in her eyes, the way her bottom lip quivered uncontrollably.

'Never mind what she did, save to say she shouldn't have done it. What she did is between her and me now. But you can't stay here.'

'I don't want to stay here. My mother said Shrimp's was a lovely place but it's not, it's awful.' There was an edge to her voice, a little defiance breaking through the fear.

'Our guests like it well enough. They keep on coming back.'

'There are guests staying here?' Catrin said with incredulity. 'In this pig sty?'

Ella glared at Catrin, her dirt-streaked face distorted with anger. 'Shrimp's has the best of reputations, I'll have you know. Our guests come back here year after year,' she snapped, running her hand distractedly through her matted hair.

'It must have been a long time since anyone came here. No one in their right mind would want to stay here now.'

Ella blinked, shook her head, looked around her as if surprised by what she saw. Then she looked back at the girl steadfastly.

'I'm sorry. I get confused these days and I think there are still guests staying here. Sometimes I think the door will open and Alice will come back. I spend a lot of my time living in the past. I find it's so much better than the present.'

The silence was alleviated only by the squeak of a mouse and the monotonous dripping of a tap into an empty sink.

'Now, I think that you'd better just go back to wherever it is you've come from.'

'But I can't go home, not tonight.' Catrin was fighting back tears again.

Ella looked away quickly. She couldn't stand tears; there had been so many tears when Alice had died.

'Well, I don't know at all. I suppose you'll have to stay here the night – just the one night, mind, and then you must sort something out in the morning.'

Catrin breathed deeply, tried to stem the feeling of sickness that was sweeping through her.

'You wait here while I go and make you up a bed.'

And with that Ella Grieve shuffled out of the kitchen into the darkness beyond.

Catrin heard a match strike and the flame of a candle lit up the dark hallway. Momentarily she saw her own reflection staring back at her from an enormous mottled mirror. She looked like a lost child, something from a Dickens novel. She listened as Ella Grieve climbed the creaking stairs, heard a door opening somewhere above her head, and then silence.

Catrin squeezed her hands into fists, willing herself not to scream.

If she could get hold of her mother right now, she'd wring her scraggy neck. She looked warily around the wreck of a kitchen. Cobwebs hung in gloomy veils from the high ceiling and clung to every sticky surface. Filthy tea towels festooned the backs of chairs. The floor was covered in a layer of sticky dust, and there were dead mice and shrivelled-up spiders all over the place. The air was thick with an overpowering smell of mildew and candlewax.

The grisly carcass of a chicken mouldered on a lopsided shelf, and there were rusty tins scattered across the kitchen table. She held her breath for as long as she could, then took a clean handkerchief from her blazer pocket and covered her nose to keep out the stench.

'You'll simply adore Shrimp's, darling,' her mother had said on the telephone. 'Everything about it is truly glorious.'

It wasn't glorious at all. It was terrible, the most awful place she'd ever seen. She couldn't stay in this ghastly place. She wouldn't. Her mother would just have to come back from Italy and fetch her. The trouble was, she didn't know where her mother was staying. She'd have to ring Sister Matilde at school; maybe she'd drive down and rescue her.

On the kitchen table in front of her lay a book and on the front in faded letters were the words *Guest Book*. What sort of people would ever have wanted to stay here in this filthy, stinking hole?

She opened the book gingerly and turned the greasy pages, glancing at the comments that people had written.

Mr and Mrs Barnaby, Wonderful stay. Marvellous food and great fun. Thank you, dear Alice and Ella.

Caroline and James Eadie, Our best ever holiday. Glorious food and such a wild time. See you next year.

The last entry read: *Mr and Mrs Aldernley. As glorious as ever at Shrimp's, truly splendid. Sorry we weren't able to stay for the wedding party.*

The comments had all been written years ago, before she was born, even. Obviously no one had stayed here since then. Surely her stupid mother must have known that the place had closed down; it looked as if it was about to *fall* down.

Catrin gripped the edge of the table tightly to steady herself.

Something small scuttled over her sandal and made her cry out in alarm.

After an age Ella Grieve reappeared, holding a candelabrum aloft, beckoning Catrin to follow her. She shuffled out of the kitchen and through a shadowy hallway which stank of sodden newspapers and mouse droppings.

A wide staircase led up into the total darkness above. Catrin held on tightly to her suitcase, tried to stifle her erratic breathing. The candle stubs in the candelabrum guttered, hissed, grew dim and then thankfully bright again. She stayed close on Ella's heels, feeling cautiously for the steps with her feet. On the wall beside them their two shadows climbed higher and higher. A bent-backed old woman with wild hair and a small girl climbing upwards into the darkness.

Chapter 8

Catrin lay quite still, her eyes closed, waiting for the rising bell to shatter the peace of St Agnes's dormitory. Her stomach growled and she smiled sleepily. It must be almost a whole day since she'd last eaten. She loved the feeling of emptiness, the way her skin pulled taut across her hipbones. She was lucky and could ignore her body's hunger pangs because she wasn't weak like the other girls, who were always rushing off and stuffing their faces at the first rumble of hunger. She could go for ages without eating. She could probably fast longer than the nuns could, maybe longer even than the holy saints.

The last thing she'd eaten had been half a slice of toast and after that she couldn't remember. Of course, she should have eaten the picnic lunch Sister Matilde had given her but she'd dumped that on the train.

The train that had brought her here to Kilvenny. Kilvenny! She opened her eyes, remembering with a shudder that she had spent the night in an attic bedroom in Shrimp's Hotel.

Early sunlight was streaming through the sash window, a myriad of dust motes swirling in the dank air, as if she were in the middle of a hazy dream. It wasn't a dream, though, and downstairs that horrible, dirty-faced Aunt Ella would be prowling around amid the cobweb curtains and dead mice. Hastily she pushed back the musty counterpane, got unsteadily to her feet and looked down at herself in dismay. She had slept in her school uniform and it was crumpled and smelt of sweat. Her legs were a mess, criss-crossed with bloody scratches from when she'd fallen from the swing, her white cotton ankle socks stretched out of shape and streaked with grime.

The room was a tip. A pile of mildewed clothes lay abandoned in a heap on the floor next to the bed, and a discarded shoe, nibbled by mice, lay in the far corner.

She needed to get out of this filthy hole as quickly as she could before she caught something. There would be all sorts of germs lurking in a place like this. Mange, smallpox, TB or even diphtheria. She must wash straight away; she couldn't possibly go out in the daylight looking like the wreck of the *Hesperus*. Sister Lucy said that cleanliness was next to godliness.

There was a small sink with a cracked mirror above it and she looked at her face, shocked at the sight. Her cheeks were dirt-streaked, her eyes puffy and ringed with bluish smudges of exhaustion and dried tears. She turned on the tap with difficulty, listened in dismay as water gurgled through the pipes and set up a terrible clanking. Without warning rusty water gushed into the sink, spattering her clothes, while the pipes shuddered and squealed in protest. She struggled to turn the tap off, opened her suitcase and looked at all the new clothes her mother had sent. She lifted up an orange T-shirt and a matching pair of shorts. She couldn't possibly wear shorts; her legs were still far too fat.

She found a fancy satin frock and stuffed it back into the suitcase angrily. Didn't her mother know she hated frocks? She tossed a pink gingham brassiere and suspender belt back into the case with disgust. She didn't need any of those ridiculous things. That was the best thing about not eating;

you could turn back the clock of growing up and go back to being a child. No wobbling bosoms to be kept under control; she even had to hide the ration of sanitary towels that Sister Rose handed out every month, because she didn't need them now.

She chose a skirt which came down past her knees, a baggy T-shirt and a pair of plimsolls, pulled a brush through her hair with difficulty, repacked her case and closed it.

Opening the bedroom door, she listened for movement downstairs. All was quiet. Hopefully Aunt Ella was still asleep down in the stinky kitchen, hanging from a hook in the ceiling by her feet like a bat.

Catrin made her way along the gloomy corridor, pushing open doors as she went and looking in. All the rooms on the attic floor looked as if they had been servants' rooms; they were simply furnished and painted cream, although the walls were stained with green mould and the curtains hung in shreds at the grimy windows.

She went silently down the narrow staircase, careful where she put her feet so as not to make a noise. On the next floor down there was a wide corridor with lots of rooms opening off on either side, and she supposed these must have been the bedrooms where the guests had stayed. She opened a door and glanced inside. There was a large double bed with a moth-eaten counterpane, the grubby sheets turned back ready for someone to climb into bed. There was a chest of drawers, a huge wardrobe and a small writing desk. By the pretty tiled fireplace there was a seating area with two high-backed chairs with faded pink velvet upholstery, and a low table. On the windowsill there was an oil lamp, and a trapped moth fluttered weakly against the glass bowl in an attempt to escape.

It must have been a lovely room once, when the linen was

clean and the furniture polished, but now it gave her the shivers. She went out into the corridor and walked to the far end, where a stained-glass window let in the light, dispelling some of the gloominess.

To her left there was a narrow corridor partly shielded by a threadbare green chenille curtain. A sign on the wall said PRIVATE.

Catrin pulled back the curtain gingerly and sidestepped the resulting fall of dust. There were four doors leading off the passage and a servants' staircase at the far end. She looked into three of the rooms, long-neglected bedrooms, dust-filled and dingy like all the others.

The last room she went into was quite unlike the others. It was a bedroom-cum-sitting-room, spotlessly clean, with highly polished furniture and a strong smell of beeswax. The bed linen was freshly starched and the sheets turned neatly back. Carefully ironed antiMacassars had been draped over the backs of the chintz chairs, and a vase of wild flowers stood on a side table next to an open book.

The fireplace was laid with screwed-up paper and kindling, and logs were piled in a wicker basket. It was as though someone might appear at any moment, set a light to the fire and settle down to read. There were framed prints on the wall, mainly scenes from around Kilvenny in the olden days. There was an oil painting of a woman in a startling blue dress. She had the loveliest of faces, with thick dark hair swept up into a glossy coil and a blue-fringed bejewelled scarf tied round her forehead. Catrin ran her finger gently across the woman's cheek, brushed the teardrop that trailed from her eye. It was such a realistic teardrop that she could imagine it slithering down the woman's cheek and dripping on to her blue bodice.

There was a pretty painted clock and an oval mirror with a surround made from seashells, and three photographs lined up on top of a bookshelf. One was of two small girls outside the Fisherman's Snug, their faces almost completely hidden by floppy sunhats. Another was of two very smart young men wearing army uniforms. A third photograph was facing the wall. Catrin turned it round. It was of her mother when she was younger, standing outside the front door of the hotel, posing for the camera. Catrin glared at it. How smug her mother looked. She had to admit that she was very photogenic even back then; everyone said that she took a marvellous photograph. And didn't she just love pouting and preening for the camera? As soon as anyone brandished a camera she was ready. If you opened the refrigerator door and the light came on, Kizzy would strike a pose. Catrin was the opposite. She hated having her photograph taken because she never managed to smile at the right moment and usually looked as if she was grimacing.

Her mother must have been about eighteen when the photo was taken. She was wearing a tight-fitting dress with a pretty scalloped hemline just below her knees. She looked so happy, so full of herself, like a Hollywood starlet.

Catrin replaced the photograph and allowed herself a sour smile. Aunt Ella didn't think her mother was wonderful, though, did she? At least there was one other person in the world who didn't think Kizzy Grieve was the bloody bee's knees.

She crossed to the window and looked down into the overgrown gardens of the hotel. There was a weed-clogged tennis court with a sagging net, and beyond that a half-empty swimming pool covered in a thick lid of slime.

It must have been beautiful here once. She imagined the sound of a tennis ball being hit, the splash of water and a shriek of delight as someone jumped into the pool. Why couldn't she have come when it was like that, instead of when it was all ruined and horrid?

A creaking made her spin round. The door of an enormous wardrobe door was opening slowly, the clothes hangers rattling ominously, and an overpowering stink of mothballs wafted around her. She shrank back against the wall. What if it was the ghost of dead Aunt Alice clambering out of the wardrobe to see who was sniffing about? She was rigid with fear and sure she could hear someone or something breathing heavily inside the wardrobe. Mother of God. What should she do? Sister Lucy said one must always keep calm in a crisis, yet Sister Lucy always flapped and grew flustered at the smallest upset.

She pressed her lips together to hold back a rising screech, eased herself slowly past the open wardrobe door. She glanced quickly inside but all she could see was a pile of old clothes moving in the draught.

A clicking and a sudden squawk made her heart leap out from behind her ribs and she screamed fit to bust.

All night Ella had been restless, drifting in and out of a fitful sleep. She had dreamt that Alice had come back to Shrimp's. She had seen her walking briskly across the sunlit, manicured lawns, calling out as she hurried towards the hotel.

Ella had run out of the house towards her, but Alice walked straight past her and marched into the house calling a name that Ella couldn't make out.

She had followed Alice up the stairs and along the corridor calling to her, but Alice merely glanced back once and Ella had seen the look of pure joy on her sister's face. Ella raced behind her, opened the door to Alice's room, stepped inside and stood transfixed. Alice was standing in front of the painting of *Woman and Child*, staring at it fixedly. As Ella put out her hand to touch Alice she had, as if by magic, climbed into the painting and disappeared. Ella had stared in disbelief. It was a conjuring trick. There was no sign of Alice, just the woman in the old painting by that Italian artist her father had so loved. She crept up to the painting and saw with a shock that the woman's face had changed into Alice's face. Alice looked out at Ella with that guileless expression of hers and then, as she opened her lips to speak, her face had blurred and the painting had returned to its former state.

Ella came to with a start. At first she thought the bells of Kilvenny church were ringing, but then she realised one of the bells was jangling noisily in the pantry. It was probably an impatient guest, maybe wanting a tea tray or a hot-water bottle. She got to her feet, pushed back her tangled hair, stumbled into the pantry and looked up at the row of bells.

Her hand flew to her neck. The bell was being rung in Alice's room. Maybe Alice had come back after all.

Catrin threw back her head and laughed, more with relief than mirth. The doors on the cuckoo clock flew open one last time and the bird gave a strangled 'Cuckoo.'

God almighty. That bloody bird had frightened her to death. She inched towards the wardrobe, shoved the door shut and stepped out into the corridor, where she came face to face with her aunt. Catrin flinched. Ella was a far more frightening sight than a silly old cuckoo and a rickety wardrobe. Ella looked at Catrin through narrowed eyes, her face white and pinched beneath the layers of grime, eyes bright with madness, hair billowing out like Strewelpeter's.

Ella pushed roughly into the room then looked back accusingly at Catrin, who was watching her worriedly.

'I thought I heard the bell ringing, thought Alice had called me,' Ella said, looking suddenly crestfallen.

'I'm sorry. That was my fault. I accidentally pushed the bell press by the window.'

'Someone up here was screaming as if a murder was being committed.'

'That was me, too. I'm sorry but I was scared when the cuckoo flew out of the clock. It gave me such a fright.'

Ella sat down heavily in one of the high-backed chairs and put her hands to her face, covering her eyes. For a moment Catrin thought that she was crying but then she stood up, shook her head and regained her composure.

'How silly of me. I was sleeping, you see, when the bell rang and I was startled. Then I heard the screaming.'

There was an uneasy silence in the room except for the ticking of the clock.

'What were you doing in here?' There was a sharp edge to Ella's voice.

'I was on my way downstairs. I just wanted to have a peep at the place before I leave. I was trying to imagine it as it must have been in the old days, that's all.'

'It was very lovely,' Ella said, a dreamy look coming over her face. 'You should have been here when we had the summer ball. There were coloured lights strung out all along the terrace, piano music and people dancing on the lawns.'

For a moment Catrin imagined her mother waltzing in the garden, enjoying everyone's admiring glances. How she would have loved that. Catrin would have hated it and found a quiet spot to hide in. She couldn't bear people staring at her, especially since she'd started to grow up.

'Why did you think Alice was ringing? You said last night that she was dead.'

'Alice *is* dead. You're too young to understand. When you're alone so much you start hearing things, things that aren't really there. You know, sometimes I think I can hear her walking about up here.'

Catrin eyed her warily. A floorboard moved beneath Catrin's feet and the wardrobe door creaked ominously.

Pull yourself together, Catrin Grieve. That's what Sister Lucy would have said. Once you let your imagination loose, you gave in to fear. Sister Lucy was full of daft sayings.

Sister Matilde was quite the opposite. What was it she'd once said? Something about imagination being part of the human soul, a restless and unbridled longing to create worlds anew.

She'd give anything to speak to Sister Matilde now. She must ring the school as soon as possible and then get the first train back to London.

'Would you like some breakfast before you leave?' Ella asked. 'I could serve you some in the dining room. There's a very fine view from there.'

Catrin looked away in embarrassment. What was wrong with this woman? She was talking as if Catrin were a real guest and the hotel was still open. She seemed to flit between the past and the present as if she wasn't sure where she belonged.

Catrin pressed her hand against her stomach to muffle the rumbling that the mention of food had triggered. She ought to eat something. She had to be careful that she didn't go too long without food in case she fainted and got carted off to the doctor. It was a balance that she'd almost got the hang of now.

She couldn't eat in this place, though. The state of that kitchen would put a rat off its food.

'Thank you, but I'm not hungry,' she lied. 'May I use the telephone?'

Ella nodded. 'If you'd care to follow me, I'll show you the way.'

They set off along the corridor. As Catrin was about to step past the rotting green curtain she glanced behind her and her mouth fell open in astonishment.

A man in a wide-brimmed hat had slipped out of Aunt

Alice's room and was hurrying along the corridor. So there had been someone hiding in the wardrobe in Aunt Alice's room all the time. But why would anyone in their right mind do that?

Catrin stood riveted to the spot as he hurried soundlessly down the servants' staircase.

So Aunt Ella wasn't as alone as she imagined she was. No wonder she thought she could hear someone wandering around up here. This was such a weird place with peculiar men who hid in wardrobes and newly found aunts who were definitely short of a few marbles.

Down in the hallway Ella pointed out the telephone booth and Catrin picked up the dusty receiver and with a shaking finger dialled the number of St Agnes's. She waited impatiently, imagining Sister Matilde pausing in what she was doing, then hurrying through the dim corridors, past the silent saints and the guttering candles to answer the telephone.

The phone rang and rang but no one answered. Surely any moment now a breathless voice would say, 'Saint Agnes's Convent School, Sister Matilde speaking . . .'

She was close to tears as she replaced the receiver. What on earth was she supposed to do? She couldn't have stayed here even if it had been a proper hotel, because Aunt Ella had said that she didn't want her here, didn't want anyone. She wiped her eyes, rang the number again, but to no avail.

'I can't get through and it's really odd because there's always someone at the convent,' she said, stepping out of the telephone booth.

'You're at a convent?' Ella enquired with surprise.

'Yes, Saint Agnes's Convent School, just outside London.'

'When did your mother become a Catholic? Or was that another of her five-minute fads?'

'She didn't become a Catholic. My father was a Catholic,' Catrin replied.

'You said *was* – your father *was* a Catholic – in the past tense.'

'That's because my father's dead, if you must know. He died when I was a baby. Now I really must go.'

Ella looked with irritation at the girl's brimming eyes. She was like Kizzy, able to turn on the waterworks whenever it suited her.

She watched Catrin walk away through the long grass, pause near the old swing and put down her suitcase.

Catrin looked back at the house and there was something despondent in the droop of her shoulders, a fragility which would have brought a lump to Ella's throat once upon a time.

She wasn't a well child at all, by the look of her; there was a shocking thinness about her that wasn't natural. Surely Kizzy would have noticed that something was clearly wrong with her own child? Then again, the feckless article only ever saw what she wanted to see.

Ella turned briskly away from the window, made her way to the telephone booth, found the address book and turned the dusty pages. With a trembling hand she dialled a London number and listened with bated breath. A few moments later a man answered and it was all Ella could do to keep her erratic breathing under control and not drop the telephone. He called loudly down the line. How awful it was to hear his voice after all these years. Ella, her throat tight with emotion, put down the telephone quietly. One thing was certain. Kizzy Grieve was playing silly buggers because Catrin Grieve's father was most certainly not dead.

Chapter 9

Catrin was dismayed when she arrived at the station. It was deserted, the CLOSED sign hanging on the window of the ticket office. She made her way outside and down towards the village.

In an hour or so she would go back, buy a ticket and get the first train to Swansea and then on to London, forget all about stupid Shrimp's Hotel, dead Aunt Alice and peculiar Aunt Ella.

The morning was already warm and the sky above Kilvenny was blue and cloudless. Rooks were circling above the castle, early bees busied themselves among the wild flowers, and butterflies hovered and dipped on currents of air.

Most of Kilvenny Castle lay in ruins but one wing still stood and the sun reflected off the latticed windows and a coil of smoke spiralled up from the enormous chimney and drifted away over the tall trees of Gwartney's Wood beyond the castle's high walls.

To kill time Catrin wandered aimlessly through the gardens, breathing in the smell of herbs and the fragrance of the small white roses that grew in profusion up the ancient walls. It was so good to get the stench of Shrimp's Hotel out of her nostrils, to blow the musty smell of decay out of her hair.

The door to the castle was ajar and a key, the biggest key she had ever seen, had been left in the lock. She knocked on the door but the wood soaked up the sound made by her small fist. She'd need a hammer to make herself heard. Hopefully, whoever lived here had a telephone they would let her use and she could ring her school and warn them that she was on her way back.

The door rasped as she pushed it inwards, the old wood catching on the stone-flagged floor. She stepped hesitantly inside and called out. Her words echoed eerily in the silence. No one answered.

She was standing in a high-ceilinged room with a fireplace big enough to house a couple of carthorses and walls covered in battered shields and gloomy portraits of the long-since dead. There was an enormous table which would seat about twenty people, with high-backed chairs set round it.

She tiptoed across the flagged floor, made her way through a door to her right and along a dimly lit corridor past sleeping suits of armour and a stuffed bear wedged tightly between a bookcase and a hallstand hung with moth-eaten coats. There was a curious smell of dying flowers and burrowing woodworm, mingling with the sweet scent of rosemary and thyme.

She stepped through a doorway into an enormous kitchen. As she stood there a shaft of sunlight pierced through the high windows and she had to shield her eyes from the momentary brightness.

The room had a dreamlike feel to it, as though she had stepped unwittingly into a fairy story. Big pots and pans hung from nails hammered haphazardly into the thick walls. A bunch of oversized keys dangled from a brass ring above the range, and giant ladles and oversized spoons splayed out of an earthenware pot on the kitchen table. Everything was massive, as if it was a room waiting for a giant to return.

Fee fi fo fum, I smell the blood of an Englishman.

Catrin shivered in the cool air.

Be he alive or be he dead, I'll grind his bones to make my bread.

Nothing in the kitchen gave a clue to who lived here; it was more like a museum than a real kitchen. It wasn't likely that she was going to find a telephone here, because everything was ancient.

At the sound of approaching footsteps out in the corridor, she held her breath and clenched her fists tightly at her sides as the kitchen door opened.

Tony Agosti, walking back from the chapel, noticed that the door to the castle was open, and made his way to the kitchen. When he opened the door he jumped with fright at the sight of the girl standing there.

The sunlight streaming through the windows cast a halo round her head and she looked like a figure from a religious painting or a ghost conjured up from another world. He blinked nervously and hurriedly made the sign of the cross.

This was no castle ghost. The girl had a mop of dark curly hair and deep blue eyes which looked too large for her small face, a face as pale as graveyard lilies. She reminded him of one of those incurably sick girls in an old-fashioned novel. She was the skinniest girl he'd ever seen, with legs like cocktail sticks and a skirt which swamped her.

'I'm sorry if I shouldn't be here,' she said anxiously, taking a hesitant step towards him. 'But I was hoping that whoever lives here would let me use the telephone – if they have one, that is.'

'There's no telephone in here, lovely girl. A couple of carrier pigeons hanging about in the garden, maybe, but nothing as up-to-date as a telephone. There's no problem your being in here, mind. Mr Gwartney from the library won't mind one little bit.'

'Does he live here?' she asked.

'No, no one's lived here for years.'

'But the door was open and there was a key in the lock.'

'Aye, Dan Gwartney is the caretaker of the castle. He keeps an eye on the place, lights the fires now and again to keep the rooms aired. The gardens are always open during the day for people to wander in and take a look round, but hardly any bugger sets foot in Kilvenny now. Gone to the dogs, we have, the last few years.'

'I should like to look round properly but I'm afraid I won't have time. I'm catching a train soon.'

Tony Agosti looked at her curiously. 'That'll be the ghost train, will it?'

'I don't know what you mean.' She eyed him warily. She didn't like to hear talk of ghosts while she was standing in the cool kitchen alone with a strange man.

'Well, there's no trains out of Kilvenny now until next week.'

She looked at him with dismay. 'But there must be. I arrived here by train yesterday.'

Tony grinned. 'That was the late train. Like I said, there'll be no more trains until next week. Very few people travel here these days, and if they do they don't tend to stay long.'

Catrin's face paled.

'I was supposed to be staying at Shrimp's Hotel for the summer,' she said.

'Were you, by God? No one stays up there any more.'

'I know that now, but I didn't before I came.' Her voice was impatient.

Tony Agosti thought that the girl was a peculiar little thing, very English and proper, old-fashioned-looking and a bit lah-di-dah in her speech. Little girls of her age didn't usually travel about the country staying in hotels on their own. Not in Wales, anyhow.

'Shrimp's has been closed for years,' he said. 'Didn't anyone tell you?'

Catrin shook her head and bit her trembling lip.

'Ella Grieve, the owner, shut herself up years ago and never comes out.'

'Does no one ever go there?' Catrin said.

'Not any more. There was a niece who used to stay there – damn, now, she was a beautiful girl, like a film star or a model.'

Catrin bristled. A model for toby jugs, maybe. Why did everyone talk about her mother's looks and how beautiful she was? They didn't know her, didn't know what she was like on the inside. If they did they wouldn't go on and on about her all the time.

As he stood there looking at this defiant little girl, Tony had a sudden vision of Kizzy Grieve running down the steps to the beach, her long, silky hair streaming behind her.

She had stumbled, lost her shoe and stopped to retrieve it, a shiny black shoe reflecting the last of the sun's rays. He remembered the golden brown of her slender calf against the hem of her red dress. Her perfume on the warm evening air as she stood looking up at him earnestly, her mascara smudged and her beautiful face stained with recent tears, her mouth opening to speak.

'Beauty isn't everything, you know,' Catrin snapped.

Tony looked up from his reverie and was taken aback to see the anger in the girl's face, her eyes bright with fury.

'No, no of course it's not.'

'Who was she, anyhow?' Catrin asked disingenuously.

'She was called Kizzy. She was Ella's niece and she used to live here with her mother.'

'Here in Kilvenny?'

'Right here in Kilvenny Castle.'

Catrin looked at him with disbelief. Why hadn't her mother ever told her this? How was it possible for strangers to know more about her own family than she did? None of it made sense. Kizzy had hardly ever mentioned her parents and never once said that she'd grown up in a castle in Wales.

'When did she stop coming here?'

'Let me see, now. Her mother, Hester, got married again and moved away. Kizzy was sent off to one of those boarding-ing schools, like orphanages for rich people, I always think. She used to come back here in the holidays, though.'

'And stay here in the castle all alone?'

'No. No, she stayed up at Shrimp's. She found the castle too gloomy for her by half. She liked the home comforts of Shrimp's – hot water, proper baths, good food and all that.'

Catrin tried to suppress a smile. Kizzy would have hated living in this dark old place with its rickety windows and cold stone floors. Kizzy hated history and all old things; she liked everything to be spanking new and usually expensive.

Catrin thought Kilvenny Castle was beautiful, full of atmosphere and bursting with history.

'And she stopped coming here altogether?'

'She went away one summer and never came back,' he said sadly.

Catrin eyed him suspiciously. He was probably another man who had fallen for her mother's sickly charms – men never seemed able to see through her.

'Did you go up to Shrimp's yesterday?' Tony asked with interest.

Catrin nodded.

'Did Ella Grieve let you in?'

'She did, as it happens.'

Tony stared at her with incredulity. 'You sure?'

'Of course I'm sure. I stayed there the night.'

'Are you staying there again tonight?'

'*No!*'

'So what will you do now?'

'I'm trying to get hold of my school. I'm hoping they'll send someone down here to pick me up as soon as they can.'

'Is there anyone else you could ring? Your mother, maybe?'

'My mother is away on holiday.'

'I suppose you'd best ring from my place. I'm Tony Agosti, by the way. I keep the Café Romana just over the road.' He held out his hand to her and she shook it shyly.

Her hand was cold, as cold as a corpse.

'Well, come on, then, or my nonna will be wondering where I've got to.'

'What's a nonna?' Catrin asked.

'The same as a granny, only harder work,' he said with a warm smile.

'I suppose I ought to tell you my name. I'm Catrin Grieve: Ella Grieve is my great-aunt and Kizzy is my mother.'

Tony Agosti stared at her in bewilderment.

Catrin looked back at him, her face draining of all colour as if a vampire had sucked all the blood out of her.

And then she fainted.

Chapter 10

Catrin opened her eyes and blinked in confusion. Above her head a ceiling fan turned slowly, whirring lazily and scattering flies in all directions. There was a smell of strong coffee and warm pastry. She turned her head and realised that she was lying on a red leather banquette from where she could see nothing except table legs. She heaved herself up on her elbows and looked warily around.

She was in the Café Romana opposite Kilvenny Castle, and Tony Agosti was sitting at a table near the window, talking quietly to the old man she'd seen reading in the library last night.

Hell's teeth. She couldn't remember walking over here. She must have fainted and been carried. How embarrassing. She lay down again quickly, straining her ears to hear what the two men were saying.

'As I said, Dan, I'd been over to the chapel like I do most days to light some candles for Nonna, and I thought p'raps you were in the castle so I went in. There she was, this little girl, standing alone in the kitchen. Gave me a right turn, it did. I thought for a moment that she was a ghost.'

'Plenty of ghosts knocking about over there – bound to be, with the age of the place.'

'We got talking about the old days and then just as I was leaving she said she's called Catrin Grieve and Ella Grieve is her great-aunt.'

'Well, stone the bloody crows!'

'She says she's Kizzy Grieve's daughter.'

'Well, I'll be damned. What the hell's she doing here?'

'She said she'd stayed the night up at Shrimp's and she was waiting to get a train back to London.'

'Bit young, ent she, to be traipsing about the country on her own?'

'That's what I thought, especially with the look of her – she looks half starved to me.'

'I've seen more fat on a kipper.'

'Why the hell would she be staying with Ella? No one in their right mind would stay up there in that dirty hole of a place.'

'They say it's filthy up there, rats and mice and mouldy food all over the place.'

Tony wrinkled his nose in disgust and Dan went on, 'There's cobwebs as thick as blankets and spiders the size of dinner plates.'

'Ugh. They say she still lays the tables and puts warming pans in the beds as if there were guests staying there.'

Dan nodded. 'It's all very sad. She doesn't seem to know her arse from her elbow these days, or whether she's living in the past or the present.'

'Poor Ella was never the same after Alice died,' Tony mused. 'It was strange, too, that Kizzy stopped coming.'

'There was a rift of some sort, I gathered, between Kizzy and Ella but God knows what it was all about. The Grieves were always very tight-lipped about their own affairs.'

'I just can't understand why any mother with her head screwed on the right way would send a child to Shrimp's, knowing the state it's in.'

'Hang on a minute, Tony. Did you say she's called Catrin Grieve?'

'That's what she said.'

'So she's taken her mother's name, not her father's?'

'So it would seem. Oh, I see what you're thinking . . .'

Catrin pulled a face. People always thought the worst, when in fact there was a perfectly reasonable explanation why she had her mother's maiden name.

'What will happen to her now?'

'Well, the only thing I could do in the circumstances was to ring Ella. Thank God, she actually answered the phone and she's on her way down here as we speak.'

'You're joking! You think she'll really leave Shrimp's after all this time? It'll be a turn-up for the books if she does. She hasn't set foot outside of there since the day they buried poor Alice.'

'She said she'd be here as soon as she could.'

'Well, I'll be off, then.'

'Why don't you stay?'

'No, thanks. Ella never could stand the sight of me.'

As he was about to get to his feet a figure passed the café window and the bell above the door tinkled a warning.

Ella stood for some time at the top of the steps, looking down on a deserted Kilvenny beach, trying to gather the courage to make her way across to the village. There, pulled up above the high-water mark, was her old boat, the *Dancing Porpoise*. It was shabby and rotting, the paint blistered and peeling, and it was certainly no longer seaworthy.

She stepped down on to the beach hesitantly. It was strange to feel the sand and shells beneath her feet again and the sea breeze cool on her sallow skin. She felt as though her blood had thinned during all the years she'd been shut away.

She was fearful of every noise and dreaded bumping into any of the villagers. Already she was contemplating turning tail and fleeing up the steps and back to the safety of Shrimp's.

She forced herself on, stopping again outside the Fisherman's Snug.

The old place looked uncared for; the winter storms had taken their toll on the thatched roof. A gull perched defiantly on the chimney, eyeing Ella with suspicion.

By the time she turned into Cockle Lane her legs felt weak with fear and the effort of walking. Once she could have run all the way from Shrimp's to the far end of the village without drawing breath.

If the news had got out that Ella Grieve had left Shrimp's, the net curtains would soon start to twitch. The Kilvenny bush telegraph would hum into action. It had never taken long for gossip to get around Kilvenny. It was a miracle that nothing had ever got out about Alice and Kizzy.

She pushed her hair off her face and straightened her back. She was a Grieve and the Grieves were known for their fortitude. Let the nosy buggers get a good look if they liked.

Kilvenny village had changed dramatically since Ella had last set foot there, and she was shocked at how dowdy and run-down everything had become. The once-whitewashed walls of the houses were grimy, and everything looked in urgent need of a lick of paint. A great many of the houses were boarded up and others near to derelict. The Boot Inn was closed, but the cellar flaps were up, waiting for a delivery from the draymen, so there must be customers who still drank there. She wondered if the beer was still brought to Kilvenny by wagons pulled by shire horses.

She caught sight of her reflection in the window of Meredith Evans Photographer's shop and gasped. She looked bad enough in the mottled hall mirror at Shrimp's, but out here in the daylight she looked a thousand times worse.

Jesus. She looked like Miss Havisham after a night on the tiles.

There was a sudden movement inside the shop and she looked directly into the face of Meredith Evans. He stared at her, his mouth falling open, bloodshot eyes wide with disbelief. She glowered back at him defiantly; the treacherous little bastard could take a running jump. She sneered at the dusty photographs in the window. It was about time he changed the display in there, it was the same as the last time she'd walked this way more than thirteen years ago.

Further up the road, the house where Mrs Tranter's Hairdresser's used to be was boarded up and the curtains in the upstairs windows were rotting where they hung. Mrs Tranter had done a marvellous trade with the villagers and the guests from Shrimp's. Had she locked herself in and gone to seed as Ella had?

There was a lump in her throat when she saw the Café Romana. When she and Alice were children they had traipsed down here to spend their pocket money. It was a great game of theirs to try and sneak into the café without sounding the bell, so as to surprise Luigi Agosti. No matter how hard they tried, it had always made a noise and he had popped up from behind the counter. He'd been a grand old man and had brought a breath of fresh air into Kilvenny. None of the villagers had ever tasted a sarsaparilla or an ice cream before Luigi came on the scene.

Ella took a deep breath and opened the door. The bell rang out loudly in the silence.

Tony Agosti got to his feet and looked at her, barely able to conceal his shock. It was an age since he'd last clapped eyes on her, and time hadn't been kind. She'd never been a fussy dresser in the old days but she'd always looked clean and well turned-out. The clothes she was wearing today would have shamed a bonfire guy, her face was ingrained with years of dirt, and her hair stuck out wildly from her head like grey candyfloss.

Dan Gwartney stood up, glanced at Ella, then cast his eyes down towards the floor. It was hard to look Ella Grieve in the face.

'Hallo, Ella,' Tony said, and there was a quiver of apprehension in his voice. 'I'm sorry I had to ring you but I didn't know what to do for the best with the girl.'

'Where was she when you found her?' Ella enquired.

'Over in the castle. She said she was waiting for a train, but like I told her, there's only one train a week now.'

'One train a week?' Ella asked suspiciously.

'That's right,' Tony said sadly.

Dan Gwartney bit his lip. Closing Shrimp's had been disastrous for Kilvenny, and Ella Grieve alone was responsible for that.

'Thing is, she was talking away to me one minute and then out like a light the next. I couldn't get an answer from the doctor's house, otherwise I'd have had him have a look at her so as not to bother you.'

'Where is she now?'

'I put her to lie down over there on the bench. She was sleeping like a baby last time I looked – still is, I fancy.'

Catrin cringed with embarrassment, closed her eyes, feigning sleep in case they came to look at her as she lay there helpless.

'What do you want us to do with her?'

'I don't want you to do anything with her. I'll take her back to Shrimp's, I suppose, get hold of her mother somehow.'

'She is Kizzy's girl, then?' Dan Gwartney asked, still avoiding Ella's eye.

She nodded reluctantly.

'You can't take a child back to that place,' he went on.

She looked fiercely at him, until he blushed crimson and looked away.

'She's family, and I won't leave her without a roof over her head.'

'For Christ's sake, woman, we all know that Shrimp's is a bloody disgrace. You can't take a sick child there,' Dan said.

Ella rounded on him. 'You save your breath to cool your bloody porridge. You haven't set foot in Shrimp's for years, so how would you know.'

'You can deceive yourself all you like, but the local kids' favourite game is to try and peer through your windows, get a glimpse of the funny old woman who lives there like a recluse.'

'Not so bloody old. I can give you a few years.'

'Perhaps it would be best if we got in touch with one of the children's homes, got her put up there for a while until something is sorted out,' Dan said.

Ella glared at him. 'Over my dead body. You keep your children's homes for those who need them. She'll be fine with me at Shrimp's until other arrangements can be made.'

'Sit down, Ella, while I make us all a drink,' Tony intervened. 'Let's talk things through calmly. We don't want to wake the girl, now, do we?'

Catrin was wide awake but paralysed with anxiety and mortification. If it wasn't bad enough that she'd been sent here to her stupid aunts, only to find that one of them was dead and the other one didn't want anything to do with her, but in the next breath they were talking about putting her in a children's home.

'Maybe she could stay with someone in the village until you can get hold of her mother,' Dan ventured.

The coffee machine hissed ferociously, steam rose up above the counter as Tony busied himself, and soon the sound of cups clinking and the aroma of coffee filled the café.

Catrin tried to swallow, but there was a lump in her throat as big as a walnut. She had to get out of this awful place as soon as she could. She wasn't going to spend another night up at Shrimp's Hotel. If only she could get home to London she could look through her mother's address book, ask her friends if they knew where she was staying in Italy. The only other hope was that her mother had said she'd write, so as soon as a letter arrived at Shrimp's she'd be able to contact her. If she got round to writing, that was; Kizzy was always making promises and not keeping them.

'You've got to see sense, Ella,' Dan Gwartney persisted. 'You were always stubborn even when you were a girl, and you must realise that Shrimp's isn't a fit place for a child to stay.'

'And you can't tell me what to do. Never mind I was stubborn. You were a bossy little bugger when you were a boy.'

'Put it this way, Ella. You take her back to that dump and I for one won't be afraid to ring the authorities. I'm in regular touch with Jerusalem House Children's Home and I could talk to someone and get some help for you and the girl.'

'Don't you patronise me with your talk of Jerusalem House and your do-gooding nonsense. When I want your help I'll ask for it.'

There was a pause, but the air was brittle with tension. Catrin was glad of the silence.

'Ella, no one's saying you couldn't look after the girl, it's just that you've not been yourself for years.'

'You think I'm mad, is that what you're saying?' Ella's voice was angry and Catrin held her breath.

'Not mad, exactly,' Tony said quietly.

'But you can't escape the fact that the Grieves are well known for their mad streak and no one who was sane would have lived in squalor for God knows how many years,' Dan said with a note of triumph in his voice.

'You can shut your trap when you like. That sister of yours up in Coronation Row used to have the dirtiest net curtains in Kilvenny. She wasn't too fussy about the grain on her washing or the company she kept, as I remember.'

'You leave my sister out of this,' Dan growled.

'He's right, Ella. We mustn't speak ill of the dead.'

Ella was silent. She hadn't known that Gwennie Gwartney had passed away. How could she know? She'd not stepped outside Shrimp's or spoken to anyone in years.

'I'm sorry to hear that,' she murmured.

Dan grunted in reply and stirred his coffee briskly.

'What about finding somewhere else for the pair of you to stay?' Tony asked.

'Where do you suggest?'

'The castle?' Dan volunteered. 'It's been empty for years but I've always made sure that it's well looked after, kept clean and aired.'

'The castle doesn't belong to me, as well you know,' Ella said.

'No, but it belongs to the girl's mother, doesn't it?'

'I don't know. I know Kizzy inherited it but I wouldn't have thought she'd have kept it – she hated the place,' Ella said.

'She's tried to sell it plenty of times, but there's not much call for draughty old Welsh castles. I never hear from her but I still get money paid through the solicitors to look after the place,' Dan told her.

'So you could stay there, Ella. Kizzy isn't likely to object in the circumstances, is she?' said Tony.

Catrin bristled. How could your mother own a crumbly old castle in Wales and never think to tell you? No way was she going to stay there with awful Aunt Ella.

'I suppose so,' Ella mumbled, 'if it's only for a few days. I can't leave Shrimp's for too long.'

'Why don't you let me walk you back up there to pick up some things?'

'I'll manage by myself, thank you, Dan Gwartney.'

'Well, I'll get over to the castle and light fires in the bedrooms to take the chill off,' he replied frostily. 'Perhaps Tony could make you something to eat. You don't look like you've had a good meal inside you for years, Ella Grieve – nor the girl, come to that.'

'I've had more good meals than you've dreamt of,' Ella snapped.

'Suit yourself. I'll be off.'

'Not before time.'

'Seems we'll be seeing a bit more of each other, as we'll be neighbours for a while.'

'Not if I see you first.'

'Look, Ella,' Tony said, 'you do whatever you have to do and then get back down here. I'll wait for Catrin to wake and then take her over to the castle.'

The bell above the door tinkled as Dan Gwartney left the café, muttering under his breath.

'Pompous old fool,' Ella said. 'I may have been away a long time but some things in Kilvenny haven't altered.'

'He means well.'

'Nosy old sod.'

Catrin covered her face with her hands. Her head ached

unbearably and she wanted more than anything to press herself down against the bench where she lay, disappear inside it and never be seen again.

Chapter 11

Catrin kept her eyes closed as Tony Agosti stood looking down at her. Her face was burning up with embarrassment and her heart beat furiously behind her rib cage.

'Are you okay?' he asked in a voice just louder than a whisper.

She pretended not to hear him. If she didn't answer maybe he'd go away, maybe they'd all go away and leave her alone.

'Righty oh, I'd better get you over to the castle and tucked up in bed. It's a good rest you need, by the look of you, my girl,' he said to himself.

Before she had a chance to object he had scooped her up in his muscular arms and carried her through the café and out of the door. So shocked she could scarcely breathe, she lay in his arms like a big baby, feeling the robust beat of his heart through the soft material of his shirt. He smelt of soap and cigarette smoke, of chocolate and hair oil, all mixed up together. She was mortified; she'd never been this close to a man before, never been carried by a man in her life.

Oh God, she'd just die if he undressed her and put her to bed. Her heart fluttered wildly as she felt the black hairs of his arms tickling the back of her knees and his breath warm on her face.

It was hot outside, the smell of stale beer wafting up from the Boot Inn mingling with the fragrance of the white roses that grew in abundance over the castle walls. High above their heads the rooks flew up from the tall trees of Gwartney's Wood, squawking as if in warning.

She felt the sudden change in temperature as they passed out of the sunshine and into the cool of the castle, goose pimples erupting on her skin like mini-volcanoes. As he climbed the stairs she swayed in his arms, acutely aware that her sensible cotton knickers were on show for the whole world to see. A door opened with a squeak and then she was laid down gently on a bed. A few moments later Tony Agosti had thankfully gone. Hastily she pulled back the heavy blankets, scrambled beneath them and pummelled the pillows in frustration.

Later he returned, pulled the sheets away from her tear-stained face, took her cold wrist in his warm hand and felt for her pulse. Her heart was beating so fast that she thought he must hear it from where he stood, and she feared that if she feigned sleep any longer he might call for a doctor and then they'd keep her here for sure. She opened her eyes, blinking and looking around her in confusion, like a princess awaking from a hundred years' sleep.

'You're okay, lovely girl. I brought you over here to the castle while you were sleeping. I've put you in your mammy's old room – I see there's still a few of her bits and pieces here to make you feel at home.'

'Thank you,' she mumbled, unable to look him in the face.

'I've brought you something to eat.'

'But I'm not hungry,' she almost wailed.

'Got to eat, girl, to keep your strength up.'

To add to her mortification, he fed her like a baby,

spooning thin chicken soup into her mouth and wiping her chin with a napkin, all the while her stomach complaining noisily and she doing her best to avoid his tender gaze.

Afterwards she must have slept for some time, because when she woke a fire was crackling lazily in the hearth and the draughts that swirled under the ill-fitting door sent sparks skittering away up the chimney. On a tallboy a candle burned erratically, casting an eerie glow around the strange room. A copper warming pan on a nail near the hearth gleamed in the firelight, and the eyes of a hook-nosed man in a large portrait shone as though he were glad of the unexpected warmth. The faded velvet curtains had been drawn across the latticed windows, but through a gap she could see a huge moon hovering in the sky.

She sniffed the air. The smell of the olden days seeped out from the ancient walls, bringing a transitory whiff of camphor, then lavender, crushed velvet and, strangely, the sharp scent of lemons. The sound of a wireless drifted up from downstairs, and hearing the voice of the English announcer made her homesick.

She checked her wristwatch. It was nearly ten o'clock. If only she were at school, she would be tucked into her bed in the narrow cubicle in St Agnes's dormitory, safe beneath the steady gaze of the statue of St Francis that stood patiently on a ledge above her bed.

An orange nightlight would burn near the door and Sister Lucy's shadow would drift through the dormitory checking that all the girls were asleep. A tap would drip in the washroom and two cubicles away Mary Donohue would snore softly. The clock over in the convent where the nuns slept in their cells would chime every hour and the arched dormitory windows rattle in the night breezes.

She watched the candle on the tallboy burn lower and lower, dreading the moment when the flame would splutter and die, thrusting the strange room into darkness. She wondered what Aunt Ella was doing now, the thought of being alone in a spooky old castle with only a mad woman for company making her afraid.

The candle hissed and the light dimmed, sending shadows darting across the uneven walls. Catrin shivered, the sort of shiver that meant someone was treading on your grave. Her heart beat wildly and her throat constricted with fear as she thought she heard the pad of bare feet out in the corridor, imagined the handle on the door turning slowly . . .

She got out of bed, locked the door, then scurried across the cold floor to the window, knelt on the window seat and yanked the curtains open. Moonlight spilt into the room and dulled her fear.

She looked down into a deserted Cockle Lane and saw Dan Gwartney's white cat crossing the road. As if aware of being watched, it turned and looked up at her, its eyes green and glittering in the moonlight. The cat mewed mournfully then slunk away into a shadowy doorway.

In Meredith Evans Photographer's shop a low-watt bulb burnt behind the ragged curtains of an upstairs room and a shadowy figure paced up and down. Melancholy music drifted out of the Boot Inn into the night. There was a cough beneath her window, someone spat out a mouthful of phlegm, and then footsteps died away.

Across the room from where she stood at the window, there was a bookcase with a selection of battered books and she wondered, had they belonged to Kizzy when she was a girl? Hardly. Kizzy only ever read magazines and the price tags on expensive frocks. Catrin couldn't for the life of her imagine her mother living here in Kilvenny Castle or sleeping in this old-fashioned bedroom. She hated old things, and in their house in London she was forever modernising and putting in new bathrooms and luxurious carpets.

She rummaged half-heartedly through the bookcase but there was nothing very interesting. There were some old school textbooks covered in stained brown paper; boring old algebra and biology. There were copies of *Oliver Twist* and *The Old Curiosity Shop*, which she'd read at school, and some dog-eared Christmas annuals. As she knelt down she saw a book stuffed in behind the others. It was just another *Girls' Annual* but it was much larger than the others. She blew the dust from the spine and opened it. She was expecting to find the usual comic-book stories but to her surprise the pages had been ripped out and in their place was an old leather-bound book on which someone had painted in gold letters, *Le ricette per i Cherubini*.

It was curious, as though someone had been trying to disguise the book. There was no point reading it, though, because she wouldn't understand a word of it.

Well, perhaps one word. She'd heard '*ricetta*' at school because Sister Tomasina sometimes said, 'You should talk to Sister Angela if you want a *ricetta* for cakes or puddings – she is a wonderful cook.'

She meant 'recipe' of course, but Sister Tomasina was from Italy and peppered her speech with Italian words.

'*Cherubini*' could mean only one thing: cherubs.

Recipes for Cherubs. What a peculiar name for a book. Cherubs were holy things which were found in old religious paintings. They were plump and dimpled and had wings and rosy cheeks. Cherubs weren't real creatures made of flesh and blood so they wouldn't need to eat. She was about to put the book back on the shelf when a sudden draught from the ill-fitting windows ruffled the pages.

The usual smell of old books tickled her nostrils, a musty,

exciting fustiness she loved. There were other smells too, the faint, sharp scents of lemons and rosemary. Rosemary for Remembrance.

She carried the book over to the fireplace, sat cross-legged on the threadbare rug and began to turn the pages, delighting in the feel of the thick, rough paper beneath her fingers.

On the first page was a picture, not the glossy type of illustration usually found in books but an oil painting on a square of canvas which had been stuck carefully on to the page. It was surrounded by a delicate frame, made from four thin slivers of wood joined together expertly and painstakingly covered in gold leaf. There was a smudged fingerprint on the page below the painting, probably left by the artist.

Catrin looked in fascination at a winter scene of a village shivering beneath a thick covering of snow which glittered in the light thrown down by a huge moon hovering in a brooding indigo sky. On the right stood an ugly church with a bell tower and next to the church was a building with bars on the windows, a giant crucifix set into the wall and a door with a grille, unmistakably a convent. On either side of the door there was a large jar, the sort of oil jar in Ali Baba stories. On the wall above one of the jars was a glass-fronted niche where a small saint stood patiently looking on, a candle stub breathing its last beneath his feet.

Opposite the church loomed a big house painted red, the colour of dried blood. It was a grand house surrounded by high walls, with smoke curling up from a tall chimney.

Her attention was taken by a dark figure walking across the square, leaving a trail of lone footprints in the snow; a furtive figure in a swirling black cloak and a strangely shaped hat, carrying a bundle in its arms.

In the foreground there was a fountain where four naked cherubs stood looking up through cascades of frozen water.

Catrin ran her fingers slowly over the surface of the picture, feeling the undulations of paint and brushstrokes. There was a tiny piece of white bristle stuck in the paint, and she remembered an art lesson where Sister Matilde, with her usual enthusiasm, had told the class how paintbrushes were made in the olden days. She'd said that many artists had shop boys working for them, who learned the secrets of painting and how to make glue and brushes and a million other things the artist needed. They, poor devils, couldn't just pop along to a shop and buy half a dozen paintbrushes as modern artists could. Oh no, they had to make them from scratch. Sister Matilde had described how these boys were sent to find the tail fur of a squirrel or else bristles from a hog – not any old hog, mind you; it had to be a white hog and a domesticated one. Mary Donahue had asked if that meant that the hog had learned to wipe its feet before it came into the house and whether it drank its tea without slurping. Everyone had laughed their heads off for ages but it was okay to laugh in Sister Matilde's lessons: she said learning should be fun. Sister Matilde told them that wild hogs were never used, but white hogs probably got quite wild when some shop boy sneaked up and helped himself to a handful of their bristles.

Catrin wondered if whoever had painted this had used a brush made with the bristles of a hog. One thing was sure: the painter must have been a genius because the picture was brilliant and the longer she stared at it the more things she discovered, and it reminded her of the pictures in puzzle books that asked you to find a number of hidden objects.

The pawmarks of an animal led across a snow-covered roof and disappeared suddenly, but looking higher up she saw, perched among the bare branches of a tree, a shivering cat looking down on the scene with eyes bright with curiosity.

She noticed the scarf next, or was it a piece of brightly coloured blue cloth that had been blown round the neck of one of the naked cherubs in the fountain, making him look ridiculous?

Then she spotted the donkey's face, half hidden by shadow, peering out of the doorway of a hovel near the church. Then her attention was drawn to a narrow side window of the blood-red house, where an oil lamp burnt dimly and someone was looking out into the night. Underneath the painting, written in faded black ink, were the words *Piazza Santa Rosa, Italia 1751*.

On the second page of the book there was a painting of a plump woman with an expression of such glee on her face that made Catrin smile without meaning to. She had dark eyes deeply set in a broad face, her skin brown as an early conker. Her round cheeks were highlighted with downy pink; her full-lipped mouth stretched into a wide grin. She was holding a loaf of bread out in front of her as if offering it to someone. It was a round loaf, with a glorious golden crust glistening with crystals of salt that looked delicious.

Beneath the title of the painting someone had written something in a foreign language. Catrin sighed with disappointment but then she saw, further down the page, written faintly in pencil by an unsteady hand, *How to make focaccia bread by Maria Paparella*.

She supposed that the gleeful woman in the painting was Maria Paparella and that this was her recipe for focaccia bread, whatever that was. Bread was just bread, as far as she was concerned; full of calories which made you put on weight. At school they always had stale white bread which curled up at the edges and tasted vaguely of onions. The baker's shop near her house in Ermington Square sold all different types of bread: brown and white, batches and bloomers, split tins, soda bread and milk loaves. In the Jewish shop on the high street they sold exotic rolls with poppy seeds, bagels and French baguettes but she'd never seen focaccia bread anywhere.

She read the recipe with interest. It was fun to read about food, almost as good as eating it but without the anxiety of counting the calories. As she read she glanced from time to time at the cheerful face of Maria Paparella, whose flesh looked so warm and comforting that she felt she could reach out and touch the soft downy skin of the woman's cheek, feel the beat of the pulse in her neck. It was so fine a portrait, so utterly lifelike, that she would not have been surprised if Maria had stepped out from the page and spoken to her.

Oh, if only that were possible! How lovely it would be to have someone normal to talk to instead of awful Aunt Ella with her scarecrow hair and mouth like a sewer.

She turned the pages of the book slowly, marvelling at the portraits of all the different people. She read their names hesitantly out loud, the Italian words awkward on her unpractised tongue. Maria Paparella, Ismelda Bisotti, Piero di Bardi, Luca Roselli and a tiny little dwarf fellow who had just the one name, Bindo. She wondered who they were and why someone had taken such trouble to paint them. It was curious, too, that a book from Italy had found its way here to the wilds of Kilvenny.

So engrossed was she that she was unaware of the church clock chiming eleven o'clock or that beyond the latticed window the moon had disappeared behind banking clouds. Far out at sea thunder growled ominously and then came the soft pattering of rain against the window. As the rain fell faster and the wind stirred the velvet curtains, Catrin turned the pages slowly, oblivious of the call of the white owl from the castle tower and the sound of hesitant footsteps in the quiet lane below.

Chapter 12

It was almost noon and the bell marking the Angelus began to ring out from the ancient church, echoing throughout the narrow streets of the small hilltop town of Santa Rosa. Pigeons flew up from the roofs of the old houses around the piazza, and a startled donkey broke into a trot, spilling lemons from his panniers as he clattered along the Via Dante.

In the garden of the Villa Rosso Maria Paparella, hands on her broad hips, stared in astonishment at eleven-year-old Ismelda Bisotti.

'Mamma mia! What do you mean when you say you've hidden the dwarf? What nonsense is this that you speak?'

'It's not nonsense, Maria. I had to hide him. He was here in the garden and Papa heard him and came looking for him. He would have beaten him senseless if he'd found him here. You know how much he hates him.'

Maria nodded knowingly. It was true that her cantankerous master, Signor Bisotti, hated little Bindo with an intensity which was quite ridiculous. It was absurd for a grown man to feel such hatred for a child. Bindo was a cheeky little beggar, to be sure, but he did have a charm that was all his own and God knows he had enough to put up with in his young life.

'Where in God's name have you hidden him?' Maria asked, looking around the garden in bewilderment.

86

'In the peelings bin.'

'Sweet saints of heaven! And he has been in there for the last two hours? The poor child will be suffocated.'

Maria hurried across the garden, opened the flap of the makeshift wooden bin where she put all the fruit and vegetable peelings. Then she stepped backwards, wafting the air in front of her nose.

'Holy Santa Lucia – we must get him out quick.'

Maria thrust her chubby arms into the bin and, with Ismelda's help, dragged Bindo out from the mound of rotting vegetables and laid the unconscious boy gently on the grass in the shade of the pomegranate tree.

He lay quite still. His face was crimson, sweat ran down his skin in grimy rivulets, and his breathing was laboured.

Ismelda shifted her weight from foot to foot in consternation, and made the sign of the cross. She had heard all about Bindo the dwarf, but she had never set eyes on him until today. He was a peculiar boy with a large head and a tiny body, as if God had muddled up the body parts and put them together in the wrong way.

As she studied his face a shaft of sunlight burst through the branches of the pomegranate tree, illuminating the freckles scattered across his snub nose.

He was beautiful.

Bindo came to slowly and, realising he had been pulled out of his hiding place in the peelings bin, opened one green eye surreptitiously. He saw the pomegranate tree above his head and beyond that an eternity of blue sky.

He winced, thinking of what would happen next. Any moment now Signor Bisotti would take his stick to him.

He swallowed hard and cursed inwardly. He hated Signor Bisotti with a vengeance. He was such a pompous old fool with his fancy clothes and his viper's tongue. Scabby old fart and wanton arse licker.

Bindo had lit many candles in the church of Santa Rosa, sent up prayers for Signor Bisotti: Blessed Virgin, may his figs shrivel and his piles grow ever bigger.

Then, with a rush of relief he heard Maria Paparella's voice and he began to breathe more easily.

'Fetch a clean rag and some water, Ismelda, quickly.'

'Will he be all right?' Ismelda asked anxiously, peering down at the prostrate boy.

'I hope so, but we must cool him down. Now run. Presto.'

Bindo opened his eyes a fraction and saw Maria Paparella looming over him, her voluminous breasts just inches from his nose. He closed his eyes and drew in her womanly smells, warm skin laced with a hint of lemon and sweat.

Maria Paparella was a wonderful woman, as big as a carthorse and full of fun. You had to watch her, though, because she was changeable. Some days she was as soft and cuddly as a laying hen, but she had the talons of a cockerel if you crossed her. Catch her on a good day and she'd maybe slip you one of those gorgeous brutti ma buoni biscuits she made, or bestow on you one of those melting smiles of hers. Oh, but if the milk had curdled or mice had got into her larder then look out. She had been known to wrestle grown men to the ground, chew them up and spit out the pips.

Maria pushed Bindo's silky hair back from his brow, and the touch of her cool fingers on his hot skin was the most tender thing he had known in all his twelve years. He sighed with contentment and closed his eyes; he could have lain there for hours.

He heard Ismelda hurrying back through the garden and then Maria was wiping his face and gently wetting his lips with a piece of cloth soaked in water.

'Do you think he'll live?' Ismelda asked, kneeling down and taking his hot hand in her own.

'Ah, he will survive. You're lucky: he's a tough one,' Maria said.

Gesù bambino! He was a beautiful child if ever there was one, with a face on him like a holy cherub. He wouldn't disgrace a Renaissance painting, with those endearing dimples and rosy cheeks.

He had been abandoned one winter's night when he was a tiny baby, left in an olive jar outside the convent, wrapped only in a dirty old shirt. Who but a monster could have done that? It was probably some desperate peasant girl, dumped by her fellow when she found she was pregnant, and without any means of supporting a baby.

'Why doesn't he wake up?' Ismelda asked fearfully.

'If he doesn't open his eyes soon I will prick the soles of his feet with a needle to make sure he is not dead.'

Bindo opened his eyes and smiled up at Maria Paparella.

She grinned back at him and said, 'Thank God for that. For a moment I thought you were a gonner.'

Bindo sat up with difficulty and looked bashfully at Ismelda.

'He could have died in there, Ismelda – if not of the heat then of the stink,' Maria scolded.

'I'm sorry but I had nowhere else to hide him. And he did stink a bit before I put him in there, but of horse shit mostly.'

'Mind your tongue, my girl. Come, we must clean him up and then we will feed him before we throw him back over the wall.'

'But what about Papa?'

'Your papa has gone over to the church to speak with Father Rimaldi, then he is going to the widow Zanelli's for lunch and after that he will take his siesta in the courtyard, as he often does these days, so I am told. I am not expecting him back until late this evening.'

Ismelda got to her feet, danced up and down on the spot, clapping her hands. 'Can we have a feast here under the tree?' she squealed with excitement.

'A feast she wants! This is the girl who barely eats enough to keep a sparrow alive. Sì. We will have a feast but hush, now. We don't want the whole of Santa Rosa to know what we are up to.'

'Okay. Okay. I'll be quiet.'

'First we must fill the bath.'

Bindo struggled to his feet. Bath? No way was he bathing. Bathing was bad for you. It wasn't good to get naked and lie in warm water. It weakened the back and made your skin wrinkle like a raisin.

Maria swiftly scooped him up into her enormous arms and carried him, wriggling and yelling, towards the Villa Rosso.

'You can go quietly and wash yourself, but any more struggling and I will scrub you with my own fair hands.'

'Okay. Okay. But nobody is to look.'

'No one will look. While you're bathing I'll wash these clothes and put them to dry.'

He stopped struggling and allowed himself to be carried into the villa.

Half an hour later Maria managed to coax him out of the bath, and, dressed in one of Signor Bisotti's voluminous old white shirts and smelling sweetly of lemon soap, he sat down beside Ismelda in the shade of the pomegranate tree.

Bindo breathed in the glorious smell of the garden; the perfume of many herbs mingling with those of lemons, oranges and limes. The sound of bees fizzing around the trailing honeysuckle filled his heart with joy and he watched in wonder as a dragonfly flew close by, its wings beating rainbows upon the soft afternoon air.

He looked shyly across at Ismelda, hardly believing his luck. He had heard many things about her but until today he had never seen her in the flesh because Signor Bisotti kept her well away from public view.

The villagers of Santa Rosa whispered about her, said she was a wild one and that Signor Bisotti kept her hidden behind the high walls of the Villa Rosso because she was an embarrassment to him.

They were wrong, though. Ismelda Bisotti was lovely. Not that she was a real beauty, not like that sniff-nosed sister of hers who had married a rich fellow and moved across the sea a few years back.

Ismelda had large, lively blue eyes which sparkled with mischief behind silky dark lashes. And her mouth. Oh, what a mouth, such a sweet little mouth, puckered and pink and softly moist. It was said that when she opened that mouth of hers she had a tongue on her like a drunken carter.

Bindo thought her the most whimsical, magical girl he had ever seen.

One day, when he had made his fortune he would seek the hand of this lovely girl and marry her. So what if God had short-changed Bindo in the body parts? At least he hadn't been standing behind the door when the looks were handed out. He had a handsome face and he had talents which would one day stand him in good stead, of that he was sure.

And one day he knew that Ismelda would fall in love with him.

Tutto è possibile. *Everything is possible.*

Fate was smiling on him at last. Only a few hours earlier he had climbed the garden wall of the Villa Rosso in pursuit of Signor Bisotti's cat. He had seen it crossing the piazza, its mouth clamped tightly on the limp body of a dead squirrel. Usually Bindo wouldn't have dared to climb that high wall, but a squirrel was too good a prize to miss. The peculiar artist fellow Piero di Bardi, who lived in the Via Dante, paid handsomely for the tail fur of squirrels, which he used to make his paintbrushes.

Bindo had nearly come a cropper, though, because Signor Bisotti had looked down from his balcony and seen him just as he cornered the furious cat. Thank God Ismelda had appeared in the garden and, swift as a wink, had shoved him into the peelings bin and saved him from a certain beating.

Maria Paparella laid a crisp white cloth on the grass and, to Bindo's delight, began to set out the most sumptuous spread of food that he had ever seen. He looked with wide-eyed wonder at the feast before him and his small belly ached with hunger.

The nuns at the Santa Rosa convent were kind enough to him, and in return for running errands and doing odd jobs they let him sleep in the stables. They fed him twice daily but mainly on thin soup and under-cooked beans which gave him the gripe.

There were slices of spicy sausage and ham on a roughly hewn wooden platter, pale cheeses wrapped tightly in vine leaves and small, orange-yolked eggs on a bed of crispy green leaves. There were dusky grapes and downy-skinned peaches. And in the centre of the cloth, a basket of golden bread which gave off the sweet smells of rosemary and olive oil and made his belly ache with longing.

Ismelda picked up one of the loaves, broke it in two, and handed him half. 'You like focaccia?' she asked.

He nodded, his mouth too full to answer. It was the most delicious bread he had ever tasted. The convent bread he was used to was dark and chewy and could be used to fill holes in the walls, but this bread was fit for angels. It was golden and crisp to the touch, dusted with salt, dimpled and stuck with sprigs of rosemary.

After they had feasted for some time Bindo looked up in surprise that they had a visitor. It was his good friend Luca Roselli, who worked as a shop boy for Piero di Bardi.

Luca stopped in his tracks when he saw Bindo, winked at his friend and grinned.

Ismelda leant towards Bindo and said, 'Luca comes here most afternoons when Papa is out of the way. Maria teaches him to cook, and one day he's going to be the best cook in all Italy and open his own eating house, isn't that so, Luca?'

Luca smiled and blushed with pleasure. 'Sì, one day I will be able to leave that hell-hole of a place where I work.'

'You don't like working for Piero di Bardi?' Ismelda asked.

'I hate it,' he said with feeling.

'But don't you learn a lot of things?'

'I don't want to learn how to make cheese glue and varnish and have to trail around farms looking for white hogs so I can make paintbrushes.'

'You don't?'

Luca shook his head sadly, and Ismelda sighed. She would give her eye-teeth for a job like that but she was just a silly rich girl and would never be allowed to work.

Luca knelt down and held out an earthenware dish for their inspection.

'Panecotta with a juice of summer fruits,' he announced. 'Maria has taught me to make it.'

'How does she know how to make all these wonderful things?' Bindo asked.

'She has an uncle, an old shoe seller, who comes up to Santa Rosa once in a while from Naples, and he brings her all the latest recipes from the grand houses there. She can't read so I read them for her and then she teaches me how to make them.'

'Next week my uncle has promised to bring me a very new exciting recipe,' Maria said, sitting down on the grass beside them. 'Something very special, which Luca and I will make for you.'

'What is it?' Ismelda asked eagerly.

Maria tapped the side of her nose and laughed gaily. 'It's a secret. You will have to wait and see.'

'Can Bindo come and have some of this secret stuff?'

Maria grinned. 'If we can get your father out of the way for a few hours, we will have another little feast all together.'

Bindo beamed and his green eyes glittered with happiness. He looked up at Luca and saw that his eyes danced with delight; he had never seen Luca looking so happy.

He put out his hand tentatively, brushed his fingers gently against Ismelda's warm cheek and sighed. This was the most wonderful day of his life.

*

In an upstairs bedroom in the Villa Rosso Piero di Bardi woke from a drunken sleep, rubbed his forehead with the back of his hand and groaned. He was soaked in a muck sweat and the inside of his mouth tasted like putrefied meat.

He sat up and looked around, wondering where in the name of God he was. Then he remembered with embarrassment the conversation he had had here with Signor Bisotti earlier in the day.

A month ago Signor Bisotti had commissioned him to paint a scene of cherubs to be hung in the church, and he had agreed out of desperation because he owed money to half the population of Santa Rosa. In a week's time he needed to have the preliminary sketches ready to show Signor Bisotti, and all he had at the moment was a blank canvas and an empty head.

What was wrong with him of late? He had never had this problem in the past – why, his hand had always itched to draw, even when he was in the most improbable of places. Sometimes when he was kneeling during Mass and a shaft of sunlight doused a cool saint in a shadowy niche or cast luminous haloes around the upturned faces of the altar boys, he would have killed to be able to take up his charcoal and set to work. Yet in the last weeks it was as if the world around him had grown stale and uninteresting and his eyes could not make contact with his hand.

His fingers felt heavy, as if his blood was transforming into a thick syrup and parts of him were turning to stone, little by little, his hands, maybe next his arms.

This morning, he had begged for more time but Signor Bisotti was having none of it. And then he had dropped the bombshell. He wanted Piero to model his cherubs on the widow Zanelli's two daughters.

Sweet Jesus, the man was mad. The Zanelli sisters were pretty enough, but in such an artificial way, all baubles and bangles and dangling ribbons. They had fine enough faces to grace the front of a snuffbox, but there was no freshness, no earthiness, and no aura of innocence about them. He had told Signor Bisotti this, said he

94

must feel the very essence of his model's flesh seep into his being.

At that point Signor Bisotti had lost his temper and screeched, 'This is the drink making you talk nonsense. Essence and aura my arse! Pah! When I ask the carpenter to make me a table, does he say, "Oh, the oak has no aura, no essence?" No. He takes my money and he makes me a table. You, Piero, will paint the Zanelli girls or I will withdraw my generous offer.'

Then Signor Bisotti had led him up to this cool, dark room and bidden him lie down until he was sober and his madness had passed.

Now Piero ran his paint-stained fingers through his tangled hair in despair. He knew that as soon as those damned Zanelli girls were sitting in front of him his hands would begin to shake and his mind would flit from one incongruous thought to another. He had surely been cursed, his talents dried up, congealed like old paint blobs on the empty palette of his mind.

He got unsteadily to his feet, went over to the window, pushed open the shutters and screwed up his eyes against the bright sunshine.

He looked down into the garden of the Villa Rosso and drew in his breath with a whistle at the scene before him.

Sunlight filtered through the leaves of the pomegranate tree, dappling the faces of the four people sitting on the grass.

There was a girl he had never seen before. She must be Ismelda, the youngest Bisotti girl, the one Signor Bisotti took great pains to keep hidden away. He'd heard the locals speak of her in hushed tones, calling her the odd child, a child who could put the evil eye on you, make milk turn sour and the hens stop laying.

She was looking intently at the little dwarf, Bindo, and the unusual blue of her eyes was so captivating that Piero could not take his own eyes off her. It was like getting a sudden glimpse of the sea, of unfathomable swirling depths. Her face was remarkable; she was no classic beauty but there was a great vitality and an animation about her which took his breath away.

Her skin was as smooth as alabaster, a cluster of freckles peppering her nose and cheeks. She had a wide mouth, lips as pink as roses, as plump as caterpillars. A mane of wild, glossy hair framed this wonderful face, hair as black and blue as a raven's wing.

Reluctantly he turned his eyes away from her and looked at Bindo, and it was as if he was seeing him properly for the first time. The boy had been miraculously transformed in some way, but what was it that had changed? His skin was paler than usual and, though darkened by the summer sun, it had a translucency that transformed his features. A smear of red fruit dissected the smooth skin of his cheek like a scar.

Bindo was looking at Ismelda with wonder in his deep green eyes, drinking her up with his gaze, his eyelashes whispering across cheeks dusted with freckles of sunlight.

Piero started when he saw that Luca Roselli, his shop boy, was down there in the garden, too. The cheeky devil was supposed to be at the house in the Via Dante, making cheese glue. So this was where he sloped off to in the afternoons – no wonder Piero could never find him when there was work to be done. Luca's eyes were closed and there was a look of such contentment on his face that Piero was astonished. Gone was the scowl he wore when he was working for Piero. He was resting his back against the pomegranate tree, wriggling his bare brown toes, looking as though he had not a care in the world.

Maria Paparella, the Bisottis' servant, sat cross-legged on the grass, her faded black dress rucked up to just below her dimpled knees. Her plump calves were as pale as early narcissi, in contrast to her large sun-browned arms; here was a woman of contrast, of light and shade, of strength and tenderness.

It was a scene of such raw and unadulterated beauty that it made the hairs on his neck quiver, and a lump grow in his throat.

Maria Paparella looked up suddenly, and she smiled as their eyes met. Piero stepped back hastily from the window, feeling suddenly bashful. He drew the shutters together reluctantly and stood for a long time in the darkened room. For the first time in months his hand itched to take up his charcoal and draw.

Chapter 13

In Kilvenny Castle Ella Grieve woke early in the four-poster bed where she had been born almost fifty-three years ago. Until last night she had barely set foot in the castle since the day her family had moved to Shrimp's Hotel. After they had gone, the castle had been shut up until her eldest brother, William, had married Hester and moved in here.

As she lay listening to the morning sounds of Kilvenny, she grew puzzled. There was the sound of birdsong and the lapping of the waves down on the beach, but something was missing. It was all far too quiet. She was used to the silence up at Shrimp's, but down here in the village there had always been lots of bustle and noise. Today there was no raucous laughter from the fish workers as they made their way down to the Café Romana, where they bided their time until the ramshackle bus arrived to take them along the rutted road to the smokehouse further down the coast. She hadn't heard the clop of hooves as the donkey cart from Duffy's Farm made its way around the narrow streets, delivering milk, eggs and gossip.

She got up, opened the window and looked over at the Café Romana. She was surprised to see that the door was firmly shut and the sign still turned to CLOSED. There was no sign of movement inside, no steam rising from the coffee machine, no workers in greasy overalls, no lingering smell of strong tobacco or pungent whiff of fish on the morning breeze.

She turned away from the window and wandered fretfully around the room. Above the fireplace there was a framed photograph of William's awful wife, Hester. Hester had been a beautiful woman but her beauty was marred by cold, scornful eyes and a cruel twist to her lovely lips. Ella looked at the sleek blonde hair framing the well-boned face, and shuddered. Hester Grieve had been a sly, calculating bitch.

Thinking of her brought Kizzy reluctantly to mind. She had been a little beauty, too, not fair like her mother but dark like the Grieves. She'd been a delightful child, full of fun and able to charm everyone around her, but after her father died she'd hardened and in her teenage years she'd been nothing short of a bloody handful. Hester had been hopeless with her, impatient and critical and hideously jealous of Kizzy's youth. When she met her second husband she'd bundled Kizzy off with relief to boarding school, upped sticks and never set foot in Kilvenny again.

Kizzy had come back to Shrimp's every school holiday, severing all ties with Hester. Ella had been fond of Kizzy, had always hoped that she would join them in running Shrimp's after she left school, but that wasn't to be. Kizzy had proved that she had far more of her mother in her than anyone had thought. What she had done to Alice had been quite unforgivable, poor, beautiful, naive Alice, who hadn't a bad bone in her body. Alice had been far lovelier than either Hester or Kizzy; she'd had looks to die for and she'd always been able to attract any man's eye, though not necessarily his heart.

Ella sat down at the dressing table and scrutinised her reflection in the mirror. There was a slight improvement on how she had looked yesterday because last night she'd soaked in the antiquated bath downstairs, her first bath in longer than she cared to remember. Her face had scrubbed up well and there was a semblance of colour in her cheeks this morning; her hair was clean, although still tangled from years of neglect.

Dear God, she must have frightened that child half to death when she opened the door to her the other night. Whatever must Catrin have thought, seeing her great-aunt dressed in that old brown overall, odd-coloured wellingtons and a face which hadn't been washed in months, even years?

Ella looked critically at herself; she had never been remotely beautiful, not even close to pretty, although her eyes were reasonable; her nose was rather on the large side though not hideous. Her mouth had always been her best feature but now it was drawn down because of all the years without smiling. She practised a smile hesitantly, and then frowned. It had been more of a grimace than a smile, so out of practice was she.

She got to her feet, took a last dissatisfied look in the mirror, and sighed. She made her way slowly down the stairs to the kitchen and set about boiling a kettle on the old stove. After a good strong cup of tea, she would have to think about what she would do with this blasted great-niece of hers. The sooner she could get shot of her and get back to Shrimp's the better.

Chapter 14

Catrin woke as the first watery light came pricking through the bedroom window, rinsing away the shadows of the night. Outside, the air was alive with birdsong and someone was whistling cheerfully.

She sat up in the big bed, yawned and sniffed. She smelt of sour sweat and unwashed hair and she realised with horror that it was almost three days since she'd last washed. When she was fully awake she'd go down to the bathroom and bath and then she must ring her school again – one of the nuns was bound to answer the telephone this morning, and her worries would be over. Sister Matilde would drive down in the old school jalopy and rescue her. Hip hip hooray, she'd be on her way out of Kilvenny for ever.

Aunt Ella would be glad to see the back of her and could hurry back to Shrimp's Hotel and lock herself in with the mice and cobwebs and strange men who hid in wardrobes for fun. Good riddance to bad rubbish.

There was a knock at the bedroom door and before she had time to hide beneath the blankets, Aunt Ella backed into the room and set a battered tray down on the bedside table, nodding curtly to Catrin. Catrin's heart sank as she looked with loathing at the boiled eggs and the plate of thickly buttered toast soldiers. She'd eaten the chicken soup last night because she was too embarrassed to turn it down, but she wasn't going to stuff herself stupid on eggs and bread.

'I thought you might want some breakfast. You look as if you haven't eaten much in a long while.'

Catrin felt her face redden with indignation. Why did people go on about food all the time? No one needed to eat three square meals a day.

'I'm fine, thank you. I don't actually have a big appetite.'

'You don't look as if you eat enough to keep a sparrow alive.'

'Looks can be very deceptive,' Catrin retorted.

Ella edged away towards the door, her mouth set in a grim line. 'Of course, if you can't eat, rather than won't eat, I could get the doctor in to take a look at you.'

Catrin bit back the urge to snap: if Ella did call a doctor to look at her, they'd know something was wrong.

'Fine,' she mumbled, leaning across for the tray.

'Do you have any plans for today?' Ella asked.

Catrin ignored her. She was making it sound as if she was on a proper holiday and not waiting to escape from a bad dream. She wanted to say sarcastically, 'Oh, yes, I'll have a swim and sunbathe and then maybe a game of tennis.' Instead she said through clenched teeth, 'I'd like to find a telephone and ring my school again, if that's all right with you.'

'There's no point.'

'I'd still like to.'

'I, er, rang them yesterday evening from the library.'

Catrin brightened visibly and sat up in bed. 'Are they coming for me today?' she asked, hope rising in her voice.

'I'm afraid not.'

Catrin looked at Ella through narrowed eyes. She could tell she was lying. 'How did you find out the number?'

'If you remember, you mentioned the name of your school

to me yesterday and I got the number from the operator.'

'And the nuns really said that I had to stay here all summer?' Catrin asked in disbelief.

'Not exactly. I actually spoke to a man.'

'There aren't any men at my school, so you must have got the wrong number,' Catrin said with triumph.

'The man I spoke to was, in fact, a doctor. Apparently there's been an outbreak of scarlet fever and none of the sisters was available to speak to me.'

Catrin glanced down at the tray of food. For two pins she'd snatch up the boiled eggs and hurl them across the room at this mad old woman.

She clamped her lips together and tried to batten down her rising anger.

'I'm sure we'll sort something out for you before long.'

'You can't keep me here against my will, you know.'

Ella raised her eyebrows and laughed. 'I've no intention of keeping you here any longer than necessary.'

'I didn't ask to come here in the first place.'

'And I certainly didn't ask your feckless mother to send you here. I expect she was desperate and Shrimp's was the last resort.'

Ella took a sidelong look at Catrin and felt immediately sorry for speaking so sharply. She was a mere scrap of a girl, bewildered and afraid. She had very beautiful eyes, rather like Ella's brother William, the sort of eyes that looked as if they'd been drawn with charcoal and smudged around the lashes. She was bound to take after the Grieves – after all, William was her grandfather.

She watched Catrin wipe her eyes surreptitiously on a corner of the sheet. Don't be fooled by tears, Ella Grieve, she told herself. Some people could turn them on like a tap.

'I don't know why she sent me here, either. She must have known you wouldn't want me.'

'I expect she thought Alice would welcome you with open arms. Alice was always a soft touch where Kizzy was concerned.'

'But Alice is dead,' Catrin said.

'Yes, she is, dead and gone, but your mother wouldn't have known that. I don't know what she thinks she's playing at. The last thing I need in my life is a child to look after.'

'And the last thing I need is a . . .'

'A what?'

Catrin was going to say 'a mad old aunt who lives in a pigsty' but seeing the stern set of Ella's face she thought better of it. 'Nothing.'

'Go on, tell the truth and shame the devil.'

'Pardon?'

'I mean, spit out whatever it is you want to say, and clear the air.'

'I don't want to say anything. I just want to go away from here, that's all.'

'You will soon enough when we can get hold of that useless article of a mother of yours.'

'But I don't even know how to find her. All I know is that she's somewhere in Italy.'

'What the hell is she doing in Italy?'

'She said she was going to meet someone she'd known at school.'

'Well, I'll find her somehow, even if I have to ring the bloody Pope himself.'

Catrin looked aghast. Was she mad? You couldn't just ring the Pope. He was a very busy man. Didn't she know anything?

Ella turned on her heel and walked towards the door.

'What am I supposed to do in the meantime?' Catrin called after her.

'For starters, eat your breakfast.'

Catrin turned her head away in fury and did not look back until the door had closed behind Ella and her footsteps had died away down the corridor.

She looked longingly at the food in front of her, ached to pick up the spoon and crack the brown shell of the egg, watch the yellow yolk rise up and dribble over the side. The smell of toast was unbearable and she imagined how it would feel to dip a toast soldier into the warm egg.

The temptation to eat was so great that if she didn't distract herself straight away she wouldn't be able to help herself. She got quickly out of bed and looked around for a suitable hiding place. She hid the boiled eggs in the back of an empty wardrobe, opened the window and stuck the toast butter side down against the outside wall of the castle. They might be able to make her stay here until they found her mother but they couldn't force her to eat.

She threw herself down on the bed, hid her face in the pillow and punched the bed with clenched fists until she was exhausted. When her anger was finally spent she picked up the strange book she had been reading last night and thumbed through the pages, losing herself once again in the beautiful paintings, transporting herself to another place, another time, far away from horrible Kilvenny.

Chapter 15

Signor Bisotti emerged from the sombre darkness of the church of Santa Rosa into the light as the Angelus bell began to chime. He stepped backwards as an old donkey, escaped from his tethering and laden with panniers of fruit, came clattering along the cobbles. Signor Bisotti ducked when a large split lemon bounced up off the cobbles, narrowly missing his head.

The good Lord must surely be looking down on him this morning, for if he had stepped out a moment sooner he might be nursing a blackened eye or missing a few of his crooked teeth.

He crossed the square, passed the fountain where the chipped and mossy cherubs splashed in the cascades of frothing water. He kept to the shade, staying close to the high walls that surrounded his house, the Villa Rosso, the largest, most luxurious house in the town. He smiled at this thought; he was very proud of his wealth and his standing in Santa Rosa.

He walked with an unaccustomed spring in his step because Father Rimaldi had given him some very good news indeed. The priest had returned from a visit to the enclosed order of nuns at Santa Lucia, some miles away. Father Rimaldi had persuaded the nuns to take Signor Bisotti's youngest daughter, Ismelda, off his hands in the coming autumn. Of course, nothing was free in this world, and in return for his trouble Father Rimaldi had demanded a payment of sorts, and that was why Signor Bisotti had agreed to commission Piero di Bardi to paint a scene of feasting cherubs to be hung in the church. That didn't come cheap, but what was money in exchange for a life without Ismelda?

Signor Bisotti sighed with satisfaction. Ismelda had been a trial to him ever since she was a baby and lately she had been even more tiresome than usual. Now that she was older it was harder to cover up her peculiar ways. Only last week she had made a slingshot, hurled a pomegranate over the wall and hit one of the old sisters from the Santa Rosa convent.

She was a noisy, foul-mouthed child, always up to some mischief or other. He had even had to move her from her upstairs bedroom into a downstairs room which faced on to the internal courtyard, because the upstairs rooms had balconies overlooking the piazza. God forbid that the nosy townspeople should see the sort of things that she got up to when she wasn't being watched. She was far safer downstairs with the added protection of bars on the window and the door being locked at night.

Why in God's name couldn't she have been more like his eldest daughter, Marietta? She was a good, biddable girl, suitably married now and hopefully soon to produce grandchildren, although she was taking rather a long time in doing so.

There had been only one dark cloud on his horizon and now that little problem was about to be solved. By the time the first leaves began to fall and the cooler winds blew up the narrow valley, he would be free. Ismelda would be safely incarcerated with the holy sisters at Santa Lucia convent, who would knock some sense into that thick skull of hers.

It wouldn't be plain sailing and there would be opposition from one quarter. Maria Paparella would not take kindly to losing Ismelda, for they were as close as if they were mother and daughter. Maria had seen to all the child's many needs since the death of his wife. Thinking of Maria dented his rising optimism. She had the most formidable temper he'd ever seen in a young woman, and telling her that Ismelda was going to be sent away to the nuns would not be an easy matter.

Still, she was a servant and servants did as they were told, did they not? That was the trouble in these modern times; the peasant people were getting above themselves. Why, that blasted little dwarf, Bindo, had actually had the nerve to climb into the garden of the Villa Rosso this morning. It was just as well for him that he had managed to escape, though how he had was a mystery. When Signor Bisotti was a boy, a cheeky half-wit like that would never have dared to insult a man of Signor Bisotti's standing. He was another one who could do with being locked up and the key thrown down a deep well.

Once Ismelda was safely out of the way he would be able to pursue his own happiness and, if fate smiled on him, that happiness might have a little to do with the widow Zanelli. She wasn't a bad-looking woman, a trifle broad in the beam but still on the right side of forty, with just enough time to give him a son and heir.

He was optimistic about his chances with the widow, particularly since he had only this morning instructed Piero to use the two Zanelli girls as models for the cherubs in his painting.

Life was looking good. Of course, he would have to smooth the waters between Maria and his intended bride because there was some animosity between then. Women were like that, were they not? Illogical creatures falling out over the least trifle. He was sure, though, that with his finely tuned skills of tact and diplomacy all would be fine – after all, he didn't want to gain a wife but lose the best cook in Santa Rosa. Maria would calm down in time; she'd have her hands full running around at the widow Zanelli's beck and call. And she'd be looking after the two sweet Zanelli girls, which would surely take her mind off losing Ismelda.

As he passed the turning to the Via Dante he wondered if Piero *di Bardi had slept off his hangover and returned to his own house. He had every confidence that the man would come to his senses; he was desperate for money.*

Signor Bisotti stepped up to the door of the widow Zanelli's house, smoothed his thinning hair and polished his front teeth with his forefinger.

He was looking forward to an afternoon with the widow Zanelli; she really was very accommodating to his needs. He pulled back his shoulders and smiled. This afternoon he would think only of pleasant things. Temperamental artists with their gobbledygook talk about essence and aura, half-witted dwarves and badly behaved daughters one really could do without.

Chapter 16

The early-morning air was soft, fresh after the rainfall and heady with the smell of flowers. Catrin stood in the overgrown kitchen garden where the scents of burdock and parsley, thyme and rosemary mingled with the horrid smell of henbane. Beyond the kitchen garden there was a low archway she hadn't noticed yesterday, and she stepped through it into a small paved garden enclosed by high walls overgrown with ivy.

In the middle of the garden there was a waterless fountain, where a small, naked stone cherub perched precariously on a plinth. His mouth and eyes were choked with moss and his body was green with age and years of weathering.

She clambered over the surrounding wall of the fountain, stepping carefully through the layers of rotting leaves and rubbish beneath her feet. She ran her hand along the cherub's outstretched arm and closed her eyes, and for a moment the cherub felt almost real to her touch. She could feel the ripple of his tiny muscles, the bend in the elbow, the delicate outstretched fingers.

Wouldn't it be wonderful if she could breathe life into this little cherub, see the old stone turn into warm flesh, the cheeks grow pink and the dead eyes come fluttering open.

The twitching of muscles, a lazy yawn and then, with gathering life, the cherub's wings would stir, move slowly, then faster, making currents of air all around her.

And then she would watch in wonder as he made his first attempt to fly, tentative, then gathering in confidence, rising higher and higher ... turning to take her hand, both of them hovering above the ruined tower, startling the rooks and then soaring up together, up into the blue skies over Kilvenny.

She opened her eyes and sighed. Sometimes she wondered if she wasn't quite right in the head. A stone cherub was hardly likely to fly, however hard she wished. She often had peculiar thoughts. Once in a Scripture lesson she'd been daydreaming and Sister Lucy asked Catrin what she was thinking and she'd said that she was wondering if rain were really angel pee. Mary Donahue had fallen off her chair in a fit of laughing, and Sister Lucy said angels were not earthly beings with bodily functions, thank the Lord, and she took away three of her house points for vulgarity. Catrin had kept quiet about her thoughts ever since.

She brushed the cherub's cheek gently with her fingers, marvelled at the detail of his face, the enigmatic smile, the slight flaring of the nostrils. She clambered back over the wall and sat down on one of the weathered stone benches set around the garden.

A desolate air hung over everything; there were cracked terracotta urns, some upturned, others broken and spilling out earth, and the flagstones were green and slippery with lichen; yet it must have been beautiful once. She imagined what it would be like to sit here listening to the gurgling of the fountain, watching the sun glint off the water and rainbows dance in the spray.

As she sat daydreaming she noticed a door on the far side of the garden and went over to investigate. She lifted the latch and a familiar smell hit her at once: the whiff of ingrained incense and the smoky holiness of church candles.

Stepping inside she automatically put out her hand to search for the holy water stoop to bless herself, and there, set into the wall, almost as if her hand knew where to find it, was a roughly carved stoop filled with ice-cold water.

She made the sign of the cross and looked about; she was in a small, dark chapel illuminated only by the muted light that filtered in through the stained-glass window above the altar. To the left of the main altar there was a tiny lady chapel set in an alcove where a spluttering candle warmed the feet of a plaster saint, and a bunch of yellow dandelion flowers had been stuffed in an old jam jar. She made the sign of the cross again, knelt down on a mouldy hassock, bowed her head, closed her eyes and clasped her hands together in prayer. She shivered, not with the cold but with a frisson of fear and exhilaration mixed up together.

The silence and coolness of the chapel soothed her and as she knelt there she thought suddenly of Sister Matilde. The nun would love Kilvenny Castle; she was fascinated by everything about history.

'I adore old things,' she'd once told Catrin's class. 'The feel of a worn step beneath my weary feet, a step where thousands of feet have trod before me, sends a delicious shiver up my spine. Or that feeling of immense joy one gets when standing in the shade of an ancient building in a sun-soaked piazza watching water play over the upturned faces of stone cherubs.'

Catrin looked back at the window and watched a sunbeam worm its way in through a small hole in the stained glass and dance playfully across the altar. The smell of incense grew suddenly stronger and mingled with the mustiness of old prayer books and damp hassocks. She glanced at the tiny saint and remembered something else Sister Matilde had said.

'How glorious it is to kneel in the early morning and watch the light slip through a stained-glass window and see the early shadows play across a lonely saint in a cool chapel.'

It was almost as if this were the very place that Sister Matilde had described, and just now everything here felt familiar to Catrin, as if she had been coming here to kneel like this for ever.

If what Aunt Ella had said about ringing her school was true, it was hardly likely Sister Matilde would come rushing down here to save her. She wondered how long it would take Aunt Ella to track down her mother and tell her to come straight to Kilvenny and pick her up. Hell's bells, her mother would be furious if she had her holiday ruined and had to come all the way back from Italy. Catrin would never hear the end of it and she'd have to spend another boring summer in London.

Then she had a truly awful thought. What if her mother contacted Arthur Campbell and asked him to look after her until she got back from Italy? She shivered, and cold fingers of fear flew up her backbone. She hadn't considered that possibility, and yet it was the most likely one because he was her godfather. She hated Arthur Campbell and his wife; an afternoon in their company always seemed like a lifetime, and the thought of staying with them for the whole summer was too awful. Arthur Campbell was a horrid shrunken old tortoise with wily eyes and a prickly beard, the feel of which made her shrivel when he kissed her.

She would refuse to go there.

That was rubbish and she knew it. You didn't refuse Arthur Campbell anything.

An hour ago she would have done anything to escape from Kilvenny as soon as she could, but now she was having second thoughts. She didn't want to stay here with moody Aunt Ella, but it would be better than being under the beady eye of Arthur Campbell.

As she closed her eyes and prayed, the image of Maria Paparella came to her as clearly as if it had been painted on the back of her eyelids. If only she could speak to this smiling woman and ask her advice, Maria would be able to tell her what to do. She looked kind and motherly but there was also a look about her that said she wouldn't put up with any nonsense. There she was again, thinking stupid thoughts: how could someone who had been dead for hundreds of years possibly help her?

She dropped her head onto her clasped hands and tried to concentrate on her prayers but her mind kept conjuring up Maria Paparella's face and she imagined a comforting hand reaching out from the page of the book to touch her, the feel of warm brown flesh against her cheek, the smell of fresh bread and the sweet scent of cinnamon. So immersed was she in her thoughts that she was unaware of the chapel door opening.

Tony Agosti stepped inside and dipped his fingers into the stoop of holy water, then his hand hovered halfway to his forehead as he saw Catrin praying in the lady chapel. She looked almost ethereal as she knelt there, the sunlight turning her face to gold.

It hardly seemed possible that this frail little girl could be Kizzy's daughter. Kizzy had always been so vivacious, always bursting with unrestrained energy, but her daughter was a ghost of a girl, as insubstantial as the morning shadows. He was overcome with compassion for her, poor little kid to have been sent somewhere she wasn't wanted. She must feel wretched, abandoned and desolate. If Ella had an ounce of kindness, she should realize that the kid needed a bit of human kindness shown to her, no matter what had gone on in the past. God, if he could have laid his hands on Kizzy Grieve's beautiful neck he could quite easily have throttled her.

The hissing of the candles stirred Catrin from her reverie and she turned and saw Tony watching her intently from the doorway. He smiled suddenly, a smile which transformed his face from the solemnity of a medieval saint to a court jester, a smile which took the chill off the chapel.

He lit four candles, placed them at the feet of the little saint, and knelt down next to Catrin, hands clasped, eyes closed, lips moving in silent prayer. She looked sideways at him; he was a very handsome man, his dark eyelashes throwing shadows across his sculpted cheeks, a nose like that of a marble saint. His eyelashes flickered momentarily; he turned his dark eyes on her and smiled, edged closer, wiped a smudge from her cheek with his thumb and whispered, 'My daily duty is now done, and for the next hour or so I am a free man.'

'Duty?'

'Now that Nonna rarely gets out, I come across to light candles for her, one for her husband and one each for my parents.'

That made three candles. He had lit four and she wondered who the fourth one was for but was too shy to ask.

She followed him out into the garden and they sat together on a bench opposite the fountain.

'Damn, you know I love this place, it's so peaceful and has such a feel of history,' he said with a sigh. 'I often wonder about all the different people who must have lived here over the years.'

'What sort of people, do you think?'

'Well, if I close my eyes I can hear the swish of a long dress as a grand lady passes through the gardens.'

'Would there have been grand ladies living here?'

'Of course. Your family, the Grieves, were very wealthy people in the olden days. If you'd lived here then you would have worn fine clothes and learnt to embroider and play the harpsichord or something like that.'

'Ugh. I should have hated it. I don't like dressing up and being all ladylike, and I'm hopeless at needlework.'

Tony chuckled. 'You take after your Aunt Ella, then: she was a tomboy.'

Catrin pulled a face; she didn't like to be compared with grubby Ella Grieve.

'Ah, you could do worse. Ella can be a funny old stick, but she's got a heart of gold underneath all that bluster.'

'She swears too much,' Catrin said.

'That's because she spent too much time with the fishermen when she was little and picked up bad habits, but hey we've all got our faults. Do you know something, Catrin Grieve?'

'No, what?'

'I for one am really glad that you turned up here out of the blue and flushed her out of hiding.'

'Why do you think she shut herself up in Shrimp's for all those years?'

Tony shrugged. 'I don't know. She had her reasons, I suppose. Damn, those roses smell beautiful today. I bet it smells better here now than it did hundreds of years ago.'

'Why would it?'

'Well, it would have stunk in the olden days.'

'What sort of awful smells would there have been, do you think?'

'Rotting food, the smell of dead rats, and there were no proper toilets, for a start.'

'A bit like Shrimp's smells now, then,' Catrin said with a sniff, and she wrinkled her nose in disgust.

'I suppose so.'

'I'd rather we didn't talk about bad smells any more. Is that the tower?' she said, pointing across the gardens.

'Aye, that's where the nursery used to be.'

'The nursery?'

'When Ella's parents were first married they moved into the castle, and once the children came along they used the tower as the nursery. It suited Mrs Grieve having the children away from the main house, as it were, looked after by a nanny. She hadn't a lot of patience with small children, according to Nonna.'

'Did my mother stay in the nursery when she was little?'

Tony shook his head. 'No. There was no money for a nanny when your mother was small; she slept up in the room where you are now. Besides, she didn't like the tower. She thought it was haunted.'

'Is it?' Catrin asked nervously.

'Maybe. They used to say that the Grieves locked the mad members of the family up in the tower and their ghosts come back to haunt the place.'

Catrin looked at Tony in alarm, and he smiled. 'I'm only teasing.'

'Good, because whenever anyone talks about the Grieves they talk about the mad ones.'

'There's a fine line between madness and genius, and I think the Grieves had a bit of both in their blood.'

They were silent for a few moments and then Catrin said, 'This garden is very different to the rest of the gardens.'

'That's because this is the Italian garden.'

'Italian?' she said with interest.

'One of your ancestors had this garden specially made. Italian gardens always had water as the main feature.'

'It's a real shame that the fountain doesn't work any more,' Catrin said wistfully.

'I can remember it working when I was younger. Mr Grieve, Ella's father, had it restored years ago. I used to come and sit here for hours with my nonna. Maybe one day we can try and get it going again?' he said enthusiastically.

'I'm afraid I won't be here that long.'

'You going somewhere?'

'Aunt Ella's going to try and get hold of my mother.'

'Is she, indeed?'

'She said she was going to ring the Pope.'

'I wouldn't put it past Ella to do that. She's quite mad, you know.'

Catrin gave him a sideways glance.

'Don't look so worried. She's not mad exactly, just a little eccentric. Where is she, by the way?'

Catrin shrugged. 'I don't know. I haven't seen her since she brought me some breakfast.'

'I'll tell you what, why don't you and I go on a little ride around Kilvenny so that you can get your bearings? You can leave a note for Ella and I'll meet you outside in, say, ten minutes' time.'

She was about to turn down his offer but when he smiled at her with that wide, warm smile she couldn't bring herself to refuse.

Chapter 17

Meredith Evans stumbled out of the Boot Inn and looked anxiously up and down Cockle Lane. His nerves had been on edge ever since he thought he'd seen someone peering in through the window of his shop a few nights ago. He'd convinced himself that it had all been in his imagination until yesterday, when his anxiety had been further heightened by seeing Ella Grieve staring at him through the dusty window. What a sight she'd been with her mad, glaring eyes and her hair as wild and tangled as tumbleweed.

She was the last person he'd expected to see down here in Kilvenny. He hadn't set eyes on her since the day Alice had been buried years ago.

He caught sight of the girl standing outside Kilvenny Castle and stopped abruptly, felt the sweat breaking out on his forehead again and his heart squeezing tightly.

For a moment he could have sworn that it was Alice Grieve standing there, as though he had been transported back to his childhood and there she was waiting patiently for him to arrive as she had always done. He chided himself for his stupidity. There was a likeness to Alice, it was true, but unlike Alice this little girl was pitifully thin, as if she'd been struck down with a wasting disease.

He gathered his wits and walked on, watching the girl

surreptitiously. She glanced nervously towards him and he took in the vivid blueness of her eyes, the pale skin stretched tightly over the bones of her face.

He yelped in alarm as a hand was laid on his arm, and he turned to face Dan Gwartney.

'Good God, man, there's a bag of nerves you are!'

'Just a bit jumpy, that's all. I'm not sleeping well of late.'

'Guilty conscience?' Dan said.

Meredith ignored him and was about to walk away when Dan whispered, 'You can tell she's a Grieve all right.' He nodded towards the girl.

'She's what?' Meredith gasped.

'Ella's great-niece, by all accounts.'

'You mean she's Kizzy's daughter?' he said, aghast.

'A bit of a turn up for the books, eh? Not much like her mother to look at and of course the father is a bit of a mystery, I gather.'

Meredith, his mouth hanging open in disbelief, was unable to answer. Dan patted him cheerfully on the shoulder and went on his way.

Meredith took a last look at the girl and then blundered into his shop, pulling the yellowing blind down over the door and swivelling the CLOSED sign outwards.

Chapter 18

As Tony and Catrin rode through the narrow streets of Kilvenny, Catrin wondered what Sister Lucy would say if she could see her now. Lord, she'd be apoplectic with fury. When Tony Agosti had offered to take her on a ride through Kilvenny she'd thought he meant in a car. When he'd turned up outside the castle on a decrepit pushbike she'd been horrified.

'All aboard for the Kilvenny express.' He'd laughed and she'd been too flustered to refuse.

She'd never ridden a bike in her life and certainly never clambered up on to the crossbar, and yet here she was now wobbling up through Kilvenny clinging on to the handlebars with one hand and to Tony Agosti's shirtfront with the other.

They passed the war memorial and took a left turn into one of the narrower streets of the village, Tony giving a running commentary as they went.

'Here we are in Donkey Lane. On the right in number five lives Tudor Davies, only one eye but he doesn't miss much, nosy old devil. Old Sarah Pugh in number nine hasn't had a wash since she was christened, and the last house on your right is empty now but was once a gin palace.'

Tony's cheerfulness was infectious, and by the time they

turned into Goose Row Catrin's face was flushed with pleasure and she looked about with interest, soaking up all he told her about the remaining inhabitants of Kilvenny.

'Years ago here in Coronation Place there used to be three pubs in a row, the Doghouse, the Bug and Bucket and the Brute and Stone.'

'Why were there so many?'

'Fishing was thirsty work, my girl, and Kilvenny used to be a busy old place.'

'What happened to it?'

'First the fish deserted us and put most of the fishermen out of work, then the smokehouse closed down, and then Shrimp's shut up shop into the bargain.'

'Did Shrimp's closing make a lot of difference?'

'Oh yes. It used to be busy nearly all year round, full of toffs and nobs from up England with plenty of money to spend down here in the village. Old Mr Watkins the butcher said his delivery boy used to be knackered from making up to four trips a day to Shrimp's. Gladys Beynon, who was the cook, used to buy nothing but the best – sides of beef, legs of lamb, mutton chops, chitterlings, pigeons and geese.'

Catrin tried to picture Shrimp's Hotel full of well-to-do guests, to imagine them walking across the lawns towards the beach, the tinkling of the piano and the aroma of cooking from the kitchen.

'If you look down there you'll see the track that leads down to the old smokehouse where they used to cure the herring.'

Catrin saw a narrow lane leading down towards the sea and, out near the rocks, the broken remains of an old building.

They were silent for a while as Tony pedalled up a steep hill, eventually coming to rest at the top and helping Catrin down off the bike.

'Take a look at that view. You won't see many better.'

Before them lay a wide sweep of deserted bay stretching away as far as the eye could see.

'Isn't that beautiful?'

It was breathtaking. Catrin had never seen anything quite so wild and spectacular in her life. White-crested waves rolled in from the ocean, crashing on to the line of shingle, throwing up foam and spray, then racing up the pale sands, making patterns of lace. How she would love to climb down there and leave a trail of footprints as she ran across the unmarked sand.

'Is that a shipwreck?' she asked, pointing to where the hulk of a boat lay half submerged in the choppy water.

'Yes, that's all that's left of the *Flino*. She was an old tub heading for Cardiff but she was blown off course in a storm and sank.'

Catrin had a sudden vision of a huge old ship tossing in heavy seas beneath glowering skies. The wind was roaring, people were screaming . . .

She felt as if her lungs were swelling up, filling with water until she could barely breathe.

She put her hand anxiously to her throat and Tony, noticing the paleness of her face, put his arm around her shoulders.

'Are you feeling all right?'

She nodded, took a deep breath and looked out towards the calm sea, glistening beneath a blue sky. Impossible to imagine what it must have been like for those poor people trapped on the *Flino*.

'Tell me the rest of the story.'

'Well, valiant efforts were made to save those on board, but tragically only a handful of people were saved, along with a cat.'

'Why was there a cat on board?'

'In the old days ships often had a cat to catch the mice and rats. It was a terrible night for Kilvenny folk, by all accounts, and they fought bravely to save the people on board.'

'Who were they?'

'Well, there were sailors, of course, but the others were passengers, poor wretches travelling to make a new life for themselves in a strange land and, sadly, most of them ended up buried in Kilvenny.'

Despite the warmth of the morning Catrin shivered. 'What happened to the survivors?'

'They were cared for in the village. In fact Nathaniel Grieve, who they say was a queer old fish, gave some of them shelter in Kilvenny Castle.'

'What happened to them after that?'

'I don't really know, but not long after the *Flino* went down there was an outbreak of cholera here and half of the village died of it.'

'Did Nathaniel Grieve die, too?'

'No, but he left Kilvenny and the castle was shut up for years.'

'But the Grieves came back?'

'Yes, one of his children came back eventually and the Grieves have been here ever since.'

It felt strange to think that she came from a long line of Grieves stretching right back into the old days.

'When we were kids we used to spend hours diving near the *Flino* to see if we could find any treasure.'

'And did you?' Catrin asked eagerly.

'No. It wasn't a treasure ship, just a cargo ship on its way to the docks with a hold full of fruit.'

'Fruit?'

'Lemons and limes and other exotic stuff bound for the markets. They reckon that the beach was awash with lemons and olives for weeks afterwards.'

Catrin looked away from the beach up to where the land climbed steeply towards a solitary house standing in the middle of the fields, staring out to sea.

'Blind Man's Lookout,' Tony said.

'How can a blind man be a lookout?' Catrin asked, frowning. 'Does anyone still live there?'

'Not any more; it's been empty for years. They say an old fellow who lived there could tell the colour of things just by touch.'

Catrin looked up at him in puzzlement. 'Do you believe that?'

'Well, I suppose it's possible.'

'It must have been a very lonely place to live,' Catrin said.

'Not for him. He had a wife and a house full of children – a bit like the old woman who lived in a shoe, so they say.'

'No one could live there now. Look, the roof's half off and there's no glass in any of the windows.'

'It must have been bleak as hell in the winter. At least Kilvenny gets a bit of shelter from the headland, but here when the winter storms come it takes a real battering. Perhaps we'll get hold of another bike for you and one day we'll ride round the coast and I'll show you the cockle women at work.'

'The what?'

'Over in Aberderi the women pick the cockles – have done since Roman times – and that's a wonderful sight.'

'Is a cockle one of those yellowish things they have in jars?'

'Ay, but fresh cockles are the best. You never tasted one?'
She shook her head.

'There are all sorts of recipes you can use cockles in.'

'What sort of recipes?'

'Let me see, cockle cakes, cockle pie, cockle soup, all sorts. Do you like cooking?'

She shook her head again.

'My favourite recipe is spaghetti alla carbonara every time. My grandfather taught me to make it the way the shepherds used to make it in Italy.'

'I've only ever had spaghetti from a tin.'

'Sweet Jesus, then you haven't lived. Surely you must cook sometimes?'

'No, I've never cooked anything in my life.'

'You're joking? You've never cooked a thing?' he said, scandalised.

She blushed.

'Everyone should know how to cook. What would you eat if you had to look after yourself?'

'When I'm at school the nuns cook, and at home a woman comes in to make my tea.'

'Well, if I was you and you have to stay here in Kilvenny for any length of time, I'd start to learn straight away.'

'Why?'

'Because Ella Grieve can just about boil an egg but she can't cook for toffee. She'll be serving you up some disasters, I can tell you,' he said with a laugh.

'She never learnt to cook, either?'

'No. Mind you, she used to go out in that boat of hers and bring back all sorts of fish. She wasn't a bit squeamish. I've seen her gut a fish and slaughter a chicken without batting an eyelid.'

Catrin blanched. 'That's a funny thing for a woman to do.'

'She's an unusual woman, your Aunt Ella. Anyhow, we'd better get back in case she thinks you've disappeared.'

'I think she'd be glad if I had.'

'Oh, don't be thinking that. Ella's bark is worse than her bite.'

'Does she bite, then?'

'No, that's just an expression. She makes a lot of noise but she's not dangerous.'

They were silent as they clambered on to the bike and freewheeled down the hill towards Kilvenny. The sea breeze caught Catrin's hair, blowing it round her face so that she could hardly see. She surprised herself by laughing out loud with utter joy, and by the time they squealed to a halt outside the Café Romana she was red-faced and weak-kneed with exhilaration.

'Thanks, Tony,' she said breathlessly as he helped her off the bike.

'My pleasure. You've been like a breath of fresh air, and I'll be sorry to see you go if you're determined to leave.'

She smiled. No one had said anything that kind to her in ages. She'd be sad to say goodbye to him, too. He was such fun, and she hadn't had much fun in her life before today.

As he was about to open the door of the café, Catrin said hurriedly, 'I don't expect I will be, but if I am here for a bit longer, would you do me a big favour?'

'Fire away, Catrin Grieve. Your wish is my command.'

'Well, seeing as I've never cooked anything in my life, I'd like to try out a recipe I found in a book.'

'What do you want to make?'

'Fock ... *focaccia* bread – I think that's how you say it. Only I don't have any of the ingredients.'

To her consternation Tony threw back his head and laughed gleefully.

'Wonderful! The first thing you want to make is Italian bread, eh? You say you have a recipe?'

'Yes, I found one in an old book.'

'If you take the trouble to make the bread, will you eat it?' Tony asked, looking steadfastly into her eyes.

She returned his gaze warily.

127

'Only, I noticed that the birds made a fine meal of your toast this morning.'

Catrin blushed and stared down at her feet.

Tony smiled. 'Give me a list of the ingredients and I'll get them. Maybe we can make a cook out of you while you're here. I'll tell you something, too. Ella always used to love her food. Maybe if you become a good cook she'll want you to stay.'

'I doubt it.'

He went into the Café Romana. As she turned to cross the road she saw a man in the doorway of the photographer's shop watching her intently. He lifted his hat to her and she was sure he was the man she'd seen sneaking out of Aunt Alice's room. She turned her face away and hurried into the castle.

Part Two

Chapter 19

Ella and Catrin settled awkwardly into life in Kilvenny Castle and established a routine of sorts in the first few days. They rose at roughly the same time in the mornings and made their separate ways down to the kitchen, where Ella busied herself making tea and usually burning the toast. Then they sat in uncomfortable silence on opposite sides of the enormous kitchen table, avoiding eye contact. Usually Ella turned the wireless up loud so as to discourage any conversation between them, and Catrin drank her tea, toyed with her toast and, when Ella's back was turned, hid it in her handkerchief to be disposed of later.

Throughout the daylight hours they skirted around each other warily. When Ella was indoors Catrin made a point of going out and she trailed dolefully around the castle gardens. If Ella took it into her head to go outside, Catrin retreated indoors. Sometimes as they crept along the dim corridors they would turn a corner suddenly and come face to face and each turned tail.

As the days wore on Catrin grew restive, embarrassed by the heavy silences. Sometimes she hovered on the threshold of speaking to Aunt Ella, but her courage always failed her and she was left tongue-tied and ill at ease. Sometimes she was aware of Ella sneaking a glance at her from behind a book as if she, too, wanted to break the silence but couldn't bring herself to. It became a constant game of avoidance and furtive glances between two people who didn't want to be anywhere near each other.

One sweltering afternoon, as Kilvenny withered under a blinding sun, Catrin made her way along the narrow lanes and alleys. The village was hushed, the rooks sleeping soundly in the tall trees of Gwartney's Wood, and the grasshoppers in the long grass by the creek worn to a frazzle. The air was heavy, tinged with the smell of baked earth and wilting flowers, the road beneath her feet erupting here and there in suppurating blisters of melting tar, the choked drains exhaling the stench of rotting leaves and bad eggs.

The streets were deserted and an air of exhaustion hung over everything. The faded blinds were pulled down over the windows of the Café Romana, and on either side of the door the geraniums slumped drunkenly in their terracotta pots. All around were the scents of sweet peas, rapidly ripening tomatoes and drying seaweed.

She looked curiously in through the darkened doorways of the tiny houses that were still inhabited, inhaling the peculiar smells of Kilvenny: Brasso and eye-watering disinfectant, mothballs and Welsh cakes sizzling on a griddle mingling with the smell of old linoleum and scalded tealeaves.

She tiptoed past an old woman asleep on a chair outside her front door, a bowl of half shelled peas on her lap; she stepped hurriedly into a doorway as a barefoot old man came down Goose Row pulling a belligerent donkey along behind him.

Bryn Jones's shop was halfway along Goose Row, and Catrin lingered outside trying to buck up the courage to go inside. When she eventually sidled in, she stood at the back of a line of women waiting to be served.

The shop was dimly lit by an unshaded lightbulb around which flies swung as if on a wire. It was unlike any other shop she'd ever been in, filled with the smell of withering cabbages, strong cheese, rhubarb and carbolic, and a whole plethora of smells that were new to her.

She'd never seen women like the Kilvenny women in their down-at-heel slippers and toffee-coloured stockings rolled down round their blotchy ankles. They wore flowery turbans and pinafores over faded frocks. Some had half-smoked cigarettes tucked behind their ears and one stiff-faced woman with a nicotine moustache had rollers the size of steamroller wheels fixed in the front of her iron-grey hair, legs as hairy as a spider's and a mouth painted carmine red.

Catrin listened to their chatter, marvelling at the sound of their voices, sometimes as loud as the rooks that shrieked above the castle, at other times soft and undulating like the rise and fall of the sea. The women gave off their own peculiar smells, oilcloth, strong soap and starch, tired lilac, sweat and camphor.

A fat, bald man in a brown overall bursting at the seams lifted packets of cereal down from the top shelf, using a cane with a hook at the end. With a flick of his hairy wrist he snatched up tins of peas and soup from the lower shelves, spun them in the air like a juggler and brought them down on the marble counter with a dull thud. He ducked below the counter and reappeared like a jack-in-the-box clutching a giant cauliflower or waving a bunch of spring onions. All the time he worked he kept up a conversation, barely pausing for breath.

'Morning, Mrs Edwards. Hot enough for you? Your usual, is it? Tin of corned beef, packet of soaked peas ...

Don't strike a match after eating them, mind, or the whole place will catch light.'

'Mr Jones! You cheeky devil!'

'One tin of sardines, a packet of coconut creams ... Your legs been giving you trouble again this week, Mrs Wyeth? ... A packet of jelly – that'll soon have you bouncing around again.

'I hear your Dai's moving up England way looking for work. Nothing round here for the youngsters any more ... A packet of tea, three tins of oxtail soup ...

'There's nice to see you, Mrs Davies. A bottle of Camp coffee and a packet of blancmange, a bar of Lifebuoy soap and a pound of sultanas.'

'Aye, and one of them nice custard tarts for a treat.'

'Always treating yourself, you are, Mrs Davies.'

'None of your cheek, Bryn Jones, or I'll take my custom elsewhere.'

'It'll be a long walk to Swansea, Mrs Davies, especially in this heat.'

'You heard all the talk about Ella Grieve, then?' the stiff-faced woman said.

Catrin pricked up her ears.

'Aye, that's a turn-up for the books. I didn't think we'd see her in the village again until Dai the Death brought her down in her box.'

'There's cheerful you are this morning, Mr Jones.'

'They say she's got her niece with her – staying in the castle, they are.'

'Rather them than me. That place gives me the heebie jeebies.'

'Is the niece that pretty girl with a funny name, Kizzy or something like that?'

'No, this is a young girl, a skinny little thing, they say, her great-niece.'

'I didn't know she had a great-niece.'

'Me neither.'

Catrin made a move to leave but an enormous woman was wedged in the doorway, blocking it.

'A bit of a darling, that Kizzy was. I seen her once over near Blind Man's Lookout kissing some fellow in broad daylight.'

'Man-mad like her mother, I expect.'

'Had more men than hot dinners, that one.'

'Dirty, lucky cow,' the stiff-faced woman cackled.

'Have you seen Ella yet?'

'Only a glimpse, *duw* there's a state on her. Hasn't put a comb through her hair or had her face licked with a flannel in a very long time.'

'I liked old Ella, though. She was a rum one, plenty of spirit she had, not like Alice.'

'Ah, but Alice was a few shillings short. They say that in every generation of Grieves there's one who's a bit simple.'

'She was a queer one, all right. When we was kids I seen her walking round the castle gardens talking to imaginary people. Put the fear of God up me, I can tell you – you'd have sworn there was somebody with her.'

'Away with the fairies she was most of the time, but harmless,' Bryn Jones said.

'They were always an odd lot. Old Nathaniel Grieve abandoned Kilvenny for years, shut up the castle and then one of his kids popped up again like a bad penny and they've been here ever since.'

'Aye, well, there's always a bit of madness in them very old families and of course there was English blood in the Grieves, too.'

Bryn Jones caught sight of Catrin, coughed and rolled his eyes in her direction. There was an immediate silence except for the shuffling of slippers and the creaking of corsets.

All eyes were turned on her but she was already pushing past the enormous woman and away out of the door.

Down on the beach she thought about what she'd heard. A few weeks ago she hadn't even known she had a family, and now it seemed that she came from a long line of mad people. Alice had been odd, by the sound of her, and her own mother was a bit peculiar at times.

What if she were mad, too? How would she know? Sometimes she said daft things and the girls in school gave her funny looks. So what? She kicked out angrily at a pebble. The girls in school could take a running jump. You couldn't win with them. When she was fat they used to call her spiteful names and now she was thin they still did; she just didn't fit in. At least in Kilvenny she didn't have to worry about any of them.

She took off her shoes, pulled off her socks and waded out into the sea. Standing there in the shallows she felt the cool, salty water caressing her tired feet and rising up over her aching calves. A rogue wave took her by surprise and swirled round her knees, sending a tremor of excitement up through her whole body.

In a moment of recklessness she tucked her skirt into her knickers and giggled. That was one in the eye for Sister Lucy. She squealed as the freezing water crept up towards her quivering thighs. A bigger wave broke around her, soaking her, and she ran backed out of the water, slipping and stumbling on the shingle, finally falling on to the dry sand, shrieking with fear and exhilaration.

She sat for a long time staring out to sea, wriggling her toes in the warm sand, the salt drying on her skin and her hair lacquered with spray, feeling better than she'd felt in ages.

She explored the beach, looking into the deep rockpools, marvelling at the little creatures she found there. She stalked a crab across the sands, running away when it stopped and stared at her.

It was beautiful here, apart from having to live with Aunt Ella. She felt free and there was so much to see and learn that was new and exciting. She ran her fingers along the rough surface of a cuttlefish, felt the silken touch of a mussel shell and the corrugated ridges of a cockleshell.

She crept barefoot up to the door of the Fisherman's Snug and opened the door, relieved to find no one inside. She tiptoed across the wooden floorboards, worn smooth by years of use, looking around her in fascination.

There was a large table which had seen better days. It was covered in grubby sailcloth, but through the rips she could see fragments of different cloth as though it had been recovered many times. Set against the wall was a high-backed settle, on whose armrests there were beautiful carvings of fruit – apples and walnuts, acorns and pomegranates.

At the far end of the room a wooden screen jutted out from the wall. She peered round it and it was some moments before her eyes grew accustomed to the shadowy light. There was a small table and chairs that were far too small for grown-ups to use. It brought back memories of a picture book she'd once had of *Goldilocks and the Three Bears*; Baby Bear's chair had been as tiny as these. How quaint it looked, and how much fun it must have been for the children who had been allowed to play here. A small stove, blackened with age, was set into an alcove, and on the wall above it hung miniature pots and pans, rusty old spoons and misshapen tin mugs. In the darkest corner there was a cabin bed with steps to climb up. The mattress was rotten and looked as though mice lived there, but once it must have been really cosy. A cracked mirror hung haphazardly on the wall and she had to stoop to look into it.

Candles were stuck to cracked saucers and a dusty hurricane lamp dangled from a length of twisted string from the ceiling. There was an ingrained reek of the sea; salt and tar, fish and strong tobacco. It would be lovely in here if the stove were lit and the candles, too. She'd like to tidy the place up and curl up on the battered sofa with a good book on a stormy night.

As she walked back up Cockle Lane she was startled to see Aunt Ella standing outside the castle looking up and down the road, one hand shading her eyes from the glare.

'There you are. I've been looking all over for you,' she said, a note of relief in her voice.

'Is something wrong?' Catrin asked.

'The postman's just called in and there's a letter for you, postmarked Italy. That should put a smile on your chops.'

Catrin took the letter and looked hard at Ella. She looked different, more awake than usual, as if she were catching up with the world after all those years locked away.

Catrin went into the Italian garden, settled herself on a bench and looked for a long time at the familiar sprawling handwriting on the blue envelope. She wavered. Once she had opened the letter everything would change; there would be an address and then Aunt Ella would get in touch and Kizzy would come back from Italy to collect her. Catrin shuddered. Kizzy would be absolutely furious to have her holiday ruined but Aunt Ella, on the other hand, would be delighted: she'd probably rub her hands with glee to see the back of her great-niece.

She closed her eyes for a moment, listened to the soft swish of the waves on the sand, the gulls mewling overhead, felt the soothing warmth of the sun on her face.

She held the envelope to her nose and sniffed, wondering if the letter had brought with it the scent of Italy, but it smelt only of cheap paper and a faint hint of her mother's expensive perfume.

Sister Matilde had told them about all the glorious smells of Italy. The aroma of fresh coffee and bread baking; of red wine, tomatoes on the vine, and sun-warmed lemons, all mixed with the tantalising scents of herbs and spices.

She opened the envelope, surprised to find that there were several sheets of thin paper folded inside. Usually it was all her mother could do to pen half a page, and then she made her writing big so that she didn't have to write very much.

She began to read, slowly at first, then turning the pages feverishly. When she had finished she sat for a long time staring down at the letter until suddenly she threw back her head and laughed. She laughed louder than she'd ever laughed in her life, startling the rooks from the trees in Gwartney's Wood until they reeled in a black squawking cloud above the ruined tower of Kilvenny Castle.

From the cover of the rose-laden archway Ella watched anxiously, wondering if the girl had taken leave of her senses. She was skipping around the outside of the fountain, waving her arms round and round like a drunken windmill and shrieking like a banshee. Whatever could her mother have said to send her into paroxysms of hysteria? Maybe she should call the doctor and have the girl looked at.

Catching sight of Ella, Catrin came to a halt, bent double and clutched her ribs to ease the stitch.

'You seem very happy, Catrin. Good news, I presume?'

'Oh yes,' she spluttered.

'Get a grip on yourself, child. Whatever has brought all this on?'

'I'm sorry, I can't help it. It's just the thought of my mother in a . . .' She trailed off again into laughter.

'Nothing can be that funny, surely?'

'Oh, but it can. I'm sorry, Aunt Ella, I'll sit down and read what she says, if you like.'

Full of curiosity, Ella sat down on a bench and Catrin joined her.

'I'll just get my breath back and then I'll begin.'

> Convent of Santa Lucia
> Near Terrini
> Italia

Dear Catrin,

I do hope you arrived at Shrimp's without a hitch. I meant to say I hadn't heard back from the Aunts, but I was sure it would be all right. Still, you'll be safely there by now and I daresay having an absolute ball. Anyhow, enough of all that. Darling, I desperately need you to do something for me.

I have had the most terrible time since I arrived in Italy. I was meant to be meeting an old friend of mine at the railway station in Naples, but they didn't turn up and to add to my troubles my handbag was stolen along with most of my money and traveller's cheques. A priest came to my aid and kindly (or so I thought) offered to find me an inexpensive place to stay.

I didn't expect a luxury hotel, of course, but neither did I expect to travel miles to this godforsaken place on the back of a bad-tempered donkey or to have to rely on the charity of some very peculiar nuns—

'Nuns?' Ella interrupted.

'It gets better,' Catrin said, barely able to hide her glee.

Honestly, you wouldn't believe how horrid it is here and it's jolly good you didn't come with me. The plumbing is outrageously ancient – the original Roman, I shouldn't be surprised. I haven't had a decent wash in days. To get to the lavatory one has to fight through herds of chickens and spiteful geese. And the food is gruesome. If I have to endure another plate of mushy beans I shall die—

'She always was fussy about her food,' Ella said.
'This is the best bit.'

The room the nuns have given me is simply dreadful – the bed, if you can call it a bed, has a mattress stuffed with straw. There's no glass in the windows so I can hardly sleep for the noise of the village dogs barking and bats flapping about all over the place.

I can't even bear to get close to the window to get some fresh air because the convent is halfway up a cliff and the drop to the river below is sheer.

There are bars on the window because one of the inmates once jumped out to their death. You can still see the bloody fingerprints on the wall! I've even seen vultures flying around – it's positively prehistoric. As if the room wasn't bad enough I have to share it with a crazy Italian woman and when I do manage to get to sleep I'm usually woken five minutes later because of the racket she makes singing and dancing about the place. I think it's a sort of lunatic asylum-cum-convent.

The telephone doesn't seem to have been invented here yet. I need you to telephone your godfather and ask him to arrange for some money to be sent to me here so that I can get home as quickly as possible. He has contacts in Italy, so should be able to help. Please be quick – I cannot endure this a moment longer. Hope you are well, darling.

Love
Mummy x

*

'So you'll telephone your godfather, he'll send some money, and soon your mother will be home and your worries will be over?'

Catrin glanced at Ella, a look of determination on her face. 'I don't think so.'

'What do you mean?'

'I'm not going to ring my godfather.'

'But your mother's asked you to – you can't disobey her.'

'Oh, I can.'

'Catrin Grieve!'

'I think being in a convent with lunatics will be good for her. She sent me down here without even speaking to you, and she wasn't worried one little bit as long as I was out of the way. Now that things have gone wrong for her she wants me to jump to attention, but I shan't and no one can make me.'

Catrin looked at Ella defiantly, her eyes burning with passion.

Ella surveyed her, the spots of high colour on her cheeks, the mouth set in a stubborn line, and she wanted more than anything to laugh out loud, but keeping her face straight she said, 'Good for you. I daresay it's high time that someone refused to dance to Kizzy's tune.'

'You do?'

Ella nodded enthusiastically. 'I should imagine that time in this convent might do her good, make her think about things.'

'You see, Aunt Ella, I didn't even know I had an aunt until a few weeks ago, and I didn't know until Tony Agosti told me that my mother used to live here. There's so much I don't know about myself, about my family, because my mother chose not to tell me.'

'What do you think she'll do?'

'She'll cry a lot, give the nuns a hard time, stamp her feet and wait for her friend to rescue her. Once everything's all right she probably won't bother to write again.'

'You seem very sure.'

'I know her.'

'Are you two close?'

'No. I'm not the kind of daughter she wanted. I'm surprised that she bothered to have a child.'

Her defiance melted away and gave place to a frightened look, her bottom lip quivering.

Ella knew what it felt like to be ignored. Her own mother had had no time for her, and that meant constant anxiety and yearning for attention, then the anger born of a mother's cruel indifference.

'What kind of daughter would be the right kind for her?'

'Someone who wants to put on make-up, go dancing, flirt with boys, who wants to be a model or a film star, all that kind of rubbish.'

'And you're not that sort of girl?'

Catrin shook her head.

'Perhaps the Grieve girls not getting on with their mothers is hereditary.'

'Didn't you get on with yours?'

'Definitely not – she disliked me intensely. My mother preferred boys and was quite open about it. She positively doted on my brothers.'

'And Alice? Did she love Aunt Alice?'

'Oh, she loved Alice in her own way. Everyone loved Alice. Alice was pretty and biddable whereas I was not. I was simply an enormous irritation to her.'

Catrin understood what she meant. Ella Grieve would not have been a prissy, quiet child; she would have been stubborn, lively and headstrong.

'And my mother didn't get on with her mother?'

'Oh, my goodness, no she didn't. This place used to

resound with their constant catfights. They truly disliked each other. Mind you, Hester was, er, fiery, to say the least.'

'I never met her.'

'No, well, you didn't miss much. She died before you were born.'

'And you didn't like her?'

'You are a very perceptive child. No, I didn't like her. The truth is, I couldn't stand Hester. She was a selfish old cow.'

Catrin hugged herself, tried to hold back a rising giggle. She wasn't used to grown-ups being direct with her; they usually hedged around the truth.

'It's small wonder that your mother turned out the way she did. She didn't have much of an example set her.'

'What sort of an example did she have?'

'Well, Hester was a proper flibbertigibbet, and that's putting it mildly. Truth is, she was a tart. One man at a time wasn't enough for her. She led my brother William a right old dance with her flirting and canoodling. She'd had a fling with most of the men in the village by the time she left.'

Catrin drew in her breath with a whistle. When the girls at school talked about their grannies, they described them as grey-haired, cake-baking sweeties, but her grandmother had been a bit of a trollop, by the sound of it.

'My grandfather was your brother, wasn't he?'

Ella nodded, a faraway look in her eyes. 'Yes. He was the eldest of the four of us and far too soft for the likes of Hester. He let her get away with too much, just to keep the peace.'

'He died, didn't he?'

'Yes, he was killed in the war. Your mother was only young at the time and quite inconsolable after his death.'

'Was she? She's never talked about him to me.'

'Sometimes people can't talk about those they love and

have lost. She spent even more time up at Shrimp's after he died, as far from her mother as she could get. She was more like a daughter to Alice than a niece.'

'Until she did whatever awful thing it was that she did?'

Ella turned her head away quickly. 'That we won't discuss. I think it's time we thought about some lunch.'

Catrin's heart sank at the mention of food. Then she thought of her mother sitting down to a plate of beans in the company of nuns and lunatics and she brightened up and followed Ella into the castle.

Chapter 20

Catrin woke earlier than usual, took *Recipes for Cherubs* from its hiding place under her bed and opened it eagerly. Her spirits lifted as soon as she looked at the painting of Maria Paparella smiling broadly and holding out the loaf of *focaccia* as though it were a gift. She wondered if Maria baked the bread for the other people whose portraits were in the book.

Had Luca Roselli, the handsome boy with the dark curly hair and small scar on his cheek, sat down to eat this bread with the little dwarf, the silken-haired, green-eyed Bindo? Had the man with the funny name, Piero di Bardi, broken bread with Ismelda Bisotti, the girl with the infectious grin and sparkling eyes? Were they all friends, who had sat together laughing loudly as they shared a meal?

There were other paintings of people who looked like a load of old misery-guts, not the sort of people who would enjoy a good laugh.

There was the frosty-looking widow Zanelli, who reminded Catrin of Sister Lucy because they both looked as if they had a bad smell under their noses. There were two mealy-mouthed little girls, twins by the look of them, pretty as pictures with porcelain skin and their hair in ringlets. When you looked closely, though, you could see that they had hard eyes and mouths which would flit from a pout to a sulk in an instant. She didn't like the snooty look of Signor Bisotti, who had a mouthful of bad teeth and shifty eyes. The scariest of them all was the hawklike priest, Father Rimaldi, who glared out from the page, a murderous glint in his narrow eyes. He wouldn't be a barrel of laughs, that was for sure.

She wondered if Santa Rosa was a real place and whether all these people had been real people, too, or figments of the artist's imagination. If they were real they would have gone to mass in the ugly old church, dipped their hands in the cool water of the cherub fountain or hurried across the cobbled piazza to pay their respects to the tiny saint in its niche on the convent wall.

She closed her eyes and tried to imagine what sort of lives they'd lived, whether they had been happy, rich, poor or sad. What had become of them all? They would all be long dead by now, but someone had wanted their memory to live on because they'd taken the trouble to preserve their faces in this peculiar book.

She replaced it under the bed, thought about washing, thought better of it, dressed and hurried out of the castle and across to the Café Romana to see Tony Agosti.

In the castle kitchen Catrin laid out the ingredients for focaccia on the table: a block of salt, a packet of yeast, a bag of flour and a bottle of olive oil. She'd never heard of anyone cooking with olive oil before. The infirmary sister at school doled it out as a medicine for earache, wedged in tight with a squeaky dab of cotton wool.

She'd blushed when Tony handed her the bottle of virgin olive oil. 'Virgin' was a rude word. Mary Donahue, who knew everything about everything, said her sister Bridget wasn't a virgin and so no decent man would ever marry her.

You could tell girls who weren't virgins because they walked with their feet splayed at ten to two and had a brazen look about them.

'Virgin' was something to do with having babies, and that meant doing S.E.X. She didn't know much about that, either, except it was dirty and painful and made you get F.A.T.

Mary Donahue said that to do S.E.X. women had to buy pretty nightdresses and they had to lift them up for the men to have a good gander at what they'd got and then the man shook a packet of seeds that landed in the woman's belly button and made a baby that came out of her B.U.M – *yuk*! It was all too horrible and made her feel sick to think about it.

She pushed the unpleasant thoughts from her mind and began to read the instructions for making the bread, and then set to work excitedly.

She mixed the yeast and the water, added the flour and salt, and mixed them all together. She began to knead the dough, softly at first, pushing her knuckles down tentatively into the mixture . . .

She imagined the mound of dough was her mother's face, and bubbles of anger began to fizz in her belly. Small bubbles at first, growing bigger, filling her up until her ribs swelled and she felt as if she would burst, as if the air was being forced out of her body and she couldn't breathe.

Katherine Isobel Grieve. Kizzy. Smiling at any man who passed.

She pinched the dough spitefully.

Kizzy bloody Grieve, who filed her nails and never looked at you when you spoke to her . . .

Slap.

Who made her lips into a bow and smoothed them with lipstick. Red lipstick. Thick and sticky as blood.

Pinch punch first of the month and no returns.

Pretty, pretty Kizzy twittering like a bird. Pretty Polly, Pretty Polly.

Slap slap slap.

Pretty Polly Kizzy who hadn't even bothered to tell her about things.

Punch.

A smear of red on white cotton ...

'Didn't your mother tell you about the curse?' Sister Lucy had said with a scandalised voice.

No. No. No.

'Don't go near boys or men. They're only after one thing.'

And it wasn't your sweets. Dolly mixtures. Jelly babies.

Slap pinch slap.

She squeezed, pinched, whacked and thumped the dough until her skinny arms ached and beads of sweat pinpricked her forehead.

She caught sight of herself suddenly in the small mirror above the sink. She stepped closer and scrutinised her face. There was a smudge of flour on her nose, an unusual glow to her skin and her eyes were brighter than usual. For a moment, despite her anger, she thought she looked almost pretty.

When the dough had risen as if by magic, she divided it into three equal lots, made dimples and pressed sprigs of rosemary from the garden into the dimples, and then she dribbled olive oil over them. Finally, she sprinkled the loaves with crumbled block salt, put them on a battered baking tray and slipped it into the hot oven.

Later, when she opened the oven door a warm fragrance enveloped her. She lifted the loaves out carefully and put them to rest on a misshapen rusty rack she'd found in the larder.

She looked down proudly at the golden *focaccia*, the sprigs of rosemary crisp to the touch, the sea salt glistening tantalisingly.

Each loaf looked just like the one that Maria Paparella was holding in the painting.

She broke off a tiny piece and popped it into her mouth.

The taste was wonderful and she chewed slowly, savouring it. She was almost tempted to snatch at the bread and stuff it all into her mouth, so great was her hunger. She swallowed hard, walked quickly away from the table out of temptation's way. She picked flowers in the garden, purple and red blooms which she put in an old blue bottle she found in the larder.

She was exhausted and yet exhilarated by the time she had finished, and she sat up in the window seat, impatient for Aunt Ella to come down for breakfast.

When Ella came into the kitchen sunlight drizzled through the windows and filled the room with a syrupy light. She blinked, surprised to see that Catrin was already up, standing next to the kitchen table like a nymph, a shy smile lighting up her face, her eyes sparkling and her cheeks flushed with excitement in a way that had quite transformed her.

'Good morning, Aunt Ella. Look, I made us some bread for breakfast,' she said hesitantly. 'I thought it might be good for me to do some cooking for a change.'

'You don't take after your mother, then. She couldn't cook to save her life.'

'She still can't,' Catrin replied with a grin.

'I must admit that I'm not much cop at cooking, either.'

'I know,' Catrin answered.

Ella looked cross for a moment, but then her face relaxed into a smile. Catrin thought she looked quite nice when she smiled.

'It's not just me who thinks so. Tony Agosti said you were a hopeless cook.'

'Did he, now? I'll be having words with him.'

Catrin grew flustered, hastened to add, 'He said lots of nice things about you, too.'

'Maybe I'll let him off the hook, then.'

'My mother said that the food at Shrimp's was wonderful.'

'That was nothing to do with me. Gladys Beynon used to do all the cooking. I was more of a dogsbody.'

'Tony was telling me all about her.'

'She came to work for us when my parents were alive, and she was with us for years.'

'Where is she now?'

Ella winced. 'I don't know if she's even still alive. She left just before Shrimp's closed for good.'

'What did Aunt Alice do at Shrimp's?'

'This and that. She was good with the guests in her own little way.'

Catrin had noticed that sometimes it was easier than others to draw Aunt Ella into a conversation, but if you mentioned something she didn't want to talk about she clammed up and an uncomfortable air grew up around them.

Catrin changed tack. 'Have something to eat, Aunt Ella.'

Ella pulled a chair up to the table and watched as Catrin poured the tea, noticing that she needed two hands to lift the teapot. Her arms were pitifully thin, the blue veins too close to the surface.

Catrin took her tea without milk or sugar.

'Your Aunt Alice didn't take milk. She had an allergy to dairy products – and cats as well. Have you the same?'

Catrin shook her head and lied, 'I just don't like milk, or any dairy food, really.'

'This bread you've made looks very good. May I?'

Ella broke some off, spread it thickly with butter and popped it into her mouth.

'Now that is gorgeous, mouth-wateringly delicious.'

Catrin wriggled with pleasure. It felt good to have made something all by herself which people enjoyed eating. Maybe that's why Maria Paparella looked so full of joy as she held out her loaf.

'Where did you learn to cook like this?'

'From an old book called *Recipes for Cherubs* which I found upstairs. It's full of recipes and paintings.'

'Well, I never. That'll be Alice's old book. I thought my mother burnt it years ago.'

'Why would she burn it?'

'Oh, she said it put daft ideas into Alice's head and gave her dreams.'

Catrin sat quite still. If the book had been burnt she would never have seen the paintings, never have read the recipes.

'Where did Alice find the book?'

'God only knows – she was always sniffing about in the castle. She called it her colouring book of clues.'

'Clues?'

'Oh, it was all gobbledygook. Alice always had her head full of nonsense; she thought the book had clues in it which would help her find the lost treasure of Kilvenny.'

Catrin sat up very straight. 'Is there treasure here, do you think?' she asked excitedly.

Ella shook her head and smiled wryly. 'There's nothing much of any value here. Alice was a fanciful child. She used to talk to the pictures in the book, make up imaginary friends, stuff like that.'

'When you saw the book, did you think there were clues in it?'

'I never saw it. I'm not much of a one for books and

Alice guarded that one as if it were gold dust. One thing's for sure, though: if this bread is anything to go by, the recipes are damn good.'

'It's called *focaccia* and it's Italian.'

'How strange that you should be making me Italian bread.'

'Why strange?'

'Because if my life had turned out differently I'd always planned on going to Italy but I never got there, and yet here I am eating Italian bread with a great-niece I never thought I'd meet.'

'Why did you want to go to Italy?'

'I had a good friend who told me a lot about it; they'd spent several years out there studying art.'

'Your friend was an artist?'

'Wanted to be one.'

'And why didn't they become one?'

'Wanting isn't enough. The desire to paint was there, but not the talent.'

'I see. And your friend, was he from Kilvenny?' Catrin asked, turning her head away.

Aunt Ella wasn't easily fooled by sneaky questions and her lips set in a straight line, but then suddenly she laughed. 'Subtlety isn't your forte, Catrin, something we have in common.'

'I don't understand.'

'Don't worry your head about it. By damn, I'm enjoying this bread.'

'I'm glad you like it.'

'You know, after all those years on my own I never thought I'd take delight in eating again or enjoy eating in someone's company, and then you turn up out of the blue and, although we didn't hit it off straight away, I somehow feel as if we were meant to meet.'

153

For the first time they sat together easily, Ella eating hungrily while Catrin tore small chunks off the bread and ate them guiltily, chewing each piece over and over to savour the taste.

'You don't have a big appetite?' Ella asked, wiping a smear of butter from her chin.

Catrin shook her head. 'Not in the mornings, but when I'm hungry I eat loads, like a horse really. I'm just lucky that I don't put on weight,' she lied with a smile.

Ella nodded but was not fooled.

Catrin put down her morsel of bread, bit her lip anxiously and said, 'I've been thinking. I know I can't go back to school for the holidays and if we do get hold of my mother she'll be furious if she has to come back from Italy, and the only other place I could go would be my godfather's, but I'd really rather not go there.'

'Who is your godfather?' Ella asked, helping herself to more bread.

'Dr Campbell.'

'Dr Campbell?' Ella spluttered.

'Dr Arthur Campbell. Do you know him?'

Ella regained her composure. 'No. I'm sorry, my tea went down the wrong way. You don't like him?'

'How did you know that?'

'Just a feeling in my water.'

Catrin looked around as if fearful of being overheard. 'No. And I hate his wife.'

'He has a wife?'

'Oh yes, he's married but they haven't any children.'

Ella got suddenly to her feet. 'That bread was delicious. I'll clear away, shall I?'

'Mrs Campbell gives me the creeps,' Catrin continued, picking up a crumb and slipping it into her mouth.

Ella busied herself clearing the table, her mind racing.

What the hell was Kizzy Grieve playing at? Why hadn't she told Catrin that Arthur Campbell was her father, instead of this sham about him being her godfather?

'What does he do, this Dr Campbell?' Ella asked nonchalantly.

'He's a psychiatrist, a very clever one, some people say.'

'But you don't think so?'

Catrin shrugged. 'Oh, he's clever but he's very bossy and asks too many questions and he ...' She faltered, almost dropping her cup.

'He what?'

'Well, he's just not much fun to be with and the thing is, Aunt Ella, I was wondering if I could maybe stay here in the castle for a while. I wouldn't be any trouble to anyone.' Catrin's eyes were wide with entreaty.

'And is that why you made the bread? To soften me up?'

'No! Well, maybe a bit. I just wanted you to like it. I've never cooked anything before, never ridden a bike or even paddled in the sea before I came to Kilvenny.'

'You've never paddled in the sea?' Ella looked horrified.

Catrin shook her head and looked at Ella hopefully.

'I suppose by rights we ought to contact your mother,' Ella said stiffly.

'It doesn't really matter, does it? She thinks I'm staying at Shrimp's so she won't be worried. I've got a return ticket to London for September, and it might do me some good to get to know the family I didn't know I had.'

Ella took the cheese and butter back into the larder and stood there for some moments, thinking. Maybe it would be all right to keep the child here for a few weeks, just so long as she managed to keep her mouth shut and not blurt out the truth about Arthur Campbell. There was no knowing how the truth might affect the child. Ella had always thought the truth was the best option because secrets could be so damaging, and Ella Grieve knew all about secrets. Holding on to them was draining, debilitating; it made you shrivel inside a little more each day.

When Ella came out of the pantry she found Catrin sitting forlornly at the table.

'I could help out here, cook some recipes from the book so that you don't have to cook,' Catrin said.

'I don't know.'

'Please?' She looked imploringly at Ella.

'Oh, I suppose it wouldn't do any harm,' Ella replied, and without warning Catrin ran across the kitchen and flung her arms round her. Startled by this show of affection, Ella flushed with awkwardness. No one had touched her in years . . .

She put her arms diffidently round Catrin's tiny body and held her close, feeling the girl's heart beating erratically behind her rib cage.

Chapter 21

Catrin made the trip up to Shrimp's alone, unlocked the kitchen door and automatically held her nose to keep out the stink. Then she looked around in surprise. Someone had been in here poking around. The kitchen drawers had been rifled through, and some of the cupboard doors were open, revealing rusty tins and grimy crockery. A window had been opened, letting in the sea breeze.

She stood nervously in the hallway listening for sounds of an intruder. Above her head the curtains of cobwebs danced in the draughts. A thick layer of dust still covered everything and the air was musty, almost sticky.

She made her way slowly up the worn stairs, turned right and slipped behind the rotting green curtain.

There was a peculiar smell in Aunt Alice's room and it took her a while to realize that the remains of a recent fire lay smouldering in the hearth. She looked warily around. Ghosts didn't light fires or eat chocolate.

She picked up a chocolate wrapper from the floor and sniffed it – she hated the smell. She sniffed it again and licked her lips. Maybe the man she'd seen slipping out of Aunt Alice's room had cleaned up the kitchen, but why would anyone do that? He might even be in here now, snooping around. She listened but the house was eerily silent.

She opened the bureau and rummaged about until she found the chequebook that Ella had asked her to bring back to the castle. She slipped it into her pocket and was about to go when the wardrobe door creaked ominously behind her.

She tensed, felt every tendon in her body creak with fear. Sister Matilde always said that the worst kind of fear was the fear of fear itself. With an intake of breath she threw open the wardrobe door and jumped back.

She breathed a sigh of relief. The wardrobe was empty except for a few old dresses which smelt of neglect and mothballs. At the bottom of the wardrobe there was a large cardboard box and she knelt down and pulled it towards her – it was very light. Written on the lid in a spidery hand were the words *To be delivered to Miss Ella Grieve, c/o Shrimp's Hotel, Near Kilvenny.* Nervously she lifted the lid, ready to jump as if she were opening a jack-in-the-box.

Nothing leapt up at her. She lifted out an ivory wedding dress decorated with sparkling gems, marvelling at the feel of the smooth satin, running her fingers over the delicately embroidered bodice. She held the dress against herself, looked in the mirror and was shocked by her reflection. The ivory of the dress heightened her pallor, made her eyes sink deeper into her face, and highlighted the dark circles beneath her eyes.

Suddenly overcome with guilt, she folded the dress back into the box and hastily replaced the lid. Why had Aunt Ella bought herself a wedding dress? She hadn't ever married, because she was still called Grieve. Maybe the friend she'd talked about had been her lover and she had been jilted at the altar like Miss Havisham in *Great Expectations* and that's why she'd shut herself up in Shrimp's for all those years. She shoved the box back into the wardrobe and closed the door thoughtfully.

Chapter 22

The storm came with barely a warning. Banking clouds obliterated the sun and a squally wind blew in off a sea the colour of wire wool. Then the rain came sweeping down Cockle Lane, battering against the windows of the castle, flattening the geraniums in their pots outside the Café Romana and whipping the leaves of the tall trees in Gwartney's Wood into a bubbling green broth.

Ella had settled in the kitchen listening to the ancient, whistling wireless and Catrin was curled up on the window seat, her head buried in her book, looking for clues to the hidden treasure of Kilvenny Castle.

She was studying a painting of someone called Ismelda Bisotti, a girl probably just a bit younger than herself. She wore a faded blue frock, and was holding out a ripe pomegranate as if making a present of it to someone unseen. Her long hair was dark and wild, tinged with a blue sheen, her black eyebrows arched above enormous blue eyes framed by feathery dark lashes. There was a smudge of something white on her nose, her head was thrown back and her mouth opened wide, showing the whitest teeth Catrin had ever seen. She was laughing fit to bust. Catrin wished she could hear her laughter and wondered what had been said or what she had seen that was so hilariously funny. Just looking at Ismelda's face made Catrin want to laugh out loud, too.

Underneath the painting was written *How to make* Gelato, *by Ismelda Bisotti*.

What on earth was Gelato?

As she stared in absorption at Ismelda Bisotti a crack of thunder broke overhead, rattling the pots and pans that hung from hooks around the kitchen, and the radio crackled and whistled furiously.

Catrin put down the book and looked out of the window. The rain was hammering down and the road was a rivulet of black water, carrying along leaves and lollipop sticks at a ferocious pace. At the Café Romana the downstairs windows were steamed up, but in an upstairs window Catrin saw an old woman peering across at the castle and waving frantically, trying to attract her attention.

'Aunt Ella, there's a funny old woman waving at me from the café.'

Ella got up stiffly and looked out through the rain-streaked window.

'Good God. I never thought to ask Tony if Louisa was still alive. I just presumed she'd passed away – she must be well over ninety if she's a day.'

'Who is she?'

'That's Tony's nonna, as they say in Italian – his grandmother. Everyone in Kilvenny used to call her Nonna. I suppose in a way she was like a grandmother to most of us.'

'Why do you think she's waving at me?'

'I expect Tony has told her all about you and she wants you to go across and keep her company. She was always a nosy old bugger and probably wants to find out what's going on.'

'Do you think I should go?'

'Why not? There's little else you can do in this weather, and she used to be great fun to talk to.'

'Will you come, too?'

'No. I'm not ready to go visiting yet. You go but put something on over your clothes or you'll be soaked to the skin.'

'Does it rain all the time here?'

'Only twice a week, once for four days and once for three,' Ella said with a straight face.

Catrin gave her a sideways look and then as she made her way along the corridor towards the main door Ella heard her laugh loudly. It was a long time since Ella had made anyone laugh; a long time since laughter had rung out in Kilvenny Castle.

Chapter 23

Maria Paparella was on her way back from the early market to the Villa Rosso. She hummed cheerfully as she walked along the Via Dante. When she came level with Piero di Bardi's house she could hear him inside, singing loudly, so she paused outside the window, breathing in the multitude of smells that drifted out of the house: dust and calfskins, charcoal and fish glue, bacon fat, linseed oil and sawdust.

She went closer to the window and peered cautiously inside. On a bench near the window there were pots of sharpened charcoal, dishes full of wax and murky water. Set out on a rickety table there were brushes of all shapes and sizes, boxes of sawdust, sand and salt. A row of bottles stood on a lop-sided shelf: vinegar, varnish, sugar and tantalising quicksilver.

She was fascinated by the flute-shaped pots that held the different colours that Piero used for his paintings.

She was unable to read the labels on the pots but Luca had told her the names of some of the colours: indigo, verdigris, lampblack, cinabrese, sinoper, vermillion, ochre, saffron ... They were such exotic, exciting names that they made her head spin and conjured up images of all the faraway places she would never see.

She caught a glimpse of Piero, his dark head bent over a canvas, completely absorbed in his work. He glanced up suddenly and there was a look of such joy in those dreamy eyes of his that she shivered with pleasure.

Here was a man in dire need of fattening up. She'd come back tomorrow and bring him something special to eat, put a bit of colour in those pallid cheeks, a little more flesh around those sunken buttocks. Something must have cheered him up, because Luca had been complaining for weeks that he'd been in the foulest of moods.

Thinking of Luca she smiled and felt for the piece of paper in her pocket that her uncle, the travelling shoe seller, had given her in exchange for two freshly baked loaves of focaccia and a walnut cake. This afternoon Luca would read the words on the paper and they would search out the ingredients for the new recipe.

She made the sign of the cross as she came level with the little saint in her niche on the convent wall, and further along she stopped outside the convent gates and looked down at the two jars that had stood outside the convent gates for as long as anyone could remember. It was in one of those jars that the baby Bindo had been abandoned one winter's night long ago.

She remembered that night vividly because it was the night when she had started working as a servant at the Villa Rosso. Earlier in the day Signor Bisotti had been asking around the village for a girl to help out, as his wife had gone into early labour with her second child and now the child was delivered but the mother was sick. Maria's mother had gladly offered her services; it had been a relief to have one less mouth to feed through another cold winter.

Maria had tearfully packed her few possessions in a bundle, hugged her mother for a long time, and then made her way through the village to the Villa Rosso. She had been no more than a child herself and had sat on one of these olive jars trying to summon the courage to walk across the piazza and knock on the door of the villa.

The snow had been falling for several hours, the wind was

biting and she had pulled her thin cloak tighter around her body and looked up fearfully at the hideous gargoyles on the church, with waterfalls of ice spilling from their wide ugly mouths.

Signora Bisotti was in a bad way after the birth, and Maria had been sent to sit with her and bathe her fevered brow with water. She had been afraid because the Signora lay so still, her breathing very shallow. She was as thin as a willow reed and pale as death, her head turned to the side, eyes rolling backwards into her head, mouth moving in silent but fervent prayer.

Later that evening she had heard Signor Bisotti whisper to Father Rimaldi that it was only a matter of time, and less than a few hours later Signora Bisotti was dead.

Father Rimaldi had risked life and limb riding down to the Convent of Santa Lucia to find a wet-nurse and had returned at dawn with a sad-faced mute who stood in to feed the famished baby.

That first night in the Villa Rosso Maria had lain in bed listening to the wind screaming around the house and the querulous cries of the newly born Bisotti child. Later she had knelt on the bed looking out of the window at the swirling snow until tiredness overtook her. When she had finally fallen asleep it was a fitful sleep, the sound of crying babies and the moaning wind interrupting her dreams.

That freezing night someone had crept past the shuttered houses and abandoned baby Bindo in the olive jar. If Father Rimaldi had not ventured out from his house just before dawn, the child would surely have perished. It was a miracle.

Maria did not see the newborn baby girl they had named Ismelda until the end of her first week at the villa. She clearly remembered peering down into the crib where Ismelda lay roaring, her tightly balled fists pummelling the air, her face red with fury. Mamma mia, *she'd been born making a noise and hadn't stopped since.*

Maria had worked in the Villa Rosso ever since that night. She had looked after Ismelda after the wet-nurse was sent away. She had sat up with her through the long nights when she was cutting her first teeth, wiped her brow through fevers and bouts of colic, and now they were as close as if they were blood relatives.

Maria turned away from the convent gates and almost bumped into Father Rimaldi. She did not like him, for even though he wore the priest's cloth, beneath it his heart was as dark as a witch's armpit.

She stepped back in alarm and said, 'You startled me, Father. I was lost in my thoughts.'

'And what were you thinking, my child? Good thoughts, I hope?'

'I was thinking about the woman who left Bindo here in the olive jar. I often wonder what happened to her.'

'It's so long ago. The poor wretch probably has a pile of children by now, and has long forgotten that unfortunate child.'

'I wonder,' she said absentmindedly.

She nodded to Father Rimaldi, made her way across the square and past the fountain, putting out a hand to brush the outstretched fingers of one of the cherubs.

Father Rimaldi watched her go with a strange expression on his face.

Chapter 24

The bell above the door of the Café Romana tinkled as Catrin stepped inside. Tony Agosti beamed at her from behind the counter. 'Ah, Catrin, so you've come to see my nonna.'

'How did you know that?'

'Ever since she heard that you and Ella were staying at the castle she's been like a cat on a hot tin roof. She's been up at the window looking out for you. I'll take you up to her. Nonna can't get about much any more but she doesn't miss a trick.'

He led Catrin behind the counter, through a curtained doorway and up a narrow staircase to the first floor.

Nonna was sitting in a wicker chair close to the window, like a bird in an eyrie looking down over Kilvenny. Close up she was a sight to behold, an old woman dressed all in black, black jumper, long black skirt and thick black bobbly stockings. She wore a black scarf over her silver hair, knotted under a cascade of wobbling chins. She was so old that she looked as if she had dropped out from between the pages of *Recipes for Cherubs*.

She looked up and Catrin knew at once from the opaque milky blue of her eyes that she was blind, so how could she have seen Catrin in the window of the castle?

As if reading her thoughts Tony said, 'She can hardly see anything these days, just shadows mainly, but she senses when people are there, isn't that true, Nonna?'

The old woman nodded and smiled, and her face creased into deep dark furrows.

'Nonna, this is Catrin, Ella Grieve's great-niece, who's staying over at the castle.'

The old woman looked Catrin up and down as if she could see her.

'Sit down. Sit down. You leave us alone now, Antonio, you don't want to be listening to the women's talking,' she said impatiently.

Tony winked at Catrin and left the room, whistling as he clattered down the stairs.

'So you are little girl who make Ella Grieve come out of hiding?'

'Yes. Only I'm not so little, I'm thirteen.'

'You very thin for a girl of thirteen,' Nonna said.

Catrin looked at her warily; maybe she was just pretending to be blind. 'I've always been thin,' she lied.

'Not so thin as this, I think. Like the stick you are.'

Catrin bristled with indignation.

'You angry I say you are too thin, eh?'

'No,' Catrin replied sulkily.

'You a bit prickly like your Aunt Ella?'

'Maybe. I don't know, I've only just met her.'

Nonna was silent for a moment and then she said wistfully, 'I glad you comes here to Kilvenny. I missed Ella all these years. Funny I never think that she be one to run away and hide her face from the world.'

'I suppose not.'

'She was a livewire when she was a girl, always in trouble.'

'Did you know her very well?'

'Well? 'Course I knows her well. I there in the room when she being born and that Ella she come out kicking and yelling. My Antonio say people like cheese and chalk when they are very different. Ella and Alice like this chalk and cheese even though they twins.'

'They were twins!' Catrin exclaimed.

'Yes, they twins but not like you say the peas in pod. They looks very different. They acts very different. Alice was very quiet girl.'

'And Ella wasn't?' Catrin asked with interest.

'No. She always in the mischief. Her mother coming down here from Shrimp's many times looking for her. She always talking to the old fishermen and her mother get mad as a nutter and shouting fit to bust. But she always brings back many fish for supper so she forgiven sometimes.'

Catrin smiled and thought that Ella sounded as if she'd been good fun when she was little.

'I tell you, Kilvenny very quiet when Ella got sent away to the boardings school but she not stay there long.'

'Why not?'

'Alice miss her twin terrible, don't eat, don't sleep, so Mrs Grieve bring Ella back home from the school.'

'Why didn't Alice go away to school, too?'

'No good sending Alice to school.'

Catrin scratched her head, puzzled. 'But why?'

'Because Alice she couldn't go to no school'

'Why not?'

'Well, she was ... how does my Antonio say? She a little bit simple up in the head.'

'Do you mean she was a lunatic?' Catrin said in a shocked voice.

Nonna shook her head. 'Oh, she not raving mad, she just not quite that full shilling as they says.'

'Is Aunt Ella all right in the head?' Catrin asked.

'Oh, there no flies on Ella. She very clever but she has trouble with the truth.'

'You mean she tells lies?'

'No. No. She too fond of the truth for her own good.'

'How can you be too fond of the truth?'

'She always say the truth. If someone have a big nose, Ella, she will say, "Hey, you got a big nose." Can't keep her tongue shut up. Lot of people don't like it, especially the ones with big noses, if you knows what I'm saying.'

Catrin giggled. 'Maybe the man she was going to marry had a big nose and she told him and he cancelled the wedding,' she blurted out.

'She never going to marry no man.' Nonna laughed loudly, displaying a handful of wobbly teeth.

'No man be able to cope with Ella. She like to be free and not doing the cookings and the washings of dirty underpants for no man.'

Catrin slapped her hand over her mouth. People here in Kilvenny said really rude things. 'Underpants' was a filthy word.

'Well, Aunt Ella *was* going to marry someone, you know,' she muttered stubbornly.

'No, never. I tell you is not possible.'

'Can you keep a secret, Nonna?'

Nonna nodded.

'There's a wedding dress in a wardrobe up at Shrimp's and it has Aunt Ella's name on the box. I know because I looked, even though I shouldn't have.'

Nonna threw back her head and cackled. 'It is a dress with diamonds sewn on all over and gold stitchings here on the front?' she asked, indicating her sunken chest.

Catrin nodded.

'That not Ella's dress. Dress belong to Alice. It cost lot of money. I remember day Ella shows it to me. Right here in this room.'

'Oh, I thought it was Aunt Ella's because it has her name on the box.'

'Alice always want a fairy-tale wedding dress and Ella buys her most beautiful dress from London.'

'Did you go to the wedding?' Catrin interrupted.

'Ah, that wedding is one I never forget. The chapel in the castle is full of flowers and all the peoples is waiting. Me and my husband, Luigi, God rest his soul, was wearing us best clothes, he's wearing new suit we bury him in two weeks later.'

She paused and wiped a tear from her eye and Catrin looked away in embarrassment.

'Only trouble is, there one person who didn't come to wedding.'

'Who was that?'

'Alice.'

Catrin looked at Nonna in astonishment. 'What? You mean she didn't turn up for her own wedding?'

Nonna nodded and let out a long sigh.

'The bridegroom, he is there waiting. Your mother is dressed all in her best and the priest is going up the bananas because Alice don't come.'

'Why not?'

'Nobody know. Ella goes looking for her but Alice is gone.'

'So the bridegroom just went away and the wedding was cancelled?'

'*Sì*. We never see him no more.'

'Poor man.'

'He will have survived, I think. I don't like him much. Me and Luigi think he got his eye on more than just Alice.'

'What do you mean?'

Nonna hesitated. 'Well, she was quite wealthy woman and I thinks he maybe after her money.'

'Who was he?'

'Let me see, Mister ... No, is no good. I can't remember name. He looks like rat and his eyes like the vulture. I remember his face, but is funny, when you gets old you forgets the names but I can remember things from when I a child in Italy very good.'

'Was that the last time my mother was here in Kilvenny?'

'I think so. She very beautiful girl, your mother. I can see her now in lovely silk dress the colour of red poppies and her hair black as coal.'

Catrin bit her lip and said nothing.

'You don't like to hear talk of her beauty?'

Catrin looked hard at Nonna. She looked almost witchlike in her black clothes; perhaps she had strange powers and could tell what Catrin was thinking.

'It gets on my nerves, if you must know. Looks are all that people seem to care about and it's not fair.'

'No, is not fair. Me, when I young I no beauty. I look like a frog who been trod on and my Luigi, he is very handsome, I never think he look at me twice but he does and we falls in love. Is not just outside of a person is important, eh?'

'No.'

'My Antonio is telling me your mother on holiday.'

'Yes, she's in Italy.'

'Where does she stay?'

'In a place near ... Hang on a minute.' Catrin took the letter from her pocket and unfolded it. 'Near a place called Terrini.'

'Ah, Terrini is not far from where I live but I never been there. When I was child we don't travel far from our own village.'

'She's staying in the Convent of Santa Lucia.'

Nonna stiffened and hastily made the sign of the cross with a gnarled old finger.

'Do you know it?' Catrin asked eagerly.

'Mother of all the saints. *Sì*, I know of it. Everyone heard of the Convent of Santa Lucia. Is a terrible place where they used to put all the people who has worse than just their shillings missing.'

'Like Aunt Alice?'

'No. The people they locks up in Santa Lucia does very queer things, screaming and shouting, banging their heads against the wall.'

'Lunatics?' Catrin asked.

'*Sì*, and the lunatics sometimes escapes and is running about naked like they children. Is not a nice place to go. When we little and we naughty my mamma say, "You don't behave and I send you to the nuns at Santa Lucia." Then we very afraid and we stops the nonsense.'

'It sounds a horrible place,' Catrin said with wide eyes and a growing smile.

'Is very, very horrible. The nuns there was very cruel and people used to think that the nuns can put the evil eye on them and make them sick.'

'What's the evil eye?'

'In Italia the evil eye is called *malocchio*. See here, I have *corno* from when I little.'

She pulled a small necklace from under her black jumper, a tiny red horn, in the middle of which was the outline of an eye. 'This is called a *corno* and protect you from *malocchio*.'

'You really believe in all that daft stuff?'

'*Sì*. And you don't? Maybe someone has put evil eye on you and that why you so thin.'

'What a load of rubbish.'

Catrin was silent, wondering how could this woman know such things when she couldn't see? Maybe she was like the old man Tony had told her about, who could tell a colour by the feel of it.

'I hear you make bread for Ella the other day.'

'Italian *focaccia*. Did you ever eat *focaccia* when you were little?'

'No, never. Is too expensive. My family very poor and eats same bread all the peasants eat. Very chewy and good for stuffing into holes in the walls to keep cold wind out in winter.'

Catrin grinned.

'Is funny thing, though. Today I have money and can buy plenty of food, but nothing taste so good as when I little girl and I come in and eat what my mamma make. All that work we have to do make big appetite. Appetite is very good thing, eh?'

Catrin looked down into her lap. She was forever battling against her appetite. It was the enemy, the gnawing, noisy dragon in her belly that roared for food.

'Sometimes we almost crying from hunger and my poor mamma she always make something simple but tasting very good.'

Catrin's stomach began to complain loudly, and she got to her feet to muffle the sound. 'I'd best be going now.'

'You come see me again, eh?'

'Okay.'

'And you brings that Ella with you.'

'If she'll come.'

'She will come in time. Ella takes a while to warm up and come out of herself. *Ciao* for now.'

'*Ciao*.'

Chapter 25

The rain continued to sweep through the village and the wind blew in off the restless sea, roaring through the tall trees of Gwartney's Wood and making them creak mournfully. Catrin was soaked to the skin in the few seconds it took to run across the road from the Café Romana to the castle. She stood beside the stove in the kitchen in a puddle of water, her clothes steaming gently in the warmth.

'Get that old coat off quickly,' Ella urged.

Catrin struggled out of the coat she had earlier grabbed from the hallstand, and a small brass key fell out of the pocket. She knelt down and picked it up.

Ella held out her hand and took it from her. 'Well, fancy finding that after all this time.'

'Is it yours?'

Ella smiled a wry smile. 'No. This is the key to your Aunt Alice's dowry box.'

Puzzled, Catrin asked, 'Isn't a dowry an old-fashioned thing? Money or jewels or something that a bride has to give to her husband?'

'It was just a joke of ours calling it that. Alice had an old wooden box which she used to call her clues box and she put all her little treasures in there, old postcards, drawings, shells and bits of glass, things she found on the beach. My brothers and I used to tease her and call it her dowry box. Only, once she did find something interesting.'

'What was it?'

'An old ring with some writing on it – Latin, I think. It was probably worth a few bob.'

'Did she sell it?'

'No. She locked it up in her box and wouldn't let anyone touch it. She was saving it for when she got married.'

'What happened to the dowry box?'

'God only knows, but if you find it you're welcome to it. You seem to have a knack of finding Alice's things,' Ella said, handing Catrin the key.

'Are you sure?'

'Well, it's no use to Alice and certainly not to me but I doubt if it's still around. I haven't seen it in years, not since . . .'

'Not since the day she didn't get married?' Catrin said.

'That subject is out of bounds,' Ella said curtly.

'Sorry.' Catrin winced, annoyed with herself for pushing the conversation too far. She needed to be careful what she said to Aunt Ella, otherwise she clammed up.

'Come here and let me dry your hair and you can tell me how Nonna is.'

'She's a bit peculiar,' Catrin said, her words wobbling because Ella was rubbing her hair so hard.

'She was a good old stick and there was nothing much that went on in Kilvenny that she didn't know about.'

'She's almost blind now,' Catrin said.

'Is she?'

'Yes, except she still seems to know what you're doing. It's almost as if she can see you.'

Ella laughed. 'People used to say she was a witch. She used to tell fortunes from tealeaves and remove spells.'

'Spells?'

'Oh, I never believed all that malarkey. But if someone was ill they would go to Nonna for a cure instead of the doctor. They probably still do, for all I know. She would drop some olive oil into a bowl of water, say some magic words and abracadabra they would be well again.'

'But you didn't believe it?'

'Not really.'

'Aunt Ella, have you ever heard of someone called Maria Paparella?'

'No.'

'What about Luca Roselli or Father Rimaldi?'

'No, I don't think so. They don't sound as if they come from round here.'

'How about Piero di Bardi?'

Ella put down the towel and indicated that Catrin should sit down near the stove.

'I've heard of him but I don't know much about him.'

'He was a real person, then?' Catrin asked excitedly.

'Oh yes, he was a famous artist and painted many great pictures. There's a painting of his called *Woman and Child* up at Shrimp's in Alice's room. It's not an original, of course; if it was it would be worth a fortune.'

'Where is the original?'

'It was owned by a very wealthy American family, I think. It's funny you should ask about Piero, because that painting was Alice's favourite when we were children. She used to say the lady was one of her friends and she blew kisses to her every night before she went to sleep.'

'Do you know anything else about Piero di Bardi?'

'Sorry, but art isn't one of my strengths, I'm afraid.'

Catrin was crestfallen.

'It's a shame you didn't meet the friend I mentioned. Piero was a favourite of ...' Ella faltered and turned away quickly.

'Why was he a favourite?'

'Let me see. Piero didn't merely paint, he told stories through his pictures, and by looking at his paintings you could feel the real person, experience their joy or their pain. His portraits were so wonderful that you could almost hear them breathe.'

Catrin could hardly contain her excitement; she felt just like that when she looked at the paintings in *Recipes for Cherubs*. It was as if they were trying to talk to her.

'I do know someone who could probably tell you all about Piero.'

'Who?'

'Mr Knowitall over the road.'

'Tony Agosti?'

'No, Dan Gwartney from the library. He's fanatical about art. In fact, there's not much he doesn't know about anything, though I hate to say it.'

'Why do you dislike him so much?'

'He's a meddlesome old bugger, always poking his nose into things.'

'Has he always looked after the castle?'

'When Hester left he offered to, though God knows why – she only paid him a pittance. Then she died and it was left to your mother. I suppose she's kept on paying him so that the place doesn't fall down. One day, I expect draughty old castles will come back into fashion and she'll sell it.'

'I hope she doesn't. I like it here. It feels as if, even though I didn't know it existed until a few days ago, I kind of knew it did exist inside me, if that makes sense.'

Ella nodded. 'Even though you've never been here before, I suppose Kilvenny Castle is in your blood – the Grieves go back for hundreds of years, you know.'

'That makes me feel funny inside.'

'You have the Grieve genes in you. You look a little like Alice.'

'My godfather, the horrible man, is always going on about genes.'

'Is he, indeed?'

'He says that genes will out in the end, or something like that.'

'You've lost me.'

'Well, he says that if someone in a family is brilliant at music, say, one of their children, grandchildren or great-grandchildren will probably have the same talent.'

'I don't think any of the Grieves were geniuses,' Ella mused.

'There were some who were mad, though, weren't there?'

'Oh yes, loads.' Ella laughed. 'But I think you and I are pretty sane most of the time, don't you?'

'I suppose. I can't imagine my mother ever living in Kilvenny Castle, even though she is a Grieve.'

'Kizzy took after her mother more than the Grieves. Both Hester and Kizzy couldn't wait to get out of Kilvenny. "I don't want to spend my life moping about with ghosts in a freezing museum" – that's what Kizzy used to say.'

'Do you think this place really is haunted?'

'I don't know. I don't believe in ghosts, not as in things that flap about in white sheets, but I sort of feel that if people have been very happy or very sad, somehow their spirit seeps into a place.'

'In the bedroom where I'm sleeping I can smell lemons really strongly and at other times lavender as if someone was in there with me, but I'm not a bit afraid.'

'It's the living one needs to be afraid of, not the dead.'

'I suppose so. I'd love to live here for ever and ever.'

'And not go back to school?'

Catrin was thoughtful for a moment. 'I sort of like

my school. I'd rather be there than at home because my mother's always out and there's no one to talk to.'

'What about your godfather? Do you see him much?'

Catrin turned her head away and Ella noted the colour rising in her face.

'I have to go there on Sunday afternoons in the holidays.'

'Do you have fun?'

'No. He ignores me most of the time now, but when I was younger he was interested in me and used to ask me questions all the time.'

'What kind of questions?'

'Oh, how was I doing at school? What was my mark in the art exam? Did I dream much? How well was I doing at Latin and mathematics? He thinks cleverness is the only thing that matters. He's just a bore.'

'So you prefer to be at school?'

'I suppose. Some of the nuns are a bit drippy but there's one I really like. She's called Sister Matilde. She's funny and knows loads of things, and she's full of life even though she's old and has been shut up in a convent. The older girls say she had a failed romance and that's why she became a nun.'

'And do you think that's what happened?'

'I don't know. But just because something rotten happens, do you think it's right to hide away?'

'I don't know the answer to that, Catrin.'

Catrin realised what she'd said and could have kicked herself. Ella had shut herself away after Alice died, and living all alone at Shrimp's was a bit like being a nun except for the prayers.

'Nonna said you went away to school once. Did you like it?' she asked, changing the subject hastily.

'I loved it.'

'Oh.'

'You sound surprised.' Ella's voice was wistful.

'I thought, well, the way Nonna said it, it sounded like you would be glad to be back because Alice missed you.'

'Of course I missed Alice terribly, but it was a great freedom to be at school. I needed to be away from Alice for my own sanity.'

'So you weren't happy when you were made to come back?'

'No. I was furious. Alice and I were twins but we were very different. I always had to be there for her, constantly looking out for her, and sometimes as a child that was too much to cope with.'

Neither of them spoke for a while. Catrin understood what Ella meant about being furious inside. She was furious most of the time, and when she wasn't she was full of a simmering anger which every now and again threatened to bubble up and drown her. It was hard to know what made her so angry. Her mother, of course, was one of the reasons. She wasn't like a grown-up at all and she didn't do the things mothers were supposed to do. Catrin had found it easier to control her anger since she'd put herself on a diet, and she was so hungry most of the time that it pushed the anger to the back of her head.

'Were you sent away because you were always in trouble?'

'It was partly that. I was a bit hair-brained and drove my mother mad because I was such a tomboy. She wanted me to be a proper girl and I couldn't be. My father was a very wise man and he realised that to send me away was the best thing for me, if not for Alice. But Alice pined for me, my mother couldn't cope with her, and I was brought back. I hated it.'

'But you stayed at Shrimp's with Alice for years after you'd grown up?'

'I did, but I didn't plan to. I had my own dreams once but they were dashed. After that I never got round to leaving. You see, I felt responsible for Alice, more like a parent than a sister. I thought something would happen to her if I wasn't around. And of course it usually did.'

'So you were afraid to leave her?'

'Yes. I was a coward, Catrin. I should have upped and left Shrimp's years ago but instead I stayed, tried to make the best of it and cared for Alice, only not well enough, as it turned out.' Ella's eyes were damp with tears, and her chin was wobbling with grief, like that of a child who could not be consoled.

Suddenly she stood up. 'Look, the rain's stopped at last. I'm going to set about the garden, see if there are any vegetables we could use. Why don't you go over to the library and pick Dan Gwartney's brains about that artist fellow, Piero di Bardi?'

Catrin watched her go, and for the first time in her life she felt enormous sympathy for someone else.

Chapter 26

Luca Roselli stepped angrily out into the Via Dante, slamming the door behind him. He scowled as he walked towards the piazza, kicking out at a loose cobblestone, muttering to himself.

'What's up, Luca?' Bindo called from his perch on the window-ledge of a long-deserted house.

Luca looked up, his face puce with fury, but on seeing Bindo he smiled. 'Oh, it's just him in there,' he muttered, nodding towards the house.

'What's he done now?'

'He's just so damned cheerful!'

'But for weeks you have been moaning that he is a misery. Is there no pleasing you, my friend?'

'He's so changeable. One minute he has a face like he's swallowed a rancid frog and does no work at all. Then suddenly he's singing and laughing and working like a fiend.'

'Artists are like that; they have to be a bit mad.'

'He has worked hard all morning full of the joys of spring, but this afternoon he will become a misery again and then my life will be hell.'

'How do you know he will be miserable?'

'Because the widow Zanelli and her daughters are coming for a sitting.'

'Why are they sitting for Piero? Can't he find anything better to paint?'

'He has a commission for a painting of cherubs to hang in the church and those two are to be models for the cherubs.'

Bindo chuckled. 'I bet I could find better models to paint than them.'

'Maybe, but Signor Bisotti has paid my master well to paint them so that he can get in the widow's good books.'

'Why would he want to get on her good side?'

'Haven't you heard?' Luca said, lowering his voice. 'All the talk is that Signor Bisotti wants to marry her.'

Bindo stared open-mouthed at him.

Luca grew flustered, blushed, put his hand to his mouth. 'Me and my big mouth. I'm not supposed to have said a word about that. Bindo, you must promise not to repeat it. I overheard the widow Zanelli telling my mother, so if she knows I've opened my big mouth she'll take a stick to me.'

'You can trust me, my friend.' Bindo winked and slapped Luca heartily on the arm. 'If she marries Signor Bisotti, she'll move into the Villa Rosso, won't she?'

'Sì. The sparks will fly then, eh? Maria already crosses the road to avoid her. Imagine those two living under the same roof.'

'They are so different. Maria will give you anything and the widow Zanelli is the opposite – she wouldn't give you the skin of her shit. Say, Luca, have you been to the Villa Rosso this week?'

'No, I haven't been able to slope off. He's kept me busy with his "Do this, do that, fetch me this, fetch me that!"' Luca said with rising anger. 'Yesterday I had to go all the way to Terrini to buy dragon's blood.'

Bindo, his eyes alight with interest, said, 'Dragon's blood? Where would you find a dragon to slay around here? Is your master mad?'

'Mad as an overheated bull – you know what these artist types

183

are like. They're not like normal people. Don't look so alarmed. Dragon's blood is only red paint. Today I have to get some bristles from a white hog – not a wild hog, mind you, a domesticated one.'

'What for?'

'To make the paintbrushes for His Majesty back there. When I've done all that, I have to make the cheese glue that he uses for joining wood. Then, when all those jobs are done, I have to find some cat's teeth.'

'Cat's teeth? Why would anyone need cat's teeth?'

'I have to grind them down and then they're used for burnishing. The teeth of any meat-eating animal will do but his high-and-mighty prefers the teeth of cats.'

A growing smile lit up Bindo's small face. 'I think I might be able to help you there. There's plenty of cats in Santa Rosa.'

'You get me some cat's teeth and I'll teach you how to make the paintbrushes you're always on about.'

'It's a deal. Luca, do you think one day you'll ever open that eating house Ismelda was talking about?'

'I doubt it, but sure as hell I won't become the artist my mamma wants me to be.'

'That's why she wants you to work with Piero, so that you can learn to paint?'

Luca nodded and spat disconsolately. 'She doesn't realise that hard work isn't enough. You have to have talent.'

'Did you see Ismelda when you were at the Bisotti house?' Bindo asked innocently.

'You've not got an interest in Ismelda?' Luca asked teasingly.

Bindo coloured. 'No! Well, maybe a little but I'm hoping they invite me again soon. Er, you don't have an interest in her, do you, Luca?'

'No way. I don't like girls, and anyway, nice as she is, that one isn't quite right in the head.'

'How do you know?'

'Because once when I was helping Maria to bottle tomatoes she

left Ismelda for a few minutes and when she came back she had tipped the tomatoes all over herself and then rolled about on the floor.'

Bindo threw back his head and roared with laughter.

'Upon the Virgin's nose, it is true. From head to toe she was covered in tomatoes. It was just before mass and she was wearing her best clothes.'

'*Mamma mia!* So you don't have a glint in your eye for her, then?'

Luca laughed, his dark curls bouncing. 'No. If I get married I don't want to come home and find my wife dressed up in the dinner, maybe wearing petticoats of pasta.'

Bindo doubled up with laughter, holding on to his belly.

'That's very fine tagliatelli you're wearing, my darling,' Luca spluttered.

'My, what a beautiful pair of gnocchi,' Bindo said.

Luca opened his eyes wide and roared and Bindo, realising what he'd said, joined him.

An old woman stuck her head out of a nearby window.'Bugger off! There's somebody trying to die in peace in here.'

'Mi scusi.' The boys moved away, whispering together.

'I think Ismelda has a soft spot for you, Bindo.'

'Has she?' he asked eagerly.

'Maria said she's never stopped talking about you since you were there.'

Bindo shivered with pleasure. 'I am going to make her a present and give it to her when I go there next.'

'What will you give her?'

'Something she will never forget.'

'You have money for such a present?'

'The best things in life are free, my friend.'

Then, seeing Signor Bisotti's old cat slinking out of an alley-way, Bindo was off in pursuit, running as fast as his little legs would take him across the sun-soaked piazza.

Chapter 27

Dan Gwartney struck a match and Catrin heard a friendly pop as the gas mantle lit. A gentle glow illuminated the shadowy recesses of the reading room in the library.

A small fire was lit in the hearth, for the evening was chilly, and the smell of coal smoke filled the room, the flames flickering and throwing shadows across the walls and floor. An enormous white cat lay asleep on a threadbare rug, its pink tongue lolling out of its mouth. Catrin eyed the cat nervously.

'You don't like cats?' Dan Gwartney asked, noticing her apprehension.

'I don't know. I've never had a pet.'

'Pedro won't bite you. He's ancient and hardly has a tooth left in his head.'

On cue the cat yawned, and revealed his few remaining yellow teeth.

'It doesn't stop him gallivanting, mind you. He's a real Casanova.'

'Is that a type of cat?'

Dan Gwartney laughed loudly. 'No, Casanova was an Italian lady-killer.'

'A murderer?'

'No. He liked the women. Had a lot of, er, lovers.'

Catrin blushed crimson.

'Pedro comes from a long line of feline Casanovas. There are plenty of his offspring around Kilvenny; his blood line will never die out.'

'A bit like the Grieves?' Catrin gave the cat a wide berth.

Dan Gwartney indicated that she should sit down on a battered leather sofa and he sat opposite her in a wing-backed chair, perusing her in silence for a while. Catrin looked around at the threadbare velvet curtains and battered armchairs. She liked this room, liked the feel of the worn floorboards beneath her feet and the smell of old books all jumbled up with a whiff of stale tobacco and nose-tingling snuff.

'How can I help you?'

'I'm doing some work about art for school and I wanted to know everything there is to know about someone called Piero di Bardi,' she lied.

'Piero di Bardi?' Dan's eyes lit up with interest. 'Ah, now, he was a very interesting man. There used to be a book about him here, but I'm afraid it was stolen a long time ago.'

'Stolen?'

'Well, stolen or inadvertently not returned. It happens sometimes, though thankfully not often. As I remember, it was a woman who was staying at Shrimp's. She had a temporary membership of the library, as a lot of the guests did in the old days, but she forgot to return the book. Sadly I've never been able to get hold of another copy.'

'That's a shame.'

The windows rattled under the onslaught of the wind and Catrin shivered. Dan got up and put more coal on the fire.

'As the book's no longer here, you'll have to settle for what I can remember about him.'

'That's fine, thank you.'

'Now, I know Piero was born around 1721 in Naples, Italy. He was the eldest son of a poor musician and he had a younger brother who died of a fever when he was about eight years of age. Piero started painting when he was very young and soon people recognised his talent. He used to paint the lids of snuffboxes for tourists and eventually he was apprenticed to a painter where he learned his trade as a shop boy.'

'Oh, I've heard of them. Artists used to employ boys to work for them and they learnt how to mix paints, make brushes and stuff, and in return the master gave them lessons.'

'You're very knowledgeable for one so young.'

'And some of the boys became great painters,' she added.

'Some of them did, but of course they had to have the talent and the desire. I expect some of them were encouraged to take up art more for the satisfaction of their parents.'

'I don't understand.'

'Some parents want their child to achieve their own dreams rather than what the child wants.'

'I see.'

She wondered for a moment what Kizzy might want her to become. A dancer? A model? Or a film star? Fat chance.

'Anyhow, Piero was commissioned by many rich people to paint their portraits, and he painted the ceilings of many a palazzo in Rome. Now, it was believed that he moved to Naples and married a girl there, and some people think that she is the woman in the painting of *Woman and Child*, but that's not proved. There's some confusion about what happened to him after that, but then he resurfaced in a small village in the mountains.'

'Santa Rosa?' Catrin murmured.

Dan Gwartney looked at her in surprise. 'That's right. So you've done a little homework already?'

'That's all I really know.' She tried to hide her excitement but she knew for certain now that Santa Rosa was a real place.

'What happened to Piero?' she asked.

'Well, there was a great mystery surrounding him.'

'What sort of mystery?'

'He lived for some years in Santa Rosa, where he did a lot of his best work. *Woman and Child* is one of the paintings from that period, along with a lot of others. Then he was commissioned by a wealthy chap to paint a group of feasting cherubs which was to hang in the church there.'

'And did he?'

'He finished the painting but he never kept his half of the bargain because one day he upped and left, taking the painting with him, and was never heard of again. That's about all I know, Catrin.'

'So no one knows what became of him or the painting?'

Dan shook his head. 'No, but over the years countless people have tried to solve the mystery.'

'Where do they start looking?'

'Oh, from time to time sketches have come to light which are believed to be Piero's, often found in the most unlikely of places, and people have gone rushing off trying to find clues to what happened to him.'

'But no one ever has?'

'No. People still try, though, and if the picture of the feasting cherubs is ever found it'll be worth a fortune.'

'And would whoever found it be able to keep it?'

Dan nodded thoughtfully.

'Piero was at the height of his powers when he went missing, and that picture would doubtless have been a masterpiece.'

'Aunt Ella was right. She said you'd know all about Piero.'

'Did she send you over here, then?'

'Yes.'

'I expect she said go and ask old Mr Knowitall, didn't she?'

Catrin shook her head, but she felt her face go pink and she knew that he could tell she was lying.

Catrin looked more closely at him. He had a sweet face for an old man. His cheeks were pink and shiny, and his bushy eyebrows lifted up when he smiled. He had hair like silver candyfloss and kind blue-grey eyes which twinkled in the firelight.

'Would I be able to find out anything about Santa Rosa while I'm here?'

Dan went over to the bookshelves. He took a small step-ladder, climbed to the top and began to search the shelves. A few minutes later he climbed carefully down, holding a dusty book in one hand.

'You're in luck,' he said. 'Here we are, *Days in Old Italy*, by Theodora Sprenker. Your Aunt Alice, God bless her, could probably recite every word in this book.'

'Could she?'

'Oh, she loved this book, spent hours with her nose in it. Anyhow, come over to the table and I'll put the reading lamp on so you can see properly.'

Catrin crossed to the large shiny-topped table near the window.

'There's a spirit stove over there in the corner and a tin of chocolate biscuits. If you fancy a brew or get peckish, you can help yourself.'

She eyed the biscuit tin longingly, then turned her back on it. 'Thank you, but I'm not hungry. What time do you close?'

'No proper time, my lovely; you can't put opening and closing hours on learning, I always think. The door's open most of the time. It's so nice to see a child who has a love of books. Most youngsters seem to spend hours stuck in front of the television.'

'We're not allowed to watch television at school.'

'How about listening to the radio or the record player?'

'We're only allowed to listen to classical music.'

'None of that loud pop stuff?'

'Only Val Doonican and Vera Lynn, but they're not very easy to dance to. Sister Lucy says Cliff Richard and Elvis Presley are the spawn of the devil, wriggling their hips and pulling goo-goo eyes like madmen.'

Dan chuckled, sat down in his chair, picked up a book and began to read.

Days in Old Italy was heavy and the pages yellow with age.

There was a date on a page near the front of the book: 1903.

She searched through the index and found the right page, then turned to the section on Santa Rosa and read eagerly.

Santa Rosa is a sombre, windswept village in winter and sweltering in the summer months. It is a charming if dilapidated medieval place with narrow streets and a pretty cobbled piazza with a fountain graced by a trio of splendid cherubs. The church is a large, ugly affair with a tower and an enormous bell which resounds around the village, calling the remaining inhabitants to prayer. The interior has no particular artistic merit, and the cheap wooden panelling spoils the acoustic effect, but there are some lovely marble saints set in shadowy niches.

Dan Gwartney looked up from his book and watched Catrin with interest. Oblivious of his scrutiny, she read on.

Many of the houses in Santa Rosa are empty now, owing to emigration on a large scale, but one can take an agreeable walk through the shady streets and drink a cool glass of wine in the cave-like bar where one can linger over a lunch of freshly made pasta. Then at your leisure amble back through the village and stroll through the abandoned Villa Rosso, a former grand villa once home to the wealthy Bisotti family. Ponder awhile in the over-grown gardens or take a siesta in the shade of the pomegranate tree.

Catrin shivered with excitement. Santa Rosa was a real place and she was sure that the paintings in *Recipes for Cherubs* were of real people, too. The wealthy Bisotti family had lived in the blood-coloured Villa Rosso and Ismelda Bisotti would have lived there too.

Before you leave Santa Rosa walk along the narrow Via Dante, for there you will find the abandoned studio of the renowned artist Piero di Bardi. It is well worth a visit to Santa Rosa, just to step inside the old house and see what life was like in eighteenth-century Italy. Remarkably, the house has been kept just as it was the day the artist left the village, never to be heard of again. Rumours abound about his fate; some say he was set upon by robbers on the road to Terrini and killed; others that he went mad and was incarcerated in an asylum. All mere conjecture, no doubt, and probably his fate will sadly never be uncovered though many have tried to discover what happened to him and his lost master-pieces.

In his studio the original flute-shaped paintpots remain just as he left them. Although the paint is long gone, the pots are labelled: indigo, verdigris, cinabrese, lampblack, sinoper, vermillion, ochre, saffron and the peculiarly named dragon's blood.

There are terracotta pots containing sticks of sharpened charcoal and handmade brushes of all shapes and sizes. There are boxes containing sand, salt and sawdust, and on a worm-eaten shelf there are bottles of vinegar, varnish and quicksilver.

Empty wine pitchers litter the floor and there is even a giant half-eaten ham hanging from the ceiling – preserved with varnish by someone for posterity. Although none of Piero's paintings remain in the house, it is certainly well worth a visit for students of art or history.

On leaving Santa Rosa, take the steep road down towards Terrini ...

Catrin sat up straight looking ahead of her. Terrini! The Convent of Santa Lucia was near Terrini, and that's where her mother was right now. Her mother wouldn't be a bit interested in artists and old houses; all that interested her was men and dress shops and how pretty she looked.

Catrin closed the book thoughtfully. How she would love to walk through the cobbled streets of Santa Rosa and have a cool drink in the bar. How wonderful to open the door to Piero di Bardi's abandoned house in the Via Dante and go inside. Maybe there would be clues there which would show why he had left in such a hurry and where he'd gone. A person couldn't just vanish, surely?

She cast her mind back to the portrait of Piero di Bardi in *Recipes for Cherubs* and wondered if it was a self-portrait. She was sure it must be because all the portraits in the book were certainly done by a genius.

Piero was a thin-faced man with dark, tangled hair which hung down to his shoulders. His cheeks were hollow and there were dark circles under his eyes, as though he hadn't slept well in a long time. There was a spark of vibrant energy, though, in those eyes, dreamy haunting eyes which looked steadfastly out from the page and seemed to look right into her soul. His hand was outstretched, holding a paintbrush in long slender fingers.

She turned her attention back to Theodora Sprenker.

Terrini is a one-street town, one of the most poverty-stricken places I have ever encountered in all my travels. Barefoot children, dressed in stinking rags but with the faces of angels, followed me as I passed through, and I could hardly bear to look upon their ravaged faces with their suppurating sores and famished eyes.

There is no inn or house in Terrini in which one would feel safe to stay, so I rode straight through, throwing a few coins to these poor children.

I rode for a good half-hour, the road winding steadily upwards, until in the early evening I came within sight of the Convent of Santa Lucia. Such a curious place I have never seen, perched as it is on a hilltop, built into the very rock itself, the walls turning a deep blood-red as the sun began to set. I took my lodgings there and have wished fervently ever since that I had not. I have recurring night-mares about the place which leave me weak and quivering with fear. The poor souls incarcerated there were dressed in a uniform of rags and spent their days screaming, banging their heads and rocking back and forth, babbling incoherently. The most crazed of the inmates were locked in cells with bars on the windows and all the while the most heart-rending moaning emanated from these cells and one could barely dare to contemplate the horrors that lay behind the locked doors. Suffice it to say that I stayed only one night, the longest night of my life.

*

Catrin giggled. She wondered if the Convent of Santa Lucia was as bad today as it had been then. She smiled, thinking of her mother stuck in such a place; Kizzy would be hopping mad to be cooped up there all this time. For a moment she felt a frisson of guilt. Maybe she should ring Arthur Campbell and ask him to send her mother some money, but if she did, she'd have to say she was in Kilvenny and then he'd be bound to come and get her. No, her mother could stew in her own juices. It would serve her right for gadding off to Italy to meet an old friend, probably some stupid man who'd taken her fancy.

She looked up from the book and saw the odd man from the photographer's shop looking in through the window at her. And then suddenly he was gone.

Chapter 28

The widow Zanelli could barely contain her delight as she unwound the rags from her daughter Adriana's hair and brushed out the glossy ringlets, coiling them round her fingers, stiffening them with a little spit in unruly places. She applied a little rouge to the child's cheeks and stood back to admire her handiwork.

Then she carried out the same procedure on Adriana's twin, Alessandra.

'Stand beside your sister, there in front of the window, so that I can admire you both.'

The girls shuffled together, hands clasped in front of them, their practised beatific smiles in place.

'Bellissima. Now you are ready for another sitting with Piero di Bardi. Thanks to dear Signor Bisotti, your beauty will be captured for eternity. And to think that soon you will adorn the walls of the church here in Santa Rosa. Mamma mia. Come, girls we must not keep the great artist waiting. Presto!'

Adriana and Alessandra dutifully followed their mamma out of the house and across the cobbled piazza, the sun glinting off their shiny tresses swinging beneath their sun hats. The widow Zanelli was careful to keep the sun at bay: she didn't want her two darlings covered in freckles or developing the coarse dark skin of the Santa Rosa peasants. God forbid. She had high hopes for these girls; good marriages and wealth surely could not elude such beautiful, dutiful daughters.

As they approached the Villa Rosso the widow Zanelli smiled. One day very soon she would stop protesting and agree to marry Signor Bisotti. Heaven knows he had asked her often enough these past weeks, and if her suspicions were right it would be timely to get wed sooner rather than later. She didn't want to be taking her vows with a great fat belly.

How splendid it would be to live in the Villa Rosso and how important she and her daughters would become in Santa Rosa. To be married to such a fine and wealthy gentleman would be an honour indeed.

She would soon stamp her mark on the Villa Rosso, and one of the first things she did would be to give that impudent Maria Paparella her marching orders. She would soon put a stop to all her airs and graces, making all those fancy meals and squandering Signor Bisotti's money. Why, only yesterday she had taken an enormous smoked ham to Piero di Bardi's house, no doubt paid for by Signor Bisotti. For far too long that impudent hussy had wielded too much power in the Villa Rosso but now her days were numbered. Maria Paparella was a simple peasant from a long line of peasant stock, and that was where she belonged and where she would return, to live among the poor, eking out her days.

As for Ismelda Bisotti, from what little the widow had heard of the child, it was clear that she needed a firm hand. Father Rimaldi had only yesterday confided that Ismelda was to be sent to the nuns at Santa Lucia. She would get her come-uppance there. She'd be sure to get a good whipping from the holy sisters. A few days shut up in a dark cellar would stop her headstrong nonsense.

Poor Signor Bisotti had had such a time of it since the Good Lord had taken that poor wife of his. Signora Bisotti had always been a frail little thing, quite a plain woman, too, if the widow Zanelli's memory served her well. Giving birth to that monster of a child, Ismelda, must have been her final undoing.

197

As the widow and her daughters turned into Fig Lane, a fat white cat hurtled past them and they almost collided with Bindo, who was hot in pursuit of the cat.

Bindo skidded to a halt, raising a cloud of dust from the baked ground. He watched with dismay as the cat made its escape down an alleyway, then stepped back hastily to allow the strutting trio to pass.

'Buon giorno,' Bindo called, affecting a low bow.

The widow Zanelli curled her lip and glared at him. She pulled the girls closer to her, so that they would not come into contact with the dirty dwarf.

The girls peered round their mother's buxom frame, held their noses theatrically and raised their eyes heavenwards.

Bindo stood, hands on hips, and watched the widow shepherd her daughters in front of her.

'Be off, you pint-sized freak,' she snarled. 'Small wonder that mother of yours abandoned you in an olive jar!'

Bindo bit his lips, closed his eyes against the pain of her words. She was talking rubbish. His mother had left him at the convent so that he could live. Hadn't Mother Ignatia said he was lovingly wrapped in blankets against the cold of the winter's night?

'Who does she think she is, eh?' Bindo said loudly. 'She has the face of a poisoned trout and those two daughters of hers would make a good pair of gargoyles for the church.'

The widow Zanelli turned and glowered at him. 'They say that when Father Rimaldi fished you out of that olive jar you were as slippery as an eel. It took two days to wash the oil off you. A mother doesn't do that to a child she loves.'

She stuck her nose in the air and marched off along the Via Dante. Bindo spat into the dust, wiped his eyes with the back of his grubby hand and went out into the sun-drenched piazza.

Chapter 29

Catrin wandered along Cockle Lane and through the wicket gate into the churchyard, where she paused here and there to read the inscriptions that were still legible on some of the crooked headstones. There were Gwartneys and Grieves buried in among Merediths and Joneses, and against the wall that separated the graveyard from the castle she noticed a row of small crosses covered so thickly in moss that the names were illegible. On one of the graves there was a small posy of withered wild flowers – dandelions, cowslips and weeds – tied with green ribbon. It was a strange posy, the sort a young child might make, someone who didn't know the difference between weeds and flowers.

She came upon Alice Grieve's grave unexpectedly in a shady corner of the graveyard, and was surprised to see that it was well tended and that a bunch of rosemary had been put there; rosemary for remembrance. Catrin knelt down and traced her fingers around the words on the headstone.

Alice Katherine Grieve
Taken suddenly after a short illness

So Alice hadn't died of a broken heart at all.

A shadow fell across the headstone and Catrin spun

round to see the man from the photographer's shop staring at her with a strange look in his rheumy eyes. She could smell whisky on his breath and hear the bronchial rattle of his chest, and she got clumsily to her feet and backed away.

'Poor Alice,' he muttered, nodding down at the grave. 'Kicking up the daisies well before she should have been.'

He pulled a bottle from the depths of his trouser pocket, swigged thirstily, then belched loudly.

Catrin stayed silent, wondering whether to make a bolt for it.

'She was a damn good woman, Alice. There wasn't a nasty bone in her body. She was gentle and trusting, not like that bloody sister of hers.'

'Ella Grieve is my aunt,' Catrin said stiffly.

He swayed dangerously, put his hands out and steadied himself on the gravestone. 'Then you *are* Kizzy Grieve's child?'

'Yes.'

He turned to face her, pinpricks of oily sweat breaking out on his crinkly forehead, a lock of lank hair hanging down over one bloodshot eye.

'I thought that night when I saw you looking into my window wearing that boater hat, that you were a ghost,' he muttered.

'Well, as you can see, I'm not,' she said haughtily.

He looked around anxiously. Is your mother here with you?'

Catrin shook her head.

He looked relieved, came closer to her. 'You're not a bit like Kizzy,' he said.

People always said that, as though it was a shame that someone as beautiful as Kizzy Grieve should have such a plain Jane for a daughter. Of course, they didn't say it in so many words but it was obvious what they were thinking.

'Kizzy never even had the decency to come back here to bury her aunt,' he went on.

'She couldn't very well, could she? She's not welcome here.'

'Why did she send you here after all this time?'

'She had to go to Italy all of a sudden,' Catrin muttered sulkily.

'Dear God, if I'd have known what would happen to poor Alice, I would have taken her away from here, kept her safe.'

Catrin wondered if he was one of the mad people Bryn Jones had talked about.

'I'll never forgive myself for not seeing what was going on in front of my own eyes. If I had, Alice might still be alive today.'

He began muttering incoherently, took another swig from the bottle before he spoke again. 'You're staying in the castle, I hear.'

'Yes.'

'Rather you than me.'

'Why do you say that?'

'It's a queer old place. Alice used to say she saw things in there.'

'I've never seen any ghosts or anything spooky at all,' Catrin said, a quiver rising in her voice.

'She didn't always see them, but she said that sometimes she could smell lemons and lavender and other times she could feel them all around her, a sudden rush of cool air and the hairs standing up on the back of her neck.'

Catrin felt light-headed; she'd smelt those smells too and she felt the hairs on the back of her own neck lifting now, a frisson of fear squeezing her bladder.

It was the living you had to be afraid of, not the dead.

'Alice could see things that no one else could see.'

'Maybe she just imagined them. I mean, wasn't she a bit simple?'

Meredith Evans glowered at her and she flinched.

'She wasn't simple, she was like a child, and children can often see what grown-ups can't because they haven't become jaded by the world. They still believe in magic and . . . and love.'

Catrin felt suddenly cold and hugged herself.

'She said it was the people from the book calling to her, trying to tell her about the secret of Kilvenny Castle.'

Catrin swallowed hard and blurted out, 'Did you ever see the book of paintings she found?'

'No, she would never let anyone see it. She used to have dreams after she found it and she drove everyone mad scouring the castle for clues for hours on end. That's when they sent her to see the doctors up in London.'

'What could the doctors do?'

'Bugger all, but they were supposed to find out why she had such strange dreams.'

'And did it work?'

'No. It was a waste of good money. Mrs Grieve had the book burnt in the end, and poor Alice broke her heart over that, and not long after, they left the castle and moved up to Shrimp's.'

Catrin bit her lips to hide her grin. They were all wrong about the book being burnt because it was up in her room, safely hidden under the bed

'Did Alice still have the dreams after the book was burnt?'

'No. Nonna helped her, got rid of the dreams until *he* came along and started raking it all up again.'

'Do you mean the man she was going to marry?'

He nodded, and spat out angrily between his teeth, 'He never loved Alice – he only pretended he wanted to marry her. I think she was interesting to him as a sort of peculiar specimen to prod and probe for his own satisfaction.'

'If he didn't want to marry her, why was he waiting for her in the chapel?'

'I don't know. The whole thing was a bloody charade; she'd got something he wanted and he was determined to get it.'

Catrin wrinkled her brow in confusion. 'That doesn't make any sense.'

'He was after something very special—'

He stopped mid-sentence, knelt down and traced the letters of Alice Grieve's name with his finger. Then he got awkwardly to his feet, tipped his cap to Catrin, steadied himself and staggered away through the graveyard. Catrin lingered until she was sure he'd gone, then made her way to the wicket gate.

Outside the Café Romana Meredith Evans was standing face to face with Ella Grieve, and Catrin could tell that they weren't having a cosy chat.

Ella made to move away but Meredith sidestepped and blocked her path.

'We were bound to meet sooner or later,' he said.

'Later would have suited me just fine,' Ella growled.

'Don't be like that.'

'I'll be exactly how I like. Now get out of my bloody way.'

Catrin could sense the hatred rising off Ella like heat waves. Her first reaction was to run away. She hated seeing people who were angry: anger was about being out of control, a sin.

'Come on, Ella, what's done is done. Neither of us can change what happened to Alice,' Meredith said, his voice placatory. He put his hand on Ella's arm and she pushed him away roughly.

'What you did, Meredith Evans, was despicable.' Her voice was cold, her blue eyes narrowed with anger.

'For God's sake, I was wrong to do what I did but you didn't want Alice to marry that man any more than I did.'

'You're right on that score, but it's the way you went about it that got my goat.'

'I thought it was for the best.'

'For the best! You knew what was going on and yet you waited until the last minute to let her know the truth.'

Meredith's hand flew to his face as if he had been slapped.

'You're never right, Meredith. They said Alice was short-changed in the brains department, but you take the bloody biscuit.'

'You seem to forget that Alice was a grown woman and some of those decisions she made for herself.'

'Grown woman, my arse. She had the mentality of a child.'

'The trouble was you only ever saw her as a child and treated her like one. She knew what she was doing that day when she left, and the fact is she didn't trust you enough to tell you the truth!'

Ella stiffened, clenched her fists and moved towards Meredith menacingly. But he stepped hurriedly out of her way.

'You were responsible for what happened,' said Ella, 'and then you let her get on a train on her own when she must have been in a terrible state. She was vulnerable, barely able to get from the village to Shrimp's on her own without mishap, never mind going off to God knows where.'

'She was calmer than you think, and she knew exactly what she was doing,' Meredith said coldly.

'Do you realise that I spent months looking for her, charging across the country checking all the places I thought she might have gone to?'

'Have you ever thought that maybe she didn't want you to find her!'

Ella glared at Meredith Evans and the fury on her face almost made Catrin buckle at the knees.

'Are you telling me you knew my sister better than I did?'

'Maybe I'm telling you your sister was trying to give you your freedom!'

'My freedom? What the hell do you mean by that?'

'She knew you were planning to leave Shrimp's and she knew that if she stayed you wouldn't go.'

Ella went pale. 'Freedom! What sort of freedom was that, not knowing where she'd gone?'

'Alice may have been childlike but she faced up to the truth, which is more than you ever did, Ella. She wanted you to be happy and to do that, she knew you had to go away.'

Ella glowered at Meredith. Then she rallied, pulled back her shoulders and snapped, 'How dare you tell me you knew what Alice was thinking!' She pushed past him, almost knocking him off balance.

Spitting out her words like sour pips, she said, 'As far as I'm concerned, this is the last time we will ever speak. I blame you, Meredith Evans, and I hate you, so keep away from me and mine, do you hear?'

Meredith watched her hurry away up Cockle Lane, then he staggered inside the shop and slammed the door, rattling the glass in the rotting frame.

Chapter 30

Ella was glad of the peace in the Italian garden; she was still shaking with anger after her confrontation with Meredith. She reached out absentmindedly and touched the arm of the stone cherub in the fountain. Beneath her fingers the stone felt warm and comforting, and her heart began to slow and her breathing grew calmer.

Christ almighty, she'd come that close to laying one on Meredith Evans. For two pins she could have knocked him through his shop window, left him sprawling among his stupid old photographs. What right did he have to say that Alice didn't trust her and that she'd treated Alice like a child? Of course she had, because Alice was a child, a stubborn child who didn't always know what was best for her. She'd been difficult enough to look after as it was, and then that stupid idiot Arthur Cambell had come along and filled her head with romantic nonsense. What in God's name did a man like him want with Alice? She was beautiful, to be sure, but sweet Alice with her contrary ways, her whims and fancies and downright oddness, would have been a fish out of water in his life. She would have driven him to distraction in no time at all, and yet he'd asked her to marry him, stood at the altar waiting for her. Jesus and all the saints of heaven, what had he been playing at?

She was still racked with guilt because, although she hadn't trusted him, a part of her had been relieved to see her sister settled and moving away, and she'd relished the prospect of the freedom she'd have when Alice had gone.

She put her hand out to open the chapel door, but then hesitated. She hadn't set foot in the chapel since the day of Alice's wedding. She took a deep breath, braced herself and went in.

It was cool in the chapel and the light that came through the window above the altar was restless. Shadows moved furtively across the walls and the candle stubs on the stand in the lady chapel flickered in the draught.

Ella made her way towards the altar, sat down in an ancient pew and closed her eyes, letting the darkness engulf her, the smell of the roses in the Italian garden drifting into the chapel.

If time turned backwards now she would open her eyes and the chapel would be full. Luigi and Nonna Agosti in their best bib and tucker sitting proudly next to Gladys Beynon, who was wriggling with excitement, checking that the pins in her hat were secure.

All around her, friends and villagers were squeezed close together, whispering ... the smells of incense and mothballs mingling with the heady scent of the freshly cut flowers that had been delivered at dawn from the florist in Swansea.

The bridegroom, standing tall and straight, staring ahead of him, the collar of his shirt stiffened with starch, white against the dark skin of his neck, his shoulders stiff with tension. His sister seated close to him, the peacock feather in her black hat quivering in the draught, vivid in the dimness of the chapel.

There was a frisson of excitement as the door opened, all ears waiting for the old organ to grind into the Wedding

March. All heads turned as Dan Gwartney's voice shattered the expectant silence.

'It's Alice. She's gone.'

The next moments had felt dreamlike, and ever since that day Ella had played them over and over in her head. Beside her, Gladys let out a sharp little cry of pain and Nonna clapped her hands together, more in relief than astonishment. Luigi Agosti had got shakily to his feet, his hand going to his heart. There was the sound of a ring dropping on the flagged floor, rolling away and then spinning as if it would never stop.

Ella had pushed past Dan, who stood in the doorway trying to bar her exit. She'd run through the Italian garden, the cascade of water from the cherub fountain loud in her ears, while above her in the tall trees of Gwartney's Wood the rooks squawked discordantly.

She had thrown off her wedding hat, kicked off her new shoes and run like a hare down Cockle Row, hurtled across the beach, up the steep steps in her haste to get to Alice.

The breeze was riffling through the bunting that had been hung up in the trees surrounding the front lawn of Shrimp's, and the clink of glasses came from the marquee on the lawn. The servants were a blur of black and white as they came running out of the hotel, staring wide-eyed at Ella as she careered past them, calling frantically for Alice.

There was no sign of Alice anywhere, and though she pressed the servants for information no one could remember seeing her leaving. Her wedding dress lay discarded on the bed in her room, the fake diamonds twinkling brilliantly in the morning sunshine. The suitcase that she had so carefully packed for her honeymoon was gone. Then Ella saw the two photographs that had been ripped in half and tossed into the fireplace.

Ella sat down heavily on the bed and pieced them together. Sweet Jesus! Poor Alice. No wonder she hadn't turned up at the church. As she sat immobile with shock she heard the train puffing away in the distance and knew without a doubt that her sister was on that train. Alice, who had never done anything independently in her life, was making her first journey away from Kilvenny on her own.

Kizzy was the first to arrive back at Shrimp's. She came running into Alice's room, her face tear stained, eyes wide with alarm.

Ella got to her feet, stood stiffly, a pulse in her neck racing as Kizzy looked to her for an explanation. Ella thrust the ripped photographs into her hands and Kizzy looked at them, threw back her head and laughed hysterically.

Ella had been incensed, consumed with fury. How dare this slip of a girl, barely out of school, laugh when she was presented with the damning evidence against her?

'It's not what you think, Aunt Ella. The man is just besotted with me.'

'Don't tell me what to think, Kizzy Grieve!'

Then she looked intently at Kizzy and for the first time she noticed that under her eyes were dark circles, carefully concealed by make-up. She saw the expensive red dress, which Alice had brought her from Knightsbridge, straining at the seams across Kizzy's burgeoning belly.

'Are you pregnant?'

Kizzy cast down her head and nodded. When she looked up, tears were running freely down her face.

'You should be ashamed of yourself!'

'I didn't mean it to happen like this.'

'Well, it's a bit like shutting the stable door after the horse has bolted.'

'I thought that despite our differences we could make a go of it.'

Ella lost control. 'Get out of here! Get out – and don't you *ever* come back.'

'But Aunt Ella, I've nowhere to go, no money.'

'You should have thought about that. Now get out and ask that two-faced bastard you've been canoodling with behind your aunt's back to look after you and your bastard child. You bloody whore!'

'But you don't understand, Aunt Ella!'

'Oh, I understand all right!' Ella screamed and she caught Kizzy a resounding slap across her cheek.

Kizzy stumbled out of the room, blundered up the stairs to her bedroom in the attic. Ella, unable to move, heard her a short while later racing down the stairs and the front door had banged loudly behind her.

After Kizzy had gone, Ella stood there for a long time, expecting the groom to storm in looking for Alice. But he didn't come. No one came. She heard later that he'd marched out of the church with his sister in tow, and they had left Kilvenny soon after. Ella had not seen either of them since, and had no desire to. She'd sworn that she'd never have anything more to do with Kizzy Grieve or her illegitimate child, but now she felt a growing affinity with Catrin, greater than with anyone else in a long time.

By the time Ella bucked up the courage to go downstairs the hotel had been silent, the few remaining guests gone and the servants keeping to their rooms.

She had crept down here to the chapel and left a note beneath the statue of the tiny saint, explaining why she couldn't leave. Then she went to the stable block, where she kept her old car, took her carefully packed haversack out of the boot and went slowly, numbly back to Shrimp's. Her hopes of freedom had been dashed and she had lost the one opportunity to be with the person whom, against all the odds, she thought she could truly love.

She had driven away from Kilvenny in the early hours to begin her fruitless search for Alice, and over the next months Shrimp's had gone into a steady decline.

Ella wiped a tear from her cheek, opened her eyes, then shielded them from the light that was streaming through the altar window, warming her like a benediction. She felt closer to Alice at that moment than she had in years, as if Alice's presence was all around her; spinning in the dust motes, glistening in the light, tangible in the very air itself.

It was all in the past now, and she'd lived too long immersed in the past. She got slowly to her feet and made her way out of the coolness of the chapel and into the sunlight.

Chapter 31

Catrin waited until she was sure Aunt Ella and Meredith were out of the way, then hurried across the road to the Café Romana.

The bell above the door jangled noisily as she went in.

At a table in the far corner a woman sat opposite a young boy of about seven, who was spooning ice cream into his mouth from a silver dish. Between mouthfuls he smiled at Tony Agosti, who was behind the counter.

'You like my banana ice cream, eh, Dai?' said Tony.

'Yes, Mr Agosti, it's lovely. Better than the toffee one, I think, but only just.'

'He's a real fiend for ice cream,' the woman said. 'He'd eat it for breakfast, dinner and tea if I let him.'

'Ice cream is good for you, but only after you eat your food, eh?' Tony grinned. 'Catrin, my lovely, what can I do for you? You want some ice cream? Freshly made vanilla or tutti frutti. Cornet, wafer or tub? Chocolate sauce? Or raspberry, maybe?'

She shook her head furiously, swallowed her rising spittle. 'No, thank you, I don't like ice cream.'

'You don't like ice cream?'

'I'll have hers,' the boy called out enthusiastically, and Tony laughed.

'Maybe a little piece of toast for you?'

She imagined the taste of the hot bread oozing with salty butter. It made her head feel as if it was full of buzzing flies, and her stomach strained at the leash.

'Okay. Just one piece, though, and not with the butter spread too thickly.'

'Hot buttered toast coming up. You want to go up and see Nonna and I'll bring it up for you?'

'Thank you.'

As she went through the curtain behind the counter she heard the woman say, 'You want to butter that kid a whole loaf of toast, Tony. She looks like she just got out of a concentration camp.'

Catrin escaped up the stairs.

Nonna was sitting up at the window, and when Catrin came into the room her face lit up with pleasure.

'Hey, you breathing very heavy. Are you okay?'

'Yes. I've just been over in the graveyard and I bumped into the man from the photographer's shop.'

'Meredith Evans, you mean. He's a funny old stick.'

'I didn't like him much. He said some odd things, and he's just had a blazing row with Aunt Ella.'

'So I heard. Is no love lost between those two.'

'Why?'

'Because he used to be in love with your Aunt Alice.'

'I guessed that, but she didn't love him back, did she?'

'For a while everyone think one day she marry Meredith, but then she fall in love with someone else.'

Just then Tony came in, carrying a plate piled with hot buttered toast. He set it down beside Catrin. She thanked him, looked at it longingly, broke a tiny piece off and stuffed it guiltily into her mouth. The taste was out of this world and sent a shiver of pleasure through her body.

That was quite enough. Just one taste. One little bit. She

mustn't weaken. If she did, she wouldn't be able to stop. She'd eat and eat and eat until all the fat came back – the disgusting dimples and the chubby knees, the rounded belly and, worst of all, the horrible bosoms that got in the way of everything.

She snatched up a piece of toast and stuffed it into her mouth. Butter dribbled down her chin and she wiped it away impatiently. She couldn't stop herself. It was always like this if she gave in. She took up the second piece of toast and ate it without taking a breath. And then the third.

'You feeling better now?' Nonna asked when she had finished.

'Yes, thank you.' Catrin looked up guiltily and wiped her mouth with the back of her hand. She was glad Nonna hadn't been able to see her stuffing her face like a pig. She made herself a promise that she wouldn't eat another thing today. Or tomorrow.

'Nonna, Meredith said that Aunt Alice used to see things over in the castle. Do you think that's true?'

'Yes, I think is true.'

Catrin sniggered nervously. 'He said she found an old book and it gave her bad dreams.'

'Ah, that book cause so much trouble! Puts the ideas in her head and Alice is very fanciful and she starts searching, searching, driving everybody mad.'

'And that's why they sent her to see the doctors in London?'

'Pah! That was waste of time. Alice tell me the doctor he make her talk about her dreams, draw pictures of the things she sees. Is all big load of nonsense because when she come back she still searching and searching.'

'And so they burnt her book?'

Nonna nodded sadly.

'You didn't agree with that?'

214

'No. Is bad to burn books and maybe something was in the book and Alice does see something other people don't see. Is possible, you know.'

Catrin was sure that the book she'd found was Alice's book, that someone had hidden inside the cover of an annual in Kizzy's old room.

'I talk to Alice and I take away the thoughts she having about all those secrets.'

Catrin tried to stifle a giggle.

'You think is funny, but is true. I tell her maybe she not the right person to be searching, maybe it not the right time and someone come along many years later and they will find out all these things.'

'I see,' Catrin said.

'You have nervous laugh because you is afraid of what you don't understand. Maybe you need to open your own eyes.'

'I do have my eyes open,' Catrin retorted sulkily.

'It's your inner eye you not using because maybe you afraid of what you see.'

'I'm not afraid of anything.'

'We all afraid of something, we just don't like to admit it, eh?'

Catrin stayed silent.

'Now, before I forgets I must tell you something I remembered.'

Catrin didn't reply. She felt wretched after stuffing her face with all that toast, and all she wanted was to get out of here and do some exercise. She tried to calculate how many star jumps she would need to do to burn off all those calories. If she didn't move soon, the butter would start to lay itself down as a greasy layer of fat.

'I remember the name of man who Alice going to marry.'

Catrin didn't care who the stupid man was. Alice had

been just a simple woman who had stupid dreams and saw things which weren't there. What did any of it matter? It was nothing to do with her.

'He is called Arthur, Arthur Campbell, and he a doctor.'

Catrin stared at Nonna's unseeing eyes. Arthur Campbell? No, that couldn't possibly be right.

'What kind of a doctor was he?'

'He the doctor of the sike-ee-eye-atry, like the man Alice sent to in London – a doctor who mends troubles in the head.'

'I know what a psychiatrist is,' Catrin said curtly. Nonna must be mistaken. It couldn't be Arthur Campbell, that was just too ridiculous.

'He come here often for the holidays with his sister and then poof! he fall in love with Alice and make a windwhirl romance and Alice is swept off of her feets.'

Catrin could hardly hear what Nonna was saying. Arthur Campbell had been going to marry Alice Grieve, who was slightly simple in the head? No! He would never marry someone unless they were very clever, because cleverness mattered to him more than anything in the world. Anyway, he didn't have a sister so Nonna must be mistaken.

If it *was* true, though, Arthur Campbell had been stood up at the altar. Blimey O'Riley! Alice may have been daft but she was very brave to do that to a man like Arthur Campbell. How furious he would have been to be made a fool of. Catrin shuddered; she wouldn't want to face him if he was angry.

She remembered Ella asking what her godfather's name was. At the time she hadn't thought anything of it, but Ella had almost spat out her tea and then scurried off into the larder. Why hadn't she said she knew Campbell? Why did she need to be so secretive?

Catrin had been so deep in thought that she had forgotten

216

all about Nonna. When she looked across, the old woman was fast asleep, snoring gently, with her chin resting on her chest, the corno necklace flashing in the sunlight that streamed suddenly through the window.

She looked like something from another age, like a portrait from *Recipes for Cherubs*. Catrin smiled. She reached out and gently touched the old woman's warm cheek. Then she closed the door softly and made her way downstairs.

The café was empty except for Tony, who was sitting at a table near the window with his head in his hands. He jumped as she got nearer, smiled and patted the seat next to him. Catrin sat down obediently. 'Nonna's fallen asleep,' she said.

'She gets very tired these days.'

'Tony, do you know what "gelato" means in English?'

'*Il gelato* is ice cream.'

'Is it easy to make?'

'Ah! Nowadays it's easy, with fridges and electric ice-cream makers. When my grandfather came here, he made his own ice cream with an old-fashioned ice-cream maker and then he had to push his ice-cream cart up and down all the steep hills in Wales. Today they've got ice-cream vans with plastic cows and noisy bells on top.'

'Only, I've found a recipe for ice cream and I'd like to make it the old-fashioned way if I can.'

'Somewhere we've still got the old ice-cream maker. I'll look it out and you can try it.'

'That would be good.'

'You said you didn't like ice cream.'

'Well, I don't particularly.'

'Then what do you want to make it for?'

'Well, it's for Aunt Ella, to cheer her up.'

'You're a very kind girl, Catrin. Ella is a lucky woman to have a niece like you.'

Catrin felt the colour rise in her cheeks and she glowed under Tony's kind words.

'You don't need to blush,' he said, touching her playfully on the cheek.

As he got up, she noticed an old postcard on the table with a picture of a cherub on the front.

'That's a beautiful painting.'

'It's the famous Napoli cherub,' Tony said. 'Fancy a cup of coffee?'

'Yes, but no milk, please.'

'Sugar?'

'No, thanks.'

It was easy to forget how many calories there were in sugar and milk.

Catrin looked at the chubby green-eyed cherub, then turned the postcard over and read the printed bit on the back: *The green-eyed cherub is one of the few Piero di Bardi paintings to have come to light. It was found by accident and sold for a fortune at auction by an anonymous seller.* Catrin scrutinised the painting again. It was just like the ones in *Recipes for Cherubs*. Tony was partly hidden behind a cloud of steam from the coffee maker, so she furtively read the message.

Antonio, my apologies for leaving without saying goodbye. I have made a terrible mistake and had to leave suddenly. I will write soon, don't worry. One day we will have the restaurant of our dreams, maybe in London, Roma or even here in . . . The writing was smudged here and the sender's name obliterated.

It sounded as if the card was from a lover, perhaps the woman for whom Tony had lit the fourth candle in the chapel. Whoever she was, she obviously hadn't kept her promise because here he was, still running the Café Romana.

Tony came back to the table, sat down and pushed a steaming cup of coffee towards Catrin. 'You had a good chat with Nonna?'

'Yes, about Aunt Alice and Meredith Evans, mostly.'

'Poor old Meredith.'

'You like him?'

'He's harmless enough. He used to be a damn fine photographer years ago, but he lost all interest. You should take a look at some of the photos in his shop – there are some good ones of Kilvenny.'

'Why does he drink so much?'

'These days this place is enough to drive a man to drink.'

'Don't you like it here?'

'Dear God, I don't know. There's nothing going on these days, and it saps your ambition.'

'So you'd rather be running a restaurant with your friend?' she blurted out without thinking.

Tony looked hard at her and she averted her eyes with embarrassment. Why couldn't she keep her mouth shut?

'Ah, so you read the postcard.'

Catrin blushed and looked down into her coffee cup.

'There was a time when I had ambition, when I wanted my own restaurant, to cook real Italian food and make a name for myself.'

'So why didn't you make the Café Romana into a restaurant?'

'Here in Kilvenny my customers want soggy pie and chips, toasted teacakes and Spam sandwiches; they don't want *ravioli*, *bruschetta* or *tiramisù*. They're not ready for change like that.'

He laughed. 'If I served up *ravioli* or *cannelloni* they'd think I'd gone mad and say, "Hey, Tony boy, what's this muck?"'

'Did you want to live somewhere else, then?'

'I had all sorts of dreams – a little café in the heart of Naples, a trattoria in Soho London – but I was let down badly.'

'Who by?'

'A friend of mine who came here to work in the café one summer. We made great plans but then they left unexpectedly.'

'Without saying goodbye?'

'Without saying goodbye,' he repeated, and there was a catch in his voice.

There was silence for a while until Tony got to his feet,

'Ah, well, it wasn't to be. Soon afterwards my grandfather died suddenly and I stayed here with Nonna. Anyway, it's not going to happen now, so don't let's be maudlin. How are you finding Kilvenny?'

'I love it. I'm having a whale of a time and I'm getting on better with Aunt Ella.'

The bell above the door announced the arrival of Dan Gwartney, who came in, removed his cap and sat down wearily.

'All right, Catrin? Tony? Cup of strong tea when you're ready.'

Seeing the postcard, Dan picked it up and turned it over and his eyes grew bright with interest.

'That's the Napoli cherub by Piero di Bardi,' said Catrin. 'I've just read all about it.'

Dan didn't answer. He was staring at the postcard, his fingers drumming absentmindedly on the Formica table.

'Have you heard from your mother recently?' he asked, pushing the postcard aside.

'No, she's still in Italy.'

'That's good. She'll be enjoying herself, then.'

Then he got up suddenly, put on his cap and left.

'You forgot your tea, Mr Gwartney.'

But the door closed, and the echo of the bell hung in the air for a long time.

Chapter 32

It was dark in the Via Dante. The shutters were closed on all the houses except one. Piero di Bardi stood at the window watching the fat moon rising above the church tower. The bats were out, cutting arcs of darkness through the air, and over in the piazza a dog howled.

He must eat and drink and fortify himself against exhaustion so that he would have the strength to work through the night. He smiled as he lifted down the huge ham from the hook in the ceiling. Signor Bisotti's servant, Maria Paparella, had come to the house this morning, bringing the ham and two loaves of the most delicious-looking bread he had ever seen. She had been flustered when she spoke to him, blushed and said they were gifts from her master, but everyone knew that Signor Bisotti was as mean as he was ugly.

As she left she had given him one of those generous smiles of hers; a smile which could lighten up a dark alley on a gloomy day. Then, before he could thank her properly, she was bustling back along the Via Dante, singing loudly as she went. He watched her enviously until she disappeared into the piazza. How wonderful to be blessed with such a capacity for happiness and the confidence to sing so unselfconsciously. She couldn't sing to save her soul and yet, awful as her voice was, it seemed to him that she could paint rainbows with her tongue.

Piero cut some thick slices of ham, broke one of the loaves in half, and settled down to eat. These days, if he didn't eat he became shaky and disoriented and his sight blurred alarmingly. He ate enthusiastically, poured a mug of wine and drank deep. Just lately, he seemed to have an unquenchable thirst.

He had wasted valuable time this afternoon sketching the blasted Zanelli girls while the widow stood at his shoulder yattering like a demented crow. He could not abide her with her polished piety and nit-picking ways. She was a scurrilous gossip, a social climber and a spiteful bitch to boot. Left to his own devices, he would never have chosen such a charmless pair of girls as his models.

He got up from the table and stood looking lovingly at a canvas propped against the wall. He had captured her spirit, that wonderful capricious light in her eyes, and the whimsical smile. He ran his finger over the painted lips, traced the outline of her face, then wiped his eyes with the back of his paint-stained hand.

If only he knew what had happened to her, whether she was alive or dead. Why hadn't she come to him? Had she never meant to make their assignation? Or had something terrible happened to her and the child? He had been so sure she would follow him and he had waited and waited, but in vain.

He wandered over to his easel and stood lost in thought. It was time to accept that she would never come. He'd kept the hope alive for all these years and deluded himself. It was time he laid the past to rest and embraced the future. He would dedicate this new work to her memory, to the memory of their love. This painting of the cherubs feasting was going to be his best work ever, although maybe his last, for he knew with certainty that his health was failing, that time was of the essence.

He hastily removed the sketches of the Zanelli girls and took up another canvas. Then he began to draw, working feverishly, his eyes bright with rekindled passion.

As the moon rose higher and the stars pricked through the

blanket of indigo sky, Piero worked on, unaware of the mischievous eyes that watched him and the tiny hand that slipped in through the open window and surreptitiously removed a paintbrush from the pot.

Chapter 33

Most days Catrin strolled down to the beach and paddled in the sea, enjoying the freedom of being able to wander wherever she chose without asking anyone's permission. At school they were always chaperoned by the nuns and only allowed to walk down to the village shop in threes on Saturday mornings. When she was at home with her mother they took taxis almost everywhere, and when occasionally she was allowed out into the garden in the middle of the square she ambled about awkwardly, too self-conscious and tongue-tied to approach any of the other children.

She kicked off her sandals and wiggled her toes in the warm sand, stared out to sea, scooped up a handful of sand and let it run through her fingers.

It was wonderful to have time to think without the nuns telling you what you should be thinking. She was mulling over what Nonna had told her about Arthur Campbell marrying Alice Grieve, but things didn't add up. For a start, he didn't have a sister, and yet everything else Nonna had said sounded as if it must be him.

He would never have married someone like Alice; he despised people who weren't intelligent. He didn't say it out loud but you could tell. When she was small he'd paid for her to have piano lessons and every Sunday afternoon she had to play for him. She'd enjoyed her lessons, even though she was hopeless, but as soon as Arthur Campbell commanded her to play she'd been a bag of nerves. She crumbled beneath his withering gaze and impatient sighs and the black and white keys on the piano became a blur.

A year or so later he'd sent her to art classes with the best teacher he could find, then dancing lessons, but when she failed to shine in either he lost interest in her. She still visited him on Sunday afternoons during the holidays but she could tell he was bored with her.

She got slowly to her feet and climbed the steep steps to Shrimp's Hotel, wandered through the long grass and stood looking at the dilapidated building. She shut her eyes and tried to imagine how it must have been in its heyday.

The windows would be open wide and the curtains blowing in the sea breeze. Maids would be waving their feather dusters out of the windows and singing as they cleaned the bedrooms. There would be guests sprawled in deckchairs on the lawns, talking and laughing. Others would be sitting at tables covered with white damask table-cloths. She would hear the tinkle of silver teaspoons against bone china and someone playing the piano as girls in black uniforms and starched white caps served afternoon tea.

She was lost in her reverie and it was a few moments before she realised that the music wasn't inside her head. She opened her eyes and listened intently. Yes, someone was definitely playing the piano in the hotel. The breeze caught the notes and whirled them around her head. It was a song that Sister Matilde had taught them in school,

'Oh soldier, soldier, won't you marry me with your musket, fife and drum ...' *'Oh no, sweet maid, I cannot marry thee for I have no hat to put on.'*

The song told the story of a young girl who fell in love and was tricked into giving a wily soldier everything that

she had, and when she had, he told her he was already
married. The last words of the song were: *'Oh no sweet maid,
I cannot marry thee for I have a wife of my own!'*

Mary Donahue said that the girl wanted her head examining for being such a trusting chump, but Sister Matilde said
that love clouded the eyes and sometimes the judgement.

Catrin went over to the french windows, screwed up her
eyes and peered into the room. She could see the piano but
not who was playing it. It was a spooky feeling, as if a ghost
were in there.

The music stopped abruptly. Then a chord was played
with a flourish and the final notes echoed on the air for a
long time.

She stared intently at the piano. Any moment now whoever was playing would stand up and show their face . . .

The hands came down on her shoulders without warning
and she cried out in alarm. She spun round, her eyes wide
with fear.

Chapter 34

As Ella walked, head down, across the cracked paving of the Italian garden, she was startled by a meaningful cough. She jumped, and put her hand up to her heart. 'Dear God, Nonna, you gave me such a fright!'

Nonna was sitting in a bath chair to the left of the rose-laden archway, a black lace shawl draped across her head and shoulders to keep off the sun.

'I think you taking a long time to come and see me, so I gets my Antonio to push me over in this contraption and comes to see you instead. You going to sit and talk with me or you going to run away?'

'I've stopped running, Nonna,' Ella said with resign-ation.

'Come here to me, Ella, my Ella!' she cried, holding out her arms. Ella stooped and kissed her affectionately on both cheeks and they held each other tightly for a long time.

'It's good to see you, Nonna, it really is,' Ella said.

'You take your times, but I very glad I see you before I dies, eh?'

'Don't talk like that, Nonna. You'll be here for ever.'

'Well, I thank God that child come here and make you come out of hidings.'

'As soon as Tony rang me I came straight away. Not that

I wanted to leave Shrimp's but I was worried about her. She's not well, Nonna, she's as thin as a stick.'

'Something troubles her badly, eh? Something very deep that make her punish herself.'

'I think so. She doesn't get on with her mother. I suppose that's history repeating itself – you remember how Kizzy and her mother used to fight?'

'Mother of God, the screams that come from this place! They fighting like dogs and cats!'

'I suppose Kizzy never had much example, really. Small wonder she turned out the way she did.'

Nonna said hesitantly, 'I know it's long time ago, but when Alice decides she don't get married, is something to do with Kizzy?'

Ella was silent for a while. Then she took a deep breath and said, 'Yes, it was.'

'None of us ever knows what happen, because the next day when we come to Shrimp's you gone looking for Alice, and when you come back we don't hardly see you again.'

'I couldn't face anyone, Nonna, and I was worried to death about Alice taking off like that on her own.'

'We don't understand what happen, because Alice seem so happy to get married and then she don't turn up to her wedding.'

'There's a simple explanation, but not one that I wanted everyone to know about. On the morning of the wedding someone sent Alice some photographs.'

'She cancel the wedding because of photographs?'

'They were photographs of Kizzy and Arthur Campbell together. They were obviously taken without their knowledge, and showed them in a very compromising position.'

Nonna's hand flew to her mouth. 'Poor Alice!'

'That's why she bolted while we were at the church, so that no one could stop her.'

'Who do you think sends her the photographs?'

'It must have been that bloody Meredith, of course. He'd always had a shine for Alice, and he must have got wind of what Kizzy and Arthur were up to and started following them. He got the evidence he wanted, and the fool made sure that Alice saw it.'

'Maybe you too hard on Meredith, maybe he think he's doing the right thing.'

'Why didn't he come to me and tell me first?'

Nonna laid her hand on Ella's. 'If you knew, you don't let her run off like that.'

'Of course not.'

'But, Ella, maybe she need to go. Maybe she need to do something on her own for once.'

'I don't know, Nonna. It was so out of character.'

'What did Kizzy say about the photographs?'

'I didn't give her time to say much. I'm afraid I lost my temper and threw her out.'

'But why she go and do a terrible thing like that? She only a young girl and he an old man to her. She know he going to marry Alice, and Alice always so good to her.'

'Kizzy was like her mother: any man she set her sights on she had to have.'

'I always think Kizzy has the hare's brains but I no think she wicked like that.'

'She was worse than wicked, Nonna. When she left Shrimp's she was pregnant.'

'*Mamma mia!*' Nonna crossed herself. 'This child is Arthur Campbell's?'

Ella nodded and sighed deeply.

'And Alice, did she know of this?'

'Yes. The note that came with the photographs made sure that she did.'

'Did you ask Kizzy if it is true?'

'Like I said, I just told her to go. I couldn't bear even to look at her.'

'But Kizzy didn't marry Campbell?'

'No. She was a scatterbrain and would have driven him mad within a few days. My guess is that he agreed to support her financially, but never acknowledged the child as his.'

'And Alice? You don't think Alice would drive him mad if she became his wife?'

'Exactly. I never could work out why he was interested in Alice, apart from her looks.'

'Does Catrin know this man is her father?'

'No. Kizzy told her some nonsense about her father dying when she was a baby.'

'Who do she think is her father?'

'God only knows. She's been told that Campbell is her godfather. She doesn't know that Alice was going to marry him.'

'I very sorry, Ella, but she know now.'

'Oh, my God.'

'I just mention I remembers name of man who going to marry her Aunt Alice.'

'Has she been asking you about him? You see, when she mentioned that he was her godfather I pretended not to know him.'

'No, she don't say much. I don't think she very interested.'

'Thank God for that.'

'No one ever going to tell this poor child the truth?'

'Not me, that's for sure. She doesn't like him, for starters.'

'Maybe that why she so sick inside, because there this big secret in her life and deep down she know something not right.'

'She's an intelligent girl. I'm surprised that she hasn't

231

questioned why she has her mother's surname and not her father's.'

'It's fine bloody mess, eh, Ella?'

'It is, and I don't think the truth would necessarily help Catrin at the moment.'

'Maybe she don't get well until she know the truth and learns to live with it.'

'Or maybe knowing the truth would make her worse. You know what I'm like for blurting things out, Nonna. I'll have to keep a firm watch on my tongue while she's here.'

'Where did Alice go when she disappear?'

'That's the funny thing. I went everywhere I thought she might go but I couldn't find her, and when she finally came back she refused to say where she'd been.'

'But surely if she'd gone to friends they would have told you.'

'That's what I thought, but I never found out. She was never herself after she came back.'

'And poor Alice, she don't live long.'

'She went downhill fast. The doctor said that she'd been diabetic for some time and her heart was weakened. All the shocks didn't help her.'

'That was last time I see you, at Alice funeral. You look so ill and yet you don't want anyone to be near you. For long time I ring you on telephone, but you don't reply.'

'I'm sorry, Nonna. I wasn't even there for you when Luigi died.'

'My poor Luigi go so suddenly,' she said, wringing her hands in her lap.

'No good looking at the past and wishing, eh? That thing they call hindsight is a bastard nuisance. I just wish I'd never let Alice get involved with Campbell.'

'Ella! She a grown woman. Okay, she not like a proper

grown-up but you can't be stopping her find herself a man.'

'I suppose not, but I don't feel as if I protected her properly. There was something not right about Campbell from the start.'

'How you mean?'

'Well, the first time he and his sister came, they did nothing but complain. The food wasn't to their taste and the rooms were too warm. We were glad to see the back of them, and yet they kept returning time after time.'

'He come back second time to see Alice?'

'No. When I think back it was really odd the way he settled on Alice. He'd never given her a second glance. I mean, he looked her up and down – all men looked at Alice, but once they realised she was slow-witted it put them all off, apart from Meredith. Dr Campbell was the same as the rest of them.'

'When he start noticing Alice?'

'Well, out of the blue, on one of his visits he started paying her compliments, then he pursued her relentlessly. When he went back to London he telephoned every day, sent flowers and wrote her soppy letters. It was all very odd.'

'And she is flattered?'

'Absolutely. She worshipped the ground he walked on. She was forever sending him silly little gifts and walking about like she was on cloud nine. She even gave him one of her daft things from her dowry box. God, she must have been in pieces when she saw those photographs.'

'Did she ever speak of him when she come back?'

'Not a word – that is, not until the day she died.'

'What did she say?' Nonna leant forward, consumed with interest.

'She said something very strange: "Arthur Campbell must never ever find out about the children."'

'What children?'

'God knows. She was rambling, slipping in and out of consciousness most of the time. It was just the fever talking, I daresay. She died a few hours later.'

Suddenly the rooks set up their squawking above the trees of Gwartney's Wood, and far off on Duffy's Farm the old donkey brayed in answer.

There was silence for a while. Then Ella said, 'It's a shame your Tony has never met a nice girl.'

'There no one here in Kilvenny he take a fancy for. I think at one time he have little shine for Kizzy.'

Ella looked up in surprise. 'You did?'

'They was always whispering together and sending notes that last summer.'

'You don't think they . . .'

'No, Kizzy don't have no interest in him, only like a brother. I worry about him, though, because he not happy.'

'He seems okay to me.'

'The Café Romana is in bad way. Not many customers, and I don't think he can keep on much longer, but he worrying about what will happen to me,' Nonna said wearily.

'What do you think he'll do?'

'The Good God only knows,' Nonna said. 'It's time I go back now, but tell Catrin that Antonio find the old ice-cream maker in the cellar – she say she want to make ice cream.'

'I don't know about making ice cream, she could do with eating it to fatten herself up.' Ella said. 'She likes to make food, Nonna, it's eating it that's the problem.'

'Is not food that is the problem. Something deep inside is troubling her. She only using the food as a weapon.'

'A weapon?'

'Something wrong in her life and she can't mend it. She don't know, maybe, what it is that troubles her. She only in charge of one bit of her life – what she eat and what she don't eat.'

'You're a wise old bird, Nonna. I just hope she'll get over this.'

'*Tutto è possibile*,' Nonna said, nodding sagely.

'Your Luigi always used to say that but I never thought to ask him what it meant,' Ella said.

'In English it is "Everything is possible."'

Chapter 35

Catrin was too startled to speak and her heart was threatening to burst out through her T-shirt as she stared up into the face of Meredith Evans, who stared unflinchingly back at her.

He opened his mouth to speak then closed it again.

'You fool! I could have had a heart attack!' she said angrily.

'I'm sorry. I didn't mean to startle you.'

'Well, you did. What were you doing in there, anyway? The hotel is private property.'

'I was just checking the place was okay, and it seemed such a shame that no one plays the piano any more, so I had a go. It used to be so lovely up here.'

'How did you get in?' she asked frostily.

'There's a door at the back near the servants' staircase that's never locked. I always go in that way.'

Catrin glared at him.

'You mean you go in there without Aunt Ella knowing?'

He smiled sheepishly.

'Was it you hiding in the wardrobe the other day?'

'No.'

She didn't believe him.

He rummaged in his trouser pocket and pulled out a

crumpled, yellowing leaflet which he handed to her. On the front cover was a picture of Shrimp's Hotel as it had once looked. Catrin looked in amazement at the mown lawns and the neat flowerbeds bursting with blooms. There were tables set out and a smiling maid in a black and white uniform was carrying a tray laden with cakes.

She opened the leaflet and saw a photograph of two women, Alice and Ella Grieve. She drew in her breath with a whistle.

Ella looked utterly different; her hair was cut in a curly bob and she was dressed in a pair of trousers and a fisherman's sweater, and was smiling widely as she held up an enormous fish.

Beside her Alice was dressed in a flowery frock, her shoulder-length hair held in place with two clips. She was smiling sweetly but her eyes had a vacant, dreamy look as though she were somewhere far away. Nonna was right about Alice and Ella; they might be twins but they were like chalk and cheese.

'She was so pretty,' Meredith said, looking over Catrin's shoulder. 'Anyway, I'm sorry I frightened you.'

She regarded him warily.

'I'd prefer it if you didn't mention to Ella that I've been inside Shrimp's. It's for her own good, you know. I've kept an eye on her for years now on the quiet. In an isolated old place like this, anything could happen.'

Once again she didn't believe him.

Meredith ran his long fingers through his lank hair, then turned on his heel and lumbered away towards Kilvenny. Catrin decided she wouldn't say anything to Ella, but she'd keep her eye on Meredith Evans. When she was sure he had gone, she let herself into Shrimp's and wandered through the gloomy rooms, every creak of the floorboards and rattle of the windows making her nervous. She trailed her fingers across the piano keys, listening to the echo of the notes hanging on the air.

She found the visitors' book in the kitchen and took it up to Alice's room, where she made herself comfortable in a chair, lighting a candle for the day had grown darker.

She was looking for signs of Arthur Campbell and his sister staying here. There was definitely something fishy about him wanting to marry Alice and something mysterious about what had gone on the summer of Alice's wedding. And it had something to do with her mother. Kizzy had done something terrible to Aunt Alice and Ella had never forgiven her and she'd never come back. Sure as eggs is eggs, Aunt Ella wasn't going to tell Catrin what had happened, but she was determined to find out.

Maybe her mother was a thief. Or a murderer. Catrin shivered.

She turned back to the book and came across an entry in July 1944 for a Dr Arthur Campbell and a Miss Deirdre Campbell. The address given was the house where he still lived, where Catrin went to visit him in the holidays. Alongside the entry, in Arthur Campbell's familiar handwriting, were the words: *Food rather rich. Rooms overheated. Water in the swimming pool too cold.*

That was typical of him; he was so fussy that nothing was ever good enough for him.

She turned the pages until she came across another entry for the Campbells. It was strange that he'd come to a place like this because he hardly ever went on holiday – he said holidays were a waste of time and took him away from his important work.

Next to this entry he had written, *Disappointed not to have our usual rooms, particularly as the rain was incessant throughout our stay.*

If he had disliked the place so much, why did he keep

coming back? And why mention the rain? Surely there must have been a roof on the room, unless there was a hole in it? On one of these visits he had met Alice and fallen in love with her. Catrin shook her head in exasperation; that couldn't be right.

She put the book down, opened the bureau and looked inside. There wasn't anything much of interest, a pad of headed notepaper, some blotting paper, a bundle of pens and pencils held together with string. There were a few old postcards with faded writing and a pile of yellowing bills on a spike all stamped PAID IN FULL.

It was hard to make any sense of the things she'd found out since she'd been here. Alice Grieve had been going to marry Arthur Campbell, but something made her change her mind at the last minute and she'd left him standing at the altar and run away. Aunt Ella and Nonna couldn't have known what Alice was planning, because they were waiting for her in the chapel, expecting the wedding to go ahead.

Absentmindedly Catrin picked up an old calendar and flicked through the leaves. It was dated 1946, the year before she was born. There was something nagging at her brain, something that didn't add up. She dropped the calendar back into the bureau and stood lost in thought. Her mother had been at Alice's wedding in the summer of 1946. Catrin was born in 1947, so in the summer of 1946 her mother would have already been – she swallowed hard and tried to batten down her unwelcome thoughts – would have already been pregnant. If she was pregnant she must have been married, and her husband would probably have been here for the wedding. It was a warming thought: her father sitting in the chapel next to her mother, waiting for Alice to arrive in her beautiful ivory dress. But of course she hadn't arrived, and that had something to do with her mother.

All this thinking was driving her mad, making her temples throb painfully.

She rummaged about in the drawer of the bureau and found an old letter from a florist's shop in Swansea agreeing to deliver the flowers for the forthcoming wedding of Miss Alice Grieve on Saturday, 15 July 1946. Another letter, from a school in Kent, told Miss Ella Grieve that Katherine Grieve would be escorted to Paddington station by a Miss Penhaligon and would be arriving at Kilvenny on the midday train on 8 July 1946.

She slammed the drawer shut and stood absolutely still, anger welling up inside her. Then she made her way up to the attics.

She stood in the gathering dusk, an orange-red glow creeping into the room, pooling in a palette of merging colours all around her. She picked up the discarded red dress and held it up in front of her. The material was faded, riddled with moth holes, and in the dying light it was almost see-through. She ran the scalloped hem through her fingers and she knew without a doubt that this was the poppy-red dress that Kizzy was wearing in the photograph downstairs, the dress Nonna had described her wearing at the wedding.

Catrin looked at the label in the frock; it was from a dress shop in Knightsbridge where her mother still bought clothes for special occasions. Kizzy would never have left behind an expensive dress like this unless she'd been in a terrific hurry. Had she rushed back here from the chapel, changed as quickly as she could, packed her things and left, never to return? It looked like it: there were rotting stockings hanging over a chair back, a spilt bottle of her mother's favourite perfume.

The dress slipped through her fingers to the floor and as if in a trance she crossed the room to the rickety wardrobe and

240

yanked the door open. Old clothes steeped in dust hung on rattling hangers, reeking of mildew. She lifted out a washed-out school blazer, the silver buttons tarnished with rust; a withered nametag on the collar read *Katherine Grieve*. How strange to think of her mother as a schoolgirl. She put the blazer back and lifted out a blue gingham dress with an ink stain across the bodice. She couldn't imagine her mother wearing these drab clothes; she was always so glamorous and particular about her appearance. Her mind went back to speech day last year, when Sister Lucy had thought Kizzy was Catrin's sister because she looked so young. Catrin had a vision of her in the refectory clutching a cup of tea, standing out like an exotic bird, incongruous and awkward in the midst of the other mothers with their perms, muted twin-sets and sensible skirts. Kizzy had been nearly nineteen when she had Catrin, eighteen when she left school in the summer of 1946.

She put her hand to her mouth to stop herself crying out.

Kizzy must have been pregnant while she was still at school, but if she was pregnant she must have been married. She couldn't have been the sort of woman who would have a baby without having a ring on her finger. That was unthinkable. There were words for women like that: trollop and tart, slut and slag.

But when could Kizzy have got married? She couldn't have married while she was still a schoolgirl, and the letter downstairs said she would be arriving back from school on 8 July, only a week before Aunt Alice's wedding.

That was stupid. She was muddling herself up with all the dates, looking for problems where there weren't any. There must be some sort of explanation.

There wasn't.

If her mother hadn't been married, that meant Catrin was illegitimate.

Or, as Mary Donahue would say, a bastard.

One of the Palfrey twins had asked her once why she had her mother's surname and not her father's. Catrin had explained patiently, just as Kizzy had to her, that she had taken her mother's surname because her father was foreign and he'd thought she might get teased having a name that was hard to pronounce.

The girl had given her a strange, knowing look and whispered to her twin, and then they'd run away together, snorting and sniggering

Why had she been so stupid and accepted Kizzy's explanations without questioning them? The more she thought about it, the more she realised how blind she'd been, how she'd ignored all the clues that had been staring her in the face. Her cheeks reddened as she recalled Sister Lucy, on her first day at school, taking her birth certificate off her mother and the long, cold look she'd given Kizzy as she'd handed it back.

Everyone had known and they must have been laughing at her behind her back.

She slammed the bedroom door and hurtled down the stairs, through the kitchen and out into the fresh air. She bent double, began retching into the long grass, then, gasping for breath and blinded by tears, ran headlong back towards Kilvenny. The sky was darkening and the gulls wheeled above her head in a screaming frenzy.

Chapter 36

Ismelda lay back in the bathtub and looked up at the ceiling, where a lizard was patiently waiting for a fly to settle. How wonderful it would be to be able to walk upside down like a lizard. How she would love to be able to walk across the ceiling, climb over the high walls that surrounded the Villa Rosso, maybe even to the top of the church tower, and look down on the village. She sighed; she would never be let out, just be kept cooped up here, bored and lonely.

She rubbed the coarse bar of lemon-scented soap between her hands until she had a good lather going. She made a circle with her thumb and forefinger and blew gently into the film of soap as Maria had taught her to do. A bubble grew slowly, wobbling dangerously, growing bigger and bigger until she could see her distorted reflection in its quivering brilliance.

It was magic. There she was inside the bubble. A girl with a big head and a small body, a little like the lovely Bindo.

Papa said that Bindo was a freak of nature, a monstrosity. Papa could be so silly. Bindo was just a boy put together differently. He was warm and funny and kind and, unlike some people, he told the truth. You didn't have to search for the truth with Bindo; it rolled off his tongue like warm honey off a spoon.

She blew another bubble and watched it float up on the warm currents of air. She giggled. Two Ismeldas. One here in the bath and one up there in the bubble. She blew a third bubble and watched as it broke loose and wafted upwards. It hovered for a moment, then touched the wall and popped.

She blew more bubbles and watched with envy as one drifted between the bars of the high window and out into the garden. The other Ismelda had escaped and soon she would be blowing over the high villa walls, away across the piazza, over the heads of the stone cherubs that the artist had made. Higher and higher she would fly, away down the valley, past the Convent of Santa Lucia where the mad people were sent ... drifting far away, even as far as the sea.

What would Papa say if he knew that she could conjure herself up many times? Didn't he always say that one of her was enough for anyone? Poor Papa. He was such an old misery.

She heard someone passing under the window, humming as he went. It was Father Rimaldi.

She didn't like Father Rimaldi. He smelt horrible and he told lies with his eyes without his lips knowing.

'It's good to see you, Ismelda,' his lips said when he saw her at early mass. His eyes said it wasn't good to see her at all. Once she had seen him kick a donkey in the piazza when no one was looking.

She washed herself more quickly, not forgetting the back of her neck or inside her ears, for Maria was sure to check. After her bath, if she behaved herself and didn't start her antics, she might be allowed out to play in the garden on her own. She must keep quiet, though, because Papa would be taking his after-breakfast nap on the upstairs balcony.

Papa couldn't bear it when she made a noise and he was always saying, 'Why can't you be like other little girls?' Like the silly Zanelli girls, he meant. The sort of girls who spent all day brushing their hair or preening and prissing in front of a looking glass. She didn't give an oxen's fart for that kind of nonsense. Oh no. When she was allowed out to play she pranced around like a performing monkey, she jigged and whooped and cartwheeled across the grass. She had even tried to swim in the grand fountain that Papa had had built last summer. She had stripped right down to her baggy drawers and frolicked like a drunken mermaid. Papa had gone berserk and screamed that she was strange in the head and should be locked up for her own safety.

She did know how she was supposed to behave most of the time, it was just that it was much more fun not to. Besides, it was tiring to be good, and hard to keep clean when the world was such an exciting but dirty place.

There were so many rules to remember. Why would she want to sip from a cup when you could tip the whole lot down your throat in one hot, gurgling gulp? If you jumped up and down, you could hear the liquid slopping around in your belly.

Going to mass was one of the worst of all things. Maria and Papa always took her to the earliest mass when there were few people around, and she was always wedged tightly between them.

Stand up. Kneel down. Beat your chest. Be quiet. Sing. Don't sing.

At that special moment in the mass when Christ was present you were supposed to sit with a bowed head. Why, when you knew that all around you the statues were opening their eyes in wonder, the gargoyles pursing their lips to sing and the light dancing in through the windows?

'Stop fidgeting, Ismelda,' Papa would mutter. 'Keep your hands in your lap.'

When all she wanted to do was reach out and catch the fizzing dust motes that floated around her.

Today she was going to sneak a spoon out of the kitchen, dig down as far as she could in the garden and see if she could find some treasures to stash away in her secret box. She might find a bit of blue glass if she was lucky, or maybe some tiny birds' bones.

Then she might stand on her head for a while underneath the pine tree. She liked to see the world from upside down.

She stood up in the bath and shook herself the way she'd seen dogs shake themselves on rainy days. Droplets of water flew off her and spattered the floor and walls. She stepped over the edge of the tub and planted her feet on the floor.

She lifted them up and looked at her wet footprints. She walked round the room, looking in delight at the patterns her feet made. After her bath she would help Maria carry out the tub and tip the soapy water on to the path and watch as the thirsty sun sucked it up.

She pulled on her robe, tied the belt clumsily and tiptoed to the window.

If she climbed on to the stool and on to the wicker box where the lemon soap was stored, she could look out into the piazza. It was her secret: the only time she was able to see the outside world.

She peered inquisitively out, though her view through the small barred window was restricted. She saw the widow Zanelli walking towards the Via Dante. Ismelda wrinkled her nose. Maria had told her all about the widow Zanelli, how she had nagged her husband until his ears melted inwards and his face wrinkled up like a pickled walnut; had nagged and moaned until the poor man gave up the ghost and died.

The widow Zanelli held her head high but she waddled from side to side as if she had piddled herself and it hadn't yet dried. With her were her two daughters, the ones Papa was always talking about.

Oh, such a pretty pair. So neat and dainty. So kind to their mother. Poor little girls without a papa of their own.

Ismelda spat through the window. Then she clambered off the box, dressed hurriedly and went to find Maria.

Maria threw up her arms and rolled her eyes. 'Holy Mother of God. Are you sick?'

Ismelda shook her head and smiled.

'Why, you haven't even fussed about what you are wearing. Usually you are running around naked and I am trying to catch

246

*you. Maybe at last you are growing sensible. All those candles
I light for you in the church are doing some good, eh?'*

'Can I go out into the garden and play?'

'Sì, but you behave, you hear? No cursing or singing. Your
papa is in a very bad mood.'

'Papa is always in a very bad mood.'

'Well, today it's a worse one because he can't find that blessed
cat of his and the widow Zanelli told him that Bindo was chasing
it through the village yesterday.'

Ismelda hid a smile behind her hand. The cat, Pipi, was the bane
of her life. Sometimes he pissed outside the door of her room and
the stink was terrible for days. When he shat in the garden there
were white worms wriggling in the steamy volcanoes he left
behind. The only good thing about the cat was that it hated Father
Rimaldi and when the priest came to the villa and got too close to
Pipi he bared his rotten teeth, and then he pounced and scratched,
spat and hissed like a tiger. Animals were very clever like that;
they were good judges of character.

Chapter 37

Ella, coming in from the kitchen garden carrying an armful of freshly picked runner beans, stood back as Catrin hurtled past. She called out to her but Catrin was already racing up the stairs and a moment later the bedroom door slammed shut and the key turned in the lock. What could have upset her like that? That bloody Meredith had better not have opened his big mouth and said anything to her. If he had, Ella would fill his trap for him. Ella went quietly upstairs and stood outside the bedroom door, listening to the unbridled sobbing. She turned reluctantly away; it was probably best to leave her for now.

Catrin lay on the bed, her ribs heaving with emotion, her heart thumping wildly. She was never speaking to her mother again – never going back to school, either. How could she look any of the girls in the face, knowing what she did now? God, it was so awful. Everyone must have known that her mother wasn't married and that she'd done a terrible thing and had a baby before she was married. It was shameful, horrible. Disgusting. Arthur Campbell and his snooty wife probably knew, too, and Aunt Ella and everyone else in Kilvenny. Why had her stupid, stupid mother told her a pack of lies, made such a fool out of her?

Oh God, she'd rather be dead than ... than like she was now. She was a bloody *bastard* and that's why no one liked her at school except for Mary Donahue – and the Palfrey twins said Mary didn't count because ...

She didn't count because she was a scholarship girl from a poor family, a rough family, who had her fees paid by a charity. Her mother had run off when she was a baby and her father was a good-for-nothing who spent most of his money on gambling and strong drink. But at least Mary *had* a father.

When Catrin eventually stopped crying, sat up, and wiped the tears from her face, she saw a letter lying on her pillow. There was only one person it could be from, and she couldn't care less about how her mother was. She hoped the bloody nuns at Santa Lucia had put the evil eye on her, or locked her up in a cell with bars on the windows. Or even better that she was sick, lying dying on her bed of straw begging for forgiveness for what she'd done. She snatched up the letter. It took up one thin sheet of paper, and had clearly been written in haste.

> Hotel Paradiso
> Via Rafaela

Dear Catrin,

At last I am back in civilisation – well, almost. I managed to borrow a little money from an English traveller who came to the convent the other day, so I have been able to escape. It wasn't a moment too soon, either, as I was half starved and bored witless. There is a limit to how many times one can sit through mass and benediction in one day. I have been feeling quite poorly ever since I left there, which is probably due to the fact that I had to do all my own washing and scrub and polish half the day in return for my keep. I never want to set foot inside a convent again as long as I live.

I am staying here for as long as my money lasts, but I need money *NOW!*

Mummy

It would be lovely to see Kizzy getting her hands dirty! Kizzy the scrubber! Catrin screwed the letter into a tight ball and dashed it down on the floor.

'Sod my mother!'

She'd a good mind to find out the telephone number of the Hotel Paradiso, ring her blasted mother and tell her exactly what she thought of her. She'd tell her that she, Catrin, wasn't as stupid as Kizzy thought, that she knew that everything she'd been told was a pack of lies ... that Kizzy was a dirty, loose woman who'd had a baby without bothering to get married. All that stuff about her father dying when she was a baby was probably made up, too. She pulled the pillow over her head and began to sob again until her eyes burnt and her throat felt as if it would close over.

Later, when she was calmer, she climbed beneath the covers and opened *Recipes for Cherubs*. As she turned the pages the smell of lemons seemed to seep into the room and she felt as if someone was in the room with her, yet she didn't feel in the least afraid. Wasn't that how Alice had felt? She held the book tightly and thought how strange it was that Aunt Alice had held it, too, and turned the pages desperately looking for clues.

She looked closely at each page, trying to fathom what Alice had seen and why she had thought there were clues hidden there which would point her towards the treasure. And what was the treasure?

The painting on the last page was one of Catrin's favourites: a beautiful garden surrounded by a high wall. There was a large pomegranate tree laden with ripe fruit, and to the left of the tree was a fountain where a plump cherub stood on a plinth, spitting a stream of water into the air.

There was a wooden bin set against the wall and a fat white cat was curled up on top of it, basking in the sunlight. She looked more closely, and saw what looked like a soap bubble drifting away over the wall.

Beyond her latticed bedroom window the enormous sun began to sink, and a soft pink light washed the room. Catrin laid down the book and closed her eyes.

She imagined that she was lying beneath the pomegranate tree, listening to the birdsong, sunlight filtering through the branches, the ripening pomegranates above her like planets in orbit ... the drone of fat bees weighed down with pollen, and all around her the smell of lemons and herbs growing stronger as the sun rose higher and higher. She could hear children's laughter ... Ismelda, Bindo and Luca Roselli somewhere not far away. Maria Paparella was singing in a croaky tuneless voice and a hand softly caressed her warm cheek, gently wiping away her tears and smoothing her forehead. The lazy trickle of water from the fountain was so soothing and the cat was purring contentedly ...

She opened her eyes and let out a cry of surprise. Alice Grieve might have been simple but not that bloody simple. She opened the book again and found the painting of Santa Rosa in the snow, the four naked cherubs in the fountain in the piazza looking up through cascades of frozen water.

Bloody Nora! No wonder Alice had always had her head stuck in Theodora Sprenker's book.

She leapt off the bed, tucked the book inside her cardigan, unlocked the door and raced headlong down the stairs, almost colliding with Aunt Ella, who had been hovering nervously about waiting to see how Catrin was.

'I was just coming up to see if you were all right,' Ella said, her face etched with concern.

'Oh, I'm fine. I can't stop now. I need to go over to the library. I won't be long.' She gave Ella a brief smile and was gone.

Ella watched her, dumbfounded. An hour ago she had been breaking her heart, sobbing fit to bust, and now her eyes, though still swollen, were bright with excitement, and her cheeks unusually flushed.

The door of the library was open but there was no sign of Dan Gwartney, although the fire was lit and the gas lamps turned on. The book by Theodora Sprenker was still on the table near the window and she turned the pages excitedly until she came to the section on Santa Rosa. 'It is a charming if dilapidated medieval place with narrow streets and a pretty cobbled piazza with a fountain graced by a trio of splendid cherubs.'

'A trio of splendid cherubs'! When Theodora Sprenker visited Santa Rosa there had been only three in the fountain, but in the painting in *Recipes for Cherubs* there were four. She opened the book and looked again at the winter painting, and there, sure enough, were four cherubs standing beneath the cascades of frozen water.

So at some point one of the cherubs had been removed. But why?

Deep in thought she closed the books, slipped *Recipes for Cherubs* back inside her cardigan and left the library. She looked up and down Cockle Lane, but it was dark and deserted except for a light burning dimly in Meredith Evans's shop. She scurried across the road and through the archway into the Italian garden.

The scent of roses was heady in the night air and the little cherub, silvered by moonlight, stood alone in his water-less fountain, staring up at the stars. She touched his outstretched arm, traced the outline of the tiny, splayed fingers and thought how extraordinary it was that this little fellow should end up in Kilvenny, hundreds of miles from Santa Rosa. She was sure that Alice had realised this was the missing fourth Santa Rosa cherub. She wished there was a way of knowing how much Alice had found out and how far she had got in unravelling the clues.

Meredith had said that Alice's mother, Hester, had burnt the book. But of course she hadn't. Alice and her family had gone to live up at Shrimp's, and Alice was afraid of Hester and didn't come down to the castle after that.

The man who was going to marry Aunt Alice had started raking all the business about the book up again and had been probing and prodding her like a specimen. And that man was Arthur Campbell!

Catrin sat down abruptly on the bench, her thoughts racing. Arthur Campbell would never have married someone like Alice unless ... unless he wanted something, and maybe that something was the secret that Alice knew about Kilvenny. If Arthur Campbell wanted something badly enough, he usually got it. He wasn't a man to suffer fools gladly, and he wouldn't have been able to cope with someone like Alice as his wife, but did marrying her mean that he would get something? Only he hadn't married Alice, because for some reason she'd run away and left him standing at the altar.

She stood up, went across to the chapel and stepped nervously inside. It was dark, a pool of moonlight shining on the altar, the faint smell of incense and burnt-down candles hanging on the air.

It was here that Arthur Campbell had stood waiting for Alice to arrive. Kizzy was here, too, wearing the expensive poppy-red dress that she was to discard later before she left Shrimp's for ever. Kizzy who had done something terrible to Alice, something that Ella had never forgiven her for. Kizzy Grieve, her mother, not long arrived back from school but already pregnant. Arthur's so-called sister would have been here, too. Everyone had been waiting for Alice ...

As she tried to think, snatches of the song Meredith Evans had been playing at Shrimp's kept reverberating inside her head,

'Oh, soldier, soldier, won't you marry me ...?'

If Alice had found out something that made her change her mind about marrying Arthur, why hadn't she just cancelled the wedding? Why let everyone turn up? Unless something had happened at the very last minute.

'Oh no, sweet maid, I cannot marry thee for I have a wife of my own.'

A rustling near the back of the chapel startled her, and she was sure there was someone hiding in the shadows, watching her. She tiptoed back down the aisle, paused half-way; there was definitely someone there, someone who didn't want to be seen. She slipped thankfully outside and looked around for a hiding place, because whoever was in there would have to come out soon, and there was no other way out of the chapel.

She wriggled in among the ivy until she was hidden from view but could still see the chapel door. An owl called in Gwartney's Wood and a bat swooped down into the Italian garden. She could hear the wireless in the kitchen and for a moment she longed to be inside with Aunt Ella and not hiding, quivering with fright out here in the garden.

The chapel door opened slowly and a head looked out cautiously. Then a cloud drifted across the moon and, though she strained her eyes, she could not see who it was.

The cloud moved on and there in the moonlight was a man stealthily crossing the courtyard. She wriggled further into the ivy and almost cried out when her back pressed against something hard.

There was a clanking in the distance and a low rumbling nearby.

The man stopped, startled by the noise, and as if on cue a lazy spurt of water gurgled out of the cherub's mouth and splashed down on the dried leaves and rubbish.

Catrin held her breath, felt behind her and realised that she'd leant against a lever which had turned on the water. The man stood quite still, silhouetted in the moonlight. A faceless man wearing a wide-brimmed hat who reminded her of the painting of the ugly Father Rimaldi.

'Jesus!' the man muttered, staring in alarm at the fountain.

The voice was strangely familiar and yet she couldn't put a name to it. The shadowy figure disappeared soundlessly through the archway, looking over his shoulder nervously.

When she was sure he'd gone she slid out of her hiding place and tiptoed across to the fountain. The cherub glistened with water in the moonlight, a steady spume of water rising from his long-parched mouth. Maybe it was a sign that she was on the right track. If only he could talk and tell her his story!

She made her way through the gardens and peered around the wall just in time to see the door of Meredith Evans's shop closing quietly.

A cough nearby made her jump until she saw with relief that it was only Dan Gwartney.

'Sorry, girl, I didn't mean to startle you like that. There's a bag of nerves you are.'

'I'm okay. I just had a fright, and I didn't see you coming.'

'What frightened you?'

She could hardly say she'd been hiding in the ivy, watching a man creeping through the garden, so she said, 'I was walking through the Italian garden and the fountain suddenly started working. It scared me, that's all.'

'Well, well. It's a sign, maybe.'

'What sort of sign?'

'That you've come home and that you're welcome in the castle. I see you were over in the library earlier. Did you find what you wanted?'

'Yes, thanks.'

'And what was it you wanted to know?'

'Er, I just wanted to read about Santa Rosa again.'

'Well, any time you need something, just pop over. I'm off up to Shrimp's to check that everything's all right.'

She was about to tell him that Meredith had been up at Shrimp's but Pedro the cat came running up from the beach, wailing like a stuck pig, and seeing Dan, leapt into his arms, almost knocking him backwards.

'There, there, Pedro. I expect the daft old devil's been stalking crabs again and got a pinch on the nose for his trouble.'

The cat was purring in Dan's arms, its eyes blazing like meteors in the darkness.

'Goodnight, Dan.'

' 'Night.'

He walked away towards the beach, talking to the cat as he went.

Chapter 38

In the garden, Ismelda took out the tin box she kept hidden behind the peelings bin. She stuffed it down the bodice of her dress and climbed lithely up into the pomegranate tree. Hidden from view among the branches, she opened the box and surveyed her treasures. The sun broke through the branches, and the silver ring flashed with a blinding brilliance. She held it in the palm of her hand and shivered with pleasure. Then she put it carefully into the pocket of her baggy drawers. Next she picked out a seashell and held it to her nose. She'd heard tales of the sea from Maria, who had an uncle who lived in Napoli. He had told Maria that in Napoli there was always the wonderful smell of salt and freshly caught fish.

She pressed the shell to her ear and listened intently. At first she heard only a faint hissing, then the magic began: the music of waves lapping against the shore and the screaming of sea birds wheeling in a blue sky. She closed her eyes. Oh, one day maybe she'd escape from the Villa Rosso. She imagined walking across the piazza hand in hand with Maria and Bindo, climbing into a donkey cart and riding away down the steep road that led to the faraway sea and the rest of the world. One day, please God . . .

There was a noise, a soft footfall in the grass, and Ismelda stiffened. She peered through the branches and saw with dismay Papa's fat white cat, Pipi, slinking through the garden towards the tree. The bloody thing would give her away if it saw her. The cat hated her, and whenever it came across her it growled and spat, curling those razor-sharp claws. She had scars on her legs from their past encounters.

The cat ambled towards the tree and looked up at Ismelda with its curious yellow-green eyes. It sat down, meowed and stared at her with interest.

'Pipi. Pipi! Where are you? Come to Papa. I have your fishy here waiting,' called Signor Bisotti from inside the villa.

'I've just seen him go into the garden,' Maria shouted from the kitchen.

Holy Saint Agnes's drawers! If Papa came and found the cat and looked up into the tree and saw her there, she would be dead, too.

'Pipi! Pipi! Come to Papa!'

Ismelda waved her one free arm at the cat, hissed and said, 'Shoo!' but the cat was unperturbed.

'Pipi!'

Just then a pomegranate broke away from the branch and hurtled towards the ground. It hit the cat with a thud between the eyes.

The cat keeled over on to its back. Its legs pointed towards heaven and they were as stiff as if they'd been washed and starched by the good nuns of the Santa Rosa Convent. The cat's eyes rolled, then flickered shut. The pink tongue lolled out of his mouth, his fat belly shuddered, and then he lay still.

Suffering Jesus! Papa loved that cat more than anything in the world. Maria had said that when the cat died, Papa would take him to the man in Terrini who stuffed dead animals.

Ismelda pushed her box of treasures into a cavity between the branches, dropped out of the tree, and pulled the cat into the bushes. Then she sat down hastily beneath the tree, folded her hands in the lap of her frock and assumed as angelic a pose as she could.

Signor Bisotti came out into the garden, squinting against the *bright sunlight.* 'Have you seen Pipi this morning, Ismelda?'

'Ah, sì, Papa; earlier on he was here in the garden.'

'How did he look?'

'Full of life, Papa. So happy he almost smiled at me.'

'That's good, for the widow Zanelli was telling me at mass that her daughters saw the dwarf pelting him with lemons last night.'

'Why would he want to hurt Pipi, Papa?'

'God knows. He's a law unto himself, that dwarf. It's about time he was run out of Santa Rosa. We don't need the likes of him here.'

'What do you mean, Papa, "the likes of him"?' she asked sweetly.

'He is an insult to the eye of a good Christian.'

'But, Papa, Father Rimaldi says that we must love all God's creatures, whatever they look like.'

'You might love the scorpion because God in His infinite wisdom made him, but you still wouldn't get too close. If you ask me, it's a pity the good nuns didn't put Bindo out of his misery at birth.'

'But I didn't ask you, Papa.'

'Why, girl, do you have to be so literal? You know even his own mother didn't want him.'

'But Maria says that all mothers love their children, whatever they're like.'

'Does she now? That woman says too much; she has a bell on every tooth.'

'She says that even a hard-faced old bint like the widow Zanelli loves her children, even though they are the biggest prudes God allowed to walk the earth.'

'Well, she had better mind that peasant's tongue of hers or she will be looking for work elsewhere.'

Ismelda bit her lip. She had been about to say that once, when Maria had drunk three glasses of limoncello straight off, she'd said the widow Zanelli was a calculating old bitch and that everyone in Santa Rosa knew that she and Father Rimaldi were as thick as thieves. Hadn't Maria seen with her own eyes Father Rimaldi sneaking out of the widow's house in the early hours? Signor Zanelli, God rest his soul, had gone to his grave as a dead husband but not as a father. Anyone with eyes in their head could see who those two Zanelli girls looked like.

Signor Bisotti sniffed suspiciously. 'I'm sure that dwarf is somewhere about this morning – I can smell him at ten paces. I shall sit in the shade of the pomegranate tree, and if he has the cheek to try and climb my walls and set his dirty feet in my garden, there'll be trouble with a big T.'

'But, Papa, how could a little dwarf climb over these high walls?'

'He may be little but he is cunning, as sly as a low-bellied snake, that one is. The church walls are thick and the windows narrow, but it didn't stop him getting in there. Father Rimaldi caught him with his feet up on the altar rail, swigging the communion wine.'

Ismelda coughed to stifle a giggle. 'Would you like me to fetch your hat and bring you a drink, Papa?'

'Are you well, Ismelda? Never before have you asked me if I want a drink.'

'I am quite well, Papa.'

She smiled up at his suspicious face. Hell's teeth! If he found the cat he'd be sure to blame its death on Bindo. He'd have the dwarf plucked and trussed like a market-day chicken and throw his gizzards to the crows.

Ismelda hurried into the villa and soon reappeared, carrying a large hat and a glass of water.

Signor Bisotti made himself comfortable, pulled his hat down over his eyes and settled down for a pleasant doze.

Ismelda sidled over to where she had hidden the cat in the bushes.

The cat lay still, a bubble of snot oozing out of his pink nose.

Behind her she heard soft snoring as Papa slept.

She knelt down and stared at the cat.

The pink nostrils quivered.

The bubble of snot grew larger. One malevolent eye opened and settled on Ismelda.

She flinched.

The cat snorted. The bubble burst. The cat got unsteadily to its feet and stumbled across the parched grass.

Ismelda glanced back at Papa. Still sleeping.

The cat stopped unsteadily and then slumped, legs splayed out. She must do something.

She raced into the villa and raced back. With some difficulty she lifted the cat to a sitting position.

She rubbed her fingers in front of its nose.

The cat snuffled, whiskers twitching, then it gave an ear-piercing wail.

Signor Bisotti threw off his hat and got to his feet just as the cat took off. With astonishing speed it ran in ever-decreasing circles round the garden, then shot up into the pomegranate tree, causing a shower of fruit to fall all around a startled Signor Bisotti.

Ismelda watched, her blue eyes wide with innocent wonder.

Finally the cat tired and sat down on the wall of the fountain, eyeing them both malevolently.

'It's a miracle!' Signor Bisotti shouted. 'He has a new lease of life.'

Ismelda wiped the snuff off her fingers, and smiled up at Papa. 'All those candles you have been lighting for him must have worked.' She grinned – and she sneezed loudly, twice.

The cat blinked and yawned.

Signor Bisotti and Ismelda stared in amazement at his mouth. His four large yellow teeth were gone.

'It's that bloody dwarf! Maria, fetch me my stick. I'll flay the skin off Bindo's wizened back when I get my hands on him.'

Chapter 39

Catrin was sitting on the window seat when Ella went into the kitchen.

'Something smells good in here,' said Ella.

'I made a new recipe, some biscuits called *brutti ma buoni*.'

'*Brutti ma buoni*?'

'In English it means "ugly but good". Ugly but good biscuits.'

'Well, I never. Luigi Agosti used to make them for Alice and me when we were small.' Ella took a biscuit from the plate Catrin held out to her, bit into it and sat down next to her niece.

Catrin picked up a biscuit tentatively. She'd followed the recipe to the letter. It was Bindo's recipe. Bindo the green-eyed dwarf.

'You looked upset yesterday, and I've hardly had a chance to speak to you,' Ella said hesitantly.

'I was very upset. I still am.'

'Anything I can help with?'

'I don't know.' Catrin fell silent and fiddled with biscuit crumbs in her lap.

'Aunt Ella, I found out something about me that probably everyone else already knows and it was a bit of a shock.'

Ella swallowed hard, dreading what was coming.

'You see, Aunt Ella, I'm a bastard – but I expect you know that, don't you?' Catrin said it so matter-of-factly that Ella flinched and put her hand on Catrin's arm, but the girl brushed it away.

'I've always believed all the rubbish that my mother told me about my father dying when I was small. That's a lie, isn't it?'

Ella nodded and fiddled with a loose strand of her wild hair.

'My mother wasn't married when she had me, was she?'

'Not as far as I know.'

'She was pregnant the last summer she was here?'

'Yes, she was.'

'But you don't know who my father is?'

Struggling with her conscience, Ella got up and wandered over to the window. It wasn't her place to tell the girl the truth; Kizzy needed to do that – and pretty damn soon.

'I'm afraid only your mother can tell you that.'

'I don't want to see her ever again, for as long as I live.'

'Come on, now. I expect she thought it was for the best. I don't suppose she meant to hurt you.'

'Well, she has! Everyone at school must know, and they've been laughing at me behind my back so I'm never going back there again.'

'I doubt if everyone knows.'

'Well, I know. I know that everything I've believed is a pack of lies. How could she be so spiteful, and why did she have to lie to me like that?'

'She was young, Catrin. She probably didn't know what to tell you.'

'*You're* sticking up for her now,' Catrin said.

'No, I'm not. I just don't want you to get too upset about it.'

'Upset? Of course I'm upset. I'm a bastard, and I don't

know who my father was, and I've got a mother who doesn't care about me.'

'I'm sure she does care about you in her own way.'

'She doesn't care at all, that's obvious. I'm not wanted, and I'm not good enough, I never have been.'

'Good enough for who? There's nothing wrong with you.'

'I've always embarrassed her, never been pretty enough. I used to be plump – fat, really – and I thought if I was thin I'd feel better, fit in more, but I don't and I never will because I'm a bas—'

'Enough! I don't want to hear that word again. Get a grip. You're not the first child to be born out of wedlock, and you won't be the last. It happens.'

'Why did it have to happen to me, though? It's just disgusting,' Catrin wailed.

'I don't know why it happened to you, but I know people in the same position and they've turned out all right.'

'I don't believe you.'

'Tony Agosti, for a start.'

Catrin looked up in surprise. 'Tony? Doesn't he have a father, either?'

'He doesn't have a father or a mother.'

'That's being an orphan, though, and that's not as bad as what I am.'

'His mother had Tony before she was married, and after he was born she left him here with Nonna and Luigi and buggered off.'

'What, left him for good? You mean she never came back?'

Ella sighed, and it was a while before she replied.

'No, she never came back. He was brought up by his grandparents.'

'How awful for him.'

'Not really: they loved him dearly. So you see, at least your mother didn't abandon you.'

'That's probably only because I didn't have any grand-parents she could dump me with.'

'I don't suppose it was easy for her being an unmarried mother.'

'She doesn't love me. She never wants to spend any time with me – look at the way she sent me here without even bothering to see if you minded.'

'But you're here now and, despite our shaky start, you're very welcome. Come on, have another biscuit.'

Catrin was about to refuse but, unbidden, her mind conjured up a picture of Ismelda Bisotti and Bindo sitting together beneath the pomegranate tree eating *brutti ma buoni* biscuits. Hesitantly she put the biscuit to her lips, and then popped it into her mouth and ate it. Without thinking, she took another.

Ella sat in silence, delighted to see her eating, and when she'd finished her third biscuit she took Catrin gently in her arms and hugged her close.

'You're a very lovely girl, Catrin Grieve, and don't you forget that,' she said softly.

'Aunt Ella, can I ask you a question?'

Ella braced herself, but Catrin only said, 'You know the statue in the Italian garden?'

'I do.'

'Where did it come from?'

'You are a funny one! What a strange question to ask in the midst of all your misery, but I can tell you the answer.'

'Brilliant.'

'A ship went down along the coast.'

'Do you mean the *Flino*?'

'That's right. The statue was salvaged from her and brought here. It was covered in muck and moss until my father decided to restore it and get it working.'

'Where was the *Flino* on its way from?'

'I don't know . . . somewhere abroad. If you're interested you could always look up the records in the library. There's all sorts of information in there in an old scrapbook someone put together.'

Catrin shivered with anticipation. Things were getting more mysterious and interesting by the minute.

'I see you've heard from your mother,' Ella said, nodding at the letter discarded on the window seat.

Catrin scowled. 'She's staying in a place called the Hotel Paradiso in Naples and she can stay and rot there, for all I care.'

'Do you think you should speak to her and tell her what you've found out?'

'No. I don't want to speak to her as long as I live!' Catrin said defiantly.

Ella thought that Kizzy had better make the most of her holiday, because she was going to have a difficult task on her hands when she came breezing back from Italy. Catrin had changed since she'd been here in Kilvenny, and was showing more feistiness by the day.

'Perhaps you'll feel differently, given time.'

'Oh no I won't. She can bloody well whistle!'

Chapter 40

Dan Gwartney had his head stuck in a book when Ella burst into the library. He got to his feet and went towards her.

'Ella, it's a surprise to see you. I was just thinking about pouring a drink. Come and join me.'

'I'm not staying long,' she said haughtily. 'I want to use your telephone, if that's all right.'

'Help yourself, you know where it is. Who are you ringing this time of the night?'

'Kizzy Grieve, if you must know.'

'I didn't think you were on speaking terms,' he said.

'Well, I haven't got much to say to her, but what I have got may give her a nasty shock.'

'You know where she is then?'

'Some hotel in Italy. Catrin had a letter from her today.'

'Ella, sit down for a minute and catch your breath. I'll get you a whisky and while you're drinking it I'll ring the operator and find out the number.'

Ella sank thankfully in a chair and took the proffered drink without protest. 'She's staying at the Hotel Paradiso, near Naples.'

'What's she doing there?'

'Visiting some man or other, I expect.'

Dan raised his eyebrows, then left the room, and a few

minutes later she heard him shouting down the line to the operator.

When he came back Ella had finished her drink and he poured her another one without giving her time to refuse.

'The line isn't very good but I'll try again in a minute, get a connection, and then you can talk to Kizzy. How is Catrin?'

'Up and down, you know,' she said, determined not to give anything away.

'She comes over here quite a bit. She likes to read, which is nice to see in this day and age.'

'That reminds me, can I borrow that scrapbook with all the cuttings about the *Flino*?'

'You taking up history as a hobby?' he teased.

'Hardly. Catrin's interested in it, and I thought it might take her mind off things a bit.'

'What things would they be?'

Ella pursed her lips and was about to retort angrily that he hadn't changed and was still a nosy old bugger, when the telephone rang, an insistent ring which made Ella flinch.

'I'll take that and call you when she's on the line.'

Ella drained her drink and then helped herself to another; she needed fortifying before she gave Kizzy a piece of her mind.

Dan came back in looking crestfallen.

'Sorry, Ella. I got through to the hotel, but it seems that Kizzy left this morning without leaving a forwarding address.'

'Bugger! I'd got myself all wound up to give her a flea in her ear, and she's flown the coop.'

'Is there any other way you can get in touch with her?'

'Not as far as I know. Thanks for the drink, anyway.'

'I'll just get you that scrapbook.'

He searched through the drawers of a large chest and

produced a battered old scrapbook. 'This hasn't seen the light of day in a good few years. If you could sign for it in the members' ledger I'd be grateful.'

The telephone rang again, and Dan excused himself.

Ella opened the ledger and turned the pages until she came to her own name, surprised he hadn't erased her from the book considering how long she'd been away. She signed for the book and then flicked through the pages until she came to a section in the back for temporary member-ships; a lot of the guests from Shrimp's used to join while they were on their holidays. Looking down the list she saw a name which made her breathe unevenly. There was the once-familiar copperplate handwriting.

Oh God, how excited she used to be when a letter arrived with her name and address written in that distinctive hand.

She snapped the book shut and leant heavily on the table. It was all a long time ago and there was no good getting upset about the past. One had to let go and yet . . .

She straightened up and turned to see Dan standing in the doorway watching her.

'Are you all right, Ella?'

'Fine. I'm fine.'

'Do you want me to see you home?'

'Do I look like a woman who needs escorting across the bloody road?' she asked sharply.

'Now, now, Ella, mind your tongue.'

'You know me, Dan. Wasn't it you who always said I was as rough as a badger's arse?'

'I think my actual words were "as rough as a badger's arse and twice as prickly".'

Ella grunted and drained the last of her whisky.

'Goodnight, Ella.'

But the door had already closed.

Chapter 41

A rook perched on one of the small stone crosses in the graveyard eyed Catrin askance and, with a strident cry, flew up into the trees.

Sitting down between the crosses, resting her back against the wall, she opened the scrapbook that Ella had given her at breakfast this morning. Someone had painstakingly stuck in an old newspaper article, some handwritten reports and ink drawings.

She read the faded newsprint and learnt that the *Flino* had set sail from Napoli carrying a cargo of fruit and wine and eight passengers. She had got into difficulties when a storm blew up unexpectedly, bringing thirty-foot waves which swamped her decks. She had hit the rocks, started taking on water and been listing dangerously. When the villagers of Kilvenny had seen her in difficulty, they'd tried valiantly to save those on board. A few passengers had managed to scramble into a rowing boat, but it had capsized and those who had clung perilously to it were soon swept away to their deaths in the freezing water. Many of the dead were washed up days later on to the beaches around Kilvenny. One body was washed up along the coast at Aberderi and was dragged up the beach by the cockle women. The captain, Antonio Ravello, who had survived against all the odds, identified those who had perished.

There was a black-and-white sketch of the *Flino* as she floundered in heavy seas beneath a glowering sky. There was another of shadowy, windswept figures stumbling up the beach carrying grown men on their backs, others buckling under the load of barrels and crates. A third showed a priest kneeling, holding the hand of someone who lay lifeless on the beach; the priest's hand was raised as if giving the last rites.

There was a newspaper report of people coming from far and wide to see what they could loot from the stricken vessel. Another report described a fight which had broken out outside the Bug and Bucket over a barrel of wine, and another in the grounds of Kilvenny Castle over ownership of a mysterious object later revealed to be a watermelon – for days after the *Flino* sank the sea was choked with olives, limes, lemons and pomegranates.

The villagers rallied round and gave shelter to those who were injured, and Nathaniel Grieve put some of the most badly injured survivors up in the old tower of the castle. One man and his heavily pregnant wife took shelter in a half-derelict house above the beach and lived there for many years after.

Catrin read through all the reports and snippets of inform-ation, but nothing struck her as being of great importance.

She put down the scrapbook, took her penknife from her pocket, knelt down in front of one of the crosses and began to scrape away the thick moss from the stone until she had uncovered the roughly engraved name hidden beneath: Orazio Russo. She set doggedly to work on the next cross until she could read another name: Agatina Marino. How sad that they had lost their lives so far from home and their families.

She was sweating by the time she had uncovered four

names, but she kept going. The next grave was the one with the posy of weeds and wild flowers. It was strange that someone should still lay flowers after all this time. There couldn't be anyone left living who remembered the passengers on the *Flino*.

She didn't know what she expected to find; the name she uncovered made her heart lurch painfully.

It was unbearably sad to see his name inscribed on a forgotten cross in a village graveyard hundreds of miles from Santa Rosa. How tragic to think that such a young boy should have lost his life when the *Flino* went down.

She traced the name with her finger, closed her eyes and tried to bring his face into her mind; a handsome boy sitting beneath a pomegranate tree, in the garden of the Villa Rosso, smiling as if everything was right with the world.

A shiver made its way up her backbone, a frisson of fear growing stronger until her whole body began to tremble.

She glanced across at Alice Grieve's grave. Although she'd never met Aunt Alice, they had something in common: a fascination with an old Italian book and a belief that within its pages there was a hidden message. Alice might have been childlike, even simple, but she'd seen something in that book which had made her think and set her on a trail she'd been unable to finish. Though Catrin had no idea what it was she was looking for, she knew there was something, and it might be connected with this little Italian boy buried here, a boy with a handsome face and a small scar on his cheek. Luca Roselli.

As she made her way dejectedly out of the graveyard, a rook perched on a tree yattered at her ill-temperedly. She stared back defiantly, imagined her mother's face in place of the rook's. She screwed up her own face and waved her arms at it.

'Sod off!'

Chapter 42

In the cool of the kitchen Maria Paparella counted out the eggs from the basket. Twelve brown eggs bought fresh from one of the old women at the early-morning market. She cracked them expertly, one by one, on the side of the large earthenware bowl, then beat them vigorously with an old spoon. Then she lifted the cloth off the earthenware jug of cream and tipped the cream into the bowl.

Luca came in, carrying a large metal pot.

'Did you manage to get it, Luca?'

'Yes. I went to see the batty old nun at the convent and did a swap for three of your walnut cakes. She says that's the last of the ice until the snows come again. Have you made up the mixture according to the instructions I read out to you?'

'Yes, and it's almost ready. We must hurry, though, or it will go off in this heat.'

'Okay. I'll read out what we have to do next.'

He picked up the recipe Maria had got from her uncle from Naples.

Maria pointed to two metal jugs on the table. 'These are what he gave me to use.'

'Yes, it says here that we must pour the mixture into the smaller jug.'

'Just one moment, I need to add the chocolate powder.'

'When you've filled it you must put it inside the larger one.'

Maria deftly poured the mixture into the smaller jug and put it inside the other one. 'Then what?'

'Then we pack the ice in between the two jugs. We must be quick, because the ice is already melting.'

Luca packed a handful of ice round the small jug, glancing down at the recipe as he did so. 'Now we put block salt on the top, then more ice, and so on.'

'What next?'

'Then you start to stir with the paddle spoon.'

'You start doing that, Luca. I need to check that Signor Bisotti has gone out. I don't want him bumping into Bindo when he arrives.'

'I think he's already done that.'

'Gesù bambino! How do you mean?'

'He caught him in the piazza not half an hour ago and accused him of stealing the cat's teeth.'

'He should be thanking him. The old brute's far happier without them. They gave him pain these past few years. Since they've gone he's a different animal, purring and rubbing up against your legs instead of biting and spitting.'

'The Signor caught Bindo a crack around the back of the legs with his stick that lifted the poor little fellow right off his feet. If it hadn't been for Piero coming on the scene, Bindo would have been beaten senseless.'

'What did Piero do?' Maria asked with interest, her face colouring.

'He got between them and told Bindo to run. And he was off like a shot.'

'I don't expect Signor Bisotti took too kindly to that?'

'The funny thing is, they just stood staring at each other.'

'Neither of them spoke?'

'No, but Piero looked at Signor Bisotti as if he was seeing him

*for the very first time, and Signor Bisotti looked paralysed with
fear.'*

'Then what happened?'

*'They just nodded at each other and walked away in opposite
directions. Then Signor Bisotti went into one of the houses in the
piazza.'*

'The widow Zanelli's?'

Luca nodded and blushed.

*'Well, at least he won't surface for the next few hours. She's got
her claws firmly into the old fool. Now, there's an old cat that
could do with having her teeth pulled. Tell you what, Luca, you go
and find Bindo and I'll finish this. Be quick, though. We don't
want it melting on us.'*

*Maria refilled the jug with ice and then salt and turned the
paddle. Soon the mixture started to freeze and stick to the sides —
it was like magic.*

*She stuck her finger into the mixture and tasted it. It was
delicious.*

*She busied herself chopping lemon and orange peel into the
thinnest strips, washed the wild strawberries, cut the tops off four
ripe pomegranates and dug out the fleshy pips.*

Ismelda's gelato was almost ready, and very good it looked, too.

*Today they would have a wonderful feast. If Signor Bisotti
did marry the blasted widow it would be the last one for a long
time. Soon all that would belong to the past. They would dine on
beans and thin soup for the rest of their days. She sighed, for she
knew she wouldn't be able to stomach being under the same roof as
that woman and her hideous offspring. But if she left, where would
she go? Her parents were both dead. And what of Ismelda? She
could never leave the child behind. She loved her and would
lay down her life for her. This evening she would go to mass and
light many candles to the Holy Virgin to beg deliverance from that
horrible fate.*

Chapter 43

In the cool of the kitchen Catrin laid out all the *gelato* ingredients that Tony had brought with him. She propped *Recipes for Cherubs* up on the table and occasionally turned the page to look at the painting of Luca Roselli. Every time she looked at that sweet face a lump grew in her throat. He was sitting on the grass, leaning against the trunk of the pomegranate tree. His eyes were closed and he was smiling contentedly as if he knew a secret that no one else did. She noticed for the first time what he had round his throat: a horn-shaped *corno* like the one Nonna had shown her. It hadn't protected Luca from bad luck.

She cracked the eggs one by one and beat them with a fork until her arms ached, folded in the cream and began to whip the mixture again, as she imagined Maria Paparella had done years ago.

It was hard work and soon her forehead was damp with exertion. She painstakingly cut the lemon and orange rind into the thinnest of slivers, removed the leaves from the strawberries, washed and drained them and sliced them.

She wanted to serve the *gelato* in pomegranates like the one Ismelda Bisotti was holding in the painting but Tony told her that they weren't yet in season, so instead she cut the tops off four large lemons and scoured out all the flesh.

Tony had also brought the ice-cream maker he'd unearthed, and he spent five minutes explaining how to use it. Under his watchful eye Catrin packed the ice and salt between the outer and inner containers, then he put the lid on and showed her how to turn the handle.

'You carry on with that,' he said, 'while I go to fetch the cake I've made. Just keep turning and then we'll add more ice and salt and then hey presto! we shall have the best ice cream ever.'

'How will I know when it's ready?'

'Take the lid off and you should see when it's started to stick to the sides.'

'Okay. When it's ready I'm going to fill the lemons with it and put the top of the lemon on like a little lid, and a mint leaf for decoration.'

'They'll look and taste wonderful, I'm sure.'

A table had been laid in the Italian garden and the pink gingham cloth fluttered in the warm breeze. The garden was alive with birdsong, the hypnotic droning of bees amongst the roses, and the sound of water splashing into the fountain.

Ella was sitting next to Nonna, who was wearing a black lace shawl to keep the sun off her face. When Catrin came out with the ice creams, Nonna threw back the shawl and cried, '*Bellissimo!*'

Flushed with pride, Catrin watched in delight as they each took one. She thought they looked like a scene out of *Recipes for Cherubs*, sitting together in the Italian garden eating home-made ice cream and enjoying each other's company.

'This is delicious,' Tony said, spooning ice cream into his mouth.

'Nothing taste quite like ice cream made the old-fashioned way,' Nonna said, smacking her lips noisily.

Catrin picked up her spoon and took a little ice cream on it. She couldn't eat much of it because of all the cream and eggs; it was so fattening.

She closed her eyes and put the spoon gingerly to her lips. The coolness was welcome after all her efforts, and the taste was divine. Just one little spoonful, that's all she was going to allow herself; a taste was quite sufficient, but she took another mouthful and relished the tang of lemon and orange on her tastebuds.

'This is wonderful!' Nonna said, waving her spoon in the air. 'You got any more of this?'

Catrin nodded happily and slipped another spoonful of ice cream into her own mouth without thinking. Soon she was digging down into the lemon, searching out the last of the ice cream.

'Now that is ice cream fit for cherubs,' Ella said, wiping a smear of it from her chin.

'It's an Ismelda special.'

'I never hear of this Ismelda ice cream,' Nonna said, wrinkling her forehead.

'Ismelda's a girl, not an ice cream.'

'She's a friend of yours?'

'No, she's a girl I wish I'd known, someone who lived a long time ago.'

Ella looked enquiringly at her.

'Ismelda Bisotti,' Catrin said dreamily.

'You wants to stay clear of them Bisottis,' Nonna warned.

'Why?' Catrin pricked her ears up.

'They not good people. They involve with American Mafia and very bad people,' Nonna said, admonishing the air with a gnarled old finger.

'The Ismelda Bisotti I'm talking about was Italian.'

'These Bisottis came from Italia, too. They start with ice-cream shops and restaurants in Naples, then they buy hotels and they emigrate to America and become very rich.'

'I've heard of the Bisottis,' Ella said. 'I remember years ago reading about one of the Bisotti daughters marrying into the English aristocracy. Let me see, I think an Alessandra Bisotti married the duke of somewhere or other.'

Catrin sat quite still. Alessandra was the name of one of the girls in her book, but their last name was Zanelli so the widow must be their mother. Widows were women whose husbands had died, so maybe Signor Bisotti had married her. Catrin pulled a face; she didn't like the look of Signor Bisotti or that snooty widow and her goody-two-shoes daughters. Poor Ismelda, if they'd become her stepsisters.

Catrin walked over to the fountain, pondering what she'd learnt. It seemed as if everyone had deserted Santa Rosa, but why? Piero di Bardi had disappeared, the Bisottis had gone to America, and Luca Roselli had lost his life in Kilvenny.

She looked across at Aunt Ella, Nonna and Tony and smiled. A few weeks ago she hadn't known they'd existed, and now she couldn't imagine life without them.

'Dear God, Nonna, that's your third helping,' Tony said with a whoop of disbelief. 'You weren't standing behind the door when God handed out appetites.'

'Ah, and that's why I nearly as big as the *elefante*.' Nonna laughed and prodded him playfully on the arm with her spoon. 'Is good to be a big woman, I think. Nobody mess with big women. All this fashions for stick-skinny models come to no good. The young girls, they all want to be so thin they almost see through. They weak with eating so little, and then they got no fire, and when they got no fire they let the men push them around.'

'No man ever pushed you around,' Ella said with a laugh.

'No, because me, I never no skinny jinny. I like my food too much.'

Catrin turned away hastily; she was uncomfortable when people talked about fatness and appetite.

'Antonio, you going to cut that walnut cake or we just got to look at it, eh?'

Catrin declined the cake politely and sat quietly on the edge of the fountain while Nonna and Ella ate cake as if food was soon to be on ration.

'Talking of walnuts, do you remember that *étui* of Alice's?' Ella said.

'What's an *étui*?' Catrin asked.

'It's usually a sort of sewing case, only this one was a painting set. It was quite beautiful and whoever had made it must have taken enormous trouble over it. It was a real walnut shell, beautifully burnished, and it had a hinged lid. When it was opened, it had the tiniest little paintbrushes and things inside. It was Alice's pride and joy.'

'Tell Catrin the story of how she find this thing,' Nonna urged.

'Well, it was really strange. My father – your great-grandfather – found the cherub statue over there in the castle and decided that he was going to restore the fountain. It took him weeks to plumb it in and make the plinth.'

'What's that got to do with the *étui* thingy?' Catrin asked.

'Be patient, I'm getting there. My father had finally finished the fountain and we were all waiting excitedly for him to turn it on. There was a great clanking and clattering as the water made its way through the pipes, and then all of a sudden a trickle of water dribbled out of the cherub's mouth. A few seconds later there was a great whoosh! and water shot out, and something flew out and landed in Alice's lap. It was a small oilcloth package and inside was the walnut *étui*. Alice thought it was a miracle, of course, and Father let her keep it. No one had a clue what it was doing in there.'

Catrin tried to contain her excitement. She knew the statue of the cherub had been washed up when the *Flino* sank, and she was sure it was the statue in the picture of the Santa Rosa piazza. Luca Roselli had lived in Santa Rosa and he was on the *Flino* when she went down.

Hell, there were so many unanswered questions. Where was Luca going to, and why did he bring the statue with him? Was he travelling alone or were there others from Santa Rosa on the *Flino*, too? And who had hidden the walnut *étui* in the cherub's mouth, and was it done in Italy or in Kilvenny?

'Do you still have the *étui*?' she asked.

'I haven't seen it for ages. Alice used to keep it in her dowry box.'

Bugger. If only she could find the dowry box, she was sure she'd learn something important.

A cloud drifted across the sun and a breeze got up, rustling the roses on the walls of the castle and sending a shower of petals over the four of them, like perfumed confetti. The chapel door opened and banged shut. Nonna put her hand to her head but too late: the breeze snatched at her black lace shawl and whipped it away, sent it looping and swirling high above their upturned heads. It came to land like a parachute, balanced for a moment on the water spurting from the cherub's mouth, then wrapped itself over the cherub's face.

Catrin leapt to her feet, retrieved the soggy shawl and handed it to Nonna, but her mind was on something else entirely. On a snowy night in a small hilltop town . . .

281

Chapter 44

In the garden Maria had set up a small table in the shade because the day was blisteringly hot. A dragonfly danced through on a current of hot air and bees fizzed excitedly among the flowers.

Pipi lay hidden in the bushes, purring loudly.

Bindo sat at the table, his feet dangling over the edge of his chair. He had made an effort to wash in the fountain in the piazza, and had slicked down his silky hair in preparation for his visit.

Ismelda sat next to him, dressed in a pretty blue frock, with a freshly washed ribbon already escaping from her unruly hair.

Bindo thought she looked wonderful, good enough to eat. Her blue eyes sparkled with delight and the colour in her cheeks was high from rising excitement. Surreptitiously he felt for her hand beneath the table and squeezed it tightly in his own sweaty one.

Ismelda winked at him. She loved to look at him, delighting in the colour of his hair, the sunlight streaking it with thin ribbons of gold and copper. She wanted to reach out and touch his snub nose with its dusting of summer freckles, to smooth her hand along his downy cheek, feel the shape of his bones beneath his hot skin.

How she would love to trace her finger around the outline of his pink mouth, a mouth which threatened to break into a wide smile at any moment.

Maria came out into the garden carrying a silver salver on which there were four rosy red pomegranates.

'Il gelato!' *she said.*

Luca handed a pomegranate to Ismelda and another to Bindo.

'It's cold!' *Ismelda shrieked, almost dropping hers.*

'Sí, is il gelato. *Very cold and made with ice. This special recipe come all the way from Napoli, and Luca and I make especially for you.'*

'Eat and enjoy,' *Luca said, handing them each a small spoon roughly hewn from wood.*

Ismelda spooned ice cream into her mouth and smacked her lips with gusto. 'I have never tasted anything so good in all my life.'

'You know, one day I may open a shop which sells nothing except gelato,' *Luca said.*

'You would never be able to get enough ice to keep going,' *Maria said.*

'Maybe someone will find a way of making ice.'

'How could they do that?' *Maria scoffed.*

'If you could find a way of keeping it cold, I could take a tray and walk around the village and call out to people to come and try some of my ice cream,' *Luca said.*

'Who in Santa Rosa has the money to buy ice cream?' *Bindo asked.*

'Maybe I go to Napoli, to all the big cities where people have lots of money. Maybe to France, or even as far as Inghilterra.'

'Whoa!' *Bindo cried.* 'That's miles away. You have to cross the seas, and it's cold there all the time, so who will want to eat cold things?'

'Promise to take me with you if you go,' *Maria begged.* 'I've never been out of this village.'

'I have only been out of this house to go to mass,' *Ismelda said sadly.*

Bindo leant over to her, pushed her hair back from her ear and whispered something to her.

Her blue eyes widened with surprise and she put her hand to his cheek. 'You would do this thing for me?'

Bindo nodded eagerly.

Maria got suddenly to her feet and put a finger to her lips. 'Quickly! Signor Bisotti is back earlier than we thought. Give Bindo a leg up into the tree, Luca.'

Luca leapt into action and lifted Bindo up into the branches of a fir tree alongside the garden wall. Ismelda watched in admiration as Bindo made his way effortlessly up into the tree. Then, quick as a wink, he was clambering over the wall. They heard a yelp and loud cursing as he made contact with the ground, just as Signor Bisotti stumbled out into the garden.

He had drunk too much, his face was red and blotchy, and he was sweating profusely. 'You'll all be glad to know my good news.'

'What good news, Papa?' Ismelda asked, wiping a smear of gelato from her nose.

'This afternoon, the lovely widow Zanelli accepted my proposal of marriage. We are to be married in three weeks' time.'

Maria drew in her breath with a wheezing sound and reached for Ismelda's hand.

Ismelda turned pale and her eyes grew wide with astonishment and the threat of tears.

'Is no one going to congratulate me on my good news?'

There was silence, apart from the sound of an empty pomegranate falling from Ismelda's hand into the grass, and the contented snoring of the toothless Pipi somewhere in the bushes.

Chapter 45

In Shrimp's Hotel Catrin stood in front of Piero di Bardi's beautiful painting *Woman and Child*, the painting that Aunt Alice used to blow kisses to every night before she went to bed.

It was curious that, although it was called *Woman and Child*, there was no child. She put her head on one side and scrutinised the woman, then turned her attention to the photograph of her mother wearing the poppy-red dress with the scalloped hemline. Of course! You couldn't see the child because the child wasn't yet born. She stepped closer to the painting and saw the soft undulation of the woman's belly beneath the blue material of her dress. This was supposed to be the woman Piero had married in Naples, so what had happened to her and her child?

She was very beautiful in an unusual way, and there was a wonderful liveliness about her face, her eyes full of passion and her mouth slightly open as if she was about to speak. If only those lips could move and tell her story.

If Piero di Bardi had painted the picture, he must have been with the woman when she was pregnant, and then for some reason they had separated and he ended up in Santa Rosa, and there was no mention of his wife and child ever living with him.

She felt her excitement growing as she examined the scarf tied round the woman's head, holding her dark hair back off her forehead. It was a distinctive blue scarf, with fringes of gold and red.

This was the moment of truth. Excitedly she opened *Recipes for Cherubs* and turned the pages until she came to the snow scene. There was the shivering cherub with a scarf wrapped comically around its neck. A blue scarf with blurry fringes of red and gold at either end. If she was right – and it was a long shot – the woman in the painting had been in Santa Rosa on that freezing night. Had she wrapped the scarf round the cherub's neck as a joke, or had it been snatched by the wind, the way Nonna's shawl had been?

Had she come to Santa Rosa to find Piero and show him their newborn child?

In the *Recipes for Cherubs* painting a priest was crossing the snowy piazza, carrying a bundle. She looked more closely. He might be carrying a baby wrapped in a shawl. Why would a priest be carrying a baby in the dead of night?

It was all too complicated, and made her head ache with the effort of thinking. She looked at the small face peering out of the window of the red house. Whoever it was would have seen what was going on, but there was no way Catrin would ever find out who the person was or what she had seen.

She turned sadly away from the painting and made her way out of the room and down the corridor, pausing at the top of the stairs. The telephone in the booth downstairs was ringing. She was in two minds as to whether to answer it; she was afraid that it would be her mother or, worse still, Arthur Campbell. She slipped out through the kitchen door and went thoughtfully back through the long grass.

As she walked up Cockle Lane she looked across at Meredith Evans Photographer's shop. She had a feeling that it had been him slipping out of the chapel the other night, the same man she had seen at Shrimp's. If he was so keen on snooping, maybe she should go into his shop and see if there was anything interesting there. The thought of being in the gloomy old shop on her own, though, made her nervous. She walked past the shop several times, glancing furtively in through the window, but couldn't buck up the courage to go inside. Then she had a brilliant idea.

Chapter 46

Meredith Evans was deep in thought as he made his way along Goose Row. As he passed the war memorial he looked up from his reverie and saw Catrin Grieve sitting on the step outside the Café Romana. He was taken aback when she smiled at him and said, 'Hallo, Mr Evans.'

'Afternoon,' he said, doffing his cap to her.

'I'm glad you came along.'

'You are?' he said, surprised.

'I've just been up to Shrimp's and I think there's some-one up there who shouldn't be,' she said, getting to her feet.

Meredith put his finger to his lips to silence her. 'Did you see who it was?' he asked in a throaty whisper.

'No, but I heard them upstairs poking around about ten minutes ago.'

'Thank you, girl. You won't mention this to anyone, mind?' he said urgently.

She shook her head, smiled angelically, and watched him hurtle off towards the beach.

The door to Meredith's shop was stiff, and the glass rattled ominously as she closed it behind her. It was dark inside and she was too afraid to turn the light on in case anyone passing down Cockle Lane saw her.

She stumbled around, looking up at the sepia photographs of Kilvenny folk that stared down accusingly from the walls. There was a large photograph of Aunt Alice, and one of Aunt Ella and some other people outside Shrimp's Hotel. She looked impatiently round the room but there was nothing of much interest. Conscious of time passing, and scared of being caught by Meredith, she crept into the back parlour.

It stank of whisky and stale tobacco and made her stomach lurch dangerously. There were more photographs of Alice; Alice sitting outside the Fisherman's Snug, holding a shrimping net; Alice standing next to the cherub in the fountain, copying his pose; Alice on the beach, posing in a bathing costume ... She looked like a film star except for that vacant look about her eyes. Meredith must have been very much in love with her to keep these photos for so long after she had died.

Catrin moved quickly into a small kitchen at the back of the house, where dirty plates were stacked up on the draining board, reminding her of a photograph she'd seen of the Leaning Tower of Pisa. A rubbish bin spewed out potato peelings and empty tins, and flies tap-danced in sticky spillages on the floor.

It was nearly as dirty as Shrimp's.

She retraced her steps to the parlour, and looked nervously up the narrow staircase. If she went up there and Meredith came back she'd be trapped, but she was here now and she might not get another chance. She put her foot on the creaking stairs and went slowly upwards, ears cocked for the slightest sound.

There was nothing of interest in the bedroom or the spare room, so she made her way silently down the stairs and through the parlour. She had just set foot in the shop when she heard the door creak open. She ducked down behind the counter, crouching fearfully in the darkness. She edged further underneath the counter between an ancient camera and a pile of mouldy newspapers.

She listened; no sound now except the ticking of a clock in the parlour. She peered round the side of the counter; the shop was empty. It must have been just the breeze rattling the door. She'd wait a while and then make her escape.

She was about to crawl out from under the counter when she heard the soft pad of footsteps as someone tip-toed furtively through the shop. Silence again, and then the sound of chesty breathing. She stayed crouched and petrified, her bladder filling up like a balloon about to burst. Any minute now she'd be discovered and then anything might happen.

She sniffed, wrinkled up her nose in disgust. There was a horrible smell, a mixture of fish and stale wee.

And then she sneezed.

The silence was unbearable, the air full of pins. She squeezed her eyes shut and bit her lips to stop herself screaming.

Something nudged her behind the knees and she toppled forward on to her face, scattering the pile of newspapers.

She wriggled round and came face to face with Dan Gwartney's fat white cat. Pedro, the Italian lady-killer. The cat studied her with curious green eyes. She looked back, drawn in by the hypnotic stare.

As she tried to put the newspapers back as they had been, she noticed a small, battered wooden box.

She looked from the cat to the box. And back at the cat.

The cat made no attempt to move, and she wasn't sure afterwards how long they'd stayed locked in a gaze, but the spell was broken when a clock in the parlour tinked the hour and she blinked, shook herself. She snatched up the box, stuffed it inside her cardigan, edged past the cat and out through the gloomy shop, past ancient camera stands and an antique brass birdie on a dusty shelf.

Chapter 47

The winds grew cooler as they blew up the valley, rattling the tiles on the church and snatching the water from the mouths of the cherubs in the piazza. The first shrivelled leaves began to fall and blow along the Via Dante, and the shutters on the houses rattled like old bones.

In the convent stable Bindo lay curled up in the straw, listening to the night sounds. A bird croaked up in the rafters and mice scurried across the dusty floor. Soon the church bell would clatter out midnight and startle the sleeping pigeons into flight.

He got up and went outside, stooping to wash his face in the water trough. He saw his reflection looking back at him, and over his head, the huge moon drifting above the roof of the church. He crept silently out of the convent gates, stood in front of the statue in her niche and crossed himself.

'Life's turning out good for me,' he said to the tiny saint. 'You've looked after me well.'

Then he made his way over to the Villa Rosso. He stood for a moment, looking around warily. Usually at this hour Santa Rosa was quiet as the grave, but he was sure tonight that not all the inhabitants were asleep.

He got a foothold on the garden wall and began to climb. When he reached the top he paused to regain his breath, then dropped soundlessly down into the darkness of the garden.

Pipi the cat emerged from the bushes and rubbed playfully against his legs. What a change in that creature since Bindo had relieved him of his teeth. Not that they'd been of any use, because the bloody things were rotten and only attached to his gums by threads. Piero di Bardi wouldn't want to buy them for burnishing. The poor cat must have been in agony with a mouthful of festering teeth.

He rubbed the cat's head affectionately and then tiptoed across the garden to the villa. He slipped in through the larder window and crossed the hallway to Ismelda's room. He listened. He could hear Signor Bisotti snoring loudly upstairs. He drew back the bolts soundlessly and pushed open the door.

Ismelda was awake and waiting for him.

The moonlight was soft, outlining the houses round the piazza in a silvery sheen. Bindo and Ismelda crossed to the fountain and sat down on the wall looking up at the cherubs.

'That one is my favourite,' Ismelda whispered, 'the one with the lopsided smile.'

'Mine, too,' Bindo said, reaching out for her cold hand. 'They say that that one is modelled on Piero's brother, who died when he was little,' he said softly.

'I've seen him through the window, and he always stops to touch its face.'

'Are you enjoying yourself?'

'Oh, Bindo, you can't imagine how wonderful it is to be outside those walls. The Villa Rosso feels like a prison to me.'

'We must not be out long tonight.'

'Why?' she asked, disappointment in her voice.

'I have a feeling in my water that things are not quite right in Santa Rosa.'

'How do you mean?'

'There's a kind of restlessness about the place tonight. Come on, let's go.'

They slipped into the darkness of the Via Dante, scaring a black cat which ran past them with a nervous wail. In one of the houses an old man coughed and groaned in his sleep.

A light shone from Piero di Bardi's house, and they crept stealthily up to the window. Bindo put his finger to his lips to warn her to be quiet.

Piero was hard at work on the far side of the room, his face half in shadow.

He finished mixing some paint, put his brush to the canvas and began to work like a man possessed. Ismelda was captivated by the way the muscles tightened in Piero's slender hands, the sudden tension in his neck, the way he tilted his head to one side and then stood back to scrutinise his work.

Suddenly, as if aware of being watched, he turned round and they ducked down out of sight. When they looked again, the room was empty.

'See what he is painting!' Bindo said excitedly.

Ismelda looked at it in awe.

Sunlight filtered through the leaves of a pomegranate tree, dappling the faces of the four people sitting on the grass. She herself was there, looking longingly at Bindo, her blue eyes lit with a curious light. And there was Bindo, his skin as soft as milk, his green eyes watching her . . .

Luca was leaning back against the tree, a satisfied smile on his lips, and Maria sat cross-legged on the grass, showing her plump and dimpled knees.

Ismelda turned to look at Bindo, her eyes wide in the darkness. 'Look,' she whispered, 'he's given us all wings.'

'Luca says he calls the painting Feasting Cherubs,' Bindo said.

'I thought he was supposed to be using the Zanelli twins as his models for the cherubs,' Ismelda said.

Bindo shrugged.

'How I wish we had real wings, Bindo, so that we could fly away from here.'

'Where would we go?' he asked.

'Somewhere far away where we could be free, if there is such a place.'

'I will find this place one day and I will take you there,' Bindo said.

'When Papa marries the widow Zanelli, life will be so terrible.'

'Have you met her yet?'

'No. She is coming to the house tomorrow with Father Rimaldi to discuss the wedding.'

Bindo sighed. 'I'd better keep out of the way, then. I thought that we were going to make brutti ma buoni tomorrow.'

Ismelda smiled and patted his hand. 'Here.' She took a cloth from her pocket and opened it. 'I brought you some Maria and I made specially for you this afternoon, after Papa told us the widow was coming to dinner tomorrow.'

He took a biscuit from her, and ate it enthusiastically. 'Am I ugly but good, Ismelda?'

'You will never be ugly to me. I think you are beautiful.'

'You do?' he asked.

She nodded and grinned.

'Tomorrow I will light a candle for you in the church and pray that you will be saved from the widow Zanelli,' Bindo said.

'Maria is going to make strangolapreti.'

'Is she?'

'Yes.'

'Let's hope it lives up to its reputation, then! When will I be able to come to the Villa Rosso again?' he said through a mouthful of biscuit.

'I don't know. When it's safe I'll let Luca know and he will tell you.'

Just then, Piero came back into the room and they ducked down beneath the windowsill.

'Come,' said Bindo. 'I need to get you back.'

They walked along the Via Dante and paused when they reached the piazza. There was a candle burning behind the shutters of an upstairs room in the widow Zanelli's house, the flickering light escaping through the cracks in the splintered wood.

'She's up late tonight,' Bindo said.

'What if Papa is there with her?'

'We must be quick. Come.'

As they scuttled across the piazza, the door of the widow's house opened. Bindo grabbed Ismelda's arm and pulled her down so that they were hidden behind the fountain.

She was so afraid that she pulled the skirt of her dress up over her head.

Bindo strained his ears.

'Goodnight, Alfonso.'

'Goodnight, my darling. I'm going to miss these nights with you.'

'It won't be for too long. I have great plans for us.'

'You won't forget me?'

'Don't be so foolish. I am determined to encourage the old fool to sell up here as soon as possible, move to Napoli and make an even bigger fortune.'

'Signor Bisotti's wealthy enough already, isn't he?'

'Yes, but I know how to make his money work in his favour.'

'You do?'

'Trust me. In the next few years we will move to America, and when we're settled I'll send for you and we can take up where we left off.'

Bindo was horrified to see the widow Zanelli kiss Father Rimaldi for what seemed like a very long time. Then he heard something that chilled him to the bone. He looked across at Ismelda and shuddered.

The priest's footsteps hurried across the piazza and the door closed softly on the widow Zanelli's house.

Ismelda whispered from under her skirt, 'Was it Papa?'

'No, it wasn't. Whoever it was has gone now. Come, we must get you back quickly.'

His head reeling from what he had seen and heard, Bindo took her hand and, keeping to the shadows, they hurried back towards the Villa Rosso.

'What did they say?' asked Ismelda.

'Didn't you hear?'

'No. I had my fingers in my ears and my skirt over my head.'

Bindo sighed with relief.

When they were safely back in the garden of the Villa Rosso, he stood looking at Ismelda.

'Here – I have a present for you.' He fished something out of his pocket and put it in her hand. It was a burnished walnut.

Ismelda looked at him enquiringly.

'Look. Lift the catch on the side.'

She fumbled in the darkness and then suddenly the walnut split in half.

'It's a little painting set for you. See, there are brushes and charcoal and a tiny palette.'

Ismelda's face broke into the widest smile he'd ever seen. 'It's beautiful. Perfetto.'

'I made it all by myself. Well, with a little bit of help from the woodcarver, who's a good friend of mine now.'

'You are wonderful and I love you.'

'You do?'

She took something out of her pocket and handed it to him; it was a silver ring and engraved on it were the words Tutto è possibile.

'This is for me?' he said in disbelief.

'It's for you. It was my mother's. It will bring you good luck,' she said, bending down and kissing him on both cheeks.

In the bushes they could hear Pipi purring contentedly. Somewhere close by, an owl called, long and low.

When Ismelda was safely in her room Bindo stood for some

seconds outside her door before sliding the bolts across so that no one would know she had escaped. Then he went back into the garden, climbed the pomegranate tree and, sitting among the moon-silvered branches, looked at the ring on his finger and thought about what the widow Zanelli had said to Father Rimaldi.

He was still there when the moon began to wane and the last stars melted away into the lightening sky.

Chapter 48

It was quiet in the castle, just the faint sound of the wireless from down in the kitchen where Ella was taking an afternoon doze. In her bedroom Catrin put the box down on the bed with trembling hands and stood looking at it for a long time, longing to open it but afraid of disappointment.

She found the key, turned it in the lock and opened the lid. The tantalising smell of camphor drifted out into the room. She lifted up a piece of rotting tissue paper and her heart sank at the sight of a pile of shells and slivers of blue and green glass; Alice's treasures. She ran her hands through them and her fingers came across something: a small necklace with an orange horn with an eye engraved in the middle, a *corno* like the one Nonna wore to ward off the evil eye.

She held it up to the light and it glowed warmly. Had this belonged to Alice? A silly charm which she thought would keep her safe?

She ran her fingers through the shells again and unearthed a tiny heart-shaped box, the sort that expensive rings were kept in. She snapped open the lid, and then drew back in dismay. Four yellowing teeth lay inside on the faded velvet. Ugh! Why would Aunt Alice keep anything so disgusting?

She closed the box and grinned. She imagined the look on Arthur Campbell's face if Alice had handed him the teeth! He would have been mortified if she had presented this old box to him as her dowry. What would he have wanted with a boxful of childish things, fragments of weathered glass, shells and four disgusting teeth? She giggled, thinking of how his mouth turned down at the corners whenever he saw something disagreeable, the way he wiped his hands on his waistcoat if he came into contact with something unpleasant. Whatever it was that he had wanted from Alice, it certainly wouldn't have been this box of old flotsam and jetsam.

Catrin wandered across to the window and looked out into Cockle Lane.

She could hear Tony singing as he worked over in the Café Romana and outside the Proprietary Library, sitting in a pool of sunlight, was Pedro the cat.

She stared at the cat without really seeing it. *Think, Catrin Grieve. Think hard.* With a whoop of glee she rushed over to the wardrobe, yanked out her school blazer and felt in the pocket for the card Sister Matilde had given her at Paddington.

At first she'd thought it was a holy picture, then that it was one of Sister Matilde's little jokes, but looking at it now it was clear that this was the same cat as the one in the picture in *Recipes for Cherubs*. The only difference was that this one was much bigger, and whoever had painted it wasn't as good an artist as Piero.

It was a large fat, white cat sitting beneath a pomegranate tree. Its mouth was open as if in a snarl and most of its teeth were missing. She chewed her lips with excitement. Could the teeth in the ring box have belonged to this poor old animal? And what in God's name was Sister Matilde doing with this picture of the cat?

She knew from Tony that when the *Flino* went down, a cat had been saved, a ship's cat. Dan Gwartney had said that Pedro was from a long line of feline Casanovas and that his bloodline would never die out. It was a long shot, but maybe Pedro was descended from the *Flino*'s cat. Maybe Pedro's ancestors had spent their days in sunny Santa Rosa, basking beneath the pomegranate tree, or looking down from the branches of a tree on to a snowy piazza.

She turned the picture over; someone had written faintly in pencil *Kilvenny Castle*.

She put her hand to her head and sucked in her breath; her brain was beginning to ache from too much thinking. Things were unravelling fast and she was learning more about the past and about what had happened to the people in the book, but there were still so many unanswered questions. There was one person she must talk to now and she had to be quick.

Dan Gwartney dropped his feather duster and spun round as Catrin burst into the library, red-faced and panting.

'Dear God! Is someone chasing you?' he asked.

'No, but may I use your telephone?'

'Of course. It's in the sitting room across the corridor – I'll show you.'

He led her into a small, bare room which reminded her of the visitors' parlour at school: white walls punctuated only by a large crucifix, the smell of beeswax polish strong in the air.

'Help yourself,' Dan Gwartney said with a smile, and closed the door behind him.

She dialled the number and waited while the phone rang and rang. She was about to give up when a breathless voice said, 'Saint Agnes's Convent School.'

'Christ, Mary Donahue, is that you?'

'It is. Who's that?'

'It's Catrin. What are you doing at school?'

'Sod all! I'm cooped up with that pair of gargoyles the Palfrey twins and I'm bored to buggery.'

'But I thought you were going home?'

'I did, but there was a bit of trouble between my dad and the law, and the law won. Oh, it's a long story and I had to come back. How are you, anyhow?'

'I'm having a good time, actually. It's dead exciting here.'

'Lucky old you. This place is like a morgue, especially with Sister Matilde gone.'

'Gone?' Catrin gasped.

Mary lowered her voice to a whisper. 'Gone all right. There's been all hell up. She went over the wall in the middle of the night and legged it!'

'You're joking!'

'Cross my heart and hope to die and stick a needle up my arse. The nuns haven't told us anything, but I overheard Sister Lucy talking to Mother Michael in the kitchen garden, and apparently she's pinched the money from the charity box and the convent car to boot.'

Catrin clutched the telephone to her ear, hardly able to take in what Mary was saying.

'Are you still there?' Mary asked.

'Y-yes.'

'Can you believe it? Maybe she's not really a nun but a bank robber.'

'I doubt it. The convent car wouldn't be much use as a getaway car – it only does about ten miles an hour.'

'Are you coming back to school? Is that why you're ringing?'

'No. I just wanted to talk to Sister Matilde about something.'

302

'That's funny, because she was talking about you the day before she escaped.'

'She was?'

'Yes, she said she hoped you'd fatten yourself up a bit while you were in Wales. She said she'd stayed at that hotel and the food was lovely. Is it?'

'Yes, it's fine.'

'It's still shit here. And are you any fatter? You looked dreadful when you left.'

'Thanks a bunch.'

'You're welcome. You know me, I don't beat about the bush.'

'Well, I am eating more, if you must know. Listen, Mary, has anyone at school ever said anything about me not having a father?'

'Are you a mind-reader, Catrin Grieve?'

'What do you mean?'

'Well, the Palfrey sisters were making some snide comments about you, saying that you had your mother's name and stuff, and Sister Matilde gave them a right ear-bashing.'

'What did she say?'

'She said they should look a bit closer at their own family tree, and one of them said sniffily that they were descended from a duke and a wealthy American family, and Sister Matilde said that if they looked back far enough down the family tree they'd probably find they had murderers there, too.'

'I bet they didn't like that!'

'You should have seen their faces; it was great.'

'I have to go now, but if you hear any more about Sister Matilde, ring me. It's Kilvenny 299. Will you do that?'

'I will.'

'An old man will probably answer, but he'll come over to the castle and fetch me.'

'Castle? I thought it was a hotel. You lucky devil!'

'Take care, Mary.'

'Cheerio.'

Her mind racing, Catrin put down the telephone. As she turned to leave the room, she saw Meredith Evans looking at her through the open window, and she was sure that the nosy devil had been listening to her conversation. He moved quickly away and Catrin wandered back into the reading room, where Dan Gwartney was dusting the shelves of books.

'Did you get through all right?' he asked.

'Yes, thanks.'

'You don't look too happy.'

'Well, the person I really wanted to talk to wasn't there.'

'You're welcome to try again later,' he said with a warm smile, and then, as an afterthought, 'Did you find anything of interest in Meredith's shop?'

Catrin blushed, and without explanation she hurried out of the library and back to the castle.

Chapter 49

Catrin hid the dowry box in the back of the wardrobe and lay down on the bed thinking about what Mary had said. Had Sister Matilde really stayed at Shrimp's? It was odd that she hadn't mentioned it when Catrin told her that Kilvenny was where she'd be spending the summer. Unless there was something fishy about Sister's visit . . .? And why had she suddenly taken off from the convent? It couldn't be to meet a man, because she was far too old for romance and stuff like that. Even more curious was the picture of the cat that Sister had given her.

Damn and bugger. She'd give anything to ask the old nun what it was all about, but she'd probably never see her again now, and school would be unbearable without having her lessons to look forward to.

Sister Matilde always said that if they had a problem they should sleep on it, let it rest and bubble away beneath the surface, and hey presto! the mind would work its wonders and out of the blue a solution would be found.

She was hard at work trying not to think when there was a tap at the door and Aunt Ella put her head round.

'There you are. Tony's just popped over and he said to tell you that he's made *spaghetti carbonara* and he wants us to join him and Nonna for supper.'

She was about to feign tiredness and refuse, but maybe being in company would give her a chance not to think and let her brain work away.

Nonna was sitting at a window table when Ella and Catrin went into the café. The table had been covered with a pink gingham cloth, and red candles burnt brightly in round-bellied wine bottles, making the wine glasses gleam in the flickering light.

'Tony, it looks just like a real restaurant!'

Tony grinned, bowed theatrically, pulled out a seat like a proper waiter, whipped up a napkin with a flourish and set it in Catrin's lap. He did the same for Ella and then poured red wine into their glasses.

'As a first course tonight we have some *bruschetta*, to be followed by a *carbonara*, a simple but tasty and nourishing dish as made by lowly Italian shepherds and as taught to me by my grandfather.'

Nonna's face was wreathed in smiles, her skin as brown and wrinkled as a pickled walnut.

Tony scurried hither and thither, reminding Catrin of the noisy Italian waiters in a restaurant near her house in London, small, dapper men in black and white scurrying between the tables, their laughter loud in the evening air.

Despite her intention to do no more than pick at the food, she was soon carried away by the conversation and laughter, and the wine made her head swim and filled her with a peculiar warmth. She picked at a piece of *bruschetta*, wiped a sliver of tomato from her chin with the back of her hand.

'That wine has put some colour in your cheeks and given you an appetite.'

'Nonna, if you can't see, how do you know if I'm pale or not?' Catrin asked with a hiccup.

'I have a new kind of sight. I feels things in here,' she said, patting her heart.

'They say that sometimes when one sense is taken away, the other senses develop more,' Ella said. 'I remember my grandfather used to talk about an old man who lived along the coast and he could tell colours just by feeling them.'

Catrin looked askance at her. 'And you believe that?' she scoffed, her mouth full of a second piece of *bruschetta*.

'Well, it was before my time – and before my grandfather's, come to that – but the man was a legend around here. He was blind and yet he could feel colour through his fingertips, describe the colour of things around him.'

Catrin took another swig of wine.

'You going to do any more of your cooking?' Nonna asked.

'Yes, I'm going to make *strangolapreti* next, whatever that is.'

'How you know about *strangolapreti*, eh? I don't hear that word in long time.'

'What does it mean?'

'In English it means "priest-stranglers".'

'What?'

'Is a dish of dumplings with spinach. Very tasty, too. My mother always make *strangolapreti* in the winter.' She made a smacking sound with her almost toothless mouth, and Catrin giggled.

'Slow down with that wine,' Ella warned. 'I don't want to have to carry you home.'

'But why is it called priest-stranglers?'

'Because often in Italy the priest come to your house to eat and you must feed him. For the peasants it hard to feed they own children, never mind a hungry priest. There was legend say that one priest eat so many of the dumplings he chokes. Others say that you feed the priest with these and he so full that he can't eat no more.'

'So they wouldn't actually try and choke or strangle the priests?'

'Maybe they do. Not all the priests is good men, you know. Some is very greedy and loves money and women more than they loves God. In our village we have very good priest who kind to the poor people.'

Tony arrived at the table, balancing four plates on his arm, and put one in front of each of them with a flourish. '*Spaghetti alla carbonara! Buon appetito.*'

'I was going to tell Catrin the story about the bad priest,' Nonna explained.

'Oh, that used to be my favourite story when I was little,' Tony chuckled, sitting down next to Catrin.

'Once upon a time in little village in Italia they have bad priest who do very wicked things. Many peoples like to strangle him, I think.'

'What sort of things did he do?'

'He very greedy for money and want to make name for himself. I don't know him, because he dead long before I was born, but he very famous in those parts for his wicked ways. I glad to say that he come to no good.'

'What happened?'

'Many of the poor people in the village have enough of him and they gets together and makes a plan. One night, when is dark and the clouds hiding the moon, they creep to his house, climb in and take him from his bed.'

'They didn't kill him, did they?' Catrin said in alarm.

'No, they don't kill him, they just teach him a lesson.'

'What did they do?'

'They blindfold him and take him up into the church tower and they tie him with rope to the big bell.'

'And they left him there?'

'*Sì.* All night long he is there. In the morning the bell

begins to ring and the people come out for early mass and then they see him.'

'Tied to the bell?'

'*Sì*, tied to the bell. The bell is ringing and there is their priest naked as the day he was born.'

Catrin gasped. 'Is that a true story, Nonna, or did you make it up?'

'Is true. My husband, Luigi, tell me, and his great-great-grandfather tell him that he seen this thing happen with his own eyes. He was on his way to mass and he look up and there is the priest tied to the bell. At first he can't believe his eyes and he think he been drinking too much wine the night before.'

Catrin looked wide-eyed at Nonna, trying to decide whether she was having her leg pulled.

Nonna continued, 'The great bell is swinging. Dong, dong. And bits of the priest is swinging too, if you see what I mean.'

Catrin blushed and was glad Nonna couldn't see her face.

'Luigi say that the mothers cover the eyes of the little children who watch. One woman with two little girls faints and he has to carry her all way home. And she a big lump for young man to carry.'

'Who got the priest down?'

'I don't know, but somebody. But you know what?'

'What?'

'That wicked priest, Father Rimaldi, was never seen again in that place.' Nonna rocked back and forth, and laughed until her eyes ran with tears.

Catrin watched her in astonishment, her mind racing. 'How do you know that he was called Father Rimaldi?'

'Because Luigi tell me. His name was famous far and wide after that.'

'That's only half the story,' Tony said, opening another bottle of wine with a resounding pop.

Catrin thought how happy he looked, how handsome in the flickering candlelight.

'How you mean, half the story?' Nonna asked.

'Ah, see, you don't know everything, Nonna,' he declared, filling her glass to the brim and winking.

'Tell us, then,' Catrin begged.

'Ah, well, you see, I happen to know this from a very good source.'

'What do you know?' Catrin urged.

'Well, do you remember Benito, Nonna, the student who came here one summer and camped in Blind Man's Lookout?'

'*Sì*, I remember. Very handsome boy who got into a bit of trouble.'

'He was a nice lad,' Ella said. 'He did some building work on the tower, and he used to spend hours talking to Alice.'

'That's him. Anyhow, you want this story or not?'

'Yes.' Catrin nodded impatiently.

'Well, Benito was an art student at the university in Rome, but one summer holiday he was working as a labourer, doing up an old villa which had been abandoned for years.'

'What's that got to do with the priest?' Catrin demanded.

'Hang on the bell, Nell. While he was working at the villa, some builders who were restoring the old priest's house opposite ripped out some old plaster and came across a skeleton.'

'Ugh!' Catrin exclaimed, dropping her fork with a clatter.

'It gave them a hell of a shock. The police were called and they had to stop work for weeks.'

'Antonio, you going to put me off my pudding with these stories?'

310

'Ah, go away with you. Nothing puts you off your food, Nonna.'

'Well, when they examined the remains they discovered that it was the skeleton of a young woman, who had had her skull bashed in.'

'Who was she?'

'It was impossible for them to tell, because she'd been there for such a long time and there was no way of finding out.'

'Oh.' Catrin's voice was flat with disappointment.

'They only knew that she'd recently had a child.'

Catrin sat up very straight, eyes shining with anticipation.

'There was one other clue about how long she'd been there.'

'And what was that?'

'Beside the body was a bag of money.'

'What did that prove?'

'The coins were eighteenth-century, so they guessed she'd been there since then.'

'Did they find the skeleton of the baby, too?'

Tony shook his head and Catrin sighed with disappointment.

'But Benito was intrigued and did a little digging.'

'Did he dig up more skeletons?'

'Not digging like that, but asking around.'

'What did he find out?'

'There was an old convent just along from the priest's house, and the nuns looked out the ledgers going back hundreds of years, and he found out something very interesting.'

'What?' Catrin could barely contain her excitement.

'In 1751 there was a child abandoned, put into a tub outside the convent, a child nobody ever came to claim.'

'It wasn't a tub, it was an olive jar, actually,' Catrin said.

311

'Come again?'

'The baby was left in an olive jar, put there by the priest.'

'In the ledger it said that the priest at the time, one Father Rimaldi, found the baby wrapped in an old blanket and took the baby to the nuns. The Last Rites were given, because the baby was deformed and wasn't expected to live.'

'He wasn't deformed, he was just a dwarf,' Catrin said, in a faraway voice.

'But the child lived?' Ella asked.

'Oh yes, and the nuns christened him,' Tony continued.

'Bindo!' Catrin exclaimed.

Tony gaped at her.

'What was the child called really?' Ella asked.

'Catrin's right, he was called Bindo. I thought it a funny name.'

'Funnily enough, years ago Queenie Probert, one of the old cockle pickers from Aberderi, had a donkey called Bindo,' Ella said.

'I remember her, she live in house called the Shambles,' said Nonna.

'That's her,' Ella said and then added, 'How did you know the baby's name, Catrin?'

'I don't know, it kind of just came to me out of the blue,' she lied. She looked away from their bewildered faces and took a gulp of wine.

'But they couldn't be sure that Father Rimaldi had murdered the woman?' Ella said.

Catrin said nothing. If they'd seen the portrait of Father Rimaldi, they'd know that he was a man capable of anything

'No,' said Tony, 'but it's more than likely, if you think about it. A priest living alone has the opportunity to do something like that. Maybe he did the mother in and then left the baby outside the convent for the nuns to find.'

'But why would he murder the woman?'

'That will always remain a mystery, I'm afraid.'

Catrin's mind was still racing. She was pretty damned sure who the woman was. It was the woman in the Piero di Bardi painting, the woman who was carrying Piero di Bardi's child. Maybe she had arrived in Santa Rosa that snowy winter's night with her baby, looking for Piero. Had she come across Father Rimaldi, and had he offered to help her and then double-crossed her? If there had been a struggle, her scarf might have come off and blown round the neck of the little cherub. Then what had happened? Had he murdered her and given the baby to the nuns?

She thought of the painting of Father Rimaldi, the hawk-like nose and the eyes with the murderous glint, and she shivered

'Anyone for pudding?' Tony asked.

Chapter 50

Maria was hard at work preparing for the evening meal. She worked without her usual enthusiasm, chopping vegetables angrily, cursing when she nicked her finger with a knife, stemming the trickle of blood on the sleeve of her old dress.

Ismelda was shut up in her bedroom in disgrace, because Signor Bisotti had caught her sitting up in the pomegranate tree this morning. What a fuss just because a child was tempted to climb a tree. He had taken on as if she were some kind of monster. Then the miserable old bastard had confiscated her box of treasures. Mother of God! How awful was it to stash a pile of childish keepsakes in a box? Hadn't he ever been a child himself? He was probably born a wizened little shitpot. Whatever had his wife seen in him? She had been a good-looking woman with a sunny temperament. Mind you, there had been some gossip that she'd been betrothed to the wood carver who lived in the alleyway behind the church, but Signor Bisotti had paid her parents handsomely for her hand in marriage.

Marie finished preparing the vegetables for the minestrone and began to make the strangolapreti. Later, Luca was coming to help her make some gelato. He, bless him, was full of himself these days with his plans for opening a shop in Naples selling this icy gelato and making his fortune.

She had her work cut out today: after all the cooking, she must

314

serve at the table tonight – it would stick in her craw to fetch and carry for the likes of the widow Zanelli and her simpering daughters. As for Father Rimaldi, maybe the strangolapreti *would do the trick and strangle the bastard.*

She crossed herself hastily. It wasn't right to think ill of a man of the cloth, but these days he was strutting around Santa Rosa as if he were some kind of prince. He was puffed up with his own importance, telling everyone that soon he would be the guardian of a church which boasted a painting of feasting cherubs by the famous Piero di Bardi. No doubt he would line his pockets with the offerings from people who came from far and wide to look at the great man's work.

She had been back to the house in the Via Dante several times, on the pretext of passing messages to Luca. Each time she had taken Piero a little offering, morello cherries steeped in wine, a fish stew or a walnut cake. He was filling out a little, but he wasn't at all well and she'd noticed that sometimes he stumbled into the furniture as if he hadn't seen it. She was worried because, despite the animation in his eyes, he looked gaunt and exhausted. They spoke little, apart from polite pleasantries, but she was comfortable in his company and he in hers, and sometimes he looked at her in a way which made her heart feel as if it had turned to panecotta.

All day long and half the night Piero was working on his masterpiece. Signor Bisotti constantly bemoaned the fact that he hadn't seen the picture yet, but Piero was adamant on that point. No one was going to see it until it was finished; no one, that is, except Bindo. Maria knew he'd seen it – he and Piero had struck up quite a friendship in the last few weeks.

Maria sighed. Life would change for ever when that awful woman came here to live. She was driving the whole village mad, waylaying all and sundry and bragging about the fact that her daughters were soon to be immortalised in paint.

In a few weeks she would be wed, would become the new Signora Bisotti and move into the Villa Rosso. Maria smiled ruefully. Signor Bisotti had been searching high and low for the wedding ring that had belonged to his first wife, because the old skinflint wasn't willing to have a new one made. He hadn't found it yet, and she was damn sure that Ismelda had something to do with its disappearance though she'd flatly denied it.

Chapter 51

Catrin and Tony were sitting on the step of the Café Romana watching a huge moon rising. The breeze was cool, with a hint of rain in the air, and somewhere far off a bell clanged dolefully.

'Why is that bell ringing non-stop?'

'That's the Waiting bell in Aberderi,' Tony said.

'What does it mean?'

'Someone's ill and not expected to live through the night. They'll ring the bell all night long until first light.'

Catrin shivered and Tony put his arm round her and hugged her.

She said, 'Don't let's talk about dying. That was a lovely meal, Tony, You know you really should open a restaurant somewhere – you'd be great at it.'

'Ah, chance would be a fine thing.'

'You know earlier when you were talking about Benito? Nonna said that he got into some trouble here. What did he do?'

Tony drew heavily on his cigarette, and it was a while before he spoke. 'He was accused of stealing something from the tower.'

'In the castle?'

'Yes. You know where the old nursery is?'

317

'I've never been up there.'

'Well, sometimes when Shrimp's was full they used the tower as an overflow. Guests stayed there and walked up to Shrimp's for their meals.'

'So if it was raining while they stayed here, they'd get soaked?'

'I suppose so.'

Catrin grinned. That was one mystery solved. Arthur Campbell must have stayed in the tower, and that's why he'd written the comment about getting soaked.

'Go on, tell me the rest.'

'Benito was in the tower, doing some painting and repairs, and one of the guests accused him of stealing. She said that she caught him going through her bags.'

'And was he?'

'I never believed a word of it.'

'What happened to him?'

'The police were called and PC Idwal, the local bobby at the time, who was a bit of an idiot, locked him in the tower while they waited for a police car to arrive from Swansea, but he did a Houdini and escaped.'

'How could he do that?'

'God knows, but he did.'

Tony threw down his cigarette in a shower of sparks. 'I got a postcard from him a few weeks later from Italy.'

Catrin gave him a sideways glance and said softly, 'The Napoli cherub postcard?'

'That's right,' he said. 'He was mad about cherubs, always going on about finding some long-lost painting by an Italian fellow – as if there was any chance of finding it here in Kilvenny!'

'He came here to look for it?' Catrin asked incredulously.

'He'd met a woman in London, another nut case who was just as mad about this artist, and she had a picture which

318

she was convinced was a di Bardi. She said she'd found it between the pages of an old book when she was staying in Kilvenny. Very far-fetched, if you ask me.'

'A picture of an ugly cat without any teeth?'

'How the heck did you know that?'

'I just have a good imagination, that's all.'

They were silent for a while. Catrin was convinced that she knew who the woman was: Sister Matilde in the days before she had become a nun. Sister had stayed here and had taken the book on Piero out of the library and never returned it.

'And Benito went away and you never saw him again?'

'That's right. He just disappeared into the sunset and left a lot of unhappy people behind him.'

Catrin fell silent again, staring up at the map of stars above and the huge, milky moon that drifted above Gwartney's Wood. Over in Aberderi the Waiting bell continued to toll.

Chapter 52

It was gone midnight by the time Catrin got back to the castle and climbed the stairs to her bedroom. She was still a little tipsy from all the wine. She undressed and crawled into bed but, though she was physically exhausted, her brain would not let her rest and she kept going over and over what Tony had told her.

'Benito just disappeared into the sunset and left a lot of unhappy people behind him.'

Benito. Benito who had been accused of stealing something from the old tower while he was working up there. The old tower where Arthur Campbell had stayed. Benito had been camping in Blind Man's Lookout.

It was Benito who had told Tony the story of the skeleton found in the old priest's house in Santa Rosa. Father Rimaldi's house.

Please let me go to sleep.

But a little voice kept niggling inside her head.

Father Rimaldi was carrying a baby across the piazza, and someone saw him from a window of the Villa Rosso. A baby who wasn't expected to live. Bindo the dwarf. Piero di Bardi's baby son?

Dong. Dong. Dong. Father Rimaldi swinging from the bells.

One of the cockle pickers had a donkey called Bindo.
Please, brain, let me sleep.

Benito. Benito. Benito. Benito the Houdini who could escape from locked rooms.

She yawned again, pressed her hands against her temples to try and chase the thoughts away.

Sister Matilde said try not to think . . .

She'd been here. It was Sister Matilde who had said how glorious it was to kneel in the early morning and watch the light slip through a stained-glass window and see the early shadows play across a lonely saint in a cool chapel.

Sister Matilde flying over the wall and escaping in the convent car.

The smell of lemons grew stronger and she was sure someone unseen was standing by her bed looking down at her. A soft hand smoothing her forehead, tracing the curve of her cheek and the arch of her brow.

Somewhere close by, she was sure, there was a contented cat purring and bees humming. Water splashed in a fountain and a pomegranate fell from the tree and landed with a thud in the parched grass.

Catrin yawned and soon after came the warm and welcome sleep of the tipsy.

Chapter 53

Night was falling, a smoky darkness drifting up the valley. The wind was cold, and it rattled the shutters on the houses as it whipped through the narrow streets, whisking the water in the cherub fountain into a whirlpool. A donkey cart clattered slowly along the Via Dante, began to speed up as it passed Piero di Bardi's house, the driver looking nervous when he heard the artist cursing and crashing around inside.

Bindo, perched on an olive jar outside the convent, saw the donkey come to a halt outside Father Rimaldi's house. An old man climbed stiffly down from the cart and, seeing Bindo, doffed his cap and then knocked on the priest's door.

Bindo looked longingly at the high walls that surrounded the Villa Rosso. He was pining for Ismelda; he hadn't seen her since the wedding of the widow Zanelli and Signor Bisotti almost two weeks ago. With the new Signora Bisotti sniffing about and keeping a tight control on the budget, Luca couldn't go there and help cook any more, although occasionally he was allowed in to bring messages from Piero to Signor Bisotti. He had told Bindo that poor Ismelda was locked in her room for hours and that Maria was wandering around looking as if she had swallowed a bag of salted slugs. The new Signora Bisotti, God rot her scabby tongue, was busy nosying around the house and the rumour was that the Bisottis would soon be moving to Napoli. If that happened, Bindo

322

would up sticks and move, too; he wasn't going to be separated from Ismelda, not even if he had to walk all the way behind them.

Father Rimaldi came out of his house and crossed the cobbled road to the Villa Rosso, whispering to the driver of the donkey cart. Moments later Signor Bisotti appeared, saw Bindo, and gave him a look of pure hatred. Bindo glared back and then scuttled away down the Via Dante.

It was late, a watery moon floating above the church tower. Bindo and Luca Roselli were sitting on the side of the fountain eating sunflower seeds, spitting the skins around them. Signor Bisotti's fat white cat came scurrying up to them and Bindo grinned.

'That cat's in a hurry, but he won't be catching much without his teeth!'

'Signor Bisotti wasn't too pleased, though!' Luca laughed, his own teeth white in the darkness.

The cat leapt on to Bindo's lap, almost knocking him backwards into the fountain.

'I'd like to pull that grouchy old bastard's teeth out with rusty pliers,' Bindo said, rubbing the cat's knobbly old head.

'The talk is that they're moving to Napoli soon,' Luca said.

'I know, and I'll follow them if they do,' Bindo said, puffing out his chest with bravado.

The cat raised a paw and tapped Bindo's chin, claws withdrawn.

'Me too,' Luca replied miserably.

Bindo stared at him, green eyes glittering with surprise. 'You?'

'Can you keep a secret?'

'Of course.' Bindo pressed his small hand to his heart dramatically.

'Signor Bisotti's spoken to my mother. He wants me to go and work for him, to set me up in a shop in Napoli where I can experiment with my cooking and especially with my gelato.'

'And you're sad about that?'

'I don't want to work for him, I want to work for myself, but my mother's over the moon and says I must go.'

'You want to watch yourself with him: his promises are made and broken several times a day. But at least we'll be in Napoli together.'

The cat grew agitated, dug its claws into Bindo's thighs and meowed plaintively.

'Ouch! Be careful, Pipi.'

'One day maybe I can even give you a job.'

'I will be rich, buy a house and marry—' Bindo stopped mid-sentence and cocked his head to one side. 'Can you hear that?'

'What?'

'Someone's screaming!'

They leapt down off the fountain and ran, the wind whipping their hair into their faces and blowing the crisp leaves into an agitated dance around their bare feet.

Chapter 54

Aberderi was a hamlet, a huddle of broken-down old cottages set around a water pump which had long since fallen into disrepair. The Ship and Bottle pub was the only place that showed any signs of life: the sound of raucous singing drifted out, along with a blue stream of cigarette smoke which floated away on the breeze.

The ride from Kilvenny along the cliff road had veered between the exhilarating and the terrifying, and when Catrin got off the bike she had borrowed from Tony Agosti she crumpled, her legs like jelly and her lungs bursting.

She tiptoed past the pub, then walked slowly past the derelict houses, the smell of seaweed and donkey shit strong in the morning air.

The last house had a sign above its door, *The Shambles*. She stopped and listened. It seemed to be the only house where anyone was home. A radio was playing and a kettle whistled piercingly. Looking through the open front door into the gloomy darkness of the passage, she jumped when a voice croaked, 'Who's there?'

She made her way slowly, anxiously, towards the voice.

In a cavelike kitchen with a window the size of an arrow slit, a tiny woman no bigger than a child was huddled in an armchair. Despite a fire roaring in the grate as though it were the depths of winter, she was wrapped in a plaid shawl. The room was stifling, and smelt strongly of fish and stewed tea.

The old woman's face was yellow and waxy, as if she had been preserved for a long time in a dank, dark place; she watched Catrin approach with wily eyes.

'Don't stand there with your mouth hanging open. Come on in, whoever you are.'

'I'm Catrin Grieve,' she said, a tremor in her voice.

'Queenie Probert,' the old woman said, examining Catrin with interest. 'I can tell you're a Grieve, all right,' she said at last. 'What are you doing so far from home?'

'I'm exploring.'

'Well, come over here and sit by me.'

Catrin edged towards her and sat down hesitantly on a stool at her feet.

'I remember your Aunt Alice well.'

'You do?'

'She often came here when she was a girl, a bit like you poking about trying to find things out,' the old woman croaked, her slack mouth twisting itself into a smile. She got awkwardly to her feet, moved the kettle off the hob, switched off the radio and fixed her gaze on Catrin again. 'What is it you're looking for?'

'A donkey called Bindo.'

Mrs Probert laughed, exposing a graveyard of teeth. 'There been no donkey called Bindo here for years now.'

'But there was once?'

Mrs Probert cackled with laughter again, and Catrin shrank back in alarm and began to wish that she hadn't come all this way.

'Don't look so afraid. Get a bit closer and listen carefully so I don't have to raise my voice.'

326

Catrin felt a shiver of excitement run along her backbone. She was on the same trail as Alice.

'There was always a donkey called Bindo here for as long as I can remember. Used to happen that when one Bindo died the name was passed on to a new donkey.'

'But it doesn't happen any more?'

'Sadly, times change and the young ones give them daft names nowadays, call them after them shrieking pop stars and footballers. Not right in my book, calling a donkey Stanley Matthews.'

'Why Bindo?'

'You got time to hear all the story?'

Catrin nodded eagerly.

'Many years ago, the body of a boy was washed up on the beach – the tide had dragged him up here; still clinging to a pallet he was. He was close to death and the cockle women brought the poor little fellow up here to die in peace.'

'He was little, then?'

'A tiny little thing like that Tom Thumb.'

'Bigger than that, I think. What happened to him?' Catrin asked with bated breath.

'He was laid out in the back bar of the Ship and Bottle, where he breathed his last,' Queenie Probert said, closing her eyes as if she, too, was giving up the ghost. She paused for what seemed an age.

'And then he died?'

'When they came to bury him in the morning, they saw a movement of his little finger.'

'He was alive?'

'It was a miracle. He was badly injured, mind, and he'd lost the art of speaking. But the strangest thing was' – Catrin could barely breathe – 'that inside his jacket was a tiny statue of a saint. That's what must have kept him safe, see.'

Catrin was silent. In the painting in *Recipes for Cherubs*

there was a niche in the wall of the convent in Santa Rosa, where a small saint looked down on the olive jar in which a baby had been abandoned one freezing night.

'Penny for your thoughts,' Queenie Probert said, touching Catrin gently on her arm.

'I was just thinking, that's all. Did he stay in Aberderi?'

'Times were hard here in those days. Most people were on the bones of their arse, and another mouth to feed was nigh on impossible.'

'So what did he do?'

'He was given a bed in the shed with the donkeys until he was well. In fact, he scratched his name in the wood on one of the donkey stalls – Bindo. That's how people knew what to call him. It's there to this day.'

'And then?'

'I fancy he went to work over Kilvenny way for Nathaniel Grieve.'

Catrin grinned. Imagine that! He'd worked in Kilvenny, had walked the same alleys and lanes as she had. It made her heart puff up with pleasure to think of him doing that.

'Thank you, Mrs Probert, for telling me all this.'

'You're welcome, my lovely. Strange how you came here with all your questions just like your Aunt Alice did all those years ago. She wanted to know all about the little dwarf, too.'

Catrin wondered what else Aunt Alice had found out.

'I'm tired now, but I enjoyed our little chat. If you go up the lane and turn left you'll see where they keep the donkeys.'

Almost before she finished her sentence, her head nodded on to her chest and she was snoring soundly.

Chapter 55

It was getting dark when Catrin went into the donkey shed, a weak light breaking through the gaps in the ramshackle roof. Up in the rafters a bird chirruped and the shadowy donkeys shuffled their feet expectantly, their large heads nodding over the doors of the stalls as if in welcome. Catrin felt as though she were stepping into a Christmas Nativity scene except for the earthy smells of damp straw and steaming donkey droppings.

Outside the wind was getting up, rattling the wooden building and bringing with it the smell of seaweed and fish. Stray drops of rain wheedled their way in through the broken roof and somewhere close by a mouse scuttled for cover.

As she approached the nearest stall the donkey lifted its head, drew back its lips and showed a mouthful of yellow teeth. Catrin stepped closer. Far out at sea the thunder rolled and she shivered.

Above each stall there was a makeshift sign with a name on it: STANLEY, ELVIS, TOMMY, GRACIE.

She stepped up to Gracie's stall, put out her hand and the donkey nuzzled her fingers playfully.

She knelt down on the floor and ran her hands over the

ancient wood of the door, her fingers finding the letters carved there: BINDO.

Here in this shed the green-eyed boy had slept, sharing the stable with the donkeys, tucked up in the straw amongst the mice and nesting birds.

She imagined him curled up at night, listening to the sea pounding on to the beach, the scream of the gulls as they followed the fishing boats in. How homesick he must have felt, away from his friends, alone in a strange land where he couldn't even speak the language. It was even worse than that, though, because Queenie said that he'd lost the use of his tongue. Thinking of his loneliness brought a lump to her throat. She patted Gracie's nose and turned away; it was time she set off back to Kilvenny before the weather came in any worse.

The donkeys were watching her in dignified silence, ancient-looking beasts with knowing eyes.

She closed the stable door and stood with her back pressed against it for a long time, breathing deeply in the salty air, feeling the rain on her face, soft as a blessing.

Chapter 56

Luca reached the Villa Rosso with Bindo close on his heels and Pipi lolloping in their wake. The two breathless boys and the wheezing cat stared aghast at the spectacle before them.

Signor Bisotti, aided by his new wife, was dragging Ismelda out of the house, and she was kicking and screaming as though fighting for her life. The air was filled with the sound of cursing and bloodcurdling screams, mainly Ismelda's. From the balcony, the two Zanelli sisters watched the scene with delight.

Bindo ran to Ismelda's aid but Father Rimaldi, who had followed the Bisottis out of the villa, caught him a resounding blow on the forehead, splitting the skin, and Bindo reeled backwards and sank to his knees.

Luca yanked him to his feet and held on to him.

'Get any closer, you fucking midget, and I'll crack that empty head of yours,' Signor Bisotti spat, hatred thick as phlegm in his foul mouth.

'Maria will come and save her,' Bindo said, a trickle of blood running down his cheek.

'She's not here. Signora Bisotti sent her on an errand this morning.'

Beside himself with misery and rage, Bindo broke free of Luca's grasp and ran to Ismelda, reaching out frantically for her flailing

331

hands. *She tore crazily at his clothes, desperate to touch him, but she was not strong enough.*

With a torrent of oaths, Signor Bisotti lifted Bindo by the shoulders of his threadbare jacket and hurled him towards a petrified Luca.

Ismelda screamed and fought like a cat until Signora Bisotti gave her a slap which knocked her backwards and Father Rimaldi, like a man practised in kidnapping, flung a rope round her and tied her arms to her sides. As she opened her mouth to roar once more, he slipped a length of cloth between her teeth and knotted it at the back of her neck.

Bindo could only watch in dismay as she was bundled into the back of the cart. He held his arms out towards her beseechingly, and from the back of the donkey cart she looked at him, tears smearing her face, her beautiful blue eyes wide with fear and anger.

Maria Paparella, turning out of the Via Dante where she had spent a pleasant half hour with Piero on her way back from a fruitless errand, arrived on the scene as the carter cracked his whip and the donkey cart set off at a trot towards the crossroads and then took the right fork that led down the steep hill to Terrini.

Seeing Maria, the Bisottis stepped hurriedly back into the Villa Rosso and the door banged shut behind them. Father Rimaldi glanced at her nervously, then scuttled across the road to the church.

Maria looked from Bindo to Luca, saw the fear in Luca's eyes and Bindo standing there bleeding and bereft, his eyes glassy with rage and impotence.

There was only one place where the conniving bastards would be taking Ismelda, and that was the Convent of Santa Lucia where the mad people were sent; a place of no escape.

She sank to her knees and crossed herself, threw back her head and howled. The leaves swirled around the three of them, the wind growing ever wilder, the first flakes of snow settling on the upturned faces of the four cherubs in the fountain.

Chapter 57

The sky was a mix of stormy hues, purple and red blending with orange, the rain driving in off the sea, sharp as pine needles. Catrin pedalled along the cliff road, the wind sweeping her hair into her face so that several times she swerved dangerously close to the cliff edge. Down on the beach the waves pounded on to the sand, spume rising high into the air, hissing as though it were whispering secrets.

Exhausted, she came to a wobbling halt, propped the bike against a tree and looked around.

The dry-stone wall that had once enclosed the garden of Blind Man's Lookout was reduced to rubble, and nettles and weeds grew in profusion in every crack and crumbling crevice. The old house was falling down: a few more wild winters and the roof would cave in and the whole place would be past repair.

Many slates had slipped off the roof and the rafters were exposed to the brooding skies. Weeds sprouted from the wonky chimney and an abandoned bird's nest threatened to topple at any moment. The window frames were warped, the glass long since gone, allowing the weather free rein inside the house. The front door hung on a rusty hinge and groaned painfully as Catrin entered.

The downstairs rooms were littered with broken

furniture, and sand had blown up from the beach, piling in drifts on the floor amid shrivelled birds' nests, sheep shit and the remains of camp fires. This was where Benito had camped out that summer long ago.

The staircase was rotten, broken away from the wall, and looking up, Catrin could see the gaping roof and the rain-laden sky above it.

She went out through the hole where the back door had once been, into the overgrown garden, where the smell of rosemary and mint was strong after the downpour.

She thought suddenly of the blind man who had lived here in the olden days, the man who could tell the colour of things without seeing them; another survivor of the ill-fated *Flino*. A man and his pregnant wife, who had scrambled up here and set up home, had a house full of children like the old woman who lived in the shoe.

At the end of the overgrown garden, sunken steps led up to another level and Catrin climbed them wearily. More steps led up from the next level and when she got to the top step she sat down with a heavy sigh.

The sun came out after the rain and bathed everything in a new and watery light. She was above the level of the house now, and could see the sea over the roof and, to her right, the smoke rising from the chimneys of Aberderi. To her left she could see the lane that led down from the station, the tower of Kilvenny Castle and the rooks circling high above it.

Absentmindedly she pulled up a handful of weeds and her hand touched something rough, a cockleshell set into the wall. She tried to pick it up but it was set fast. She knelt down and pulled up more weeds until she was soaked with rainwater and spattered with earth. The shells had been painstakingly arranged to form letters: *Tito, Lucia, Caterina*.

She wandered back down the steps and through the

desolate rooms of the house. As she went into the front garden and made her way across the overgrown flagstones, an image of Maria Paparella drifted before her eyes, a woman with an expression of such glee on her face that it made Catrin smile. Those warm, dark eyes, the skin of her face as brown as an early conker, her cheeks highlighted in downy pink, the full-lipped mouth opening and beginning to sing tunelessly but joyfully.

All around Catrin, now, was the sound of children's voices on the wind.

She could see the face of Piero di Bardi as he was in *Recipes for Cherubs*, a thin-faced man with dark, tangled hair. His cheeks were hollow and there were dark circles under his eyes. Wonderful, dreamy, haunting eyes . . .

He had eyes which reminded her of Nonna, eyes which were losing their sight.

The children's voices were closer now, mingling with the cry of gulls.

'Tell us the colours of the paints in your workshop, Papa!'

Indigo, verdigris, lampblack, cinabrese, sinoper, vermillion, ochre, saffron.

Mamma, make us some *brutti ma buoni*. Please, Mamma.

Tito, come quick, Bindo is coming.

Hey, Bindo.

She put her hands to her head, pressing her fingers against her throbbing temples.

She knew without a doubt that they had all been here. Piero, the man whose life had been all about colour, a man who could tell the colour of something by its touch. Maria looking after him and all those children they'd had. She was suddenly struck with a thought. Did Piero know that Bindo was his son, and did Bindo realise who his father was, or had they lived their lives unaware of the truth?

Chapter 58

Sister Annunziata, newly arrived at the Convent of Santa Lucia, unlocked the door to the cell at the top of the turret and stepped inside hesitantly. This cell was kept for difficult newcomers, so that their screaming should not stir up those on the lower floors. They usually stayed up here a week and then, if they complied with all that was asked of them, they were moved to other cells.

The little rich girl who had arrived screaming and biting like a wild animal two weeks ago gave no sign of doing as she was asked. According to the other sisters, she refused to wash or to eat and sat all day and most of the night staring ahead of her. When she did fall asleep through sheer exhaustion, her sleep was fitful and she cried out pitifully.

Sister Annunziata watched the girl anxiously. She was huddled in a corner, knees drawn up to her chin, head bowed in submission or fury – it was hard to tell. Her shock of wild, unwashed hair covered her face like a veil, and there were bruises on her thin arms and angry weals round her ankles from when she had been restrained.

Sister Annunziata opened the door and listened in case any of the other sisters had followed her. She had firm orders merely to check on the girl and report back, but the child was in a terrible state and it couldn't be right to leave her like this.

For some moments Sister Annunziata struggled with her con-

science, but then she thought that surely God in all His wisdom would not want her to abandon a child. She dipped a cloth into the stoop of water set into the wall. Kneeling down, she lifted the child's face and pushed her hair back so that she could see her properly. Her face was streaked with grime and there were dark circles beneath the bluest eyes the sister had ever seen. She gently cleaned the child's face, spoke soothingly to her and wetted her parched lips from a tin cup. The girl put out her hand tentatively and touched Sister Annunziata on the cheek, a touch full of gratitude.

She lifted the girl on to the pallet bed, covered her with a coarse blanket and then sat with her for a long time, stroking her forehead until, fearful that one of the other nuns would come to see where she was, she leant over and kissed the girl's cheek tenderly.

A few weeks later, she was passing through the market place in Terrini, head bowed and eyes lowered as she had been instructed to do by her superiors, when she heard a piercing whistle nearby. She did not look up, for fear of catching someone's eye, because the locals believed that the nuns from Santa Lucia could put the evil eye on them. She walked quickly on through the market place but the whistling seemed to come from all around her. She stopped in front of an enormous wine barrel and slowly raised her eyes. She jumped in alarm as a young dwarf popped up from behind the barrel, grinned at her and winked.

'You're a nun from Santa Lucia?'

'I'm not supposed to talk to anyone,' murmured Sister Annunziata.

'Well, don't. I'll ask the questions and you just nod or shake your head. How about that?'

She shook her head and made to move away.

'You know Ismelda Bisotti?'

Despite all her good intentions she nodded enthusiastically.

'Is she well?

She inclined her head.

'Would you give her this?'

He held out a pomegranate towards her.

An emphatic shake of her head this time.

Bindo thrust his hand down into his shirt and pulled out a piece of string tied round his neck.

'See the ring I keep on this string next to my heart? Ismelda gave me this ring. I'm going to marry her one day, so it's all quite proper.'

Sister Annunziata put her hand to her mouth to stifle a rising giggle. This little fellow was so comical, so serious and sure of himself.

'Please,' he begged, going down on one knee theatrically.

'Get up at once, you fool. People are beginning to look at us.'

'If you don't take it to her, I will follow you all round the market and call out that you were once my betrothed but that you forsook me to become a bride of Christ.'

Sister Annunziata's mouth dropped open in horror. She had no doubt that this brazen fellow would carry out his threat. Imagine if word got back to the convent! She would be mortified and dragged before her superior.

'Very well!' she hissed through clenched teeth, and she snatched the pomegranate and hid it beneath the folds of her habit. 'Now go away and leave me alone!'

After his first meeting with Sister Annunziata, Bindo went to Terrini market every week, hitching a ride on a donkey cart. He followed Sister Annunziata surreptitiously, passing her his gifts to Ismelda when they were sure no one was watching. He brought a lemon, a paintbrush, a slice of walnut cake, and often he sent a note tucked between two slices of focaccia telling her all the news from Santa Rosa. Maria was getting fatter. One day soon Piero's masterpiece was to be unveiled in the church at Santa Rosa. Her father now had a son and heir, an ugly child with a nose on him the size of a carrot.

In return Ismelda sent him notes and sometimes a small painting which she did to cheer him up.

Chapter 59

Ella was rattled. She'd looked everywhere for Catrin, but couldn't find her. Dan Gwartney said he'd seen her wobbling off on Tony Agosti's old bike, heading off past the war memorial, but she'd been gone for hours and the weather was threatening to come in rough.

In frustration she decided to walk up to Shrimp's to see if Catrin was up there. She needed to see the place again, because she couldn't ignore the fact that one day soon she'd have to think about moving back in, and there was a hell of a lot of work to be done before she could.

Catrin's unexpected arrival had done her a favour, dropped the scales from her eyes and made her come to her senses, start looking outwards again. No doubt Kizzy would make contact eventually and Catrin would be whisked away out of her life for ever. The thought of life without Catrin filled her with sadness. She'd lived for years without any desire to see Kizzy's child, and yet after a few weeks in her company she couldn't bear the thought of losing her.

The rain started as she was walking up the steps from the beach, and with her head down she made her way through the long grass.

She let herself into Shrimp's and stood staring around her, wondering how she had let things sink to this sorry state. Looking back, there hadn't been a particular moment when she'd given up, but after Alice died she'd slowly shut down, lost interest in herself and her surroundings. She'd stopped taking bookings and let the staff go.

She closed her eyes and tried to conjure up how the kitchen had once been. This had been Gladys Beynon's kingdom and was always kept spotless. Gleaming copper pots and pans reflected the light from the range, where the fire was never allowed to go out, and there was always tea brewing on the hob for all the tradesmen who brought baskets of meat and crates of fish. Halloran, the old gardener, came in with armfuls of carrots and cucumbers, radishes and peas in the pod grown in the kitchen garden.

It used to be a hive of activity and the smells were mouthwatering. There was always the aroma of fresh bread and scones baking and the tantalising smell of hot butter being drizzled over the potted shrimps in the earthenware ramekins; the salty tang of lobsters and bream, cod and hake, kippers, cockles and mussels.

Alice coming into the kitchen arm in arm with Benito, whom she often met when she was walking back from Duffy's Farm where she went every morning to collect the cream and eggs. Alice carrying armfuls of wild flowers which she used to make up her posies. Alice telling Gladys, with the enthusiasm of a child, that Benito had found the remains of an Italian bread oven in the garden at Blind Man's Lookout. Benito offering to make one for Gladys if she wanted. Gladys huffing and puffing and saying Welsh bread had always been good enough for her and she wasn't having any foreign nonsense in her kitchen.

How they'd laughed then, Benito saying that some of the fish she was cooking had maybe been born in Italian waters and swum all the way to Kilvenny.

There was always talking and laughter, and in the

background the bells in the pantry constantly ringing, chambermaids running hither and thither carrying with them the smells of polish and fresh linen. Kizzy waltzing in and checking her make-up in the mirror on the back of the pantry door, glancing furtively at young Tony Agosti, who had brought up some tubs of homemade ice cream from the Café Romana. Benito sitting between Alice and Kizzy, tucking into a breakfast of bacon and lava bread and cockles brought over from Aberderi.

If only she'd had the courage, she should have handed over the running of Shrimp's to Gladys and offered Tony Agosti the chance to work with her; they would have made a great team, and she could have left Kilvenny and made a new life for herself somewhere far away, out of reach of gossips and philistines.

She closed the kitchen door and made her way up to Alice's room, where she stood for a long while staring at the painting of *Woman and Child*. She felt close to Alice at that moment. Alice as a child, blowing kisses to this woman in the blue dress, hiding under the table in the Fisherman's Snug. Alice as a woman, looking forward to marriage and having lots of children. She had even chosen names for them: Lucia, Maria, Pepito.

It was almost dark as she went downstairs. The telephone began to ring. She stood stiffly listening to the shrill sound. No one had telephoned Shrimp's in years; she'd stopped answering calls after Alice had died. She waited until the ringing stopped and then went out through the kitchen, locking the door behind her. She had taken no more than a few paces when the telephone began to ring again. She let herself back in, hurried to the booth and lifted the receiver. She flinched when she heard the hysterical voice on the other end of the line.

Chapter 60

It was summer at last and the sun rose early, bringing with it a luminous light which drifted up the river, chasing away the bats, rinsing the sky of stars and transforming the river to a twist of pink and yellow light.

Ismelda stood at the window looking down into the valley below. If she leant right out, she could see the deep pool below the convent where the nuns did the washing. They looked so small from up here, their heads bent as they knelt scrubbing sheets against the stones. Sometimes a soap bubble drifted up towards her, a rainbow orb glistening in the sunlight, and she thought longingly of the Villa Rosso, of Bindo and Maria, of Luca and Piero, of all that she had lost.

Sister Annunziata had told her that they had been several times to visit her but each time they had been turned away. As the days went on she became more despondent. Once a day she was allowed out into the yard for exercise, but the other inmates terrified her: dribbling old women who rocked back and forth, groaning; others who moved around as if in a trance and, the worst by far, the ones in shackles who screamed and shook on the spot as if trying to remember the steps to some strange dance they'd learnt long ago.

At meal times she sat in the refectory looking apathetically at the bowl of stewed beans that was served each day; all appetite gone. She thought longingly of the days in the Villa Rosso when she'd sat beneath the pomegranate tree with her friends, the sun breaking through the branches and dappling them with light.

High summer passed, and all too soon the cold winds of autumn came boisterously up the valley, clattering the shutters and making the inmates of Santa Lucia howl with misery at the thought of approaching winter.

Chapter 61

The moon was floating above Gwartney's Wood, the first uneasy stars pricking through the bowl of inky sky, when Catrin wobbled back down Cockle Lane on the bike.

Dan Gwartney, standing at the window of the library, waved as she passed the window but she was in no mood to talk to anyone. The lights were out in the Café Romana, and Meredith's shop was in darkness.

She left the bike in the courtyard of the castle, looked around for Aunt Ella and decided that she was either over talking to Nonna or she had gone to bed early.

She went into the kitchen, cut herself some bread and cheese, grabbed an apple from the fruit bowl and hurried upstairs. She found *Recipes for Cherubs* and turned to the picture of Bindo. She smiled down at his cheeky face, traced the dusting of freckles on his snub nose and sighed.

If everything she'd worked out was true, Piero di Bardi and Maria Paparella had survived the sinking of the *Flino* and set up house in Blind Man's Lookout. Bindo had been saved and come to work for Nathaniel Grieve in Kilvenny, where poor Luca Roselli was buried in the churchyard.

She yawned and her stomach rumbled noisily. She was starving after all the exercise, but the bread and cheese must wait; there was something she needed to do. She went over

344

to the wardrobe and got out Aunt Alice's dowry box.

She'd been wrong about one thing. Arthur Campbell certainly wouldn't have married Alice Grieve just to get his hands on the rubbishy trinkets she'd stashed in the box. Maybe he really had loved her.

She opened the box, tipped out the contents and dropped the box on to the bed – and heard something rattling inside. She shook the box, tipped it upside down, and saw the false bottom. Carefully she turned the box round in her hands and examined it, slid out the bottom of the box and tipped out a pile of small paintings.

She gathered them up and laid them around her on the bed.

They were similar to the ones in *Recipes for Cherubs*, although the hand that had painted these was less sure, less steady.

There were four paintings in all.

The first was of a red-cheeked young nun winking cheekily beneath her wimple, the fingers of one hand crossed as if she was wishing someone good luck. In the other hand she held a leather-bound book with gold writing on the front that looked as if it had been recently painted: *Recipes for Cherubs*. A book which had been put together over two hundred years ago and had somehow ended up here in Kilvenny and given Catrin as much pain and pleasure as it probably had Aunt Alice before her.

She turned to the second painting, and her hand shook as she held it. There was Bindo as Catrin had never seen him before, his face white with shock, tears streaming down his dirt-streaked cheeks, his lips shaking with sorrow. Standing beside him was Luca, holding on to Bindo with one hand, the scar on Luca's cheek livid against the extraordinary pallor of his skin.

Above the two forlorn figures of the boys the sky over

Santa Rosa was darkly brooding, while around their bare feet leaves swirled in a wild eddy. Catrin could feel the pain seeping out of the painting and she shivered as they, too, would have been shivering in the cold night air . . .

She wrinkled her nose in disgust at the third painting. There were the two Zanelli sisters done up like dog's dinners, wearing identical dresses of frothy cream lace, their hair in glossy ringlets and tied with red ribbons. They looked as smug as guts, their pink mouths twisted into satisfied smiles, eyes hard as dried prunes. Signor Bisotti stood behind them with a smile which revealed teeth the colour of graveyard headstones. Standing next to him was the widow Zanelli, one hand laid across her chest, revealing a gold band on her ring finger, and on her face a smile which could turn butter rancid.

Happy families. The new Bisotti family in the days before they went to Naples and made their fortune selling ice cream and then on to America where they had become millionaires. She supposed Ismelda had left Santa Rosa, too, and gone with them, poor girl.

The final painting made her draw back in alarm. It was a view from a great height, looking down to where a river meandered between huge boulders. There were birds on the wing, seen from above, floating on currents of air. It made her head spin and she felt a tightness pressing down on her ribs, forcing the air out of her lungs and making her gasp.

Catrin put down the painting and sat staring ahead of her. When she'd first seen the paintings in *Recipes for Cherubs* she'd been full of wonder. They had cheered her up when it had seemed that life wasn't worth living; the recipes had given her an interest in food and making things for other people to enjoy. Maria, Luca, Ismelda, Bindo and Piero had felt like friends, not just pictures in a book, and yet beneath the surface there had been something unpleasant bubbling away all the time.

There was such a difference between the paintings here and the ones in *Recipes for Cherubs*. There was no feeling of joy, of celebration or appetite for life in these. They were pictures of loss and separation, of misery and pain.

She heard someone calling her name, and before she had time to hide the dowry box, Aunt Ella came rushing into the room, her face puce with exertion, her breath coming in ragged gasps.

'What's the matter, Aunt Ella?'

'I've just spoken to your mother on the telephone and she's spitting teeth and feathers.'

Part Three

Chapter 62

Kizzy Grieve stepped down off the train, smoothed her clothes and patted her hair. Then, looking around, she frowned and wondered if she'd got off at the right place. Kilvenny station had always been spick and span, with pots of bright flowers set along the platform and baskets of flowers hanging outside the waiting room. But now the kiosk that used to serve tea and biscuits and hot soup in the winter was boarded up, and there wasn't a soul in sight. It was all run-down and grubby and there was no station-master or porter to carry her suitcase.

She sighed. What she really wanted right now was a large gin and tonic and a long, hot bath. First, though, she'd have to face the Aunts and she wasn't relishing that at all. As for Catrin, when she got her on her own she'd give her an absolute ear bashing. How dare she ignore her letters and not send any money? She'd had an absolute nightmare of a time in that godforsaken hellhole of a convent. She cursed under her breath. If she ever found out who had sent her on a wild-goose chase, there'd be hell to pay. It was pretty damned obvious now why she'd been sent the stupid postcard in the first place.

When she'd arrived back in London she'd opened the door of the house in Ermington Square and realised immediately that something was wrong. The hallway was in chaos, the telephone table upturned and the cupboards under the stairs emptied out, umbrellas and hats tossed all over the place. The drawing room had been ransacked and every door and cupboard in the kitchen emptied, drawers opened and the contents strewn all around.

The rest of the house was in equal turmoil and yet when she'd hurtled into her bedroom to check her jewellery box it was untouched. As she'd stood with her hand poised over the telephone to report the burglary to the police, it had started to ring and she'd been so relieved to hear Arthur Campbell's voice on the other end of the line. He'd offered to come straight round, organised someone to come and do the clearing up and had taken her back to his house for the night, then driven her to Paddington this morning.

And now here she was back in Kilvenny. She wandered out of the station and into the lane to look for a taxi but the lane was deserted. Damn and blast! It would take for ever to walk all the way to Shrimp's. As soon as she could she'd get out of this dreary backwater and sort something out with Catrin's school, arrange for her to stay there for the rest of the holidays. Kizzy needed a proper break after everything she'd been through of late.

She teetered down the lane towards Kilvenny, her high heels clacking noisily on the tarmac, her suitcase banging against her legs.

When she turned into Cockle Lane she stopped suddenly. Kilvenny had never been the most exciting place in the world, but this was far worse than she remembered it. It had been pretty in its ramshackle way, but now half the houses were boarded up and the others in dire need of a paintbrush. There was something else missing, too; that awful smell of bloody fish.

A light went off in the Proprietary Library as she passed

the window. She wondered if Dan Gwartney were still alive; he'd always seemed as old as the hills. She was sure he'd had a bit of a thing for Aunt Ella, but it certainly hadn't been mutual. The telephone in the library rang and made Kizzy jump. She swore under her breath. She'd only been back in Kilvenny five minutes and already her nerves were in shreds.

The Café Romana was still there, but it lay in darkness, which was odd because it had always been full in the evenings. She smiled then, thinking of the days when she'd lingered for hours over a sarsaparilla, making eyes at the local boys. She supposed Tony Agosti had long since left for the bright lights of the city; he'd always had ambition, that boy, and he was so good-looking.

Outside Meredith Evans's shop she stopped to catch her breath and glance at the photographs on display. God almighty, it was like a time warp in there; none of the photographs had been changed.

Meredith had been an odd little fellow and absolutely besotted with Aunt Alice. Maybe when all the hullabaloo had died down after the wedding Alice had married him. In fact, Mrs Alice Meredith might be in there now, fast asleep upstairs, cuddled up to Meredith.

That whole affair between Aunt Alice and Arthur Campbell had been very odd. Whatever he'd seen in Aunt Alice had been a total mystery, and it would never have worked out between them. She'd done Aunt Alice a favour, really, by flirting with Arthur, although she hadn't meant it to turn out the way it had. God, it had been awful when Aunt Alice didn't turn up at the chapel, with everyone there waiting expectantly. There was worse to come, though, when Ella had shown her the photographs of her and Arthur Campbell together. She'd never been in any doubt about who had taken them; it was Meredith, and the motive pure spite. Oh, well, that was all water under the bridge and probably all for the best as far as everyone was concerned. She'd thought it was the end of the world at the time, but it had given her the opportunity to escape from Kilvenny and Arthur Campbell had provided for her and Catrin well.

She looked down Cockle Lane towards Kilvenny Castle and shuddered. She'd hated that spooky place when she was a child. It was so ancient and cold, full of whispering noises and peculiar smells that came from nowhere. When she got back to London she'd put it on the market and get shot of it.

As she came level with the castle she stopped in her tracks. There was a flickering light in her old bedroom windows, as if the fire had been lit, and there was a light on in the kitchen.

She crept up to the latticed windows and peered inside. An old woman with the wildest hair she'd ever seen was sitting near the stove and opposite her sat Catrin, cross-legged in a high-backed chair. She looked very different from the last time Kizzy had seen her. She'd put on some weight, and her skin was bronzed, her face animated in a way Kizzy had rarely seen. Kizzy bristled. How could she sit there looking so bloody cheerful when she'd left her own mother abandoned in a convent full of lunatics?

She looked at the old woman again and realised with a shock that it was Aunt Ella. The years hadn't been kind to her – she'd never been a good-looking woman but she'd always made the best of herself in a casual way. What were they doing down here at the castle, instead of up at Shrimp's?

She was about to march in and disturb this delightful domestic scene, but then she had second thoughts. Aunt Ella wasn't likely to kill the fatted calf at her homecoming so perhaps it would be best if she went up to Shrimp's first, to find out what was going on. If Aunt Alice was there it would be easier to break the ice with her – she was always the easier of the two to twist round Kizzy's finger.

She backed away from the window and hurried down Cockle Lane where she stood looking at the Fisherman's Snug. She thought longingly of those long, hot summers when she'd been home from boarding school and how she used to hide under the table in there for a kissing session with whoever she was with at the time. She sighed and slipped off her shoes to relieve her pinched toes, and to her surprise the door of the Snug opened and someone stepped out of the shadows.

'It's been a long time,' a voice said coldly.

Kizzy screwed up her eyes against the darkness. The man came closer: she swallowed hard. The pulse in the man's throat was beating quickly, his face drained of colour in the moonlight.

'So you came back at last, then?' he said through gritted teeth.

'Hallo, Meredith. Well, you'll be glad to hear I'm not staying long. I've just come to pick up my daughter.'

'That's a shame. She seems happy here, and she looks a damn sight better than when she arrived.'

'Ah, well, that's good. I need to get back to London with her as soon as possible.'

'Where are you off to now?'

'Up to Shrimp's, actually, looking for Aunt Alice.'

'You won't find her there.'

'I see,' Kizzy said. So she was right, he must have married Aunt Alice after all. Kizzy slipped her shoes back on and followed Meredith back up Cockle Lane, huffing and puffing loudly, hoping he'd do the gentlemanly thing and carry her suitcase.

He walked resolutely on and stopped by the wicket gate that led to the graveyard.

'She's over there,' he said.

Kizzy looked bemused as she followed his gaze. Then he pulled something from his pocket and the beam of a torch danced across the gravestones, coming to rest on one.

Alice Katherine Grieve
Taken after a short illness

Kizzy looked from the grave to Meredith and then down at her feet in embarrassment and annoyance, realising with irritation that she'd laddered her stockings and she'd put them on new this morning.

'Have you at last come back to apologise for what you did?'

'I didn't even know she'd died,' Kizzy said sulkily.

'Because you never bothered to find out.'

'No, because Ella Grieve unceremoniously threw me out. You know what Ella's like. She wouldn't listen and she had no intention of forgiving me.'

Meredith looked away in disgust. 'Alice broke her heart when she found out what you'd been up to with that bloody Campbell.'

'And you can honestly tell me that you were sad about that?' Kizzy taunted.

Meredith bristled with anger. 'Everybody knew I hated him, but I never wanted her to be hurt, never thought she'd leave Kilvenny. She left, you know, and didn't come back for a long time, and by the time she did she was seriously ill.'

'And that was my fault, too, I suppose?' Kizzy snapped.

'I think the fact that you were pregnant had a lot to do with it.'

Kizzy laughed uproariously. Meredith glared at her, clenching and unclenching his fists as if contemplating hitting her.

'So you knew I was pregnant? I'm not the first and I won't be the last girl to fall for someone's charm and be left holding the baby.'

'What you did to Alice was despicable, and you think it's funny?'

Kizzy curbed her laughter, fell silent and then looked at Meredith as if she had suddenly realised he had two heads. 'I don't believe it! You think that I was pregnant by . . .?'

Meredith nodded slowly, deliberately.

'Oh my God! You think that Catrin's father is . . .?'

Kizzy put her hand to her head and then looked beyond Meredith at a figure emerging from the shadows.

'Dan Gwartney?' she said.

Meredith turned and saw Dan Gwartney standing there, a glowing cigarette clamped between his lips.

'Welcome back, Kizzy. It's been a long time.'

Chapter 63

The icy wind whistled around the tower of Santa Rosa church, and the bells clanged loudly. In the piazza people milled around, stamping their feet to keep warm, blowing on their fingers, as they waited impatiently for the doors of the church to open. Today was the grand unveiling of Piero di Bardi's painting of Feasting Cherubs. There were shivering peasants dressed in rags, huddled together for warmth, a clutch of priests from nearby villages chattering like starlings, and excited children running hither and thither, calling loudly to their friends.

The crowd grew quieter as the door of the Villa Rosso opened. Signor and Signora Bisotti, dressed in their finery, heads held high, emerged into the piazza followed by Alessandra and Adriana on either side of Father Rimaldi.

The crowd clamoured behind them but as they entered the church they grew quieter, pressing urgently for seats near the front, where a large canvas was covered by a crimson cloth.

The Bisottis stood together while Father Rimaldi looked around impatiently for Piero di Bardi. Where the hell was the fellow? After a few minutes he sent a little lad scurrying off to the Via Dante in search of him. The child returned, red-faced with the cold, and whispered to Father Rimaldi, who in turn whispered to Signor Bisotti.

The crowd began to grow restless and Signor Bisotti, eager not to lose his moment of fame, spoke hurriedly to Father Rimaldi.

'I paid him last night, so the fellow's probably already drunk. These artist types are so unpredictable, so unreliable, not like normal people at all. Let's just get on with it. These peasants don't smell too good when they're all cooped up together.'

Father Rimaldi addressed the congregation, eulogising about the generosity of Signor Bisotti and how a small village like Santa Rosa would now be on the map, boasting a work of art from the renowned Piero di Bardi, who sadly was indisposed at present.

Then, after a ferocious dig in the ribs from his wife, Signor Bisotti stepped forward and with a flourish whipped a corner of the crimson cloth away from the painting.

Signor Bisotti's eyes rolled upwards and he squealed with pain as Signora Bisotti's nails dug into the soft flesh on the inside of his wrist.

Alessandra and Adriana began to howl plaintively, screwing up their faces into masks of misery. Father Rimaldi's face turned as white as the altar cloth and the crowd craned their necks to see what all the fuss was about.

Chapter 64

In the silence of the kitchen the clock ticked loudly. The only other sound was the intake of Catrin's breath as the door opened and Kizzy made her entrance, breezing into the room and demanding immediate attention.

'Well, it's all very nice and cosy in here,' she said sarcastically.

Catrin jumped to her feet with alacrity and stepped behind the chair she had been sitting in.

'Ah, at last the absent mother deigns to show her face,' Ella said, folding her arms firmly across her chest and staring defiantly at Kizzy.

Kizzy Grieve, as beautiful as ever, immaculately dressed with not a hair out of place and flawless make-up, was back in Kilvenny and determined to make her presence felt.

Kizzy gave Ella a cursory glance, then turned on Catrin, hands on her slim hips, her face set in anger.

'Well, madam,' she said, 'I'd be very interested to know why I was left abandoned in Italy because you ignored my request for money!'

Catrin bit her lip and looked to Ella for reassurance. Ella smiled at her and winked to give her courage.

'I'm waiting for an answer to my question.'

Catrin looked away, wringing her hands in agitation.

'Maybe you'll have to wait a long time,' Ella growled

'This is my daughter, Aunt Ella, and I'll be the judge of how long I have to wait.'

'Yes, she is your daughter and it's a pretty sorry state of affairs that you sent her down here without asking if it was okay. Now, as it happens it was fine, but you, feckless idiot that you are, didn't know that!'

'I was desperate, as it happens, and how was I to know you'd let Shrimp's go to the dogs?'

'You've been up to Shrimp's?' Ella asked.

'No, Dan Gwartney told me all that's been going on here.'

'Well, I think that now you've decided to grace us with your company it's you who have some questions to answer, not Catrin.'

Kizzy looked perturbed, anxiety drawing down the corners of her painted mouth momentarily.

Catrin took a deep breath and braced herself. 'I didn't send you any money and I didn't want to ring Arthur Campbell because I thought he'd come and take me away from here.'

'So you thought it fine to leave me languishing miles from home in a lunatic asylum.'

'I wanted to teach you a lesson, if you must know, let you know that you can't always get your own way.'

Catrin's voice was high, a wobble of fear tightening in her throat. She'd never in all her life answered her mother back, and she was afraid of the consequences.

'Teach me a lesson? Do you think I'm a child? You left me stranded, and I had to beg a voyage back on a bloody boat from Naples and I was put in a cabin that was full of crates of onions and dried fish.'

Ella turned her head away to hide her amusement and Catrin, seeing her, had a terrible urge to giggle.

'I was sick of doing everything you asked me. You didn't

even tell me I had family here until it suited you to go gallivanting after some man.'

'Well, if you must know, the man in question sent me a postcard inviting me to Italy and then he didn't bother to show up – I went all that way for nothing. To cap it all, when I got home the house had been burgled,' Kizzy said with a pout. Catrin thought that she looked more like a ten-year-old than a grown-up.

'I know you've told me lies, too,' Catrin faltered, biting her lip.

Ella got up and went to her.

'For goodness sake we can do without the theatricals, Catrin,' Kizzy said, slumping into a chair, removing a shoe and rubbing her toes.

Ella snorted. 'That's bloody rich coming from you, Kizzy Grieve. There wasn't a day went by when you didn't make a drama out of something when you were a teenager.'

'That's rubbish. I was highly strung and sensitive.'

'I think you have some explaining to do.'

For the first time ever, Kizzy looked as if the wind had been taken out of her sails and Catrin looked at Ella with admiration.

'Catrin knows you were pregnant the summer you left school.'

Kizzy stiffened. 'I suppose you couldn't wait to tell her that. You always were a stickler for the truth except where it concerned you.'

Ella glowered at Kizzy. 'You have a very bright daughter – which is a miracle in itself. I told her nothing but she put two and two together and found the truth.'

'You told me I had your surname because my father's name was foreign.'

Kizzy was breathing deeply. That hadn't exactly been a lie, had it?

Ella wrung her hands in anxiety. The truth had to come out, and any minute now Catrin would know who her father was, and God knows how that would make her feel.

'It wasn't very easy for me, either, you know,' Kizzy wheedled, stepping towards Catrin.

Catrin edged closer to Ella, who put a hand on her tremulous shoulders.

'I want to know who my father is.'

The three of them stood in awkward silence, unaware that the door had opened and someone had come quietly into the room.

'It's not a difficult question, is it?' Catrin said in a barely audible voice.

'I think you should tell the child his name.' Ella's gaze was resolute.

There was an expectant silence.

As Kizzy opened her mouth to speak, someone said, 'I'm her father.'

The three of them turned to see Tony Agosti standing white-faced in the doorway.

Chapter 65

Over in the library Dan Gwartney was sitting in his usual chair opposite Meredith Evans when Ella came hurrying in.

'Am I interrupting something?' she asked

'Sit down, Ella, and join us in a drink.'

She sat down heavily and said, 'You heard the news, then?'

Dan and Meredith nodded.

'Nonna's over the moon,' Dan said. 'She thinks the world of that little girl in the short time she's been here.'

'That was a turn-up for the books,' Meredith said. 'How did Catrin take it?'

'Shocked but delighted, I'd say. I've just been up to check on her and she's sleeping like a baby.'

'We were worried it might set her back.'

'It seems, though, that I have an apology to make to Kizzy, and that will stick in my craw.'

'You thought the father was Arthur Campbell?'

'I was convinced of it, especially after seeing the photographs you sent Alice of Kizzy and him together.'

'I didn't send any photographs,' he protested.

'Come on, Meredith. It's been a day for uncovering the truth, so why don't you own up and clear the air?'

Dan coughed and Ella turned to him.

'It was me who sent the photographs and the note to Alice,' he said sheepishly.

'You what?'

'I sent the photographs and the note.'

'But why?'

'I knew what was going on between Kizzy and Campbell – I'd seen them in Gwartney's Wood together – and I thought Alice should know.'

'Didn't you think of telling me first?'

'I sent them, Ella, because I thought ... I know it was wrong of me, but I knew he was a rotter and I thought if Alice didn't marry him she'd stay at Shrimp's and that would keep you here, too.'

Ella fell silent, and Meredith looked away in embarrassment.

'There, I've said it. Bloody old fool that I am, I never gave up on you.'

'Christ, I need to apologise to you, Meredith, as well,' Ella said, running her hands through her hair in agitation.

Meredith smiled wryly. 'If it's any help, Alice had decided to cancel the wedding before she saw the photographs.'

'Why?'

'Arthur Campbell wanted something desperately from Alice, and he couldn't get it unless he married her.'

'What was it?' Ella asked.

'He wanted her book of recipes and paintings and she'd said they would be part of her dowry and be given to him on her wedding night.'

'Why on earth would he want that old thing?'

'Because that book is worth a fortune,' Meredith said patiently.

'It's a child's colouring book.'

'No, it's a book of paintings by Piero di Bardi.'

Dan blew a breath in disbelief, and Ella gasped.

'The book my mother wanted burnt, the one Catrin's been copying her recipes from?'

'That's the one. Whatever your mother burnt, it wasn't that. Anyway, Alice had shown Campbell the book. There were some loose paintings in the back and Alice had given him one, and then she found out he'd sold it for a fortune.'

'I'm completely lost now,' Ella groaned.

'She gave him a picture of a cherub. She thought it was worthless, but later she saw a postcard of the very same picture, the *Napoli Cherub*.'

'Good God!'

'I did some research for her and found out that it had been sold by an anonymous seller – Campbell, obviously – and she realised he'd betrayed her.'

'The bastard!' exclaimed Ella.

'So you see, he would have done anything to get his hands on that book, and when she didn't turn up for the wedding he must have been furious. He went through the castle like a dose of salts looking for it.'

'He wasn't the only one looking for Piero di Bardi paintings, though. Do you remember Benito, Ella?'

She nodded.

'I think Alice showed him the book, too, but swore him to secrecy.'

'And then he was accused of—'

'Trying to steal something from Arthur Campbell's sister, which was all very convenient, looking back.'

'But he escaped from the tower and ran off.'

'Never to be heard of again?'

'Tony had a postcard from him a few weeks later from Italy,' Dan said. 'I saw it a few weeks ago but there was something odd about it which got me thinking. You see, I don't think it was Benito's handwriting.'

'So someone else sent the postcard,' Meredith ventured.

'Exactly. I'd seen Benito's handwriting when he came into the library to study. The writing on the card was a good likeness, but it wasn't his.'

'Why would someone send Tony a postcard?'

'To put people off the scent,' Dan said.

'What do you think happened to him?'

'I don't know, Ella, but my guess is that Campbell wanted him out of the way. Whether he used blackmail or something worse we'll never know, but the thing is, Ella, if Campbell knows Catrin has the book she could be in danger. That man would stop at nothing.'

'I thought I saw him the other week, up at Shrimp's,' Dan said.

'So if he's been snooping about, he could well have found out that Catrin has the book,' Meredith said.

Ella shivered. 'You know, sometimes I fancied I could hear people walking about upstairs.'

'I used to sneak in sometimes, just to check that you were still alive,' Dan said.

'Me too,' Meredith added sheepishly.

'Well, if Campbell does come here, we'll be waiting for him,' Ella said.

'Oh, he'll come,' Dan said with certainty.

Chapter 66

The cart pulled up outside the Convent of Santa Lucia in the middle of the night, stirring up a cloud of dust. Someone climbed down from the cart, ran to the door and tugged the bell-pull. The sound of the bell echoed through the gloomy corridors and Sister Annunziata hurried to see who was there before they woke the whole convent up. She opened the grille and saw three tense faces, then a fourth as Bindo was lifted to eye level.

'What do you want at this time of the night?'

'To see Ismelda,' Bindo said emphatically.

'Don't be absurd. You know she's allowed no visitors.'

'You must tell her, then, that we are leaving but we will be back for her.'

'You're going somewhere?'

'Out of the country,' the woman said. 'We're leaving as soon as we can, but you must let her know that we haven't deserted her.'

'Be sure to tell her it may be a while before I can come again, but I will never desert her,' Bindo said. 'There's a basket here with some food for her,' he went on. 'Will you make sure that she gets it?'

Sister Annunziata nodded and replied, 'Now you must go before any of the other sisters come to see what's going on.'

When she was sure they had gone she unlocked the door and took in the basket.

Standing at the window of her cell, looking out into the night, Ismelda had heard her friends' voices. She heard the bell clang, and she danced up and down as she waited for someone to come for her, to usher her down to the visitors' room. The door would open and the four of them would be standing there, their faces breaking into smiles, the distinctive smell of their skin bringing warmth into the cold confines of the convent.

But no one came. Through a veil of tears she watched the cart drive away, listening until the sound of the rough wheels on the rutted road died away.

Later, Sister Annunziata brought her the news from her friends, and she tried to tempt her with some focaccia, some dainty little cheeses wrapped in olive leaves, some brutti ma buoni wrapped in a linen cloth, but Ismelda pushed the food aside, slumped down on to her straw mattress and stared up at the ceiling in despair.

Sister Annunziata was packing the food back when she saw a book in the bottom of the basket.

She took Ismelda in her arms and together they turned the pages of Recipes for Cherubs. As the wind grew stronger, whistling feverishly around the convent, Ismelda's eyes grew bright with a fierce intensity Sister Annunziata had never seen before.

Chapter 67

Kizzy waited in the Fisherman's Snug, sitting on the thread-bare old sofa, smoking a cigarette while she waited for Tony. She had almost given up hope of him coming when the door opened and he came in, shutting the door quickly behind him.

'I thought I was never going to get a chance to speak to you on your own,' she said, planting a kiss on his cheek. To her dismay, he backed away from her. He'd always been putty in her hands when they were teenagers, and she'd liked the feeling of power.

'I haven't got long, Kizzy, so get to the point.' He was edgy and stood by the window keeping an eye out in case anybody came past.

'I wanted to thank you for what you did,' Kizzy said, smiling up at him.

'There's no need to thank me,' he said coolly, surprising her.

'But it was chivalrous of you to rescue me like that.'

'Whatever you like to think, I didn't do it for you.'

She was covered in confusion and stepped closer to him, but he turned away again.

'Then why did you admit to being Catrin's father?' she retaliated.

'I did it for Catrin, because I couldn't bear for her to be hurt by what you were going to say.'

'Oh, and what was I going to say? That I didn't know who her father was?'

'I don't know,' he said.

'And you stood there and lied through your teeth. Do you think that will make her feel any better when she finds out?'

'It was foolish of me, but I'm fond of her. She was in a terrible state when she came here, and I'd hate her to be hurt any more.'

'You used to be fond of me,' Kizzy said, pouting.

'Only as a friend.'

'I remember getting up to a little more than what friends do, here in the Snug,' she said provocatively.

'That was a mistake. We were just children.'

'So who do you think is Catrin's father, then?'

'I haven't a clue.'

'Three guesses?'

'Don't be so bloody childish.'

'Benito,' she blurted out.

Tony took a step backwards, ran his fingers across his dry lips.

'How shocking is that?'

'I don't believe you.'

'Just look at her, Tony, look at her closely. You don't want to believe me, that's the problem. He led you a merry dance, didn't he?'

'I'm not going to listen to any more of this.'

Kizzy sidestepped him and stood with her back to the door.

'Either you listen to me or I tell my daughter, Miss Goody Two Shoes, that you're a liar.'

He turned to look out of the window.

371

'Benito and I met when I was on a school trip to Italy. That's why he came over here that summer, to be near me.'

'You never told me that. You pretended you'd met him for the first time that summer.'

'I'm a good liar, Tony. We used to meet up at Blind Man's Lookout; sometimes I even smuggled him into Shrimp's for our nights of passion.'

Tony bit his thumb to stop himself cursing her.

'Of course, by that time I was already pregnant and he'd promised to marry me.'

Tony didn't respond.

'Quite a Lothario, wasn't he? And he had the measure of you, all right.'

'What do you mean by that?' His voice was barely audible.

'I expect he told you he loved you, promised to open the restaurant of your dreams somewhere. Am I right?'

Tony turned to face her, his face taut with emotion. 'You knew all that? You knew he was stringing me along?'

'Oh yes. He'd left a trail of people all over Europe with broken dreams. I expect you gave him money?'

Tony nodded and looked closely at her; she was enjoying this. 'And you, Kizzy, did you give him money?'

She nodded. 'Oh yes, almost everything I'd been left by my mother. And I gave him a child he didn't hang around long enough to see.'

'And what did he promise you?'

'Undying love.'

'Me too,' Tony said in barely a whisper.

'Then we were both duped. I expect he's still out there making men and women fall in love with him,' Kizzy said. 'He never minded which sex he went for, as long as there was money behind it.'

'Do you ever hear from him?' Tony asked hopefully.

'Not a word until recently,' she replied, and his heart missed a beat.

She told him about the postcard and the trip to Italy.

'Do you think the postcard was from him?'

She shook her head. 'No. I've been thinking about it a lot, and I think someone wanted me out of the way, because while I was in Italy my house was burgled.'

'Did you lose much?'

'I've got precious little left to lose – I'm in a bad way financially.'

'But you've got the house.'

She shook her head. 'It belongs to Arthur Campbell. He's looked after Catrin and me since, er, since I was dumped by our Italian friend. And before you ask, no, he doesn't think he's Catrin's father.'

'He didn't strike me as the type to play Mr Bountiful.'

'Well, he's seen us right. Without him I wouldn't be able to pay Catrin's school fees.'

'Maybe she won't need to go back to boarding school.'

'Well, she's not coming home to me. I'm not cut out for full-time mothering.'

'You're honest at any rate, Kizzy.'

'A few days back here and I'm ready to bolt. It's my nature.'

'Where will you bolt to?'

'I've a friend holidaying in the South of France, and if I ever get out of this bloody place I'll be winging my way down there pretty damn quick.'

'And Catrin?' he asked.

'I could arrange for her to go back to school early.'

'She's happy enough here, don't you think?'

'With her new father?' Kizzy said with a laugh. And then she was out of the door and hurrying up Cockle Lane, leaving behind the faintest whiff of expensive perfume.

Chapter 68

Sister Annunziata hurried into the refectory, looked round the room and immediately saw the empty seat. Seeing her concern, one of the sisters whispered, 'The Bisotti girl has asked not to eat this evening because she is feeling unwell.'

Sister Annunziata nodded her thanks and smiled discreetly.

No doubt Ismelda had been feasting on the delicious food her friends had sent and probably could not face the watery beans and tough bread that were dished up nightly. When the meal was over she would try to slip away and spend some time with Ismelda.

Sister Annunziata looked sadly at the faces around her, dull-eyed and devoid of hope. She prayed that one day things would change, that more compassion would be shown to these poor souls whose minds were afflicted.

As for Ismelda, sweet Jesus, such a child should never have been put here. She was clever and capricious and a joy to be around. It was sinful that she should be incarcerated in a place like this because her father wanted her out of the way. Ismelda was a gift from God; she was wise beyond her years and had so much to offer the world. Half the inmates here didn't deserve to be locked up. They needed respite, peace and love to make them better, not shackles and chains and hours shut away in solitude. One day she hoped that she might be granted the strength to speak out and try to change things.

The last of the sun's rays played across the faces of the inmates and sisters seated at the long table; the faces of the mad and the sane all bathed in the warm glow of the late autumn sunset. The convent bell began to chime and the sister on duty looked up from her reading of the Scriptures as if aware that something was afoot. There was a restless silence in the room, a pent-up excitement exhibited in the twitching of noses, the feverish brightness in the expectant eyes of the inmates.

The echo of the bell clung to the air, along with a whiff of incense and the smell of candle smoke.

There was a sudden intake of breath as though everyone in the room was breathing at the same rate, everyone turning their face towards the largest of the arched windows.

A silence fractured by intensity.

Then a fleeting vision, as of a giant bird freefalling beyond the window, silhouetted momentarily against the archway of golden sky. Wild dark hair billowing out around a pale face, enormous eyes, a mouth opening, the cry of triumph . . . or was it terror?

A cacophony of twisted spoons banging on the wooden table and a raucous cheer growing ever louder.

The nuns rushed to the windows, the swirl of their threadbare habits making the dust rise.

The high-pitched scream of a postulant rent the air.

Outside the bats were swooping and somewhere a dog howled.

Sister Annunziata pushed her way to the window and watched aghast as the small body, arms outstretched like a crucifix, floated downstream until the darkening waters swallowed her up.

In the turret Sister Annunziata lit the oil lamp and watched as the crucifix on the wall grew momentarily dark then light in the flux of moving shadows. The smell of life clung to the room, a faint aroma of coarse convent soap, fresh herbs and recent tears.

She stood by the narrow window and tried to imagine how it had felt to climb out on to the perilous ledge and then step out into oblivion. She was overcome with giddiness, crossed herself feebly, wiped the beads of sweat from her forehead and breathed deeply in the cool night air.

Moonlight dappled the dark pool far below, and the river ran on heedlessly downstream towards the faraway sea.

Only a few hours had passed, and yet time seemed suspended.

She knew that what she had witnessed today would return to her, again and again; an image that would come to her in her dreams or in the lonely quiet hours.

She stripped the bed of its coarse blankets and packed Ismelda's few belongings into a trunk, but though she searched she could not find the walnut paintbox that had been Ismelda's prized possession. She found the scraps of canvas wedged beneath the bed, and she held them in trembling hands. The smell of oil paint still lingered and the paint had barely dried on the last page. A strand of dark hair was trapped in the paint, the imprint of a finger in vermillion on the last empty page . . . Her tears fell then, bitter tears against the futility of it all.

She extinguished the lamp and closed the ill-fitting wooden shutters against the night. The bats were already circling the turrets, the dogs barking in the small towns scattered across the valley. The nun's lips moved in silent prayer and the cries of the mad and the misplaced echoed in her ears.

Sister Annunziata closed the book gently, held it against her breast then slipped it beneath the folds of her habit.

No one must steal it. The story was not quite finished yet . . .

Chapter 69

Kizzy was leaving Kilvenny, and Catrin could barely contain her delight. Dan had arranged for a car to pick her up and take her to Swansea. There she would do the rounds of hairdressers, manicurists and dress shops before heading back to London and then on to the South of France. She'd half-heartedly offered to take Catrin with her, but Catrin had politely declined; she and Tony had exciting plans for the rest of the summer.

Catrin stood waiting dutifully outside the castle while Kizzy trailed around saying her goodbyes, kissing everyone on both cheeks like a film star, making Dan and Meredith blush deeply.

She stepped up to Catrin and took her face in both hands. Catrin squirmed. This was Kizzy's theatrical idea of mother love; an intent look into her child's eyes, a false tear trailing down her cheek, and then a swift walk away; she'd seen it in a film somewhere and adopted it as her own.

'Goodbye, darling. Write to me,' she whispered and then she turned and walked to the car without looking back.

As an afterthought she opened her handbag, took something out, turned and held it out to Catrin.

The girl went to her mother and held out her hand.

'Here,' Kizzy said. 'Aunt Alice gave me this, but I never really liked it. I couldn't see the point, really.'

Catrin looked down at the walnut *étui* that nestled in the palm of her hand.

She looked up to thank Kizzy, and for the first time ever she saw the beginnings of a real tear in her mother's eye.

Carefully Catrin lifted the catch on the side of the walnut, revealing tiny paintbrushes, small sticks of charcoal and a little artist's palette with paint marks on it. It was the most beautiful thing she had ever seen.

'Aunt Alice loved that. If she'd met you she'd have liked you to have it.'

But Catrin wasn't listening. She was peering down at the initials someone had painstakingly inscribed on the lid: I.B.

She said, 'Ismelda Bisotti. It belonged to Ismelda Bisotti.'

'No, dear, it didn't, it was Aunt Alice's.'

'Sorry, er, Ismelda was – *is* a friend of mine.'

'It's just as well I didn't call you Ismelda, then.'

'Why? Were you thinking of it?'

'Oh yes. I always loved that name,' Kizzy said, smoothing her hair.

'You did?'

Kizzy nodded and winced. The breeze was getting up and she didn't want to stand here all day talking about girls' names and have her hair blown all over the place. She climbed into the car, and waved demurely to Ella and the others standing outside the castle.

'What made you think of Ismelda as a name?' Catrin asked as the car began to pull away.

'Because it's the name of the girl in the . . .' Her words were carried away by the breeze.

'What did you say?' Catrin yelled, but the car was already accelerating past the war memorial.

Catrin stood holding the walnut tightly in her hand, and she didn't move until the car was out of sight.

Chapter 70

When Signor Bisotti and Father Rimaldi arrived at the house in the Via Dante, Piero was long gone. They stamped from room to room cursing loudly, opening closets and peering inside. The studio was just as it had always been, but Piero's canvases were gone and there was no sign of the painting of Feasting Cherubs. Signor Bisotti slammed his fist down on the table, shaking the flute-shaped pots of paint and scattering charcoal all over the floor.

They hurried back along the Via Dante to the convent, where Father Rimaldi headed straight for the stables. There was no sign of Bindo. His few belongings were gone and one of the nuns who came running out to see what the disturbance was said they hadn't seen him since yesterday.

An hour later they were both apoplectic with fury. Maria Paparella's room in the Villa Rosso had been emptied, and most of the food in the larder had gone. Then Signora Roselli came running to say that Luca, the ungrateful little sod, had upped and offed without a word.

As Signor Bisotti and Father Rimaldi stood together in the piazza, they were aware that they were being watched. There was no one around but the eyes of the village were on them.

'When I get my hands on that bastard Piero, he'll rue the day he played this trick on me.'

'They can't have got far if they've loaded all those paintings on to a cart.'

'The people are up in arms over that painting. They think we've made fools out of them; it won't be safe for us to stay for long. The signora and I will travel down to Napoli tonight. What about you?'

'They won't lay their dirty hands on a priest,' Father Rimaldi said confidently.

'Whatever possessed the man to do such a thing?' Signor Bisotti moaned. 'You don't think he has any idea of what we did?'

'How could he?' Father Rimaldi said querulously.

'I don't know, but a few weeks back when I was giving that bloody dwarf a beating Piero looked at me and at the dwarf very strangely, as if he had worked something out. It gave me quite a turn, I can tell you.'

Father Rimaldi rubbed his chin thoughtfully. 'I had the same feeling when Maria Paparella was speaking to me about the night the baby was abandoned, as if she, too, knew something or was trying hard to remember something.'

'If they do know, we must make sure they keep their mouths shut,' Signor Bisotti said, his eyes narrowing.

'We must keep calm and try to be logical. If Piero knew the truth, he would have done more than just paint a picture that made fools of us all.'

Signor Bisotti sat down abruptly on the side of the fountain. Nausea rose in the pit of his stomach as he thought back to that awful moment in the church when the cloth had been removed and the painting revealed.

Sweet Saviour, he'd been expecting to see a masterpiece and instead there was a painting of himself and Father Rimaldi naked as the day they were born. There were devil horns growing from their heads and long tails protruding from their naked behinds. Signora Bisotti had been painted, too, and her daughters: the three of them staring down from the church, three revolting gargoyles *with gaping mouths and bulging red-veined eyes, a shower of golden coins spewing from each of their mouths like vomit.*

Signor Bisotti put his head in his hands. Signora Bisotti would never forgive him for this public humiliation. She had stormed off to the Villa Rosso and shut herself in the bedroom. He himself had stood in horrified silence as the church emptied around him. He could still hear the laughter of the peasants echoing in his ears, the visiting priests hurrying away, twittering like scandalised sparrows.

'I won't rest until he's found and punished – until they're all found and punished,' he said, getting to his feet. 'I'll have men sent to Napoli to look for them; you can bet that's where the four of them would have headed.'

'The five of them,' Father Rimaldi said grimly, and he nudged Signor Bisotti in the ribs. Bisotti, realising what he meant, spat on the cobbles and stormed off towards the Villa Rosso, hell-bent on swift revenge.

Chapter 71

When Kizzy had gone Aunt Ella suggested a walk up to Shrimp's, but Catrin refused. She was restless and wanted to be on her own to think about her mother's parting words. Which girl could she have been talking about? It was infuriating, and she wouldn't be able to speak to Kizzy for weeks now to find out what she'd meant.

She watched Aunt Ella walk off towards the library with Dan and raised her eyebrows. Grown-ups could be dead funny. One minute they hated someone, the next they were best friends. Ella was forever popping over to Meredith's shop, the Café Romana or the library, which was really odd because she'd avoided Dan and Meredith until Kizzy came back.

Catrin headed towards the beach, but no sooner had she sat down when Meredith came whistling along and plonked himself down next to her. She talked politely for a while and then, frustrated at not being left alone, got up and went back to the castle, where she collected *Recipes for Cherubs* from her room.

Then, checking no one was watching her, she went into the graveyard and sat down in a shady spot; she ought to get some peace in there.

She was distracted, though, by Nonna, who was standing

in the upstairs window of the Café Romana, looking over at the graveyard. Well, not really looking, because she was blind, but it still made Catrin feel as if she was being spied on.

When Nonna moved away from the window, Catrin heaved a sigh of enormous relief and turned her attention back to the book.

Bugger. There was Dan coming in through the gate, beaming at her. He sat down next to her and started making small-talk.

She gave up, closed the book, and sat talking about this and that until eventually Ella called her in for tea.

Chapter 72

Maria Paparella was worried. She was fretting over leaving Ismelda behind, despite Piero's promise that, although they had to get away from Italy, he would come back for Ismelda. She was anxious because for the past few weeks she'd been having bad dreams and there was something niggling at the back of her mind, something she knew was of great significance.

She sat at the window in the inn in Napoli, waiting for Piero to return. He'd gone to see an old friend who'd agreed to store his canvases until he could send for them. When darkness fell, they would take them to the friend's house, but they must be careful because Luca had seen Father Rimaldi and Signor Bisotti down at the docks, asking questions.

She left her seat and walked across to where the paintings were stacked against the wall. Carefully she peeled back the oilcloth and looked at the top one.

'Mother of God!' she shrieked, and she sat down heavily, her breath forced, whistling, out of her heaving lungs. She got shakily to her feet and looked again at the painting of the woman, a woman with a lovely face, her lips parted as if about to speak, her hair held off her face by a blue scarf fringed with gold and red.

At that moment Piero came hurrying up the stairs, banging into the walls and cursing roundly because his sight was worse than ever.

'We have to move, Maria. I've just heard that the Flino is to sail earlier than we thought. We must leave the paintings; my friend has promised to come later and will have them taken to a safe place.'

'But, Piero, I need to talk to you.'

'Not now, Maria. Signor Bisotti has people everywhere looking for us. I've sent Luca on ahead, but I can't find that bloody Bindo anywhere.'

The Flino was ready to sail. The cargo holds had been filled with every type of fruit imaginable, and the air was redolent with the scent of lemons and limes. The captain, Antonio Ravello, was itching to be off because there was talk of the weather turning bad.

Standing on the deck, Piero di Bardi hung on to Maria Paparella's arm. 'You were going to tell me something earlier?' he asked.

'It's just that I've been having some strange thoughts, and today I saw something which gave me a great shock.'

'Tell me now. Distract me and stop me worrying about that bloody Bindo.'

'Years ago, when I was only a child, I saw something in Santa Rosa which has always bothered me.'

'Go on.'

'It was the first night I stayed at the Villa Rosso, the night of the great snowstorm – Signora Bisotti had just given birth to Ismelda. I couldn't sleep, you see. I was missing my mother and I was afraid. I sat up looking out of the window and I saw Father Rimaldi carrying a baby wrapped in a shawl.'

'That's not surprising. Wasn't that the night when Bindo was found?'

She nodded. 'There was something strange because there were two sets of—'

A roar of laughter broke out down on the dock, and Maria and Piero leant over the railing to see what was going on.

The crowds parted, making way for Bindo, who was pushing a barrow almost as big as he was.

'What in God's name has he got there?' Piero demanded.

Bindo came to a standstill, wiped his sweat-soaked hair from his forehead and called up to them, 'I couldn't fit everything of mine in the cart yesterday so I had a few things sent down from Santa Rosa, keepsakes to remind me of my birthplace.'

Two hefty sailors hurried down the gangplank, took the handles of the barrow from Bindo – and almost dropped them.

'Hey, little fellow, what the hell have you got in here that weighs so much?'

Bindo lifted back the cloth and Piero and Maria burst into peals of laughter. There lay one of the cherubs from the fountain in Santa Rosa.

'I couldn't leave that little fellow behind. Piero will want to remember his brother, and I'm sure we'll find a home for it somewhere.'

Maria looked at him, thunderstruck. 'He's only gone and stolen the little saint, the Stella Maris from outside the convent,' she screeched in disbelief.

'One must have something from home to remind one of one's past. That little saint has guarded me since the night I was abandoned in the olive jar,' Bindo said.

'He's brought that mangy old cat as well!' Piero yelled. Sure enough, Pipi was fast asleep, snoring contentedly, between the tiny saint and the smiling cherub.

'Well, this lot will probably sink the bloody ship,' Maria said. 'Hurry up, Bindo. If you get left behind and Signor Bisotti gets his hands on you, he'll have your gizzards for ornaments.'

'Come, Maria, you must finish your story or it will never get told,' Piero said softly, taking Maria's hand and kissing it.

'Like I said, there were two sets of footprints in the snow.'

'What does that mean?'

'That Father Rimaldi went over to the Villa Rosso and then back across the piazza. Do you see?'

Piero wrinkled his forehead. 'You've lost me, I'm afraid.'

'Think. If he'd just come out of his house and found Bindo, he'd have walked straight to the convent and would have had no need to cross the piazza.'

'I don't see what you're getting at.'

'One thing has always puzzled me. The first time I saw Ismelda there was something wrong. She was too big for a newborn baby. I didn't really see that then, because I was just a child, but I've seen enough newborn babies since to know I was right.'

'And yet she was newborn?'

'So it was said.'

'What are you implying, Maria?'

'That Signora Bisotti had given birth to a child who was deformed, a child Signor Bisotti could not bear to look at.'

'And?'

'I think that it was Ismelda who was abandoned and that the babies were swapped.'

Piero looked at her in wonder. 'So Bindo is Bisotti's son?'

'Well, there was always talk about Signora Bisotti and the woodcarver, but who knows?'

'You never thought of telling him?'

'Would you want to find out that Bisotti was your father?'

'Best keep it to yourself, then,' Piero said.

'The other thing is, Piero, the woman in the painting of Woman and Child was wearing a very beautiful scarf.'

He smiled then, and said, 'I had it made for her in Rome; it was made especially to my own design by an old woman, a weaver of great talents.'

Maria put her hand under her cloak and pulled out the scarf. 'Is this the one?'

Piero looked down at it and his eyes widened in incredulity. 'Where did you get this?'

'I found it the morning after the snowstorm. It was wrapped round the neck of one of the cherubs. I couldn't believe my luck, finding such a beautiful thing. I've kept it ever since, locked away as a treasure.'

'She was in Santa Rosa that night. She came looking for me,' Piero said. 'She was carrying my child.'

'Hey, there, wait for me!' It was a frantic shout, and Luca came running towards the Flino, pushing through the crowds. He leapt from the quay on to the moving gangplank, and clambered up on to the deck.

'Where have you been?' Bindo asked.

'I met a nun from Santa Lucia – she'd come down here looking for us,' he panted, barely able to get his words out.

'What's happened?'

'She had news for us from the Convent of Santa Lucia.'

'What kind of news?'

'Bad news. It's Ismelda,' he wailed. 'She's dead.'

As the boisterous crowds on the dockside waved to the departing Flino the four of them stood, heads bowed, the wind whisking the tears from their eyes and blowing their hair about their anguished faces.

The ship moved slowly away into the choppy waters and the blue sky above turned slowly from cerulean to indigo and finally lampblack. It was the last time they would see the sky above Italy, the last time that Piero would ever see the sky.

Chapter 73

It was dark when Catrin made her way across to the chapel. She needed some peace; wherever she'd been today there had been someone on her tail. She slipped quietly inside, lit the candles on the stand in the lady chapel and sat down near the altar, glad of the space to think.

She'd been impatient for Kizzy to leave this morning, couldn't wait to see the back of her, and Kizzy had duly gone, heading off for the bright lights or the luxury villa as she always did. And yet in those few moments when she'd handed her the walnut *étui*, Catrin had felt close to her for the first time ever, as if Kizzy had been trying to apologise in her own way for being a rubbish mother.

She thought she heard a movement in the chapel. It was probably only a mouse scuttling about. She closed her eyes and clasped her hands. Her head was still reeling from the bombshell that Tony had dropped the other night. Before Kizzy came back, she'd been playing the scene over and over in her head. Kizzy would tell her the truth, and Catrin would scream and shout and have a fit of hysterics. It hadn't been anything like that, though. She'd been delighted to hear that he was her father. She was shocked – after all, her mother had done s.e.x. with Tony and then she'd been born. But it was a better shock than she'd thought she was going to get. She couldn't think of anyone better to have as a father. And yet ... she didn't quite believe that it was true. Still, who cared? A pretend father like Tony was better than any real one she could imagine.

She stayed quite still, the coolness of the chapel soothing her as it always did. She needed to get her thoughts into some kind of order. Aunt Ella had been fussing over her all the time recently, checking on where she was going and what time she would be back, and that wasn't like her at all. Dan and Meredith had been just as bad, popping up wherever she went.

She breathed deeply. The smells of incense and candlewax filled her nostrils, along with the smell of wild flowers and rosemary. Rosemary for remembrance. As she opened her eyes, a sliver of moonlight slipped through the arched window above the main altar and danced across the walls of the chapel, playing around the feet of the tiny saint in the lady chapel.

The dandelions in the jamjar glowed like miniature suns, sending out rays of golden light, and the candles grew brighter. She got slowly to her feet and walked up to the altar, picked up a dandelion and held it to her face. Then for some inexplicable reason she lifted the altar cloth, and crawled underneath the altar.

She ran her hands across the smooth flagstones until she found something. She sat back on her heels and looked at the floor and then slowly she made the sign of the cross. She crawled out and fetched a candle from the stand by the altar. As the candle cast its glow around her it illuminated two memorial tablets laid side by side in the floor.

Bindo
Born 1751, died of cholera in Kilvenny, 1771

Ismelda Grieve
Beloved wife of Nathaniel Grieve, mother of Charles
Born 1751, died 1819

Ismelda hadn't died in the convent! She had made it here to Kilvenny and married Nathaniel Grieve. That meant that Ismelda was one of Catrin's ancestors, her own flesh and blood.

As she knelt there, head bowed, gazing at the final resting place of Bindo and Ismelda, she heard the chapel door open and close quietly, and the key turn in the lock.

She got out from under the altar and looked around, but there was no one there. She inched towards the door, heart thumping, ears straining for any sound. Then she saw him.

Father Rimaldi was standing in the shadows at the back of the church, his hooked nose protruding from beneath his wide-brimmed hat. She opened her mouth to scream but he put his hand up as if to silence her. Then he walked slowly towards her, a cruel smile spreading across his pale face.

'So good to see you, Catrin. it's been too long,' he said, thrusting his hand towards her. She put her hands behind her back. It was a conjuring trick of some sort. The dead couldn't come back to life – that was impossible.

Then a slow realisation crept over her. She was looking at a man she knew, but she hadn't recognised him at first because he'd shaved off his beard and beneath it his skin was an unearthly pallor.

Arthur Campbell smiled that familiar superior smile of his, which always made her heart twist into a knot.

'I see you've found the family skeletons,' he said, gesturing at the memorial tablets.

'Ismelda Bisotti and Bindo,' she said quietly.

'My, my, your cleverness astounds me, Catrin, and to think I'd given up hope on your academic intelligence.'

Catrin stayed silent.

'A little research led me to find out all about those two,' he said.

'And what did you find out?'

'That the two lovebirds married and had a child, but poor Bindo was carried off in the cholera epidemic.'

'I know that, it says so on his grave.'

'What you don't know is that Nathaniel Grieve, who was childless, married Ismelda. It was a marriage in name only, by all accounts – he was very forward-thinking, apparently, and let her live her own life – but the child, Charles, took his name, the Grieve name.'

'So I'm not really a Grieve.'

'Quite right. I expect Nathaniel was afraid the family name would die out and he saw a solution to his problems. So you're related to both Bindo and Ismelda, which is why I was so interested in you when you were a child.'

'I don't understand.'

'I sent you to art lessons, if you remember – expensive ones, I might add – hoping that the genes would out in the end. I wondered, you see, if I had a budding Piero as a godchild, but I was disappointed on that score.'

'What has Piero got to do with me?'

Campbell laughed. 'More research, my dear, my own family research, in this case. I had access to the journals of one of my own ancestors, and in them was a deathbed confession which made very interesting reading.'

Catrin barely heard him. All she could think about was that she was related to Ismelda and Bindo.

Campbell continued, 'A certain Gregorio Rimaldi, one-time priest of Santa Rosa in Italy, admitted that he had committed a dastardly deed and swapped two babies.'

'Bindo,' Catrin said. 'Bindo was left in the olive jar.'

'Bindo was of no interest to me, but Ismelda Bisotti was, because she was the daughter of Piero di Bardi.'

Catrin breathed deeply, trying to clear the light-headedness threatening to overwhelm her. That explained the paintings she'd found in Aunt Alice's dowry box. They had a resemblance to Piero's, but the hand that had painted them was less steady, the colour not as intense, though they were very good.

'She was a very good artist,' Catrin said. 'I've seen some of her paintings.'

Campbell looked at her with narrowed eyes, eyes which were full of shrewd interest. 'I don't suppose you've found the painting of the *Feasting Cherubs*?'

'No, and I don't think it ever will be found.' She said, glaring at him, eyes bright with anger. 'You wanted to marry Aunt Alice to get your hands on *Recipes for Cherubs*,' she said coldly.

'Ah, yes the elusive book,' he said, and the cold anger in his voice made Catrin wilt. 'Well, I take my hat off to you, Catrin. The ugly duckling has become an intellectual swan. Do go on.'

'But you didn't get your hands on the book because Alice didn't marry you.'

'Quite right, but my troubles are now at an end because I know that you have the book and I've come here to relieve you of it.'

'And you think I'll give it to you and let you walk off with it, just like that?' she said, astonished.

'That's up to you entirely.'

'And if I don't give it to you?'

'Well, I'm sure we could arrange a little accident to someone you're close to.'

'You scheming shit!'

'Now, now, Miss Grieve! I paid good money to have you educated as a lady.'

'You think a book is worth harming someone for?'

'I'm sure it won't come to that. We can come to some sort of civilised arrangement. The book can be sold: there'll be no shortage of buyers – that book will blow the art world apart. We could all take a cut. Kizzy's money worries will be over, Shrimp's Hotel can be restored and Tony Agosti can have the restaurant of his dreams.'

'No! You think you can have everything you want, but you can't.'

'Can't I?'

'That book is very special. It tells the story of people's lives and deaths. It's a love story, a story of hope and despair, of appetite and hunger, but most especially of hope—'

'Bravo! How elegantly put! The nuns have done a fine job by you. But I'm not interested in love stories, Catrin, it's art I'm interested in.'

'You look just like Father Rimaldi,' Catrin said suddenly.

'It may interest you to know that I am descended from an English duke and an Italian woman. A woman, indeed, who once lived in Santa Rosa, the widow Zanelli, who married a rather grand man.'

'Signor Bisotti!' Catrin snorted. 'He was an ugly pig if ever you saw one! I'm not surprised he's an ancestor of yours,' she said, and then giggled with nerves at her daring.

'Ah, well, you see, fate has a way of unravelling things. I am descended from the marriage of Signor Bisotti and the widow Zanelli, but it seems the widow gave out her favours rather frivolously and I believe from family stories that I am descended directly from Father Rimaldi and the widow Zanelli. Rather quirky, don't you think, to be descended from a priest?'

'A priest *and* a murderer,' she said, her voice twisted with hatred.

Campbell had his back to the arched window above the main altar and the moonlight cast his face into eerie shadows.

Catrin's eyes widened and she was about to scream in terror when she saw the little statue of the saint floating in the darkness behind Arthur Campbell's head as though dark forces were at work. He noticed Catrin's frozen stare, but before he could turn, the little saint came plummeting through the darkness and landed with a sickening thud on the back of his neck.

'Take that, you snivelling bastard,' said Aunt Ella.

Part Four

1978

It was sweltering, a blinding sun burning down on Kilvenny, reflecting off the latticed windows of the castle. In the tall trees of Gwartney's Wood, the rooks were silent and only the grasshoppers chirruped exhaustedly.

Up at Shrimp's Hotel, a small girl came out of the front door and looked around in delight. All the windows were open, and brightly coloured curtains caught the breeze and billowed outwards. The thwack of a tennis ball echoed across the gardens, and someone shrieked as they jumped into the cool water of the swimming pool.

The girl sniffed and grinned. It always smelt lovely at Shrimp's. In the kitchen they were busy making afternoon teas. She caught the tantalising aroma of the potted shrimps that were covered in a thick layer of butter and served in little brown pots. She breathed in the smell of fresh bread baking, and scones, cream horns and walnut cake.

The tables were already laid on the lawns, and soon the maids would come down from their rooms in the attic, spick and span in their black dresses and white aprons, and teaspoons would tinkle against china cups and piano music would drift out from the drawing room.

Today was a very exciting day. Mummy had said she could walk all the way down to Kilvenny on her own because she was a big girl now, nearly six.

She walked importantly across the lawns, smiling up at the coloured lights hung in the trees. When it got dark they were switched on and it made the garden look like fairyland.

She climbed slowly down the steep steps to the beach, slipped off her sandals and giggled as the warm sand trickled between her toes.

She walked to the upside-down boat and ran her fingers along the wood. It belonged to Great-great-aunt Ella and was called the *Dancing Porpoise*. Tomorrow Aunt Ella was coming all the way from Italy with her friend, and she'd promised to take her out in the boat to catch fish; that would be fun. Aunt Ella's friend used to teach Mummy when she was a little girl; she used to be a nun, whatever that was. Grandma Grieve was coming, too, with a man friend. She wasn't so much fun; she smelt of stinky perfume and moaned a lot.

She walked along Cockle Lane and looked in through the windows of the Photographer's shop. She liked the pictures in there: they were of people from the olden days. The old man who lived there was the one who played the piano up at Shrimp's.

Later, she was going to spend her pocket money in the Café Romana. She liked going in there because the bell above the door played a tune when you went in and a man called Dai jumped up from behind the counter and made you an Italian ice cream. It was the best ice cream in the whole wide world: toffee, banana, vanilla, tutti frutti – and there was even a special one named after her.

She opened the squeaky graveyard gate and tiptoed in; it was where dead people were buried. On some of the graves there were little posies of dandelions, daisies and butter-cups, that Mummy put there.

She wandered back out into Cockle Lane, stretched up and peeped in through the window of the library; the old man in there had a wood named after him and was called Mr Know-it-all. He had hair like candy floss and he was nice and smiled a lot. He was in there now, fast asleep with a fat white kitten curled up on his lap. As she watched, the kitten opened one green eye and stared at her.

She listened. Someone was calling her name – two people, actually, Mummy and Grandpa Tony. He must have finished his work in the kitchen and been let out for a rest.

'Ismelda!'

'Ismelda!'

She hurried back to the beach and opened the door of the Fisherman's Snug. Aunt Ella used to go in there when she was little, and the fishermen had taught her to swear real good. She looked around for a hiding place and crawled under the table.

If Mummy and Grandpa Tony walked right past the Fisherman's Snug and didn't see her, she'd creep up behind them and scare them.

She kept very still, her finger pressed against her lips like they'd learnt in school.

She felt something brush against her hair and looked up to see a spider dangling from a thread.

She watched it with interest, and then she blinked in surprise. Why would someone hide a painting under an old table?

A face was staring down at her ... the face of a cheeky-looking boy with the greenest eyes she'd ever seen. There was a girl, too, and a smiling woman with fat knees, a hand-some boy with a small scar on his cheek.

Whoever the people in the painting were, they were

dead lucky because they had wings. Gosh, she wished she had wings. Maybe she could have some one day.

Grandpa Tony always said, *'Tutto è possibile.'* For people who didn't know Italian it meant, 'Everything is possible.'

POCKET
BOOKS

Also by Babs Horton

A Jarful of Angels

The remote town in the Welsh valleys was
a wonderful, magical – but sometimes dangerous –
place in which to grow up. It was there that Iffy,
Bessie, Fatty and Billy experienced a plague of
frogs one summer, stumbled upon a garden full
of dancing statues, found a skull with its front
teeth missing – and discovered just what it was
that mad Carty Annie was collecting so secretly
in those jars of hers.

But at the end of that long, hot summer of 1963,
one of the four children disappeared.

Over thirty years later, retired detective Will Sloane,
never able to forget the unsolved case, returns to
Wales to resume his search for the truth. His
investigation will draw him into a number of
interlocking mysteries, each one more puzzling
than the last.

ISBN 978-0-7434-971-1

PRICE £6.99

**POCKET
BOOKS**

Also by Babs Horton

Dandelion Soup

In the remote Irish village of Ballygurry, middle-aged Solly Benjamin is roused at midnight to find a child on his doorstep, a length of cord tied loosely around her neck. The attached tag bears his own name and address.

Who is she? And why would a complete stranger send her to him? As Solly attempts to find the answers, other Ballygurry inhabitants are drawn into the mystery.

Their enquiries lead to the secluded monastery of Santa Eulalia on the medieval trail to Santiago de Compostela. As the Ballygurry pilgrims begin to thaw in the Spanish sunshine, a number of interwoven mysteries from the past gradually unfurl to rekindle old hatreds – and restore old passions.

ISBN 978-0-7434-4972-4

PRICE £6.99

**POCKET
BOOKS**

Also by Babs Horton

Wildcat Moon

The Skallies, a row of tumbledown houses built on
the windlashed coast, was a place for people down
on their luck. A place where people came to hide.

Ten-year-old Archie Grimble, with his crippled
leg and one good eye, lived a miserable existence
there until a chance encounter with an unhappy little
girl and the discovery of a locked diary set him on
a mission to unravel the mystery of a boy who
drowned off Skilly Point in August, 1900.

But Archie's investigation was to have unexpected
consequences. A shocking murder and an
unexplained abduction were to shatter his exciting
new world forever.

Only many years later, on his return to the ruined
Skallies, does Archie stumble on the final pieces of
the puzzle – and the extraordinary truth about the
fate of Thomas Greswode is at last revealed.

ISBN 978-0-7434-9595-0

PRICE £6.99